FAMILY LIFE

The Second Inspector Starrett Mystery

Paul Charles was born and raised in Magherafelt in the north of Ireland and is one of Europe's best known music promoters and agents. He is the author of nine Inspector Christy Kennedy novels, the most recent of which, *The Beautiful Sound of Silence*, was published in 2008. The first Inspector Starrett novel, *The Dust of Death*, was published in 2007.

Also by Paul Charles

The DI Christy Kennedy Mysteries:
I Love the Sound of Breaking Glass
Last Boat to Camden Town
Fountain of Sorrow
The Ballad of Sean and Wilko
The Hissing of the Silent Lonely Room
I've Heard the Banshee Sing
The Justice Factory
Sweetwater
The Beautiful Sound of Silence

An Inspector Starrett Mystery:
The Dust of Death

Other fiction:
First of the True Believers

Non-fiction:
Playing Live

PAUL CHARLES
FAMILY LIFE
An Inspector Starrett Mystery

First published in 2009 by Brandon
an imprint of Mount Eagle Publications
Dingle, Co. Kerry, Ireland, and
Unit 3, Olympia Trading Estate, Coburg Road, London N22 6TZ, England

www.brandonbooks.com

2 4 6 8 10 9 7 5 3 1

ISBN 9780863224041 Hardback (2009)
ISBN 9780863224157 Paperback (2010)

Mount Eagle Publications/Sliabh an Fhiolar Teoranta receives support from
the Arts Council/An Chomhairle Ealaíon.

Cover design: www.design-suite.ie
Typesetting by Red Barn Publishing, Skeagh, Skibbereen

Dedication and thanks

Thanks a million to Steve and all the Fab Brandon team; to Terry for the red pen and the eagle eye; to Charlton Davidson, a fine solid "feet and inches" gentleman, for info on all things antique; to John McIvor for Starrett support above and beyond; to Paul Buchanan for his very revealing lyric, "Family Life"; to Andy & Cora for ever and ever. And to Catherine for the continued daily magic.

Chapter One

Tuesday: 26 August 2008

"Hey, Ma, where's Joe?"

"Ach, Ryan, come on, 'mammy,' or even 'mum' sounds so much better than 'ma,'" Mrs Sweeney replied.

Just then a huge Audi 4×4 pulled into the tidy farmyard, did a U-ie and reversed towards the back door. The racket the engine created while idling was enough to rattle the elegant but old farmhouse windows in their frames.

"There's your brother and his family – go on and help them in, and be sure Bernadette doesn't bring in that flipping excuse for a rat she carries about with her everywhere she goes."

"That's her pet hamster," Ryan said, opening the kitchen door and disappearing to do his duty.

"Jeez, with all that racket I could have sworn you'd arrived in a Massey Ferguson," Ryan said as he closed the back door to the farmhouse behind him.

"I'm still sooooo annoyed over them changing our Mercedes Estate for this heap of . . ."

"Bernadette, mind your tongue," her father scolded, interrupting her mid-flow.

Bernadette continued running across the farmyard to greet her favourite uncle. When she was out of earshot of her parents and her sister Finula, she whispered, ". . . shit."

"Hi, Bernie. Have you got President Bertie with you?" Ryan Sweeney asked, looking for the betraying bulge in the numerous pockets of her trendy pink dungarees.

"Noooo way. Granny threatened to put him in the oven if I brought him again."

Ryan ruffled her shoulder-length blonde hair, saying, "Right, g'on in and give your grandmother a big hug."

Bernadette disappeared into the house, scrunching her nose up into her pretty face.

As nine-year-old Finula passed her uncle, she awkwardly and formally shook his hand, asking, "Is Joe here?"

"He's out somewhere, Finula," Ryan replied to her heels and the back of her black curly-haired head.

He crossed the yard to the couple unpacking the 4×4.

"Ryan," Mona said curtly.

"Mona," Ryan replied, equally coldly.

"How's Ma, Ryan?" Thomas asked.

"She's fine, Tom."

"And the auld man?"

"I haven't seen Dad yet; he was upstairs getting ready when I arrived," Ryan replied, helping them with their luggage.

Thomas Sweeney – dressed stiffly in a black pinstripe suit, a crisp white shirt, a green and white broadband tie and sensible black leather shoes – made a subtle fuss of nudging his brother out of the way so he could take both the wheelie cases.

"How've you been since the farm meeting, Tom?"

"Bringing up a family, Ryan," the red-cheeked and straw-haired Thomas replied as he ploughed past him and waddled off after his wife who, by that point, had reached the back door.

Ryan was left standing in the middle of the farmyard, both his arms, in his blue shirt, the same length and the remainder of his slim frame clothed in tan chinos and Nike trainers. His hands were disproportionately large, and he swung the right one up to run his fingers through his thick, longish jet-black hair.

He studied his parents' blue house. He loved the magnificent house, he always had, and in a way he'd been very sad to move out. For him it was the perfect living accommodation. The house's character suited his character. It was a large, roomy house, and although he was standing at the rear of the house, he was viewing the original front of it. This was the first part of house to be built, sometime in the 1870s, Ryan believed. Then in the early 1900s, one of Ryan's ancestors had build a mirror image on the other side and decided, because of the amazing view over the land from its vantage point, to make that the front of the enlarged Palladium style house. It was like a smaller version of a stately home and had been the subject of many articles and documentaries when Ryan and his brothers and sister had been growing up. Ryan hoped it would stand for ever.

The silence of the yard was broken by two Mini Coopers, one green and one light blue, speeding into the yard and screeching to a halt, their proud silver bumpers forming a straight line about three feet from him.

A brunette girl in her mid-twenties hopped out of the green Mini and ran over to her brother.

"Teresa," he uttered just before she caught him in a passionate hug. Ryan didn't return the hug, preferring instead to let his arms hang by his sides. His sister's eyes were red and she was sniffling, and he acted like he was keen to avoid her on-coming or out-going cold or flu.

"Ach, Ryan, just think: if I'd been two years earlier, I'd have got your looks, and as I'm always saying, they'd have worked a lot better on me."

"I think Maeve might just disagree with you there."

"Is she indoors?"

"Not yet; she's coming straight from work."

The two passengers from the other Mini then interrupted them. The younger of the two walked over to Ryan and kissed him on the cheek, as the other walked to meet Teresa and kissed her briefly on the lips.

"Hi, Breda," Ryan said.

"Hi, Ryan," Breda replied. "Is Joe inside?"

"No, not yet."

"Ach, he's not still out with the cattle, is he? He's going to stink all night. I've been trying to ring him all afternoon to tell him to get home early, have a long bath and get cleaned up. I've bought him a new shirt," she said, holding up as evidence the Dunne's bag she was carrying in her right hand.

"Hi, Sheila," Ryan said to his sister's companion.

"Hello, Ryan," she whispered in what sounded like a painfully hoarse response but which was, in fact, her normal voice. She too came over to Ryan, kissed him on the cheek and hugged him affectionately.

"Jeez, I'd love to continue to hog all you beautiful women for myself, but we better get in and prepare for dinner."

"Right," Teresa agreed sarcastically.

"Oh, yes," Sheila replied. 'What age is Liam?"

"Da's sixty-four."

"Ah shit," Sheila said, "I forgot to bring him a birthday present."

"Don't worry about it," Ryan said, rounding them all up like a herd of cattle towards the back door; "you're all off the hook. We got him a family present. Joe organised it."

"I have it here," Breda chipped in. "Joe asked me to bring it over. He didn't want to risk leaving it around the farm; he said his dad always found everything."

"What did we get him then?" Sheila asked, as they neared the back door.

"It's a surprise," Ryan said, as he opened the door and shooed them all in.

Fifteen minutes later he was back out the door again as a modern, lime-green VW, complete with a dainty flower pot in the front window, pulled into the yard and, unlike the 4×4 and the two

Minis, parked more considerately over by the whitewashed out-house, which bordered the other side of the yard.

"Sorry I'm late, love," Maeve Boyce said, climbing out of her car. She hugged Ryan and they kissed on the lips. "Is everyone else here?" she continued, as she handed him her handbag and stole a few seconds to retouch her make-up to hide the tiredness that an invigorating hot shower would have more successfully banished. She quickly brushed her long, straight brown hair, which fell in a fringe half an inch up from her eyebrows and then fell symmetrically down the sides of her face to six inches below her shoulders.

"You look great," Ryan said, handing back her bag.

"Thanks, love, even though you don't or, at least shouldn't, mean it. I suppose everyone is here?"

"Yeah, well, everyone except Joe."

"Oh thank you, God," she said raising her grey-blue eyes to the heavens. "I do hate being the last to arrive. Where is he?"

"No one seems to know," Ryan said, now also herding her towards the door. "Let's get in there before Thomas and Mona strangle Sheila."

"Oh God, that means Teresa has brought the auld skinhead boyfriend."

"Ah, don't start, Maeve. Teresa and *Sheila* are very happy."

"Sorry, Ryan," Maeve said, taking her dark blue suit jacket off and revealing a semi-transparent white blouse, which in turn revealed a sight that brought a lecherous grin to Ryan's face. "Ah, that's the look I like to see, love. Let's see if we can't sneak away early from this and steal some quality time for ourselves."

"I'm your man," Ryan said, falling in five steps behind her, mesmerised by the movement within the tight, knee-length, royal blue skirt.

She waited for him a few steps before the door and then turned and asked in a quieter voice, "What's happened so far, Ryan?"

"I was here first, Ma was cooking, Dad was still upstairs – probably still is. Then Thomas, Mona and kids arrived. Bernie is still going through her 'My parents are bores and I wish everyone would stop saying I'm pretty' period. Finula was as disappointed as Breda that Joe isn't here yet. Ma was in a great mood until Teresa arrived with her posse. Mona made a fuss over Ma, Ma made a fuss over Teresa. Mona is frequently reminding Tom in whispers, 'Talk to your father.'"

Maeve interrupted him to ask, "Have *you* talked to your dad yet?"

"I still haven't had a chance," Ryan replied as Maeve grimaced. "Then Tom took Teresa to one side and warned her off being openly affectionate to Sheila in front of Bernie and Finula. Teresa was subtle enough not to make a scene by slapping him on the face, which is exactly what she looked like she wanted to do. Instead she just smiled sweetly and knuckled him with all her might on his upper arm just below the shoulder. She nearly drew tears."

"Right so," Maeve said, opening the door. "Just another typical day down on the Sweeney farm then."

Chapter Two

Both Breda and Finula's eyes were glued to the other side of the back door as Maeve opened it. They didn't try to hide their look of disappointment when they discovered it was not Joe opening the door.

Liam, the father of the family, had joined the kitchen hubbub. If anything, he looked fitter than his son Thomas, who was only in his thirty-fourth summer. That probably had a lot to do with Liam's permanent smile and twinkling blue eyes. He was decked out in his Sunday – not to mention births, marriages and funerals – best black, pinstripe suit. He boasted a full head of thick jet-black hair and a neatly trimmed black beard. His weather-beaten face, neck and hands testified to his years in the fields.

"Right, we're all here," he announced. "If Mother's ready, we can all sit down to dinner."

"But Joe's not here yet," Finula protested, beating Breda to the call by a microsecond.

"I think we'll find that Joe is attending to some farm business, and he'll join us as soon as he's good and ready," Liam announced in his sing-song Donegal accent, opening both hands towards the dinner table and inviting those present to take their seats. He looked first at Thomas and then at Ryan before he continued, "You see, Finula pet, our Joe's a farmer, aye, and when you're a farmer you can't just clock out of the office when you feel like it."

In ones and twos, they drifted to their usual seats at the large, battered oak table.

The mother, Colette, took the seat at the foot of the table because it was closer to the oven and her preparation area. Colette faced down the table towards her husband, who was silhouetted by the light coming in from the window, which acted as a link between the kitchen and the trees, hedges and rolling hills of their farmland. She too had nipped upstairs to change into a loose, flowery blue dress, suitable for an August evening, and a matching blue cardigan.

At the dinner table, to Colette's left sat her second-born son, Ryan. Ryan was her favourite, if only because Joe was the apple of his father's eye and Thomas was the oldest, who'd married and had left home eleven years earlier. Next to Ryan sat Maeve Boyce, Ryan's best friend for ten years and *girl*friend for the last five of those ten. Next to Maeve sat Sheila Kelly; tall, big built, with sandpaper skin, shaved head and without a speck of make-up, she was always, but always, dressed head to toe in black. Next sat Mona Sweeney, wife of Thomas and four years his senior. She was dressed in a more glamorous style than she could carry off and would have benefited immensely from Maeve's classy dress sense, instead of wearing the ridiculous creation she was trying, unsuccessfully, to fit into. Mona sat, mentally and physically, between Sheila and Bernadette, who in turn sat beside her granddad.

Down the other side of the table, and to Liam's immediate left, sat his younger granddaughter, nine-year-old Finula, who in turn sat beside her father, who was sitting opposite his wife. Next to Thomas was his sole sister Teresa, who sat opposite Sheila. Then there was twenty-four-year-old Breda Roche, who was a double for Sinead O'Connor in everyone's eyes. She was blessed with a naturally youthful beauty, which she would probably carry all her life. That was providing she didn't submit to her sweet tooth and the few extra pounds it was always in danger of leading her to.

Next to Breda was an empty seat awaiting the arrival of Joe Sweeney.

The eleven gathered around the table chit-chatted away in their various, sometimes overlapping, groups for about twenty minutes.

"Whist, what's that?" Liam said suddenly, holding out his hand to them all to quieten down.

"There's someone knocking on the door," Thomas said through the new-found quietness.

"I'll get it," Bernadette offered immediately.

"No," Colette ordered sternly, "Ryan will get it."

Ryan disappeared to answer the door.

About a minute later he returned into the kitchen, the blood completely drained from his pretty boy face.

"Ma," he announced from the doorway, "it's Inspector Starrett. He says he needs to speak to you and Dad about our Joe."

Chapter Three

On the other side of the rarely used front door stood the garda inspector, the permanently bent forefinger of his right hand furiously tapping away against the black shiny material of his trousers. He'd already clocked from the number of domestic vehicles in the yard to the side that Liam and Colette Sweeney had a full house.

The news he had was hard enough to deliver to a single person, let alone a full house. His sergeant, Packie Garvey, was wordless, clicking his heels and staring up to the skies, probably, Starrett thought, so he wouldn't have to look the mother or father in the eyes when they came to the door.

Starrett grimaced, trying to ensure that when the time came for him to do his duty he would have a full breath; he couldn't afford to quaver as he delivered his devastating news. He heard footsteps in the hallway. He raised his right hand to run his fingers through his longish brown hair.

When Colette arrived at the door with her husband by her right side, Starrett's compassionate ice-blue eyes could not hide what was obviously in his heart, and Colette, instead of going through a process of damage control, deduction and elimination of accident, drunkenness, detention, crime, sickness, tax-evasion or smuggling, went straight to her worst nightmare-case scenario.

"Oh my God, Liam, our Joseph's dead!"

When Starrett didn't contradict Colette Sweeney, her legs went from under her; she shuddered and buckled to the floor like a high-rise building being collapsed by having the ground floor blown out from under it.

There was a buzz of activity in the general direction of the kitchen as the door opened and three generations of the Sweeney clan piled into the grand hallway.

Liam Sweeney turned in the direction of the commotion and shouted, in his no-nonsense tone, "Tom, get all the wains and girls back in the kitchen and close the door after you. Ryan, help me with your mother."

Teresa protested the most belligerently, but eventually she was restrained and removed to the kitchen by Sheila and Breda.

Liam and Ryan Sweeney, Sergeant Packie Garvey and Inspector Starrett carried the comatose body of Colette Sweeney into the sitting room and laid her on the sofa. The sofa wasn't quite long enough to take her full body, so her feet dangled slightly off the end by the armrest. In the confusion one of her shoes had come off, and Ryan betrayed his grief by making a wild fuss over finding his mother's shoe.

Liam went over to an ornate, glass-fronted rosewood cabinet, opened the bottom door and carefully removed a bottle of Bushmills, unscrewing the cap as he recrossed the room again in a stride and a half to his wife's side. He poured a little whiskey into the bottle cap and passed it under his wife's nose several times until, very slowly, she started to stir again as if awakening from a deep sleep.

Probably only two minutes had passed since Liam and his wife had met the gardaí in their hallway, and still not a word had been spoken. When he saw that his wife was OK, he left her to the attention of his son and nodded to the gardaí to follow him out of the house.

"What's the score then, Starrett?" he asked the second he'd shut the front door behind the three of them.

"Liam, a couple of tourists discovered Joe's body down in the courtyard of one of the warehouses on the quayside about two hours ago."

"Ah Jesus, Mary and Joseph, what on earth was he doing in there? He was meant to be over in Milford today, seeing a man about taking more produce from us. Joe was a great one for selling direct to the stores. 'Cut out the middleman, Da,' he'd say, 'and you can make twice the price and deliver better quality goods.' In the courtyard you say, the one beside the Heritage Centre?"

"Aye, Liam," Starrett replied as his sidekick Garvey looked on earnestly.

"Any idea how long he'd been there?" Liam asked. The big man kept on pushing with his own questions. It was as though he were trying to delay the inevitable for as long as was humanly possible.

"Well, we know he wasn't there just before six o'clock yesterday. There was a surveyor in there checking the stability of the walls. Then, as I said, about a couple of hours ago, just after five o'clock, these two fans of *The Hanging Gale* . . ."

"*The Hanging Gale?*" Sweeney interrupted.

"Remember all that carry-on about ten years ago when they made that television series with the McGann brothers?"

Sweeney nodded and tutted.

"Ah, anyway, Liam, these two fans from Dublin are up here on a holiday, and they wanted to go and see where the film was shot, and sure the auld gate on the front barely keeps out the wind, so they nipped in the yard and they found Joe in the far right-hand corner."

"Found? Had he fallen down or something?"

"No, Liam."

"Was he a victim of a hit-and-run incident and they dumped the body there? I hear there are boy racers in souped-up jamjars with smoked windows who speed around the town a lot these days, Starrett."

"There were no marks about the body at all," Starrett replied.

"No marks at all?" Liam persisted.

"No marks, Liam."

"Well, at least that's something; at least he wasn't murdered," Liam said, appearing to take some comfort from this thought.

"Look, we'll know a lot more when the pathologist has had a proper chance to examine the body."

"Examine the body" seemed to be the words that brought the severity and finality of the situation home at last to Liam Sweeney. He put his head in his hand, shielding his eyes.

Starrett put his hand on Sweeney's back and looked down at the gravelled ground. Garvey looked off into the distance, moving very slowly from foot to foot.

"Ah, Starrett," the eldest Sweeney cried, "why this? Why now? Why Joe?"

Chapter Four

S tarrett made his excuses with Liam. He needed to return to the scene of the investigation. It had been out of respect to Liam Sweeney and his family that Starrett had visited the farm so soon after the body was found. Starrett didn't know Liam Sweeney very well, but the detective's father was quite a good friend of the farmer's, and Starrett always worked on the premise of treating others as he wished to be treated himself. He hadn't expected the entire family to be gathered together though, and so he'd left Sergeant Garvey behind to ensure all remained in the same room on the farm under Packie's eagle eye until he returned.

By the time Starrett returned to the quay, the pathologist, Dr Samantha Aljoe, who'd obviously just arrived, was by her car, a pink Volkswagen VW130. She was awkwardly balancing on one leg and leaning against her car as she tried to pull on a one-piece, opaque suit over her figure-hugging trouser suit.

"Ah, Starrett, my white knight to the rescue," she said, breaking into a generous, teeth-perfect smile, "would you ever come over here and help a damsel in distress."

"Dr Aljoe, I presume," Starrett replied, walking across the quay to her and noticing that Garda Nuala Gibson was following his every move. "How can I help?"

"Well, for now I suppose I'm going to have to settle for a shoulder to lean on," she replied in her educated Home Counties accent. Starrett arrived just in time to catch her as she finally lost her balance and fell into his arms. She remained there about ten seconds longer than she needed to and whispered to him, "That is, of course, unless you've come to your senses and are willing to consummate our relationship."

Starrett considered her words. He considered her stunning good looks, her perfect figure and the intoxicating mixture of aromas that filled his nostrils. She most certainly had a figure to die for. A figure to die for. Now what's that phrase all about? Why would you wish to die to have, or possess, someone else's figure? And surely, if you did, what good would it be to you anyway because . . . you'd be dead, of course.

He considered Nuala Gibson's glare burning straight through these thoughts into the back of his neck and replied, "Bejeepers, Samantha, are all you girls from across the channel so backward about coming forward?"

"Only when we're thwarted in our attempts at fulfilment," she replied, still not trying to disentangle herself from his supportive arms.

"Goodness, woman, you could flirt for Team UK at the Olympics," he said. "Can I just remind you that there is a body on the other side of that wall which needs your other area of expertise?"

"Oh," she tutted, standing up straight and using one of her latex-gloved hands to daintily slap the back of the other, "consider me well and truly chastised, Inspector."

With that she took a surgical case out of the boot of her car and allowed herself to be escorted by Starrett into the courtyard.

Joe Sweeney looked as if he were lying there just pretending to be dead. Even though Starrett had already seen the body, he still had to look at it two or three times more to convince himself it was a corpse. It was always the same for the detective. He never took lack of life for granted.

He left Dr Aljoe to examine the remains of Joe Sweeney and went for a walkabout around the courtyard. It wasn't yet the scene of crime, because he wasn't still sure a crime had been committed.

Starrett reckoned the courtyard, nearly completely overgrown with weeds, hadn't been used properly since it was the location in

the local, gloomy, yet gripping, tongue-wagger, *The Hanging Gale.*
In the opposite corner to where the body was found, there was a
rusted iron spherical frame with a diameter of about four foot.
Starrett couldn't figure out what that was originally used for. Was it
perhaps a discarded prop?

There were other rusted bits of metalwork lying around; some
pieces obviously fitted together, while other disjointed pieces had no
apparent home. There was a severely rusted, low two-wheel trailer
and a couple of empty five-gallon oil cans.

He nodded to Garda Francis Casey to come over to the corner
of the courtyard.

"Tape this area off please, Francis. Any news yet from the
owner?"

"Garda Gibson located him up in the Bridge Bar; he's on the
way over now."

"Good. Have him open that gate and ask him to supply you
with the names of everyone who has keys for it."

"No problem," the mild-mannered Casey replied. "I'd say it
hasn't been used a lot until quite recently though. The gates cut two
arcs through the overgrown weeds. Apart from that, most people get
in here by using the hole in the gate. The Dublin tourists admitted
they gained access that way."

That's what Starrett liked about the young garda: he'd already
started to analyse the scene and was in the process of drawing conclusions.

"Anything else get your attention?" Starrett asked.

"Well, I'd say the body was carried over to the corner rather than
being dragged across. And that rusted iron grid ball has been moved
recently," Casey replied, pointing over to behind where Dr Aljoe
was on her knees, leaning over and examining Joe Sweeney's corpse.

"Good, Francis. Anything else?"

"No, apart from the fact he was in great shape and he'd gotten
drenched to the skin in a big shower earlier," Casey replied, and
then, noting a new arrival to the scene, added, "Ah, there's the
owner. Excuse me, sir."

Starrett watched as Casey ran the short distance back to the gate. Looking up to the skies, the inspector couldn't remember any rain having fallen during the day. Then again, the rain was so frequent in Donegal people did try to ignore it. He looked down to the weeds. He hunkered down and ran the three straight and one crooked finger of his right hand through some of the taller weeds of the blanket growth. They were bone dry. He wandered over to the corpse and, without disturbing Dr Aljoe's inspection of the head, put his hands in the victim's denim trouser pocket. It felt more cold than damp, but still damp enough for him to feel moisture. He removed one of the Nike trainers, and the sock was equally moist. He knew that the Donegal rain was heavy and persistent, but he'd never heard of it wetting anyone's inside pockets and socks before.

"Our man's been drowned," he said to Aljoe's back.

"Sorry?" she said, turning around on her hunkers to face him. "Are my *professional* services now *also* surplus to your requirements?"

She turned back to Sweeney's head, removed one of her surgical gloves with a loud snap and ruffled her fingers through his jet-black, curly hair. "His hair is bone dry though – the sun?"

"No sun in this corner, doctor," Starrett replied, looking up the side of the 250-year-old stone wall.

"He went for a swim, fully clothed, came in here to dry his hair and then died? I don't think so."

"Tell me this, Samantha: after you wash your lovely hair, how long does it take to fully dry out?"

"Well, I use a hairdryer, but I don't see any thirteen-amp plugs around these walls," she said, breaking into a sympathetic smile for Starrett. "Drying mine can take anything up to forty minutes."

"So with the fresh air and no hairdryer . . . say it would take a couple of hours for his hair to dry by itself?"

"Yeah, I'd agree with that."

"There's something about the look though. His hair still looks like it's been attended to. Brushed back from his face. He looks like he's just come out of the gym or swimming pool, had a quick shower, dried his hair quickly and combed it back, maybe even with his hands, for proper attention later."

"I know the look you mean. I tie mine up in a towel until I get a chance to use the hairdryer. Mind you, I'm not 100 per cent sure about the time to dry it, so if in the name of research you want to come back to my place and observe the entire procedure first hand . . . no? I thought not."

Starrett stood up, put his hands in his pockets and looked down to either distract himself or to study Joe Sweeney.

"Don't bother about me, Starrett," she said, standing up to face him. "I need to be less than serious around corpses; it's the only way I can keep my mind clear enough to do my job properly. You know I don't mean anything by it, don't you?"

"Of course I do, doctor. We all have our own little dances to distract ourselves," Starrett said, distracted by a question running around his head. "Would you like to hazard a guess as to a time of death?"

"I'd say the early hours of this morning," Aljoe replied, studying the colour and rigidity of the body. "Not earlier than one and no later than five o'clock this morning."

They were both silent as they thought about death. For Starrett, when she gave the time of death, even though it was approximate, she was in a way officially confirming the end of a life. There was no way any little dance that Aljoe or Starrett attempted was going to lessen this fact.

It was as if he were being told, *OK, this unfortunate is deceased. Now for goodness sake, man, you get on and do what you do, and see if you can find the person with something to answer for.*

"Someone dried his hair," Starrett continued as Aljoe replaced her surgical glove and returned to her work. "Someone cared about him, someone knew him enough to care about him."

"You mean they didn't mean to kill him?" she asked, as she examined the corpse's fingers. "They were fooling around, and it all went very wrong and they panicked, feared the repercussions from the parents or brothers and hid the body in here? Maybe it was one of the brothers or even the father? Did he have any brothers?"

"Jeez, Sam, you're on a roll. You'll have solved the crime by sun-down," Starrett said, as his face cracked back into the lines of a well-marked smile.

"Well, the profiling shit seems to work for Cracker."

"Aye, but as often as not the big fella was wrong," Starrett muttered before answering her question. "Joe had two brothers, Tom and Ryan, and one sister, Teresa."

"Ah, the waste," Aljoe said, perhaps to herself, as she carried out a closer inspection of Joe's hands and arms.

Chapter Five

Garda Casey, by this point, not only had the gate opened – the padlock was so rusted it apparently hadn't worked properly for years and was only really used as a visual deterrent – but he'd also gained access, through the courtyard, to the surrounding buildings. The warehouses all along the quay were four storeys high – the fourth storey occupying mainly the loft space – and all the visible woodwork was painted in a distinctive colour of ownership. The warehouse in question was painted an eye-catching lime green, which indicated it was the property of Letterkenny property developer Owen Bonner.

Bonner himself hadn't come out to help the gardaí; no, he'd sent one of his lieutenants, a talkative Declan Dunford, to do the necessary. Owen Bonner of late had been bending over backwards to keep on the right side of the law in a desperate attempt to take his family business kicking and screaming into the twenty-first century as a legit business. Starrett knew Bonner would be spitting flames when he discovered that a dead body had been discarded on one of his many properties. At the same time, just because the body was discovered on Bonner's property didn't necessary mean that the developer *wasn't* involved. The end result was that the elderly and rugged Declan Dunford probably had his quiet evening at the Bridge Bar severely disrupted by Bonner's endeavours to appear helpful to the local gardaí in their on-going enquiries.

Starrett also knew that if Bonner *weren't* involved in the incident, he'd be carrying out his own, equally efficient, investigation.

He'd tipped Francis Casey off on this point to encourage the garda to develop a relationship with the affable Dunford.

The scene of crime team was now in full swing, going through the courtyard with the proverbial toothcomb. The photographer shot the remains from every conceivable angle and then went to work on how the body fitted in with its surroundings. Dunford chatted away ten to the dozen with Garda Casey, but Starrett noticed that Bonner's lieutenant never once looked Casey directly in the eye. As the evening wore on, more and more official vehicles arrived, and the balmy August evening also helped to draw an incredible number of sightseers. The gardaí seemed to be having trouble controlling them. Although they eventually managed to push all the gawkers back to the tapes at either end of the block of ancient warehouses, some of the more adventurous, most likely the press, Starrett figured, turned up in small boats trying to get an advantaged view waterside. Sadly their vessels were too low and the stone-paved quayside too high for them to be successful. Generally though, it was a good-natured and respectful crowd who were happy to do as Starrett's team bid them.

Starrett wondered how the Sweeney family were getting on up at the farm. He strolled across to the water's edge and looked deep into the River Leannan. It was deep enough to accommodate largish fishing vessels. He walked on towards the far corner where the quayside turned ninety degrees to the right, while the clear water continued on straight and eventually flowed into Lough Swilly, which in turn fed the choppy Atlantic Ocean at Fanad Head. His mind was about to wander across the mighty ocean to America when his thoughts were disturbed by Dr Aljoe's distinctive intonation.

"Right, Starrett, I'm off. I've done all I can do here. That's me until I can get him laid out on my table."

Starrett had a flash of something, something to do with water, but her words had interrupted his unique processs, and the moment of insight passed. He'd learned over the years never to try and chase the lost thought.

Aljoe, obviously mistaking his lack of response, continued,

"Look, I'm really sorry about earlier, I . . . ah . . . well, the truth is, as I mentioned to you, I like to distance myself from the corpse . . ."

"You were perfectly fine, Samantha."

"No, really, Starrett, I need to tell you. If the crime scene is too reverential and I get too preoccupied with who the corpse might have been, I simply go to pieces and can't do my work."

"Truth is, I love the banter as well," Starrett replied, breaking into a grin, wide enough to display his teeth. He'd endured too many an agonising hour in his London dentist's chair not to want to have at least some benefit. "I mean, just look at yourself . . ."

The doctor seemed to rise a few inches.

"Now that's much better, Starrett," she purred; "that's the look I prefer to see in your eye. But from what I'm hearing, it's a look that's reserved for Maggie Keane these days."

Starrett thought about the woman in question and not for the first time since he'd awoken that morning. He thought about how two women couldn't be more different, and yet he was strangely attracted to both. He mentally chastised himself for having such thoughts around the scene of a crime, if in fact that was what this was turning out to be.

He broke off the conversation by allowing the grin to drop from his face and looking at Aljoe.

"OK, Starrett," she laughed, "I get the hint. I'm outta here. I'll get you the autopsy report early tomorrow morning."

His smile returned.

"We could discuss it at the Coffee Dock in the morning if you like?" Dr Aljoe said over her shoulder as she walked away from him in the direction of her shocking pink automobile.

"I'll ring you later," Starrett said, chastising himself once again for noticing just how sensual her rear was.

Chapter Six

Starrett left Gardaí Casey and Gibson and the SOC forensic team behind at the warehouse to complete the search of the scene and the adjoining warehouses.

He needed to return to the Sweeney farmhouse before too much more time had passed. There wasn't a lot more he felt he could learn from the scene where Joe Sweeney's body had been found. He didn't know for sure, of course, but he didn't feel it was the scene of the crime. The youngest of the Sweeney clan had been dealt with somewhere else and then unceremoniously dumped with the ghosts of *The Hanging Gale* – that was, of course, assuming television dramas were capable of leaving ghosts behind.

If there had been ghosts in the overgrown courtyard of the warehouses, what might they have reported on the comings and goings that marked the demise of Joe Sweeney? Starrett realised old man Sweeney wasn't going to want to hear that Starrett was seeking the assistance of ghosts to help him ascertain what had happened to his youngest.

"Not a lot," Packie Garvey replied, when Starrett asked what had happened in his absence.

The first thing Starrett did when he returned to the farm was to replace Garvey in the family room with Nuala Gibson, leaving her with the waiting eleven members and friends of the Sweeney family.

"Liam left the girls to attend to his wife," Garvey added, "and told the boys he didn't want any discussions about the recent event in front of his grandchildren. Three times he told Thomas to 'whist in front of the wains.'"

"Nothing else, Packie?" Starrett continued as he wandered around the good room, where the furniture was so unused that the room looked like one of the new furniture showrooms up in Derry. They'd entered the front part of the house to ensure those under discussion wouldn't overhear their conversation.

"'Fraid not," Packie started. "Joe lived here with his parents, and as far as I can tell, the rest of them are here today because it's Liam's birthday."

Then Packie told Starrett what he'd learned about who'd arrived and when and in what order.

"How's the mother?" Starrett continued, disappointed that his usually alert extra set of eyes and ears hadn't enjoyed much fodder in his absence.

"She seems happy to hide under the cloak of shock. Maybe Liam whispered to her to lie low, you know?"

"Maybe," Starrett agreed. "Anything else?"

"Thomas Sweeney's eldest daughter, Bernadette, wanted to sit by her Uncle Ryan, but her dad made her go back to tend to her granny with her mammy. Thomas was the one who seemed most preoccupied with the rest of the group, always observing the interplay."

"Who seems most upset?" Starrett asked as he absentmindedly picked up a few photos.

"The kids, but that's just because they haven't been told what's happened, I fear," Packie replied and he watched in silence as Starrett picked up photo after photo from the top of the drinks cabinet. Starrett seemed lost in the various scenes caught in the timeless, fading ten by eights in front of him. "How do you want to do this?" Packie eventually asked.

"First off, let's go and take a look at Joe's room. Do you know which one it is?" Starrett asked, as he started towards the grand staircase.

"Yes, it's the middle one at the front. Colette went in for a few minutes; I felt I should leave her to it. I had it locked immediately she came out," Garvey said as he produced a Yale key.

Joe Sweeney's room didn't really give a lot away about the owner, apart from the fact that, if his room was anything to go by, he wasn't a man keen on creature comforts. It was a clean, good-sized but not fashionable room. It was painted off-white, and the walls were picture-free apart from a Chipperfield's Circus poster centred above his bed on the wall facing the front windows. The only comfortable chair in the room was positioned right by the middle of his three windows and enjoyed a view way, way down the glen to the spectacular twists and turns of the water. The armchair was battered and covered in Black Watch tartan material. Starrett sat in it and tried to get a sense of the man. There was a small round table to the right of the chair and on it was a book – *The Stones of Summer* by Dow Mossman – looking very much as if it had been ignored. The pages were still tight but faded in the bright light to an off-yellow, suggesting it might have been an unwelcome Christmas or birthday present. The bed was double size and made up, with a bedside table and reading lamp keeping guard. Colette Sweeney had laid out her son's dark blue suit on his perfectly made bed. The suit, white shirt and black tie were stretched out on the bed, looking as if someone had stolen a body from within. By the side of the bed sat a pair of black leather shoes with a pair of dark blue socks neatly folded into the left shoe.

On the far wall from the bed was a pale wood Ikea desk and matching chair. The desk had a few blank papers thrown carelessly over it. A Robert's radio, a mobile phone charger and a lamp were all plugged into the thirteen-amp sockets fitted in the skirting board under the desk. (Starrett hated to see old skirting boards contaminated with electrics, Eircom leads and points.) To the right of the desk, there was a large, say thirty-inch by seventy-inch, indent made on the fitted, sea-grass carpet. The clean space was so new it looked like something had been moved from there recently. To the left of the desk was a bookcase packed with manuals, files and books, mostly on cattle and farming issues. *Joe was obviously not big on recreational reading*, Starrett thought.

"Well, Packie, let's have one of the team pack up all of Joe's paperwork and take it down to Tower House for closer examination."

"Right. Shall we take the contents of the drawers as well?"

"Everything, please," Starrett said. He waited on the landing for Garvey to lock the door to Joe's bedroom again. "Now as far as I can see, the important thing is that we really need to get to know the family, and I'd say our best starting point would be Joe's girlfriend, Breda Roche. Why don't you go back to the family room and send Garda Gibson and Breda Roche to meet me in the front room."

Chapter Seven

A few seconds later, Nuala Gibson entered the good room accompanied by a very distressed Breda Roche.

Starrett offered the girl the seat he'd been using while waiting. He went to the drinks cabinet and poured a small Bushmills for Roche. She downed it in one, shuddering as it worked its way into her bloodstream.

Breda Roche's spectacular looks were sharply focused, Starrett felt, due to the fact that she'd totally shorn her hair. With her lack of hair and subtle make-up, she'd perfected the Sinead O'Connor look, but the overall impression was somewhat gentler than that of the frequently troubled singer. Starrett was drawn to comforting Breda; he wasn't so sure he'd feel the same were he sharing a room with Sinead.

"How did you meet Joe?" Starrett asked.

Starrett always felt that the clothes people wore sometimes come to mock them when grief came calling suddenly. For instance, when Ms Roche had been at home earlier that day, choosing an outfit to impress her potential in-laws, friends and her boyfriend, her loose, deep red, knee-length, gypsy chic skirt and Doc Marten boots probably felt very good. Starrett also noted, from the tightness of her top ringed in two shades of red, that it might just have been her boyfriend in particular she wanted to impress. But now that he, he who she hoped would most be amazed by her look, was dead . . . well . . .

Breda seemed to snap out of a preoccupation, and a smile passed over her face as briefly as the shadow of a cloud passing over Donegal's rich landscape on a windy day.

"I, ah, Sheila, well Teresa really," she began, trying to catch her thoughts into some shape. Her thought process seemed to calm her somewhat.

Gibson looked up from her notes to give a quick nod of credit in Starrett's direction. The detective was too busy studying Breda Roche to notice.

"OK," Roche began again, this time sitting up in her chair and unhunching her shoulders, "I knew Sheila Kelly for quite a while. We were mates . . . friends," here her brown eyes dropped to the floor, "good friends really, and her brother was my brother's best friend. Anyway, we used to hang out together, and one night we bumped into Teresa Sweeney down at the Bridge Bar – you know the Bridge?"

"Bejeepers, sure don't I know it well," Starrett said, keen to keep the conversation light at this stage.

Roche smiled in spite of herself. She was still circling around in her conversation, appearing reluctant to get to the point where she met Joe.

"Just so you know a bit about our joint history, Sheila didn't seem as taken with Teresa at first, but Teresa and I seemed to hit it off near enough immediately. We arranged to meet up a few weeks later in Letterkenny and went to the cinema to see *Once,* an amazing film, and the music is just incredible. Teresa and I love music, but Sheila's not really so fussed. We came back to the farm here afterwards. Mr and Mrs Sweeney always have an open house, and people are coming and going all the time. And that's the night I met Joe. He'd not long stopped work, and he was sitting in the kitchen sprawled out by the table in his wellies, dirty shirt, threadbare jumper – two sizes too big for him – and dirty denim jeans. He was chatting away twelve to the dozen with his mum. I can see the scene vividly in my mind now. When Joe sat at the table, he would always take up so much room; he'd rest on his elbows and have his feet extended at forty-five degrees. He was so enthusiastic about absolutely everything. He was excited to see his sister; they were very close when they were growing up. He made such a fuss over her, and then he wanted to know everything about me and the film we'd just seen."

"How long did it take him to ask you out?" Gibson asked.

Roche smiled at the memory.

"Actually there was a bit of subtle matchmaking going on behind the scenes at first."

"He was a shy boy, was he?" Gibson prompted.

"Not so much shy as so preoccupied with the farm that girls just didn't seem important to him. Like going to the cinema for instance: he was all excited that first night about hearing what Teresa and myself thought about the film, and he kept on questioning us about *Once,* and he seemed to know a great deal about films, but in all the time we dated, I've never been able to get him to take me to see a film. I don't think I've ever known him to go and see a film. He wasn't greatly fussed about the telly either. He'd watch the RTÉ news and sport, but that was it. It was kind of the same with me: yes, he seemed to like me, but no, he wasn't prepared to do anything about it."

"So what happened?" Gibson asked. Starrett knew that inside Garda Nuala Gibson would be screaming, *Land the plane, woman, land the plane for heaven's sake!* But outwardly she was poised and controlled and conducting the interview perfectly.

"Well, Sheila, who'd been out with Teresa and myself a few times at this stage – you know, we went to the places where young girls go and we did the things young girls do. Anyway, Sheila decided that we three girls and Joe should all go out for a night together. So Sheila, as ever, organised the night. First we went go-carting at the Carting Centre on the Letterkenny to Ramelton Road. That was a great hoot. Then we went to the Water's Edge at Rathmullan for a bite and then back to the Bridge Bar for a drink. When we got to the Bridge, we got split up after Joe bought us a round of drinks. It was packed in there, as usual, so Joe and I went outside to sit on the wall, and Sheila and Teresa went inside to hear Brendan Quinn do his set."

"And that's when he asked you out?" Gibson nudged.

"Ah, no, actually I suggested we go to the cinema together. I mean, I didn't feel like I was asking him out on a date or something.

He was cute, he scrubbed up well, he was funny, he was lively, he was great company, but I'd never really considered him in a romantic way," Breda said. She looked like she could see Gibson's next question coming, because she held up her hand in a stop sign before continuing: "I don't really know why, maybe it was because when Sheila, Teresa and I went out we had so much craic that boys never really came into the picture much. But I found out that they'd orchestrated it so Joe and I would be by ourselves that night at the Bridge Bar. When I asked him to the cinema, he said dismissively that he had no time to be sitting in the dark watching films. I must have looked like I'd felt that he'd shot me down, because he immediately said, 'Sorry, I didn't mean it like that. I'd much prefer to go out and do something else with you.' So the short of it was that the following day, which was Sunday, he took me to climb Muckish. Now, not my ideal date, I will admit, but it was great fun altogether, and we started going out after that."

The plane had landed, somewhere on top of the rugged Muckish Mountain, and Gibson looked suitably relieved.

"And youse were serious about each other?" Gibson asked.

"Not at first. I mean I wasn't particularly looking for a boyfriend, but the more I got to know him, the more I realised what a wonderful caring person he was, and . . ." Roche said and stopped.

Starrett found himself liking the sensual sound of her voice. It wasn't really a Donegal accent, even though she'd been born and bred in Milford; it was more like a mid-Atlantic purr, very cute and extremely pleasing to Starrett's ear. Roche's hesitancy had grown into a blush, which, because of her shaven head, also rose to her crown.

"Well, there's no real reason not to tell you. It just seems like a very private thing to be telling the gardaí, but he was a brilliant kisser; when we kissed I'd just melt, and I'd never really experienced that before."

Starrett immediately thought of Maggie Keane as Roche looked to Garda Gibson with a "Do you know what I mean?" look on her open, readable face.

"That's the sure sign," Gibson agreed with a conciliatory grin. "So you were serious about each other?"

"Yes," Roche replied.

"Tell me," Starrett began, "did Joe have many friends?"

"Not really. I mean, he worked very long hours on the farm. He hadn't been to university or anything, so he didn't have a social circle like most of us have. He got on great with his brother Ryan."

Starrett was going to ask about the relationship with Joe's other brother Thomas when Roche continued: "Ryan's around the farm a lot more than Thomas, and Thomas is married and has his own family now. He lives just a wee bit too far away – over at borderlands – just to drop in on them any more."

"Does Ryan live on the farm?" Starrett asked.

"No, he lives and works in Belfast, but he bought one of those new houses up in Coylin Court, and he and Maeve come up as often as they can."

"And . . ." Starrett asked and paused, "do you know of anyone . . . anyone who might have . . ."

"Hurt Joe?"

Starrett nodded.

"No. Joe was not the kind of boy to have enemies. He got on with his life, he worked hard, he didn't get involved in politics, he never . . ." Roche said, but her growing sobbing made it impossible for Starrett and Gibson to make out what she was saying any more. Her sobbing broke into full-scale crying, and she looked to Starrett as if he should know what she was trying to tell him and seemed frustrated by the fact that he didn't.

Gibson walked over and put a hand on her shoulder, and Starrett took Breda's glass over to the drinks cabinet and poured her another, more generous, drink.

She eagerly took the glass but couldn't find a way between her crying to get her breath sufficiently to swallow the golden-brown healer. She dribbled the whiskey back into the glass and handed it back to Starrett, apologising with her eyes all the time.

Starrett was frustrated, but he could do nothing but suspend the interview for now.

"Garda Gibson will take you back to the family. We can talk

later when you're feeling better," he said, helping her up from the table, thinking that they needed to talk to someone who'd be a bit more uninhibited about the information they gave and maybe not quite so upset.

Chapter Eight

"I think I'd like to see the older of the two wee granddaughters. What's her name again?" Starrett asked after Gibson returned from taking the quietly sobbing Breda through to be comforted by Teresa.

"That would be Bernadette."

"Bernie, right?"

"No, sir, apparently not," Gibson replied, very quickly. "Not even her dad gets away with that abbreviation."

Bernadette surprised Gibson and Starrett by not being in the least bit fazed by the circumstances. If anything, she seemed relieved to get away from the family room, and it was she who started off the proceedings when they were safely behind closed doors in the good room.

"You're the garda inspector who's going out with Katie's mum, aren't you?"

"Well, Maggie Keane is a friend of mine," Starrett replied, unsure of his ground and nervous of where this conversation might go. He couldn't be sure, but it looked as if Garda Gibson seemed to be taking some pleasure in his discomfort. "A very good friend," he added, just in case this was going to be reported back.

Bernadette smiled at him. It was a knowing smile; a smile he'd also been unsettled by the first time Katie had used it on him.

"Breda says that Joe's a great kisser," the eldest of the Sweeney grandchildren offered unsolicited.

"Really?" Nuala Gibson asked, saving Starrett the embarrassment of having to go there.

"Yes," Bernadette continued, appearing excited by the gossip opportunity, "but apparently not as good a kisser as his sister."

"Sorry, who's Teresa's boyfriend?" Starrett asked as Bernadette and Gibson rolled their eyes at each other, implying, *What page is he on?*

"Sheila, silly; they're part of the pink posse actually," Bernadette boasted.

"Oh, right," Starrett offered, deadpan.

"Yes, but even better than that. Breda is best friends with Teresa's girlfriend Sheila, and I think Breda and Sheila used to be girlfriends, or 'friends with benefits,' as Sheila puts it, but then Sheila started up with Teresa," Bernadette continued in a rush of words, followed by a sigh for breath.

Starrett looked at Gibson, thoroughly confused. He couldn't believe what he'd first heard, and, if it were true, how would an eleven-year-old have been able to pick up on it?

"Did you get all that?" he asked.

Bernadette ballooned her cheeks and slowly exhaled the air in her show of frustration.

"*OK,* Sheila and Teresa are gay, and Breda used to be. Sheila stole Teresa from Breda, who then became Joe's girlfriend," Bernadette clarified for Starrett's benefit, having the manners not to add "duh" at the end of her reply.

Starrett wondered if Bernadette knew what the word gay meant. As if reading Starrett's mind, Bernadette added. "And of course, as Auntie Teresa told me, a gay person, or as she puts it, a lesbian, is the girlfriend you have when you're waiting around to find a boyfriend. She says it's brilliant because you can't get pregnant. Jo, the elder sister of Mary, a friend of mine at school, got pregnant and she's only turned sixteen. She's taking time out to have the baby, and then she's coming back to college next year to finish her education while her mother looks after the baby."

Starrett thought of Maggie Keane and her son and two daughters and what was before them all. In fairness to Maggie, she had warned Starrett.

He really didn't know where to go with this. Innocently, Bernadette was potentially directly implicating Breda Roche, Sheila Kelly and Teresa Sweeney.

"Bernadette, could you tell me this: are Sheila, Teresa and Breda all still good friends?" Gibson asked.

"Oh yes, very much so. Sure, even though Breda's found her boyfriend, she still keeps her hair short. They all still used to go down to Belfast for nights out together. I tried to find out where they go to, because you know, in a few years' time Mary, she's my best friend, and I will want to get down to the city to get away from the boys for a weekend."

Starrett put his head in his hand. Bernadette had obviously been very successful at eavesdropping on her elders' conversations, and as Maggie had explained to him, the more the elders would have tried to exclude her, the more she would have had her eagle ears primed for the valuable information. It's not that she would have been mature enough to fully understand the inference of the words, but that didn't matter; she was picking them all up, that was the important bit at this stage in her life. She'd have them translated by the elder sisters of her friends at a later time.

"What can you tell us about your Uncle Joe?" Starrett asked. He found it funny how personal investment could force him to view interview conversations such as the one he was currently having in a completely different light. Normally, he'd probably just be extremely happy to pick up the vital information being so generously shared with him. But because of Maggie and her daughters Katie and Moya, he now had a vested interest into what he dreaded was ahead of Katie and Moya and indirectly their mother and, once more removed, himself.

"Joe was lovely," Bernadette began, shocking Starrett by how quickly she was referring to her deceased uncle in the past tense. "He was very fond of my younger sister Fin – that's Finula – and she him. In fact he was probably her favourite person in the whole world. *Oh, my God!* I'm such a *loser*. I've just realised what this will mean to Fin. I can't *believe* I didn't think of that *before*."

Gibson went across to Bernadette's chair and patted her on the back in comfort.

"Joe," she said, starting back up again, "Joe was a lot like my granddad. You know, like he was happy being a farmer. Ryan, he's my favourite uncle, and my dad aren't really farmers. They're 'professional men,' as my dad likes to remind my mother. My mum is always telling my dad he should be getting part of the farm, and my father is always saying, 'But what would I do with it? I don't want to be a farmer,' 'Why, you'd sell it of course, dumbo,' my mum would say. My dad says they can't possibly split up a farm it has taken nearly 150 years to put together. I mean, my dad's right, isn't he?"

"That's the accepted wisdom, Bernadette," Starrett replied. "What does your dad do?"

"Both my parents are solicitors," she replied, rolling her eyes in a "but someone has to do it" dismissive way.

Starrett wondered what kind of job it took to impress youngsters. He had found himself wondering quite a lot about kids lately. Maggie Keane's kids seemed fine, maybe even excited, about him being an inspector in the gardaí, but that probably had more to do with Maggie than it did with the current trends in today's youth culture. When Starrett was growing up around the streets of Ramelton, a solicitor trumped a police inspector any day of the week, and two solicitors in the one family, well, quite simply, they did not need to show any more of their cards to win the hand outright. Not to mention the fact that their joint earning power was probably five times that of Starrett's.

"What kind of legal work do they do?" Gibson asked.

"I don't really know," the young Sweeney replied, "but I do know that the prostitutes also solicit, so I'm not so sure I really care to discover exactly what it is they do."

Neither Gibson nor Starrett followed Bernadette's precocious smile.

"Now listen, young lady," Starrett started, but reigned himself back in, "the food on your table and the clothes on your back have to be paid for by someone's hard work."

"Yes," Bernadette replied immediately, offering Starrett her sweetest innocent smile, "but my mum reckons that when Granddad dies, Joe will be worth more than all his brothers and sister put together."

Starrett stared at her kindly, his blue eyes offering her advance sympathy for what was sure to be her next thought. But he was wrong.

"Now that Joe's dead," she began in a considered tone, taking great care over smoothing her dungarees in a very deliberate way, "who'll get the farm when Granddad dies?"

This time Starrett had to agree that it was a good question and a question he needed to find the answer to.

"I think that'll do us for now," Starrett said, standing up and nodding at Gibson, "but we'll need to talk to you again."

"That'll be fun," she said as she also stood up.

Starrett wondered just how many home truths he was going to learn from this child. He felt slightly guilty for uncovering the family dirty linen so easily.

Just before Bernadette left the room, she detoured to the corner where Starrett was sitting, leaned over the edge of the chair and whispered to Starrett, "I know you and Mrs Keane have kissed."

She turned so that Starrett could see her eyes but Gibson couldn't. She nodded once to him very slowly and very deliberately, as if to say, "But that will be our wee secret."

"You get on very well with Moya Keane, don't you?" Nuala enquired when she and Starrett were alone again, and then, without waiting for a reply, she added, "Maggie says it's because you don't treat her as a child, but as her own person."

Starrett would just love to have asked, "What else has Maggie Keane been saying about me?" But he knew he'd never get away with it.

"Moya's a wee dote; it seems she is the self-appointed gatekeeper of her mum's feelings," Starrett replied, to get past this moment.

"Oh, don't you believe it. Joe and Katie are right there with her every step of the way too," Gibson said positively.

"There might even be a bean garda sitting in the wings as well?"

"Ah, nah, I'd say we're all in there pretty much centre stage," Gibson said as she continued to update her notes on the Bernadette Sweeney interview.

Chapter Nine

"Who do you want to speak to next?" Gibson asked just as there was a knock on the door. She went to open it and immediately stood back into the room, opening the door to the full.

The gangly Major Newton Cunningham lowered his head, even though he didn't need to, as he walked regally through the door frame. As ever, he was dressed in his Donegal tweed suit, a mustard waistcoat, a country checked shirt and a Royal Ulster Rifles regimental tie. His long grey hair was combed back and fell over the back collar of his shirt and jacket. He strode straight across the wooden floor, his brown and white leather brogues crunching out the five steps to Starrett, muttering some kind of greeting to Garda Gibson as he passed.

Gibson left the room, closing the door behind her. Starrett could hear the muffled sounds of her addressing someone on the other side.

"I had to come down and see Liam," the major began in his regimental clipped tones. "I don't think the press is too far behind me."

Major Newton Cunningham pretty much left Starrett to get on with his work undisturbed. He couldn't remember the last time the major had turned up on an investigation.

"Of course, Major," Starrett replied, offering a seat to his boss.

Major wasn't an officially acknowledged garda title. No, the major had served in the Royal Ulster Rifles in their 1950 Cyprus campaign. Back in the 1950s, as the young An Garda Siochana was reorganising, the major had been one of those willing and able to breathe the much-needed new life into the guardians of the peace. His seventy-three years were threatening to catch up with him, but remarkably, after all he'd been through and the damage the various battles had wreaked on his body, he showed no sign of slowing up.

"Fine man is Liam; solid family," the major continued, happy to sit down on something solid. "I believe the boys all did well in their education. Joe, the youngest, seemed to be least afraid of getting his hands dirty. I believe the daughter wears soft shoes, but thankfully that's no longer a hangable offence."

Starrett knew the major was trying to give him as much information as possible, and the asides were just codes to the importance of the information. In the distance Starrett could still hear the mumbled voice of Gibson. He was just about to make some reference to Teresa when the major continued.

"Pick up anything yet?"

"We've just started," Starrett replied, as his brain did a fast rewind of his two interviews thus far.

"Look, Starrett, I can see you're going to be up to your eyes here, so the other reason I've come up to see you is to give you a bit of good news."

The major looked at Starrett, a pained smile spreading across the elder's face. Starrett knew in that second he wasn't going to like this particular good news.

"Right," he said, waiting.

"I've got a new recruit for your team," the major started, but before Starrett could offer his protest, the major raised a hand, palm towards his junior, "and I know how much you like them young. Romany is fresh from his final refresher down in Templemore, and he graduated top of his group . . ."

"Look, Major, can we possibly leave this until after this case?"

"It's clear to me, Starrett, that you're going to need all the help you can get, and maybe it's time we started to incorporate some of these modern detecting methods they're developing at Templemore into our investigations. Garda Browne is up to speed on all these recent developments, and he is keen as mustard to get stuck in."

Starrett was trying desperately hard to think of something to say, something that wouldn't get him fired, when Newton Cunningham played his ace card.

"I served with his grandfather, Starrett, in the Royal Ulster Rifles. His father died when he was very young. His mother came to me toward the end of his training to see if I could personally help him make a go of this, if I'd become a father figure for him, if you will. I couldn't possibly refuse her, Starrett."

Both Starrett and the major knew that Starrett would put up no further resistance; the reason Starrett was currently a garda inspector himself was because his father had had a similar conversation with the major.

"OK, Major, I'll see him later today back at Tower House."

"There's no need to wait until you get back to the station," the major said, rising awkwardly. "As I said, he's keen as mustard and a perfect addition for your team. Romany . . ." the major called out in the direction of the closed door. He quickly corrected himself to, "Garda Browne!"

The door opened, and a confident young man marched in as if he were still on the parade ground at Templemore. His arms swinging mechanically, he marched right up to the major and Starrett.

"Right, Garda Browne," the major started. "This is your superior, Inspector Starrett, and you won't do better on this island if you listen to every word he says. Not only should you note everything he does, but you should do everything he does."

And with that the major hobbled off without further explanation, leaving both Starrett and Browne idling in his wake.

Never one to put too much emphasis on first impressions, Starrett immediately felt there was something distinctly unlikeable about this novice garda, Romany Browne. He couldn't quite put his finger on it. Surely it couldn't be his movie idol, perfectly sculptured looks? His permanent semi-tanned complexion? Or his jet-black unkempt hair that every female Starrett knew was going to want to run her fingers through? Or his perfect snow-white molars? Starrett's set themselves were as good as any in the county, but Starrett now felt that if there were to be a dentist's advertising campaign, then he would be used for the before-treatment shots and Browne's would be the after-treatment photos. And then, as if that wasn't enough, Starrett was convinced that the novice was wearing a made-to-measure uniform, and it was made to measure in a way that showed off his perfect gym-toned body.

Starrett was going to let it go there . . . that was until he noticed Browne's shoes. Surely they weren't regulation? Yes, the uppers were black leather, but as Browne had walked across the floor earlier, the soles, made from some malleable honeycombed material, not only took his weight but also seemed to give him a spring to his step.

Starrett smiled to himself as he thought, *That wasn't a bad wee inner rant for someone who doesn't put much store on first impressions.* He smiled because he accepted that he had made his career – his third and final career – on first impressions.

"Right, Garda Browne, keen to go are we?" Starrett started.

"Yes, sir, I was only waiting for this moment to arrive . . . like, for all of my life," Browne replied, in an accent more Oxbridge than Templemore.

"Do you know what's going on here?"

"Yes, sir. The major briefed me on the way down: youngest son of the Sweeney family found dead in mysterious circumstances. Never been in trouble before, obviously a member of the family is involved . . ."

"OK, OK, Romany," Starrett interrupted with a sigh. "I hate rules, but rule number one is, never jump to conclusions."

"Yes, yes, of course, always follow the evidence," the novice offered in interruption.

Starrett was about to hit him with rule number two, but he had a more immediate problem: he first had to find the evidence before he could advise that it be followed.

"What I want you to do, no . . . what I need you to do," Starrett began, realising he was bordering on patronising, "is stay in the kitchen dining area with the family and keep your eyes and ears open and your mouth . . ."

"Shut," Browne offered.

"*Cor*-rect," Starrett said. "Right, off you go and relieve Sergeant Packie Garvey."

"The hurling champion, Packie Garvey?"

Starrett just looked at him.

"Right, right; I'm off then to relieve Packie Garvey," he replied, pronouncing Packie's name in obvious disbelief.

"Tell Packie to bring Liam Sweeney, the deceased's father, in to see us, and could you also send Garda Nuala Gibson back in to me."

Browne paused and, for a split second before he left the room, appeared to be turning back towards his new superior. Starrett could tell Browne had found something to say about Gibson but had, very wisely, thought better of it.

"So, who's the dishy garda?" Gibson whispered the second she entered the room.

It had begun.

"Yes, he's a shiny button, isn't he?" Starrett replied, inviting her to take her place at the table, by her notes, again.

He sat beside her and impatiently drummed the permanently crooked forefinger of his right hand on the brilliantly polished circular table.

Chapter Ten

Sometimes Starrett worried about how much his work involved talking. *Really,* he thought, *what else do I do? Talking, and listening to people talking: was that really a way for a grown man to earn a living?* It was a thought that disappeared from his mind the minute Liam Sweeney strode into his room.

The farmer looked as if he were doing a double take at seeing Starrett and Gibson looking so comfortable in a room in his house.

He looked like most farmers do while dressed in their Sunday best: uncomfortable. His black pinstripe, two-piece suit, with mismatched cream shirt and a brownish tartan tie, looked as if it hadn't yet made too many weekly excursions from his wardrobe. He was slightly stooped at the waist. Starrett couldn't work out if it was from too many days working the fields of his farm or from the terrible, unbearable weight that had just descended upon his shoulders. He was wearing red carpet slippers, secured on to his feet with a new piece of white elastic sewed on to each side. The slippers squeaked a rubbery sound, mocking the rest of his outfit, as he walked over to his drinks cabinet.

"What'll ye have, Starrett?"

Starrett knew better than to refuse the man in his time of trouble.

"I'll have the same as yourself," Starrett replied, then grimaced before adding quickly, "just make mine smaller."

"Right," the elder Sweeney replied; "and yourself, miss, you won't be drinking on duty, now will you?"

"No, thanks," Nuala Gibson replied.

"Grand," Sweeney replied more in a sigh. "I wouldn't want the inspector here to be caught driving home under the influence."

He poured himself a generous straight Bushmills and started to pour one for Starrett. Starrett protested that there was already more than enough in his glass.

"Ach, sure that wouldn't fill a hollow tooth," he replied as he poured in just a wee bit more. He handed Starrett his glass, they touched glasses gently, and Sweeney downed his in one. He returned to the drinks cabinet, replaced the glass and screwed the top back on the half full bottle of Bushmills.

Starrett raised the glass to his lips and gingerly let the liquid no more than kiss his top lip. He placed the glass back on the table and said, "I'm very sorry for your loss, Liam."

Sweeney chose not to sit with the gardaí at the table, but instead went to his soft seat by the unlit fire. He stared deep into the fireplace, as if looking for something. He rose, took a box of matches from the top of the photo-laden mantelpiece, and in a few seconds the fireplace roared into life, helped, in no small way, by the magic of firelighters.

Rather than continue their chat from where he was unable to look into Sweeney's eyes, Starrett went and sat on the sofa to his right. Sweeney seemed comforted by the heat from the growing flames.

"Starrett, have you any idea at all who did this to my son?"

"Well, Liam, that's what we're in the process of trying to discover right now. We'll question everyone who knew Joe, and we'll try to build up a picture of him. Somewhere there in the middle of all of this information we gather will be a clue or a hint of a motive. But it's a long, slow process, Liam; to do it right we have to take our time and be patient."

"Tell me this, Starrett," Sweeney began, his pure Donegal accent affected by neither TV, movies nor trends, "why did you join the gardaí?"

Starrett decided to go with the flow.

"When I was growing up in Ramelton, I always felt the only

thing worthwhile doing as a job of work was something which had a natural necessity, like being a farmer, like yourself Liam, or a carpenter, a teacher, a doctor or a guard – you know, the kind of jobs that are important to our community. In the end I felt being a garda and a detective was the only one I could do, so that's what I did."

"That sounds a wee bit too much like a thought-out answer," Sweeney grunted.

"OK, how about this: it was the only job I was offered when I came home from London."

Sweeney said, rising up a little in his chair and looking at Starrett for the first time, "I like that one much better. Tell me this, Starrett, did you ever notice that when Irish people move across the water they always say they're in London if they're living in London, but if they're living anywhere else – Manchester, Liverpool, Birmingham, Portsmouth or wherever – they always say they're in England?"

"I'd never considered it before, but you know I think you're right," Starrett replied, appearing to consider it as he fleetingly kissed his Bushmills again, this time even less passionately than the first time. "Any of your boys or Teresa ever go over to England or London?"

"Thomas went to Manchester University. I've a brother in Salford, and Thomas stayed with him for the first couple of terms. Ryan and Teresa went to Queen's and Joe always stayed on the farm. He was educated at the Gael Choláiste in Letterkenny, but he didn't go on to third level."

"Did he always want to follow in your footsteps?"

"You know, Starrett, that boy was wise beyond his years. I see my children haring around from here to there and just about to anywhere, like nanny goats on poteen. They're all desperate to acquire all these worldly trimmings, like houses and cars and designer clothes. Even the kids nowadays, from they're no age, want grand holidays in exotic places. Their lives are just flying past them. But Joe always seemed to realise it's not so much what you acquire in your life as what you *make* of your life."

"He was blessed then, sir," Gibson said.

"I do believe you're right," Sweeney said, awkwardly turning around in his chair to look at her, as if he'd forgotten she was there. He turned back to face the fire. "You know, when I think about it, I'm just as bad as the rest of them."

"Come on, man, sure you're a farmer," Starrett protested.

"Ah yes, Starrett; but don't you see, my problem is that I am an ambitious farmer. My great-grandfather, Tommy Sweeney, and his brother Joseph, known as Blackie, started to farm this land back in 1876. Blackie, now there was a character. Didn't have a single hair on his head, or anywhere on his body, they say," he added, glancing at Gibson. "Apparently he was very self-conscious, but he'd never wear a wig; he claimed they were too itchy and always getting caught up in brushes and briars and what have you. Aye, he used to cover his head with black boot polish. Anyway, it was around that time that the first bit of this house was built. There's the date cut in stone up in the attic, so maybe they might even have started to farm the year before, but my dad reckons it was in 1876 the Sweeney family started to earn a living from this land."

Starrett saw this as an opening to ask his real questions, but before he had a chance, Liam started back up again.

"Actually, there's a great story about this house and how they started the farm. Tommy and Joseph Sweeney weren't particularly well off, but they were handy men who could turn their hand to anything. Anyway, the man who used to own this land, before my family, Denny Desmond, he had my great-grandfather and his brother build him this house. It would have been a grand house in its day."

"It's still a grand house, Liam," Starrett offered.

"Aye, so anyway, the house is finished, fitted out and everything, and Desmond doesn't come across with the agreed payment for the work. He just wouldn't pay them. They politely came up to the farm each day, and Desmond would just fob them off, not even bothering to invent excuses. He'd just make jokes at my great-granddad and his brother's expense. They started to shame him by following him everywhere, pestering him in public about their outstanding payment.

"Eventually in a pub one night – I think it must have been Tootie's; it's known as Conway's now, but that's the only one that's been around for that long – he shouts at them to get off his back. This goes on for a while, until eventually he says, 'OK, what I'll do is this: I'll give you an acre of my land in full and final settlement for your work.' 'Any acre?' Tommy asks. 'Any acre you want,' Desmond replies, keen to get the matter settled and get back to a quiet life again. 'Will you come into a solicitor's office with us and sign a paper to that effect?' Tommy asks. 'Aye, I will,' Desmond agrees in front of a pub full of witnesses. The very next day, true to his word, he signs the freshly drawn up promissory note. It was further agreed that Desmond, Tommy and Blackie and the solicitor would then go up to walk Desmond's land so the Sweeney brothers could pick the acre of land and complete the registry of the title deeds under their name.

"An hour later they are standing on a beautiful arable acre situated on the front corner of Desmond's land. 'This will do us,' Tommy and Blackie said in unison. 'But you can't possibly have this acre; my new house is built on this acre.' 'You said we could have any acre, and this is the acre we want.' Desmond looked to the solicitor for support. The solicitor quickly advised the irate landowner, 'The signed agreement clearly states that the aforementioned Thomas and Joseph Sweeney can have any acre they choose on your land.'"

"They got the land, and the house came for free?" Gibson couldn't help herself saying.

"Indeed they did, and fully entitled to it they were too."

"That's a great story altogether," Starrett added, chomping at the bit to get on with the interview.

"Anyway, by the time my father passed it on to me – on his deathbed in 1984 – it had grown from the original 1876 single golden acre farm to just under 400 acres. My father and his brother, David, enjoyed very prosperous years, and they'd bought up the land of those less fortunate around us. They split the one farm into two in the seventies. I don't remember there being a row or anything. In fact, I never really knew what went on until much later when my dad knew he was dying. My understanding, though, is that it was very amicable.

"His brother, my Uncle David, lived on, didn't die until a lot later, and he'd let his farm get run down. None of his kids seemed to want to bother about it until my uncle died, and then they all started squabbling over the land. They didn't want to work the land, but they wanted their share in cash. After six months of squabbling amongst themselves, they eventually agreed to sell it to a developer from Letterkenny. The property boom hadn't then started, so it wasn't like the goldmine it would become, but it was still a fair few bob.

"Anyway I sat them all down and I said, our grandparents and our parents had worked too hard to build this up for it all just to be blown away again. What they hadn't realised was that my father and his brother had foreseen such a situation and had made provisions in their deeds that if one ever sold their farm, the other would have first option to buy at 'the current agricultural rate,' which was obviously quite a bit less than the commercial rate they'd discussed with the developer."

"How much less, Liam?" Starrett asked.

"We're talking over 600,000 punts. This would have been the late nineties."

"Bejeepers, Liam, that's a lot of change," Starrett sighed.

"You mean a lot of motive?"

"Well, that too, now you mention it," Starrett replied. "So your cousins, who would they be?"

"Dave, Lawrence, Adam and Beatrice. She's got a different surname now she's married, so she now would be known as Beatrice Hewson."

"And their whereabouts?" Gibson asked, pen ready to transfer the valuable information to her notebook.

"Jeez, Starrett, I'm not the man to be asking questions like that.

Now Colette would know that a lot better than me; she does the Christmas card list. Mind you, I'm not sure the last time we'd have received any from them. But that was the point I started to make, don't you see. I was over-ambitious. I mean, what did I need another farm for? Why did I put all of the members of our two families through all of that stress? Was it simply because I could have the biggest farm in the parish? But there you go, sure wasn't I equally guilty of committing the sin of coveting, a sin that I'm accusing all my children bar one of?"

"So why do you think Joe was different?" Starrett asked.

"You know, I've thought about this a lot, and I just don't know. He took a contentment from working the land that I never remember enjoying."

"Was he always like that?" Starrett asked.

"From when he was a wee boy. He's obviously the youngest, and I thought as a result he'd be spoilt, but from no age at all he'd shun the fancy toys he'd been bought for a chance to be with the animals."

"Well, he was obviously in his element here; I've never seen as many fine cows . . ." Starrett began.

"Aye, well I'll tell ye, the herd is all Joe's doing. The highest yield of milk in the county and up in the top five in the Republic. And Joe put that together all by himself you know. He studied breeds and breeding for ages and then went out and hand-picked the foundation of his herd and then nurtured them. But you see that's what I was trying to tell you: the boy was never in a hurry. He knew what he wanted to do, he knew how he wanted to go about doing it, and most importantly he *enjoyed* doing it. Now you see, if he was here now . . ." Sweeney stopped talking abruptly. He bit his bottom lip and wiped his right eye before continuing, "Aye, if Joe was here now, he wouldn't be boasting about having the best herd in Donegal; no, he'd talk to you for ages about their stock, their grazing, the style of milking. He avoided all unnatural elements. You know, we've the lowest vet's bills in the county . . . but there I go again boasting. Des McGinley, you know, the vet from down Milford way? He was always saying he'd be out of work if all the farmers were as attentive as our Joe. Joe would always say he wasn't sure if that was a compliment or a complaint."

"Liam, I know this is going to be an awkward question for you, but I have to ask it," Starrett started. "Can I assume that when you retire, the farm would have passed on to Joe?"

"Oh God, yes," Liam replied immediately, a large smile sweeping across his face. "Sure the rest of my wains would have it divided up into housing site parcels and sold to developers before we'd have a chance to sit down for breakfast tomorrow morning. They're just as bad as Lawrence and the rest of my nephews."

"Did Joe know that, that the farm was going to be his?"

"Aye, Starrett, he did. We talked about it a lot," Sweeney replied, but didn't seem to want to expand on his answer.

"Was he comfortable with it?" Starrett pushed.

"In a word, no. He felt that his brothers and sister were entitled to their share. I told him that would be the end of the farm. He said he could easily make do with the quarter he'd get. We argued about it . . . actually argued might be too strong a word. Let's just say we had several heated discussions over the last few years about it."

"And did you resolve the issue?"

"We've both seen too many great houses and farms fall into desolation in this county over the years, just because the heirs couldn't agree on how the spoils should be divided. So, in my will, I said that the farm was to be left to Joe on condition he didn't sell all of it until he was fifty years old. I made provisions that he could "donate" single acre plots to his siblings if he wished, but again on condition it was only for personal use. If they wanted to sell it they could sell it, but only back to Joe and only at the going agricultural rate."

"What if they built a house on it?" Starrett asked.

"Same rule would apply, Starrett – no loop holes. I didn't want the integrity of the farm tarnished in any way. But there you go; we're back to me wanting a monument to myself."

"What would happen if the farm were to go bankrupt?"

"Starrett, there's not a cent owed on this land of ours. No man or no bank holds any papers or mortgages on our farm. Thanks to Joe, this farm is a very healthy business."

"So how did you and Joe resolve it?"

"Well, there's the thing. As I said, Joe wasn't personally ambitious but he was very enterprising. He thought there is a right way and a wrong way to do everything. Over the last few years he'd been developing the sales side where instead of selling our produce to distributors, who sell on to shops and supermarkets and dictate the prices by the sheer volume they buy, Joe decided to start to sell direct to the shops and supermarkets himself, cutting out the middleman of course. He'd get physically sick when he'd go into a shop and see what they'd be selling his produce for. He started to make inroads, and he wasn't greedy. He also started to include the neighbouring farms in his network. Again, just to show you the measure of Joe as a man, he could easily have charged them a commission for the service and they would have willingly paid it, but he thought that would also make him into a middleman. He believed in the old style of farming, where farmers would always help each other out in times of trouble."

"Fair play to him, Liam, fair play," Starrett said.

"Aye, but look where it got him," Liam muttered, just above his breath. He sighed, shook his head a few times and added, "But anyway, he came to me a couple of months ago and said he agreed with me that the farm shouldn't be divided up, but what he'd like to do was to cut his brothers and sister in on a share each on the sale of the produce."

"Now that seems like a very fair compromise," Starrett said, smiling to himself in admiration at how canny Joe had been.

"Yes," Liam Sweeney agreed, beaming from ear to ear with pride.

"Tell me, Liam, when was the last time you saw Joe?"

Liam thought for a short time before answering, "You know, now I come to think about it, I haven't seen him since last night."

"What time would that have been?" Starrett continued.

Again Liam seemed to be backtracking through his memory bank, "I, ah, tea time, no, no, I tell a lie, it was just before lunch. Yes, that's it, it was lunchtime yesterday, or just before. He had an early lunch yesterday because he was off somewhere in the afternoon. I didn't ask, he didn't mention, but he was working hard on a Milford connection for his set-up. I know he was skipping dinner last night because he was out somewhere, and then this morning, with John Lea back from Dublin, Joe was skipping milking duties because he was going off early doing his distribution rounds with the stores and shops."

"And how did he seem yesterday when you saw him just before lunch?"

"He was fine, as usual – he didn't get down. He was happy-go-lucky, and he was ribbing me about getting a speech together for my birthday do."

"Liam, an awkward question . . ."

"I told ye man, go ahead with your questions."

"OK, Liam, now that Joe is dead, what happens to the farm?"

Sweeney looked over to the bottle of Bushmills, studied it as if he were considering another shot, then grimaced, rolled his eyes and said, "Well . . ."

But just at that moment they were disturbed with a ruction coming from the other side of the house, from the kitchen as far as Starrett could guess.

"I . . ." Liam started again, but the disturbance was growing in volume all the time, and much as Starrett would like to, they couldn't ignore it any longer.

They hightailed it out of the room led by Gibson, then Sweeney, followed closely by Starrett, who was having a very bad feeling about what they might be running into.

Chapter Eleven

Colette Sweeney was lying on the kitchen floor rolled up in a ball and crying fervently. Bernadette and Finula fussed around her, but their attention was more focused on the scuffle going on over by the window, where Sergeant Packie Garvey was trying, single-handedly and unsuccessfully, to protect Garda Romany Browne from the majority of the family. The Sweeney clan was, surprisingly, led by Teresa Sweeney, followed very closely by Sheila Kelly and Breda Roche and, bringing up the rear, Thomas, Ryan Sweeney and Maeve Boyce. Mona Sweeney seemed to be the only person in the kitchen not involved in the kerfuffle.

"For heaven's sake, Tom," she was shouting, "not in front of the girls."

Gibson was straight into the mêlée of flying fists, high-kicking feet and hair-pulling, and one by one, she and Liam Sweeney were able to pull the aggressors away. Starrett helped Garvey pull Browne to the opposite corner of the room, Starrett gaining only a thick lip for his troubles.

"OK, OK," Starrett shouted, "what the f . . ." then he noticed Bernadette's mouth form the shape of an "O" as she anticipated his next word in shock, ". . . flip is going on here?" he finished, without missing a beat.

Eight adults all started talking at once as Liam went to attend to his wife and help her back up to her chair.

Starrett clapped his hands together twice, and very loudly, to gain their attention.

"Quiet please!" he started. "Could one person tell me what happened, please? Ryan, you please tell me what's been going on here."

"That shit, that excuse for a garda, just from nowhere ups and says, 'Look, this is so easy. It's so obvious that one of the family murdered Joe. It's nearly always a family member, so why don't you make it easier on yourself and just tell me which of you it was?' And then when that subtle approach didn't work, he tried, 'OK, we know it's one of you, and whoever it is is just too yellow to admit it. Now, I bet someone else knows who the culprit is, so why don't you do the rest of the family a favour and shop him?' My mother just collapsed in a heap at that."

Starrett looked first to Browne, who didn't even look slightly embarrassed; he seemed more intent on straightening his bespoke uniform and fixing his hair. Surprisingly enough, he'd managed to escape with just a few grazes above his right eyebrow. Garvey, who was still holding Browne securely, reluctantly nodded to Starrett that Ryan's account of the event was correct.

"Jeez, man, what were you thinking?" Starrett said, feeling like clipping him around the ear as someone would do with a mischievous child. "On second thought, don't say a f . . ., don't say a word, or we'll all be hung up from the rafters here. Sergeant, arrest this man immediately."

"What? What?" Browne screeched, Little Richard style. "For heaven's sake, Inspector, have you lost your senses? I'm a member of An Garda Síochána."

"Yes, and that means you're meant to guard the peace, not disturb it. Sergeant Garvey, charge Browne here with disturbing the peace and remove him from the property."

Garvey, despite the vocal protests and disbelief from Browne, did as he was ordered.

Starrett noticed that his action had the desired effect on the Sweeney entourage. They collectively relaxed, becoming preoccupied with comforting each other and rearranging their clothes and hair and, in the case of Sheila Kelly, having an ugly gash on her left cheek attended to. She seemed quite proud of her war wound and was deep in conversation as to whether or not the resultant abrasion would heal into a scar. When Starrett had joined the gardaí, his father's only advice had been, "Be very careful before you pick a fight with a scarred man." The inspector would have to check what the accepted wisdom was about picking a fight with a scarred woman.

Starrett apologised to the Sweeneys and accepted that, thanks to Romany Browne and the lateness of the day, all useful questioning for that day was over. Gibson took everyone's details while the equally efficient Maeve Boyce made arrangements for those not able to be accommodated at the farmhouse to be put up at Frewin, a country house on the outskirts of nearby Ramelton. Starrett insisted that Maeve and her boyfriend Ryan, Teresa and girlfriend Sheila, even though they all lived relatively near by, all stay at Frewin.

Breda Roche didn't want to stay there by herself; neither did she want to stay on the farm. The more time passed, the more upset she became, and she insisted that she wanted to go back to her parents' house in Milford. In the circumstances and due to the fact that she was going to be under the same roof as her parents, Starrett made an exception for her. Garda Gibson was happy to drive her there.

Starrett bid his goodnight to Liam and Colette, promising them he would return first thing in the morning.

"So, young man, you were enjoying an Inspector Hercule Poirot moment, were you?" Starrett said, to the wall in his office. He was so mad he couldn't risk showing his face to either Browne or his trusted Garvey. Garvey was clearly embarrassed for Browne and taking no comfort from Browne's situation. If anything, Garvey looked more upset than the novice, which was making Starrett even madder by the microsecond.

There was no audible response from Browne.

"Well, Garda Browne, let's hear what you have to say for yourself?" Starrett said, slowly turning around and taking off his zipped windbreaker to reveal his now day-old blue shirt. "So, you've been reading your Agatha Christie, have you?"

"Who?" Browne replied, appearing bemused.

"*Who?*" Starrett barked.

Browne looked as if he didn't know whether to laugh or cry, like a kid who had been caught doing something and isn't quite sure whether his deed was good or bad and doesn't want to own up in case the praise he covets turns out to be the punishment he dreads.

"Okay, Romany me lad, I'll tell you. Agatha Christie is a famous crime writer, some say *The* crime writer, which is maybe a disservice to Doyle and Dexter. But we don't need to get into that here. One of Dame Agatha's legendary detectives is Inspector Hercule Poirot, who would do what you just tried to do in the kitchen back there at the Sweeney Farm. Now the main difference between Hercule and yourself is that the Belgian usually had some clever bit of evidence up his sleeve to confront his suspect with. On top of which, he'd have the gumption to wait until the end of the investigation before declaring his hand."

"But it's all so tacky, Inspector. It's just a little domestic storm in a teacup. One of them did it. You know that. I know that. And they know we know that, so why not just get the whole thing tidied up quickly so we can get on to some real crime?"

"And you tell me this with the benefit of the new modern techniques they're teaching down at Templemore this days? At this rate, Romany my lad, all you're going to be doing for the foreseeable future is directing the traffic outside the Bridge Bar," Starrett said, shaking his head in disbelief. "You're a lost cause. I know that. Packie here knows that. The only problem is that you still don't have a clue what you did wrong."

Starrett felt that if looks could kill he'd be dead at that moment.

"I'll speak to the major in the morning about where we're going to transfer you, but in the meantime, I consider you to be a danger to this case, not to mention your own life if the Sweeney family manage to get their hands around your neck again. Sergeant, lock him in the cell downstairs."

"You're not serious," Browne protested to Starrett's back. He was by the front door, putting his jacket on again, and he could hear Browne's continued pleading with Garvey.

If Garda Romany Browne were ever to make anything of his career in the gardaí, then today would make an interesting introduction in his biography.

Chapter Twelve

Starrett walked out of Tower House, the garda station, turned right, headed over to the River Leannan and slowly strolled down to the right, along the newly raised footpath which bordered the clear clean waters feeding into the Swilly. It was just after midnight, and the last night's full moon and the slowly settling dusk combined to illuminate the scene. In the distance, down by the warehouses, he could see the lights of the garda SOC team as they painstakingly worked their way thoroughly through the site. He enjoyed this walk . . . well, that was if he ignored the recently refurbished blocks of flats, which had been remodelled out of two sets of warehouses. The planning office had allowed the developers to lose the incredible charm of the original buildings, and the results were more in keeping with the overdevelopment of Letterkenny than with the heritage allure of Ramelton. "When in doubt, render it," seemed to be the rule of the moment.

By the time he reached *The Hanging Gale* courtyard, he had wiped all thoughts of the ugly box out of his mind and refocused on the demise of Joseph Sweeney. Nuala Gibson had returned from Milford and walked over to Starrett as he was staring through the gate.

"How's young Breda?"

"She settled down a bit by the time we arrived at her parents'," Gibson replied.

"Did she say anything interesting?"

"No, mostly that she couldn't believe that this was happening to her."

"To *her?*" Starrett asked immediately.

"Yes."

Starrett tutted, shook the gate a few times to see how secure it was and asked, "Anything else?"

"No, apart from the fact that she took a call from someone on her mobile," Gibson replied. "She said she couldn't talk but to text her, and she promised she would call back later."

Sergeant Packie Garvey joined them.

"Have they found anything here?"

"Well, nothing apart from ciggy packets, a few beer cans, several empty Disprin packets, Coke cans, discarded Durex . . ."

"Ah, Jeez," Starrett sighed, "too much information, Packie. Tell me, Sergeant, how many do I have left in your stash?"

"Inspector, I'm not sure I want to know this," Gibson protested immediately.

"What," Starrett began confused, "I know it's a bad habit, but . . ."

"Nuala, the inspector means how many cigarettes does he have left in the stash I carry for him in the hope that he'll be able to cut down," Garvey explained with a large grin, "Inspector, she thought you meant Dur . . ."

"OK, OK," Starrett interrupted, "no need to draw pictures. Well, how many?"

"Thirteen."

"Thirteen? Come on, Packie; I couldn't have smoked seven since lunchtime yesterday. Are you sure you've not been at them yourself?"

"Your system is obviously working then," Gibson offered, a wee bit too superior for Starrett's liking.

"No need for sarcasm, young lady," Starrett said, sticking his open palm out towards Garvey. "Thirteen's too unlucky a number to keep overnight, Sergeant – you know, with the full moon and all of that. Let me reduce it by a single digit to ensure your luck continues."

Gibson walked back into the courtyard. Starrett couldn't be sure, but he thought he heard her tutting to herself as she strode away.

Starrett lit up and sighed very contentedly as the nicotine hit his bloodstream. How could something so good be so bad? He immediately thought of Dr Aljoe. He smiled to himself. Now she was just downright bad, but bad more in a mischievous way. He thought back to the night down in Rathmullan when they nearly did the evil deed, right there on the moonlit beach. She was the one who'd eventually found the resolve to pull back so they could catch their collective breaths. He now realised that if she'd not had that moment of doubt, he'd have, quite simply, ruined any chance he might have enjoyed with Maggie Keane, she who'd recently returned into his life with her three kids, after a twenty-year period when they'd not communicated at all.

However, as willing as the aforementioned Dr Samantha Aljoe now appeared to be, Maggie Keane was, in equal measure, just as hesitant.

Starrett finished his cigarette, and the image of Maggie Keane disappeared from his mind's eye as wistfully as the smoke from his last cigarette. He wandered over to the fishing trawler moored just down from the courtyard and, just to be sure, stubbed his ciggy out on the hull. He was sure he heard some noise on board. The boat was the *Endeavour,* and, as usual, it was lit up like a Christmas tree.

"Packie, would you ever do me a favour and hop on board there and see if there's anyone below deck?"

Packie obliged.

Starrett heard a bit of muffled conversation, and a few seconds later Packie reappeared on deck with two blond fishermen dressed in regulation off-white, heavy, roll-neck sweaters, dark blue shapeless trousers and green wellingtons. They looked like members of the Russian navy.

"Inspector," Garvey said as he hopped back on to terra firma, "this is Jan . . . Jan . . ."

"Janak," the elder of the fishermen said, "and this is Konrad, Konrad Zajaz and I'm Janak Krawiec," he said in a very strong Polish accent.

"Good . . . evening . . . gentlemen . . ." Starrett said, finding himself slowing down his speech to a crawl.

"It's fine, Inspector. We both speak and understand English."

"Yes, yes, so I've noticed, very good," Starrett replied, cursing himself. "Tell me, lads, are youse here every night around this time?"

"Yes, but usually we sleep," Konrad answered, glaring at Garvey.

"And what time would you go out fishing?" Starrett asked.

"It varies with the tide. We need it to be quite high to get out of here," Janak replied.

"And when youse went out this morning, what time did youse sail off at?"

"Around midnight," Janak replied.

"Did you notice anything strange along the quay?"

"It was dark," Konrad joked.

"Yeah," Starrett sighed, "but with the near full moon, did you notice anything else?"

"There was someone further down there fishing," Janak said, nodding in the direction of the dock.

That got Starrett's attention.

"Yes?" the Inspector prompted.

"As Konrad said, even with the moon, it was dark, and they were covered in yellow waterproofs."

"Was it a man or a woman?"

"I couldn't tell. We were too busy trying to steer this tub out of here safely. If it was a man, he wasn't a tall man."

"Did you see a face?"

"No. He, or she, had their back to us until we passed, and then we'd our back to whoever it was, and, as I said, we were more interested in navigating."

"Is it usual for someone to be fishing down here at that time of the night?" Starrett asked.

"Sometimes, but not all of the times," he replied. Konrad seemed to have no intention for further involvement in the conversation.

"Is this yours?" Starrett asked, nodding in the direction of a mechanical bucket digger, which was parked midway between the boat and the gate to the *Hanging Gale* courtyard.

"Yes," Konrad replied. "We use it to scrape the fish out of our hold and swing them ashore into the back of a lorry."

"Right, lads, thanks for your time," Starrett said, realising he'd gotten as much as he was going to out of the trawlermen, at least for now. "You should probably get back to your kip for now, but we might need to talk to you again. Could you please give your details to Sergeant Garvey here."

Without further ado, Konrad and Janak did as bid and disappeared below deck.

"Packie, it's probably a good time for our own gang to get to their beds so we're fresh as daisies in the morning."

Starrett watched Packie pass the information along the team, taking pride in the fact that his young gardaí seemed somewhat more reluctant than the trawlermen to retire for the day.

Chapter Thirteen

Starrett felt restless. He hated the fact that just because it was night his investigation had to stop, while his brain couldn't stop. He wanted to go and see his father to get some background on the Sweeney family. Reluctantly deciding it was too late, he went home and started to scramble himself up some eggs. He lifted the phone and speed dialled Maggie Keane three times before he eventually let it ring through.

"You're not asleep then?" he said into the phone, which was wedged precariously between shoulder and ear as he took his saucepan, bottom covered with sizzling butter, off the flames.

"I thought you might call."

"Are you not tired?" Starrett said, dreading the answer.

"Not a bit, Starrett," she replied, with seeming genuine enthusiasm. Maybe that was just his interpretation. "There's something serene and lovely about the house late at night after everyone has gone to bed. Sometimes I just sit here in the dark or wander around the house in my bare feet. It's the only time I really get to slow down enough to truly enjoy how lovely this house is."

"Is it dark there now?"

"Starrett, your voice has gone all funny. If this is one of those smutty calls, you can just feck right off. I've heard all about what goes on over in Engl . . ."

"Nah, nah, hault your horses there, woman," he said, consciously changing his voice from the suggestive tones. "I was just trying to work out if you'd, you know, retired for the evening?"

"As in retired and didn't want any late night callers?"

"Well, yes, actually," he said. Eventually she dragged everything out of him she knew he wanted to say. He hadn't remembered her being like that the first time they'd dated.

"Ah, Starrett, you big eejit, I've been waiting for you to call," then she dropped into her more seductive persona. "Come on over."

"Right, I'll be right over so," Starrett said, dumping the saucepan in the sink and not even bothering to rinse out the browning butter.

"Aye, but Starrett . . ."

"Yeah?"

"You're not staying over."

He already knew that (he'd never stayed over), but he was disappointed that she felt she had needed to say so to him.

Seven minutes later, at 01.47 in fact, he pulled up outside her house (originally her parents' home) on the Shore Road, not too far from his parents' house. The magnificent Georgian house, well worthy of Maggie's praise, had been built at a time when a merchant family's townhouse really was an outward sign of their success. It had been built with all of the finest materials from all ports west, and beyond, and designed on a scale big enough to impress. Yet it was cosy enough to heat and economical to maintain. In the three and a half years since her husband's untimely death from cancer, Maggie had certainly not let a dark cloud descend over her house. It was airy, bright, colourful and absolutely packed with physical signs of those who lived within. Joe, at twenty, was the eldest. He was now spending most of his time down in Belfast attending Queen's University. Moya and Katie were both officially eleven at the moment, born eleven months apart; but for one month, one unbearable month according to their mother, they shared the same age. The house hadn't been kept as a shrine to Niall, Maggie's deceased husband, but at the same time, nor had all of his effects been removed to make it look like he'd never been there. Like her parents, his impact on this house was still clear. Starrett liked that. He liked it that humans with their life, mentally and physically, shaped the spaces they had lived in.

He was even happier that in the previous six months, during his time back in Maggie Keane's life, he himself was starting to mould the future footprint of the unique house. Bejeepers, as he would frequently be quoted – as in a send-up – by Moya, there were even a couple of photographs of himself included in the various galleries around the house. Starrett was flattered, but Maggie always protested that it was nothing to do with her. She proudly protested that it was all Moya and Katie's work.

Maggie had the door opened and was waiting for him there, by the back porch, arms folded and lit splendidly by a glorious nearly full moon. He strolled self-consciously towards her from his BMW, which he parked discreetly to the right of the house on the road end of her lane. She kissed him – a friendly peck on the cheek.

"Moya will be annoyed she missed you," Maggie said. She helped him off with his windbreaker, which she placed on the back of the coat-laden door. Starrett took considerable comfort every time she did that. There was something about his jacket being visible amongst the inhabitants' outdoor wear that made him feel indisputably connected with this family of mother, two daughters and son. Starrett realised there was a possibility, a distinct possibility, that he was feeling a wee bit oversensitive, even vulnerable, due to the fact that he'd just that night been witness to another family whose life was in freefall due to a loss from within, and that the son in that instance was also called Joe.

Maggie Keane, to Starrett's regret, still wasn't 100 per cent comfortable with him physically. When he'd come in, she'd sat him down at the table in the centre of the large kitchen and started to massage his neck, and goodness didn't it feel great. But then she seemed to realise what she was doing, suffer some negative thought on the matter, and pulling herself up short, she dropped her hands to her side mid-massage and shook them awkwardly, as if they'd betrayed her by being too forward and too intimate. Yet she clearly wanted him there. She had always made him feel very welcome on the fourteen times he'd been to her house over the course of the previous several months. He could remember with great clarity the majority of those visits, starting with his inaugural invitation as her official date to Joe's twentieth birthday party less than six months ago.

He'd not really known what to expect. Did he think he'd end up in bed with her? Well, she was now a widow, and they'd had previous intimate knowledge of each other. Agreed, it had been two decades earlier and just once, but yes, he kind of had been expecting to go to bed with her. She'd been attentive, friendly and generous with her time. She'd held his hand on a few occasions, laughed and joked and cracked her extremely awkward smile several times, and – and this was a big *and* – she'd given him a goodnight kiss which was anything but chaste. But immediately thereafter, if anything, they'd seemed to take several steps backwards on the intimacy side. They'd kissed five times since – and yes, he *could* recall in great detail each and every one of those kisses – and the strange thing, Starrett found, was that those six kisses had been enough. Not more than enough, just enough. They'd been enough because they'd been fulfilling, spiritually and physically fulfilling, but more importantly for him, they'd been enough because they'd convinced him that the core of whatever it was she was after with him was not just friendship.

But then, as in earlier this evening, she'd allowed her demons to rise to the surface and say things like, "But of course you can't stay over." Why would she feel the need to say that? It wasn't as if he'd been guilty of using all his guile to try and bed her. That had never been his style. He'd never in his life chased women or gone on the pull. For him it had always to be a natural encounter. Could that maybe be the problem? Did his lack of experience make her nervous in his arms?

And just now, even though something had turned her off, it wasn't like she became preoccupied with it. No, she was, as ever, attentive and charming, and they talked together with the ease of a couple of people who'd been friends all their lives. She'd prepared him a bowl of fruit and yoghurt. He liked it that she cared enough about him to insist he eat healthy late at night rather than give in to the temptation of a late night fry-up. For all of that, she never tried to talk him out of his morning visits to Steve's Café.

She was dressed in a long, dark blue dress, which looked like it was made of material so soft and malleable that it could have very easily been a nightgown. Perhaps that's why he'd never seen it on her before. She kept the night chill at bay with a black wrap that circumnavigated her elegant, slender neck a few times. He loved her neck. He loved her eyes; sad, sad eyes, but they always engaged him, held him and drank him in. He loved the way her long eyelashes cast flickering shadows across her eyes and gave the illusion that he could look even deeper into them. Her black unruly hair had clearly reached the end of its day, and she was no longer trying to pin it back into the elaborate style it started each day off in.

Starrett felt positively guilty about deriving so much pleasure at just looking at her.

She made him some mint tea; help him sleep, she said.

He told her about the death of Joe Sweeney. She winced at the mention of the Christian name, and from her brief glance at the phone, he knew she had an immediate vision of her own son. He loved the way she listened to him, sitting beside him at the table as he talked. She, probably unconsciously, he thought, took his right hand in both of hers, and as he told her about the troubled times of another family, she stroked and played with his imperfect forefinger.

She had such a calming effect on him. He found that talking to her served to give him a clearer vision of what had happened thus far in the Sweeney case. He kept flashing back to the boat outside the Heritage Centre, just by the *Hanging Gale* courtyard, and the two Polish trawlermen. Maggie and Starrett finished their tea, and she took both their cups to the sink to rinse them. She stayed on her feet, signalling that it was time for him to go.

"You have to help the family through this, Starrett," she said. "I mean, I know that's stupid, that's what you do; I meant, they need you to resolve this for them . . ."

Maggie helped him on with his black windbreaker; she smoothed out his shoulders through his jacket from behind. He tentatively headed for the door when she dropped her hand to his arm, turned him around and pulled him towards her. He had been right; it was her nightdress, and he could feel her naked body through the material. Their kiss, their seventh kiss, was as pure a kiss as Starrett had ever experienced in his life. He wondered if this might be one of her secrets: that by not being fully intimate with Starrett, she was teaching him to celebrate the true joys of the kiss.

This was what he was thinking as the kiss ended. They continued hugging.

Starrett didn't know how long this lasted, but it ended tenderly as she whispered very quietly in his ear. Her voice was very soothing and gentle, and he couldn't really hear what she was saying properly, but her tone, more intimate than normal, sounded like she had something important to say to him.

Although her words didn't seem to make sense, it sounded as if she said something like, "You have take men's . . . . . . (something – a short word) four we can move Ron."

This sentence didn't register fully with Starrett until later, because immediately she continued, in a louder voice, "Now you better go, or you'll have a lot of trouble walking down the lane." This clearly understandable sentence most definitely proved that, whatever it was Maggie had whispered, it hadn't been an invitation to dally any longer.

Starrett waited until she closed the door behind him before offering his reply to the cold night air:

"Oh, bejeepers, I'm way beyond that stage now."

He awkwardly hobbled down the lane to his car, took out his notebook and wrote down the words he thought she'd whispered. Twenty minutes later he was in bed in his own house on the Rathmullan Road, reliving the scene over and over before finally falling asleep with a mixture of a frown and a grin on his face.

Chapter Fourteen

Wednesday: 27 August 2008

Next morning Starrett gave Steve's Café a miss and used breakfast with his parents as an excuse to quiz his dad on the Sweeney family.

For as long as Starrett could remember, his mum and dad were up at the crack of dawn getting on with their busy lives. Both were retired, but they still enjoyed such full and busy days.

His mum was, for want of a better word, a healer. She was the seventh daughter of a seventh daughter, and although Starrett was an only child, he was considered to have inherited her sixth sense. It was not something he was preoccupied with, nor actively pursued, but he would sometimes admit to being surprised himself by some of the insights he seemed able to tap into. His mum hadn't felt a need for her son to follow in her footsteps. "A *very* mixed blessing" was how she'd always describe it. Starrett would readily agree when he witnessed how absolutely shattered she was at the end of her healing days.

They say we develop our ability for memories when we are four. One of the first memories to be filed in Starrett's memory bank – and he could recall the image in his mind's eye as though it were yesterday – was sitting in his home with his mother. His dad was out. There was a knock on the door, and the young Starrett insisted on opening it.

He was greeted by an old arthritic woman with tears of pain streaming down her face. His mother soon caught up with Starrett and shooed him to one side as she put her arm around the woman and gently coaxed her into the house. Starrett remembered the old woman immediately straightening up slightly at the blessed touch of his mother.

Starrett carried on playing around their feet as his mother sat the woman down in the living room and talked to her in a voice barely above a whisper. Starrett couldn't make it out. But he did remember at one point his mother standing above the old woman and placing a hand on either side of her head. His mum seemed to go into a trance-like state for some time. Starrett couldn't remember how long the trance had lasted exactly, but he did remember the old woman leaving his house looking and moving like the middle-aged woman Starrett years later realised she was at the time of the incident. Starrett remembered little else except that, after the proceedings, his mother was so tired she had to lie down on the sofa herself to rest. Starrett remembered the last part only because he was annoyed his mother didn't have the energy to play with him.

Starrett could recall several other such incidents from his youth, and perhaps that is what had drawn him towards thinking that he wanted or, more like *needed*, to join a religious order.

She'd long since given up her "healing," sincerely declaring that her "good was all done."

His dad was a great friend of Major Newton Cunningham, Starrett's superior. Starrett senior had served in the military alongside the major but, unlike the major, had remained there until just before Starrett had first left Ramelton to seek his fame and fortune. Starrett's journey had started with a spell in Armagh, followed by a much longer spell in London, where he'd found his first calling: dealing in rare vintage cars. To this day Starrett hadn't a clue how his mother and father survived financially. They just did, they always had. They had a beautiful old house with a large garden overlooking the water just around the corner, in fact, from where Joe Sweeney's body had been found less than fourteen hours earlier. When Starrett, who still received a generous income from the vintage car business back in London, had offered his dad assistance in the monetary department, his dad would always shush him up with a, "Oh, you'll need that more than us, son. We're fine, we're set for life." The only income, apart from an army pension, Starrett was aware that his father enjoyed was from selling the produce of his garden at the farmers' market in the nearby town hall every Saturday morning, and in his garden was where the son found his father at 07.05 that Wednesday morning.

"Bejeepers, that was a rum do around in the warehouses, wasn't it?" Starrett's father offered as a greeting.

"Aye, it was that," Starrett replied. "You know Liam quite well, don't you?"

"Quite well, aye. A good man, a sound man. I haven't been out to pay my respects yet. They're saying up at Whoriskey's that it's a closed wake for now."

"We're to blame for that," Starrett apologised quietly. "What about the boys?"

"You mean Ryan, Tom, Joe *and* Teresa?"

Starrett clicked his teeth and ran his fingers through his hair, his bent forefinger looking like a shark fin swiftly cutting through water. He mentally chastised himself for his brief intolerance, accepting as justification that his parents had just grown up in different times. He made a mental note to check exactly what Tom Sweeney's wife Mona thought of her sister-in-law's sexual preference.

"Well," his father continued as he leaned further over his flower border at a gravity-defying angle, clearing away dead ivy leaves and branches which were threatening to overgrow the wooden grill he used to train his roses along. He'd violently rip out as much as he could of a root and then chop the soil up with his garden fork. "I have to admit I'd seen a lot more of Joe over the last few years. He was nearly always with Liam. They got on famously and had an obvious respect for each other. I haven't seen much of the other wains since they left home to start their own families."

Starrett's dad looked at the offending ivy. His weather-beaten face broke into a grin.

"You know, families and their lifelines are a lot like this ivy."

"Right so," Starrett replied, waiting for the pay-off.

"You can nurture it all you want," he said, pointing over to the side of his house, "like over there, where I've been encouraging it to grow to cover up the outline of that lean-to shed you and I knocked down a few years ago, and I'll be buggered if I can get it to take. But here, where it's nothing but a nuisance, you can hoke around and cut it out trying to destroy it time and time again, but come the end of September it'll be all over the place again."

"So you're saying Liam wanted his kids settling down and having their own familes and they wouldn't?"

"Apart from Tom."

"What's wrong with Tom's family?" Starrett asked earnestly.

"Ach, sure you know, isn't your woman Mona a Dublin girl."

"Yeah? And?"

"Well now, I think Liam feels that city girls don't really have a good sense of the land, if you know what I mean," Starrett's dad said as he rose from his knees to sit back on his heels.

"I'm not so sure I do," Starrett said, smiling at his dad.

"Well, I think Liam heard some carry-on about how Mona was trying to get the rest of the clan interested in selling off some of the farm to developers. Liam says to me, he says, 'Sure, I wouldn't have been as bothered if she just come straight out and discussed it with me. Apparently she wanted to raise capital for the heirs. I think your woman really believes she's on the board of directors of Sweeney Heirs' Farm Inc.'"

Starrett's dad had a good laugh at that one.

"Was there real bad blood over it?" Starrett asked.

"Well, there was a bit of static all right. Liam wants to keep the farm going as a viable concern. He didn't want it compromised by selling off bits of it to be turned into a housing development. How many empty houses do we need in the county anyway? His point is that the farm is not the farm of the family; it's his farm. It's his to do with as he wants, and he wants to give it to Joe for the simple reason that Joe loves farming."

"Well, surely that should have been that then?" Starrett asked.

"A slight complication, son, in that Joe really is . . . sorry, really *was,* a good decent-hearted lad, and he didn't think it was fair that he alone should benefit from the farm."

"And was Mona really the instigator in this? What about Tom?"

"Oh you should always be wary of someone who walks at least a step or two behind his wife."

"Ach, sure, that's only because city girls walk faster, Dad."

"Aye, I did hear they were faster all right," Starrett's dad replied, and then he muttered something Starrett couldn't make out.

"What about Ryan, where was he on all of this?"

"Oh now, Ryan and Mona . . . aye, now they wouldn't really get on. No, oh no."

"Really," Starrett replied, "and why's that then?"

"Well, Tom, now sure he wouldn't want Mona and Ryan dealing with each other."

"And why on earth not?"

"Sure, didn't Ryan and Mona have a thing? Aye, they dated for a good while. Liam thought it was serious. He was convinced it was going to take, you know, and then Ryan broke it off, aye, and there wasn't a happier man in Donegal than Liam; but sure a couple of months later, didn't she only go and show up at the farm on Thomas's arm."

At this point Starrett's mum called them in for breakfast.

Chapter Fifteen

S tarrett left his parents' house and headed straight up to the Sweeney farm. On the ten-minute journey, he mentally went through the people he and his team still had to talk to:

Joe's mother, Colette Sweeney

His brothers, Ryan and Thomas

Ryan's girlfriend, Maeve Boyce

Thomas's wife, *and* Ryan's ex, Mona

Joe's sister, Teresa

Teresa's girlfriend, Sheila Kelly

and

Finula Sweeney, Thomas's youngest daughter, whose favourite uncle was the recently deceased Joe Sweeney.

And then he had to have repeat chats with the ones he had talked to yesterday.

And *then* they'd have to track down the disgruntled cousins and have a chat with them.

Owen Bonner's name would have to be on the fast-growing list as well.

As he pulled into the Sweeney farmyard in his black BMW with its instantly recognisable number plate of 00 DL 07, he wondered had he missed anyone? He was distracted as he noticed the growing media pack in his rear view mirror.

Garda Francis Casey came to meet Starrett. He advised Starrett that Garda Nuala Gibson and himself had taken turns guarding the farm all night. He had nothing to report, and on his way back to the farm this morning, he'd checked in at Frewin, the country house where Garda Joey Robinson was on duty. Nothing untoward had occurred there either. They'd accompanied the Frewin guests back down to the Sweeney farm.

In fact, the only overnight revelation Casey had for Starrett was the fact that a certain Romany Browne had kicked up a stink all night long, back at Tower House.

Starrett tutted something to the effect, "He still seems to be having difficulty learning how to fit in." Starrett noted that Casey didn't seem to be particularly sympathetic to a colleague's discomfort.

Casey advised Starrett that Liam Sweeney had asked Gibson if the gardaí could refrain from continuing their investigation and questioning until after the family had a chance to sit down together for breakfast. Nuala was welcome to join them, but, Casey reported, Liam was desperate to try and restore some form to his family's life, if only for his grandchildren's sake.

"I'm sure you'd be welcome as well," Casey offered on Liam's behalf.

"Ah, no," Starrett replied, starting to walk away from the farmhouse in the opposite direction of the main road. "I'll just go for a wee dander while we're waiting."

The Sweeney farm was among the rich rolling hills. For miles in any direction, you could see a stunning patchwork quilt of evergreen forest, green pastures, recently cut hay fields, yellow ferns and the ever-changing colours of the Swilly. The scene was bordered by hedges composed of a mixture of stones, wood, chain link fence, barbed wire, nettles and whatever was strong enough to grow in that particular area. The land rolled and tumbled away towards the Crockanaffrin Mountain, which rose on the other side of Lough Swilly and shaped the horizon with its craggy lines, some of which touched the low clouds. The whole landscape was peppered liberally with buildings. Starrett could see a shiny corrugated zinc roof, intermittently reflecting a dazzling white light; a grey stone church of indeterminable denomination with a tiny, but heavily populated, graveyard; an off-white bungalow with a curly spiral of smoke winding its way up and disappearing into the fluffy clouds. To the right, over by Inch Island, he could see the rain coming in as the clouds visibly gave up their moisture in falling grey transparent sheets, which looked like sails on a gigantic ship blowing out at a precarious angle as it slowly glided across the landscape. And each and every day of the year, the inspirational and passionate Donegal light would colour this same scene completely differently. They were views which never failed to take Starrett's breath away. Starrett reckoned they were also the rich scenes, which, if his soulful paintings were anything to go by, continually took away the breath of Martin Mooney.

The views inspired Starrett to believe in something, he knew not what for certain, but definitely something greater than mankind; certainly greater than the member (or members) of mankind who had left Joe Sweeney lifeless in the *Hanging Gale* courtyard.

There were quite a few Friesian cows roaring away with all their might, looking to be milked, or maybe they were just suffering from the vicious early morning chill. Starrett wondered if cows actually felt the cold. There were numerous birds in various flocks flying around and squawking away as if Jonathan Livingston Seagull himself was about to pay them a visit. In the near foreground, a mother cat looked as if she were leaving a runt behind. Where did that unmaternal instinct come from?

Colette Sweeney was a mother, and she had been subjected to the gut-wrenching experience of the youngest of her offspring dying first. Starrett looked back to the grand farmhouse and imagined the location of the bedroom the mother of the family had shared with Liam since the day they were wed. Starrett thought he could imagine what she was going through. It must be like feeling some alien ramming its fist down your throat, grabbing your heart and ripping it out up through your mouth before you had the chance to enjoy the mercy of your last breath.

He felt himself choking up.

He hated having to kick his heels while at the same time being desperate to get on with the investigation. He was crossing the farmyard to where Casey was busy (kicking his heels), when Gibson opened the door. She saw Starrett and smiled, a smile of obvious relief.

"Right so," she said. "Liam says he's ready for us."

Chapter Sixteen

"Starrett, when can I have my boy back home?" Colette Sweeney asked when she and her husband were in the privacy of the good room with Starrett.

"I'm afraid it'll be a while, Colette."

"Ah, but I can't abide to think of him up there in the cold mortuary in Letterkenny General Hospital or wherever it is they do their examination. Liam, can we ever get him home? He deserves to be home," she pleaded, looking alternately from Starrett to her husband.

"Colette, I know the woman who does the post-mortem, and I can assure you . . ."

"Post-mortem? Ach, Liam, they're not going to cut up my beautiful boy . . ."

"There, there, my love," Liam said, as he sat beside his wife on their good sofa in front of a fireplace chilled by the white marble of the Georgian surround. He used his arm first around her shoulders in comfort, but then he tightened it firmly as he continued, "Now, Colette, we discussed this: we've got to keep this together for the family; they're all looking to us and we can't let them down. We've got to get through this."

Then he looked Starrett straight in the eyes and said, "We'll do our grieving privately, when Starrett discovers who did this to our Joe."

Colette took a large gulp of air, as if she were sucking in her husband's energy and strength. She noticeably stiffened up her body and rose about six inches.

"Yes, yes, you're right of course, Liam. We need to let Starrett get on with his work."

Starrett was about to take this opportunity to start his interview when she continued. "I'll do all you ask, Liam, but will you promise me you'll go up and see Joe and make sure he's OK?"

Liam looked to Starrett.

"Look, I'm going to Letterkenny around midday to meet with Dr Aljoe and see what she's discovered from her examination," Starrett started.

"I'll come with you," Colette cut in immediately.

Starrett clicked his teeth quietly and looked at Liam.

"That's just not possible, my love," the husband whispered. "The family, they need us – they need you."

"Will you at least go with Starrett and see our son?" she implored her husband.

Starrett nodded yes discreetly to Liam.

"Yes . . . my love, I'll go and see our . . ." Liam stopped, choked up, and tears unashamedly flowed down his cheeks.

Now it was his wife's turn to comfort her husband. She hugged him, and instead of trying to shush him up, she encouraged him to cry, to let it out, to let him start the mourning he was forbidding her to express. Starrett thought it was clearly for *all* of the family Liam wanted his wife to be strong.

He left them in the good room of their house amongst their treasures and the memory-laden walls of photographs and paintings. He left them to start the long and very painful healing process.

His next interview was equally frustrating, if for somewhat different reasons.

When Starrett and Gibson returned to the kitchen cum family room, the person who stared at him most was Teresa's girl-friend, Sheila Kelly. Starrett reckoned Kelly was in her mid-thirties. She wore her sexuality in the black of her see-through shirt with cotton flared sleeves. Starrett wished that it hadn't been see-through. Starrett figured that the reason he'd never ever had the inclination to visit a nudist colony or nudist beach was quite simply because one, females and males alike, never knew what they were going to have to look at. She wore a pair of narrow rectangular-shaped glasses with heavy designer black frames. Her hair was cropped to the skin, a number one barber shave, Starrett reckoned, and her face enjoyed not a speck of make-up. She wore black denim jeans and black Doc Marten boots, but for all of that, Starrett thought, there was something warm, friendly and funny about Sheila Kelly.

"Why would I need to tell you everything I know about Joe?" she replied in what sounded to Starrett like a painfully hoarse voice.

Starrett laughed heartily.

In the course of his garda career, he'd met the weirdest and most varied troop of people you could ever imagine. Sheila Kelly was way up there when it came to not wishing to blend quietly into the background.

Well, it was quite simple really, Starrett reckoned. Joe Sweeney was dead and Starrett needed to find out why he was dead, how he died, and then, if necessary, who had killed him.

Yes, but why did he need to do that? He didn't have to do this. Surely he could earn money in a host of other ways. Apart from which, his percentage of Kensington Classic Cars – whom he had worked for while in London and eventually progressed to partner – generated him more than enough money to get by.

He did what he did because he loved to solve the puzzle of the crime, and he said as much to Sheila Kelly.

"Oh, that's OK then," Miss Kelly replied.

"Tell me all you know about Joe," Starrett said again.

"Joseph, sure he wouldn't hurt a fly, even if he wanted to. He was very close to his sister. They were very tight. I think it drove Ryan and Thomas mad sometimes, just how close Joe and Teresa were."

"Why do you say that?" Starrett asked. "Were they jealous?"

"Well, envious might be a better word. Yes, that's exactly it, they were envious; they could never be as close to either Joe or Teresa as they were to each other."

"I have it now: was it Ryan and Tom, and Joe and Teresa?" Starrett asked.

"No . . . not really, no," Sheila started off hesitantly. "The only thing Ryan and Thomas had in common was that they were both envious of Joe and Teresa's special relationship."

Starrett felt she hadn't yet finished, so he kept looking at her and hoped that Gibson would not feel a need to break the silence.

"Well, I suppose, at least Teresa told me, in the early days, before Mona came along, Ryan and Thomas were very close, but then . . ."

"We know Mona dated Ryan before she married Tom," Starrett offered, hoping for bigger fish.

"Right so," Kelly said, but she still seemed to be drawing herself up short.

"Do you know why Mona and Ryan stopped seeing each other?" Gibson asked.

"Well, Ryan is the cuter of the brothers, so that was the initial attraction in that relationship, and, well, a strong-minded girl has to be careful; she has to choose very carefully the time when she grants her favours," she said in a voice which sounded so painful it made Starrett uncomfortable. Kelly, unaware of Starrett's discomfort, was focusing all of her attention on Nuala Gibson. "If her favours are the only attraction, well, then eventually her favours cease to be an attraction and, well . . . let's just say, by the time she got to Thomas, she'd learnt her lesson, and I bet she didn't share any of her carnal mysteries until their wedding night."

"Was there any resentment between the three of them?" Starrett asked.

"This is a very funny way to find out about Joe," she replied quickly, looking at both Starrett and Gibson. She gave a shrug. "I think Ryan felt bad for his mum. He felt guilty for being the one who introduced Mona to the family in the first place. It was pretty obvious to all of us that Mona was only interested in herself . . . look, I'm not very comfortable talking about all of this."

That's funny, Starrett thought; he figured she was very happy talking about this stuff.

"OK," Starrett finally replied, "Let's get back to Joe. When did you last see him?"

"The last time I saw Joe," she began, a smile crossing her freckled cheeks, "would have been when he and Miss Boyce dropped around to see Teresa and myself for dinner."

"And when was that?" Starrett inquired.

"Two Fridays ago."

"And that was the very last you saw or heard from him?" Starrett said, this time unable to hide his disappointment.

Sheila Kelly looked as if she were going to say something, decided not to, but then reversed her decision and continued, "Well, actually, I did speak to him on the phone the night before last. He rang to speak to Teresa and I answered the phone, and so we had a quick chat before I passed him over to Teresa."

"How did he seem?"

"Fine, same as usual, friendly, funny . . ."

"Did he . . . ah . . ." Starrett said, finding himself interrupting her but then stopping.

Kelly looked at the detective, then Gibson, then Starrett again and then rolled her eyes at Gibson.

"Tell me this, Miss Kelly," Starrett said, scratching his chin and looking directly into her eyes, "what were you doing between the hours of 01.00 and 05.00 yesterday morning?"

"Ah, the auld alibi question?" she croaked, sounding like Bonnie Tyler with a very sore throat. "Well, that's an easy one – we were holding one of our famous midnight shindigs."

"What, on a Monday night?" Starrett asked in sheer disbelief.

"One of our gang, Anita Pickering, is off to work in NYC, the lucky bitch." She spotted a sign of disapproval in Gibson's eyes. "What? Bitch? Oh God dear, would you ever get out of the house a bit more, for heaven's sake? It's what she is, get over it!" And then in a sweeter mood to Starrett, "Anyway, Anita has been a good mate, and we thought we better throw something for her, but we ran out of time. Her family had her all booked up over the weekend, so we opted for the Monday."

"What time did it start?"

"The terribly earnest and sincere dears started gathering around eleven-thirty, and the hags were all there by just after midnight and got things swinging."

"I imagine there were lots of people there if we needed to . . ." Starrett started.

"Yes, and I imagine there were lots of complaints about the racket we made; there always are. If you check your reports, I think you'll find out about us chapter and verse, although I don't think many of the verses will come from the Bible."

Chapter Seventeen

Garvey and Casey were each conducting their own interviews. They left the main group of the family in the kitchen under the watchful, sly eye of Garda Joey Robinson, while Garvey took Thomas Sweeney, the eldest son, to the sitting/television room. This was located at the front of the house on the opposite side of the hallway from the good room where Starrett and Gibson were conducting their interview with Liam and Colette. Casey took Ryan to a whitewashed outhouse, which functioned as a storage space for animal food, at the other side of the farmyard.

Garvey made Thomas comfortable before taking his notebook from his top pocket. He always operated under his golden guideline of "How would Starrett do this?" – not because he didn't have an opinion of his own, for he certainly did, but because he, more than any, had borne witness, first hand, to Starrett's results.

"How are your children holding up?" Garvey asked.

"Ach, I'm not sure they're fully aware of what's going on, to be honest. Bernadette's cute enough, and her ears are trailing the floor. She's excited about time off school, but I'm not sure . . . well, it's the first time in her life someone she knew has died on her," Tom Sweeney replied, looking like he wasn't exactly holding up too well himself.

He hadn't shaved that morning, so his straw-textured, copper hair, permanently red-flushed cheeks and five o'clock shadow gave him a very world-weary air. He wore a permanent frown, like someone whose face had been carved in stone and was either afraid to, or couldn't, move a muscle in case he cracked his "approach me at your peril" appearance. He looked, Garvey thought, like Peter Ustinov, caught off camera.

"She's certainly a sharp one . . ." Garvey began.

"Aye, her granny is always saying she's as handy as a wee pot. She's picked up on her granny being desperate to see Joe, so now all she's talking about is wanting to see Joe when he's brought back to the house. I wonder will they put him in here or across the hall in the family room? The family room would be a much better room for visitors paying their respects, but we'd have a lot more stuff to move out. This room's really just for the telly, and my father still prefers to read his newspapers in here. I need to speak to my father about that, and then Ryan and I will have to set it up. Tell me, Garda Garvey, do you think I should let her see Joe's corpse?" Tom asked, as his eyes continued to dart around the room as if checking how and where they could best fit a coffin into the room.

Packie found himself not having a clue until he thought, *What would Starrett say?* and answered immediately, "Well, if she really wants to see him, it's probably wrong not to let her."

"Yes, you're probably right. I don't think I'll let Finula see him though. She absolutely doted on her uncle."

"What ages are your girls, sir?"

"Bernadette is eleven going on thirty, and Finula is nine, a young nine, but it's been so comforting for me to see how protective of Finula Bernadette has been."

"How often do you bring the family up to the farm?" Garvey continued.

"Oh, nowhere near as often as we'd like. My wife's a city girl, Garda. She hates the smell of the farm, and the flies drive her absolutely mad. My worry is that my daughters will grow up the same way," Tom Sweeney replied.

"So, when was the last time you were here?"

"Let's see, I think as a family, the time we'd all have been up here together would have been St Stephen's Day."

"You haven't seen your parents since Christmas?" Garvey asked. The minute the question had slipped from his lips he regretted it. It wasn't so much a question as a put-down. Starrett would never have done that. "Never ever distract your witness from your questions," he was always saying.

"No, no, no," Tom continued, barely avoiding a smile, "Christmas was the last time the family was up here. I drop by regularly on my own."

"Can you remember the last time you were here yourself then?"

"Aye, let's see now," Tom began.

Garvey couldn't be sure, but he had a feeling Tom was the kind of person who knew exactly when he had last been up on the farm. If pushed, he could probably recall what the weather was like and what his mother was wearing and which animals had been in the nearby fields.

"Yes, Teresa, Joe, Ryan and I had a meeting here at the beginning of the summer."

"Would you like to have stayed on and worked the farm yourself, Thomas?" Garvey inquired, asking his first incorrect question of the interview.

"Tom, please call me Tom. My wife thinks Thomas sounds old and fuddy-duddy."

"Right, Tom," Garvey continued, persisting with the question, "and would you like to have stayed on the farm?"

"Ach, you know, farming is not what it was, and if you want to bring up a family properly you have to be there for them," Tom Sweeney replied, rolling his eyes before continuing, "And then Mona, ach sure, I'd never have gotten her to live on the farm, even if I'd nailed her feet to the floor.

"When I was growing up, though, we all mucked in, even Teresa. Aye our Teresa could stand shoulder to shoulder with my dad and my brothers and me when it came to the old manual labour. But then, sure, one by one, me, Ryan and Teresa all went off to college and found that pushing a pen is a lot less strain than pushing a plough behind a horse."

"As the eldest, were you not expected to stay and run the farm?" Garvey asked, again immediately regretting his question as a very non-Starrett question and, he reminded himself once again, one that could equally be interpreted as a put-down.

"That tradition has very much bitten the dust these days," Tom said, looking over an imaginary pair of glasses at Garvey. "Besides, at the time I would have been considering working on the farm as opposed to going to college, the auld man looked like he'd be going for ages, and I didn't fancy being nothing more than cheap labour."

"When did you decide to become a solicitor?"

"I can't remember exactly. I do remember considering being a teacher, but Mona soon set me right on that one. Her dad was a solicitor, and she was always going that way. Her dad retired a good few years ago and passed the practice on to Mona and me."

"You enjoy the work?" Garvey asked, remembering some of the less scrupulous solicitors he and Starrett had come into contact with.

"Conveyancing is good solid work and generates dependable money, but, well, we're not all like Joe, and I don't mean that in a bad way. It's just that he was put on this earth to farm the land. He totally gets it, and he takes so much pleasure from it, but sure look where it got him."

"What, you think that his death has something to do with his work?"

"Well, it's my experience that the reason behind murder is either to do with money, business, jealousy or weemen. This in turn can be broken down into two groups: money and weemen."

Garvey didn't comment, so Tom continued: "Well, Joe and Breda seemed fine, and there was no other weemen he was involved with or interested in."

"He told you that?"

"We didn't have that 'best mates' kind of relationship. But look, after his work on the farm, he'd barely enough time to conduct a relationship with Breda. She was always complaining about how he always smelled of the animals."

"Tell me, what were you doing early yesterday morning?"

"How early?"

"Say, between midnight and about seven o'clock?" Garvey asked, giving himself a very wide berth.

"Mona and I were dead to the world," Tom replied, instantly regretting it. "Sorry, sorry, I didn't mean to sound so insensitive."

"It's OK. Words you've taken for granted all your life will now take on a different meaning. It'll take you some time to get used to it."

"Yes, I realise. My wife and I don't start work until ten o'clock, so we're rarely up before eight. She gets up first to get the kids ready for school."

"Do you have any theories as to why Joe might have been murdered?" Garvey asked.

"Is this officially a murder investigation?"

"Ehm, um," Garvey stammered a bit before recovering to reply, "at the moment we're collating our information to ascertain exactly what happened. Do you have any ideas though?"

"Well, as I was saying, with Joe I think we can rule out jealousy and weemen, if they're not the same thing, so that leaves us with money stroke business."

"Do you have any information in that area?"

"Well, if I was the gardaí, I'd be looking at the distribution companies Joe was bypassing by selling direct to the shops and supermarkets. Quite a few of the local farmers were either joining Joe's set-up or following his lead. I reckon some of the more established companies must have suffered due to Joe's success with his new venture."

Chapter Eighteen

Francis Casey, who'd never interviewed anyone solo before, went with Ryan to the whitewashed outhouse. Casey was much more of a backroom detective, happier handling files, paperwork, computers and research than dealing face to face. He rarely would have interviewed, and certainly not by himself, but Starrett needed his young team all out in force on this one. He needed statements from all who were in attendance at the dinner party, and he needed to take them as soon as was physically possible.

As they crossed the yard, they were refreshed by the gently falling mizzle. Casey, who was stepping out with Garda Nuala Gibson, held his hand up to try and keep the moisture away from his Afro-style hair. It wasn't that he was particularly vain or used the thick curls to gain a much-needed three inches to his five foot six inches; the style also had the advantage of needing little or no attention, although Nuala was always saying it was very unhealthy for your hair not to be combed or brushed at least twice a day.

Ryan Sweeney was definitely the looker of the family. Whereas Tom was stern, Teresa was unfeminine, Liam was weather-beaten, looking much older than his sixty-four years, and Colette had inherited to some degree a classic look, in Ryan it all came together in perfection. His looks, his classy Brooks Brothers dress sense, his healthy, slightly tanned complexion, his fat-free physique, his friendly blue eyes and his healthy longish, straight, thick black hair were . . . well "perfect" was the word that kept coming back to Casey. However, unlike Romany Browne – and Casey cursed himself for allowing himself to think of him – Ryan Sweeney's look was natural and uncultivated. Casey conceded to himself that both Browne and Ryan Sweeney were the type of men women were attracted to. In this instance he knew what he really meant was they were the kind of men he felt Nuala Gibson would be attracted to. Not surprisingly, Casey assessed, Ryan had, in Maeve Boyce, by far the most stunning of the Sweeney family women.

Ryan, despite the events of the previous evening, was clean-shaven, and his sculptured good looks reminded Casey of Robert Kennedy. He was dressed in black chinos, a blue shirt, a Queen's University tie and tan Camper slip-on shoes. He had a great smile, a smile that could have launched a very successful political career if he so wished.

"How're my ma and father doing?" Ryan asked as soon as they were inside. There was a rich variety of feed and animal smells. Casey didn't find it unpleasant.

"I think they're fine," Casey replied, not having a clue. "You were the first to arrive at the farm yesterday?"

"Yes," he smiled, looking like he enjoyed being first. "My ma was in the kitchen, and my father was upstairs."

"Do you have a lot of these family get-togethers?" Casey asked, starting off, as Starrett had suggested, by just following the conversation.

Ryan pumped up his cheeks and exhaled the air through barely opened lips.

"Not as much as we used to," he replied eventually, paused and then added by way of explanation, "When it was just us Sweeneys, we used to have them a lot, most Sundays in fact, and certainly Christmas and birthdays, but then, along came the girlfriends and wives and children, and, well, people start to get into a different family life, don't they? But we all try now and again to make the big birthdays, and we all try to drop by at some time or other on Christmas Day. My ma loves that. Christmas is her time of the year. Do you visit your parents at Christmas?"

Casey was a little taken back by the question because he and

Nuala Gibson were still trying to figure out how they could visit both sets of parents this year. Last year, when they had just started dating, it was easier. They just stole whatever time was possible to be with each other over the holiday period, but now that they were "officially dating," they had a responsibility, he felt, to visit both households.

"Well, I still live at home," Casey admitted, "but this year I'm hoping that somehow we'll manage both my own parents and my girlfriend's family."

"Yeah, lucky enough Maeve is totally chilled about it. Her parents are dead and . . . oh . . . look, I know you don't need to know this. Why don't you ask me your questions?"

"OK," Casey replied, visibly relieved. "What time did you arrive?"

"I must have got here just after six o'clock."

"Where did you come from?"

"I live and work in Belfast."

"I thought you lived here in Ramelton?"

"Well, my father persuaded me to buy a house in Coylin Court – you know, high up there on the hill behind the Bridge Bar?"

"Oh, yes."

"He said it'd be a great investment. At the time I bought it my salary was in sterling and the cost in euros, so I got a great deal."

"What do you work at?"

"I do marketing for the Waterfront Hall."

"Oh," Casey replied, "and Maeve Boyce?"

"We live together in Belfast. She also works in the Waterfront Hall. She's the box office manager."

"But I thought you were the first to arrive?"

"I was," Ryan replied and then broke into a smile again. "Oh, I see what you mean. Maeve couldn't get off as early as me. They were going on sale with the tickets for the Ray Davies concert, and there's always great demand for him, so she felt she should stay behind until the rush was over. She drove up after me."

"Right. I see," Casey replied.

"Right, good."

"Marketing? What exactly does that entail?" Casey continued, remembering Starrett's advice to always try and find out as much as you can about what people do. Later on in the investigation, it may become important to know what knowledge certain people have and what they had easy access to. Starrett's example was that if someone has just been poisoned, then you first look at the gardeners in your group of people.

"Well, the venue manager books the artists and then he hands it over to me, and it's my responsibility that the concert sells out. I do that by ensuring the artist in question has profile on the radio, TV and in the newspapers. If we can't get any reaction in the media, we have to resort to posters and paid advertisements. With someone like Ray Davies, all you need do is announce the show in all the proper places, and his reputation will sell all the tickets. With someone like Grannie Duffy, an amazing new act from Monaghan, we start off in the smaller room, the BT Studio, and we go to all our contacts in the media and try to persuade them to write about her, talk about her, get her on TV and radio – you know, drum up a bit of interest in her."

"What kind of act does she perform; high wire, trapeze?"

"Ah no, she's from a different Duffy family," Ryan replied without even the slightest hint of irony. "She's not a circus act; she's an amazing guitarist and singer."

"OK," Casey said, wondering if Nuala Gibson, who was big into her music, had heard of her.

There didn't seem to be any apparent common denominator between marketing and murdering so Casey decided to move on.

"What time did you leave Belfast?"

"I left the office around three o'clock, went to our house to pick up our overnight bag and got out of town before the rush."

"When did you last see Joe?"

"We had a family meeting on the fourteenth of June, my mother's birthday."

"All of youse?"

"Just the siblings."

"Just you and Teresa, Thomas and Joe?" Casey asked, picking up on something Sergeant Garvey had missed.

"Yes."

"But, if it was farm business, would your father not have been present?" Casey pushed, feeling he'd discovered an error in Ryan's answer.

"OK, I should tell you all about this because it's probably important, and it's better that you don't pick it up as gossip."

Casey nodded positively and wrote a couple of things, including Ryan Sweeney's departure time from Belfast, in his notebook.

"OK, my father wanted to give the farm, lock, stock and barrel, to Joe."

"Would that have been unusual?"

"Well, that's a very interesting question because, legally, it's my dad's farm, so he can do with it whatever he wants."

"But?" Casey pushed, just a heartbeat too quickly.

"*But,* there are some members of the family who felt it should have been divided up and sold and the proceeds divided equally among the four of us."

"I see," Casey said. "Then surely if your dad had already made that decision, there would have been no need for a meeting?"

"Good point, Garda," Ryan said, through a strained smile. "Actually, Joe was the one who set up the meeting. He'd been trying to get us together for ages, but it was very difficult."

"Difficult because youse all live all over the place?"

"No, difficult in the same way it was difficult to organise the Vietnam meeting in Paris."

"Ah, you mean the shape of the negotiating table difficult."

"Exactly . . . well, something like that," Ryan confirmed immediately.

"What were *your* problems?"

"Well, I have to admit, I was the major stumbling block."

"How so?"

"I didn't want any spouses or partners at the meeting. It was no one else's business but the Sweeneys'. And Thomas wanted Mona to be there."

"I see," Casey replied.

"Actually, that's not completely correct. Mona was demanding that Thomas insist she be there."

"What about Teresa's girlfriend, Sheila Kelly, where did she stand on all of this?"

"Actually, I think they were hiding behind Thomas and Mona, as in, if she's going to be there, then Sheila has to be there."

"And Joe's girlfriend, Breda Roche?"

"Joe thought there was no need for her to be there. Apparently Sheila tried to get Breda to get Joe to invite her. That didn't work out."

"And your girlfriend, Maeve Boyce?"

"Wild horses wouldn't have dragged her there. She felt Teresa and Mona wanted all the girlfriends there in case they needed backing on votes."

"A bit like the party whip?" Casey suggested.

"A lot like a party whip," Ryan agreed. "So in the end, I gave them an ultimatum: if there was anyone there other than the four Sweeneys, I wouldn't show."

"So you got it resolved?"

"Yes, but then didn't Mona only show up anyway with Thomas and the kids."

"What did youse do?"

"Well, we moved the meeting out here actually, and Joe told Thomas that if he wanted to bring Mona he wasn't welcome; he'd be totally excluded from whatever was decided if he tried to bring her out here. So the four of us came out here and Joe told us his plan. His plan was not to upset our father by either not accepting the farm or by dividing up the farm after it was signed over to him. What he did want to do, though, was to form a company to deal with the sales of the farm produce, and the company would be owned by the four of us."

"Equal splits?" Casey felt compelled to ask.

"No, fifty-five per cent to Joe and fifteen percent to each of the remaining three of us."

"And how did that go down?"

"Fine between the four of us," Ryan replied, and sighed before continuing, "but when Mona heard, she went absolutely ballistic, which only served to greatly upset my ma and father.

"Mona wanted the farm sold and the proceeds split up. She'd always wanted a piece of the farm. I don't know if you're aware of this or not, but before Mona married Thomas, I dated her for a short period of time."

Casey already knew, but he felt it was proper to write something down in his book as Ryan continued.

"Anyway, it didn't last long, for obvious reasons . . ."

"Which were?"

"The woman hasn't a natural bone or thought in her body, and once you get beyond the look and shape of her body, and you have to remember I'm talking fourteen years ago when she was . . . stunning, there was nothing there."

"Did you leave her for someone else?"

"As in Maeve?" Ryan smiled.

"Well, yes."

"No, I didn't actually meet Maeve until a few months later, and we didn't start dating until about five years after we met."

"What time did Maeve arrive at yesterday evening?"

"She got here about 6.45."

"But I thought you said she stayed behind at the Waterfront Hall to oversee the Ray Davies tickets going on sale?"

"As it transpires, they sold out in record time – just over thirty minutes – and she was able to leave a lot earlier than she'd predicted."

"So youse could have travelled up together after all?"

"Yes, as it turned out we probably could. No, actually we couldn't; there was another reason. She was meant to go back to Belfast this morning. I was going to stay the rest of the weekend. I rent out my house here for most of the summer, and the final rental of the season came out last weekend, so I wanted to spend some time cleaning it up and doing a bit of maintenance. It's incredible how hard a family can be on a house when it's not their own."

"What, ehm, what was your day like down in Belfast, before you left to come up here?"

Ryan Sweeney forced a smile.

"Let's see: I got into the office around 9.30, did my emails and snail mail and then scooted around town to see Eddie MacElwaine at the *Belfast Telegraph*. Then I made a few stops at Radio Ulster. That would have taken a few hours, and then it would have been time for lunch in Deans at Queen's. I got back to the office about 2.30, tidied up my stuff and headed off."

"Did Maeve travel with you into work?"

"No, as I said, she needed to bring her own car in so she could drive up here."

"Did she leave the house the same time as you?"

"No, the VW was still there when I left."

"But you didn't actually see her?"

"Look, Francis, I eh, in the course of my work, sometimes I have to work quite late at night, schmoozing at the concerts, going out with contacts and all that stuff, and Maeve, God bless her, needs her sleep, so if I'm back very late I'll let her sleep on undisturbed and I'll kip in the spare room."

"So, you'd have been asleep in the spare room at between one to five yesterday morning."

"Yes, that's what I said."

Garda Francis Casey couldn't resist eyeballing Ryan at that point. The young garda wondered how it was possible to have a girl-friend as beautiful as Maeve Boyce and not sleep with her every sec-ond God gave you. He had the decency to say nothing though, as he wrote down a few more words in his book.

"So," Casey said after a few moments, "on your trip around Belfast yesterday, you'd have bumped into quite a few people?"

"As in people who could provide me with an alibi?"

"Well, yes," Casey replied awkwardly.

"I'll give you a long list of names and contact details if you need them," Ryan responded immediately.

"Yes, that would be handy."

"No problem. When we're finished here, I'll pull my diary and do up a list for you."

"Great, Ryan. Actually, I think we *are* finished here for now. I'll go in with you. I'm chatting to Maeve next."

"I'll send her out if you want."

"Nah, it's OK, I'll go in with you," Casey replied, trying to sound as nonchalant as possible.

Chapter Nineteen

Starrett noticed Colette Sweeney comforting her husband as she led the way up to the privacy of their bedroom. Since it was still too early to head up to Letterkenny to see how Dr Aljoe was getting on with the autopsy, he decided to get the initial set of interviews concluded as soon as possible. Gibson would interview Teresa Sweeney while he interviewed Tom Sweeney's wife, Mona.

He spared a moment for a quick thought on Romany Browne. He realised he was courting the wrath of Major Newton Cunningham by keeping the young Browne detained at Tower House down in Gamble Square, but he hoped the severe shock treatment would work. Otherwise, he feared Garda Romany Browne was a hopeless case. The major would surely be more upset by that outcome.

As this moment passed, Mona Sweeney was shown into the front sitting room and formally introduced to Starrett.

"You're going to interview me by yourself?"

"Why yes," Starrett began, looking somewhat surprised.

"It's just that I'm a solicitor myself, and I thought in these circumstances men weren't allowed to be alone with members of the opposite sex."

"Bejeepers, it's the '*opposite* sex' now, is it? Isn't that a grand turn of phrase?" Starrett chuckled. "Sure it makes you sound like you're from another planet. Now I know Dublin has its strange ways, but it's my belief we're all still inhabiting the same planet."

When he noticed his attempt at ice-breaking humour was going down like a lead balloon, he said, "No, no, you'll be OK, Mrs Sweeney. We're just going to have a wee chat. I've not cautioned you at this time. If there is a need for a more official interview, we'll do it all by the book, chapter and verse. Tell you what I'll do for good measure, I'll keep the door open and help will always be near by if you feel you're being compromised."

"So, if I don't want to, I don't need to answer your questions?"

This is turning out to be interesting, Starrett thought, *very interesting.*

Mona Sweeney looked as if she'd not had much sleep during the previous night. Her make-up was heavily applied, and her hair, which Starrett imagined to have been once healthy and lush, now looked brittle and dyed to death. She was dressed in a very masculine manner, with a brown trouser suit and a yellow shirt, with one too many buttons undone. Starrett had a theory that the more women like Mona Sweeney lose their once-attractive figures, the more they flaunt their breasts. Her one concession to the farm was the fact she wore a pair of black trainers and had the bottom three or so inches of her trousers rolled up to compensate for her lack of high heels. She had small eyes set back in her head and a permanent harsh look on her face, like someone who was continuously walking through the rain.

Starrett thought about what might have attracted first Ryan Sweeney and then his elder brother Tom to this woman. What was he missing? Maybe the chance to have seen her over a decade before. He found himself comparing her to Dr Aljoe. To Starrett's mind, Dr Aljoe, who could always afford a smile, even for strangers, enjoyed the demeanour of someone created for couplings. Mona looked like someone who treated that particular kind of merger as a necessary toiletry experience. Then he chastised himself, not for having such ungenerous thoughts about Mona but about thinking of Dr Aljoe and not Maggie Keane in such an instance.

"Sorry?" Mona said after a few seconds. "I didn't quite hear you?"

"Of course not, Mrs Sweeney. You, as a solicitor, would know perfectly well that I cannot detain you without following certain procedures."

"Good, I just wanted to make sure you were aware that I was aware that I was here voluntarily."

If this if voluntarily, Starrett thought, *I'd hate to be holding you against your wishes.* He said, "I thank you for your co-operation, Mrs Sweeney. If you've a mind to, maybe we could start?"

"Mona is fine," she replied, with the air of someone who felt she'd won the upper hand.

"This is all very sad, isn't it, Mona?" Starrett began.

"Yes, it is, Inspector," she said, picking both creases in her trousers, between her thumbs and forefingers, and following the sharp line down to her knees.

"And particularly for you, Mona," Starrett offered, sounding every bit the sympathetic, caring local garda.

"I mean yes, but why *particularly* me? I mean, he was my brother-in-law, yes of course, but obviously the direct family will suffer more significantly in the nature of a personal loss."

"Sorry, I meant particularly for you, since you dated him before you married his brother."

"Inspector Starrett, I never dated Joe Sweeney," she said, sounding like a schoolmarm chastising a misguided student.

"Ooops," Starrett said, making a big fuss of getting out his notebook and checking through the pages in an Inspector Columbo moment. "Sorry. Yes, you're correct, it was Ryan, the *other* brother you first dated."

Mona looked towards the open door of the room, rose from her seat on the sofa and tiptoed over to close the door very slowly and very quietly. For all her efforts the door still ended its arc with a loud creak and a sharp metallic click as she found the catch quicker than she'd anticipated.

"Yesss, Inspector," she hissed, "could you be just a tad more discreet?"

"Oh, sorry. I didn't realise it was a secret," Starrett continued.

"How long did you and Ryan go out together?"

"Oh, just long enough for me to realise he was like most men in that he had great difficulty committing to a relationship."

"Did you find him cheating on you or anything?" Starrett asked.

"Inspector! I don't really think this has anything to do with this case."

"Bejeepers, Mona, sure it's much too early for me to know that."

"No, Inspector, Ryan did not, to my knowledge, cheat on me. We dated for about six months. It wasn't going anywhere. We split up. Luckily for me, in the course of dating Ryan, I had the good fortune to meet and enjoy some time in the company of his brother Tom, and, well, several months after Ryan and I stopped seeing each other, I bumped into Tom at a do and we got talking and . . ."

"Now you're happily married with two beautiful children?" Starrett offered.

"Exactly, Inspector Starrett," she replied, appearing happy that Starrett seemed to be ready to draw a line under that part of their chat.

"Bernadette, now she's a fine child. I have to congratulate you on how she turned out."

"Why, thank you, Starrett," she replied, visibly thawing.

"Yes, she's very observant."

"Yes . . . but like all children, she possesses a very vivid imagination," Mona added quickly, back on the defence again.

"How would you describe your current relationship with Ryan?"

"We don't have a relationship," she spat quietly, glaring over at the door.

"Well, you must," Starrett began energetically. "I mean, he's your brother-in-law, and whether you like it or not, you obviously come into contact with him frequently at family gatherings."

"What on earth has this got to do with Joe's death?" Mona Sweeney hissed, her Dublin roots coming through quietly but very clearly.

"Well, I'm just trying to ascertain the dynamics of the family," Starrett protested.

"Um, OK . . . look, he used to be my boyfriend, we slept together a few times, years but *years* ago. I'm now happily married to his brother. When Ryan and I meet up at his parents' house, we're civil to each other. We haven't had two words in private with each other since we split up. If it wasn't for Tom's family, I'd be happy never to see him again."

"What about from his side?"

"You'd have to ask him that," she replied snidely.

"OK, I will."

"But when you're doing so, ask him why he had me barred from the June fourteenth meeting up at the farm – maybe he's not as over me as I am him."

"What meeting was this?"

"Sidebar," she said, taking in a long, long breath of air: "for some time now, Tom, Ryan, Teresa and Joe have been . . . let's just say, been in discussions as to what will happen to the farm when Liam retires."

"And the farm is owned by?" Starrett asked, knowing where this was going, but hoping for what he might pick up along a less well-trodden route.

"The farm is owned by the family," she replied, pronouncing her words very slowly, definitely, deliberately and every other way that ended in 'ly,' as only solicitors can.

"OK, so the family owns the farm, and they all got together to decide what to do when Liam retires, correct?"

"Well, not exactly. Liam wasn't at the meeting."

"But surely until he retires he's the boss?" Starrett guessed.

"Liam wants to give the farm to Joe; as far as he's concerned, it's a done deal."

"OK, Mona, correct me if I'm wrong. You're a solicitor and all of that, but if the farm belongs to the family, and Liam is the head of the family, and the head of the family decides to give the farm to Joe, then surely it's his call?"

"Well, it's not as simple as that. Times change. We're in the middle of a property boom the like of which Ireland has never seen before . . ."

"But I thought we were in a slump?"

"Ah, pay no attention to that; that's just orchestrated by the government to get their house in order at the expense of the property market. The big developers are not worried about this little hiccup. In fact, if anything, it will end up playing right into their hands; they'll be able to suck up everything for near nothing in the lull and make a bigger killing in the end."

"Right so, but bejeepers, isn't it still Liam and Joe's call?"

"Listen, Starrett, I have a client, a very patient client I have to say, who is prepared to offer us eleven point eight for the farmland, the house and the fishing rights."

"Eleven-point-eight? Goodness, that's a very big earthquake."

"Eleven point eight million euro!" she hissed, barely managing to keep her volume in check. "Now that's nearly three million euros each for Tom, Ryan, Teresa and Joe . . ." Mona stopped, mid-sentence.

"Or nearly four million euro each for Tom, Ryan and Teresa," Starrett offered. Her eyes instantly proved the words matched her thoughts.

"I *see* where you're going, Inspector; that *is* a hell of a motive."

"Bejeepers, it is, but we shouldn't get ahead of ourselves. Let's get back to this meeting. You say Ryan had you barred from the meeting. How so?"

"Ryan said if I was there he would leave, and Joe, who'd called the meeting, told Tom I wasn't welcome at the meeting either. If I attended he'd be excluded from whatever was agreed."

"Did you go?"

"No, I wasn't prepared to let Ryan have his way and have an excuse to hijack the meeting."

"So, what happened at the meeting?"

"Joe, the apple of his dad's eye, had come up with this idea of keeping everyone happy. He'd keep the farm, but he'd siphon the income from the sales of the farm's produce into a separate company, and the four of them would split the company profits, giving over half the shares (and control) to Joe and dividing the remainder between the three other siblings."

"And wasn't that fair?"

"Well, on two accounts it wasn't. First: if they were to follow my suggestion, I calculated it would take at least thirty years for them to achieve the same income as my developer is offering."

"But Joe, Liam and Colette would be out a house and a roof over their heads," Starrett protested.

"Yes, but Joe would have a shit-load of money from his share and they could find somewhere else to enjoy the rest of their lives. Old man Liam has, I believe, a tidy wee nest egg up his sleeve or under his mattress."

"Yes, but some people are not interested in buying out the rest of their lives; they need to do something. They need a reason to get up in the morning."

"Inspector, they'd have nearly three million fecking reasons to get up each morning."

Starrett could do nothing except laugh.

"You said you had two reasons," he eventually said. "What was the second?"

"The second was that Tom was being offered 15 per cent of the sales of the produce of the farm: the milk, the vegetables and the cattle. For heaven's sake, Inspector, he was the eldest son. He was entitled to the whole shebang."

"Yes, Mona, but as you said just a few moments ago, times change."

Chapter Twenty

Teresa Sweeney didn't look that much older than Joe, so Nuala Gibson figured that her bedroom in the farmhouse would still be intact. Her theory that mothers are reluctant to destroy the memories of happy times proved spot on, and a few minutes later, Teresa led Gibson into a late nineties time capsule. The walls were covered in photographs of Soft Cell, Haircut 100, Paul Young, Kim Wilde and Spandau Ballet, and posters of k.d. lang, William Shatner (looking very proud in his *Star Trek* uniform), a *Bend It Like Beckham* movie promo, Ellen DeGeneres, Anne Heche and Daniel O'Donnell. Daniel O'Donnell wore fake John Lennon glasses, long hair and a beard, courtesy of clever ink work with a black felt-tip pen. The microphone he was holding had been crudely Tipp-Exed out and replaced with a large, smoking spliff.

Gibson laughed out loud, and Teresa also broke into a smile as though remembering the fun she'd had doctoring the King of Donegal's photo.

The wall space that wasn't covered with posters and photographs was filled with bookcases packed to the brim and beyond with books, mostly about exotic foreign countries but also about travel. Gibson noticed several novels by Patricia Cornwell and even more by master crime writer John Connolly. Apart from the Cornwell and Connelly novels, there were no other collections – just a mismatch of individual airport type novels. All the novels were paperbacks, whereas all her travel books were hardbacks. Teresa Sweeney flopped on her single bed and invited Gibson to sit on the wooden chair by a small table which served as a desk, with pens, papers and a couple more books scattered around.

Gibson wondered about a younger Teresa spending hours in this room, plotting her life; wondering about why her parents didn't understand her; why so and so was so rude to her; about her exam results; about having enough money for clothes; about her sexuality. Gibson wondered exactly when Teresa had discovered she was gay. Had it been in this very room? Or after she'd left home and mixed with a different crowd? What must it feel like to now be back here again, having to consider the untimely death of her favourite brother.

Teresa Sweeney sat upright on her bed and swung her legs over the side on to her blue and extremely fluffy bedside rug.

"I know you, don't I?"

"Well, I think we know *of* each other rather than we *know* each other. We were in the same year in the convent in Milford."

"OK, you're *that* Gibson. A friend of mine used to fancy you something rotten."

Gibson had the suss not to ask Teresa if the friend in question was male or female.

"Right," Teresa said solemnly, "we better get started."

Teresa wore her hair brown and short, but not shaved to the skin like her girlfriend. It was cut to about half an inch from her scalp, and Gibson imagined, by its thickness and rigidness, that it must have been cropped recently. She had panda's eyes. Gibson wondered if this was due to lack of sleep or from the end of a bad cold or flu; she was still continuously sniffling. She could only be in her mid-twenties; surely she shouldn't, at this stage, have her lifestyle so transparent on her face. Still, to Gibson, she didn't look healthy at all. The Sweeney girl really did look a lot like her father. On Ryan, the look was definitely what could be classed as cute, but on a girl, a girl who avoided make-up, it wasn't attractive. Her skin had the slight hue of dessert wine, but her smile transformed her entire face, betraying her soul. When she infrequently broke into it, it took ages for it to disappear, and just as it was about to completely disappear, a dimple appeared in the centre of her chin. Teresa must have been very self-conscious about her dimple, because as it appeared out of the end of her smile, she looked embarrassed which, with the dark circles around her boodshot eyes, made her look very vulnerable.

Gibson thought Teresa had what men would class as a good (full) figure. She was dressed in expensive-looking blue jeans, a red Ralph Lauren short-sleeved polo shirt and red and white ankle-high Converse trainers with stars emblazoned on them.

"I'm so sorry about the loss of your brother," Gibson began. Teresa's dimple appeared back on her chin, minus the smile, and as it twitched slightly from side to side, asymmetrically, her nostrils flared up as though she was about to start crying. She bit deeply into her bottom lip, fluttered her eyelids and fanned her cheeks furiously with both her hands.

"I'm not going to cry, I'm not going to cry. I promised Sheila I wasn't going to cry."

"Maybe it's better if we jump straight into my questions?"

Teresa took a deep breath and straightened up her upper torso.

"Good idea, Nuala; fire away."

"I understand you and Joe were close?"

"Yeah, we were best mates, even in our teens, when brothers and sisters are meant to grow apart for a time. We were still each other's best friends. Joe and I always told each other everything."

As Teresa said the word "everything," she stared straight into Gibson's eyes. Was she giving Gibson the answer to a question the Sweeney girl didn't want asking?

"Also in a family like ours, there was a certain element of safety in numbers."

Gibson's eyebrows suggested, "How so?"

"Well, brothers are notoriously vicious with each other, and when Joe, Tom and Ryan were growing up, they used to take lumps out of each other. Then they reached the stage where the auld self-preservation override clicked in with Tom and Ryan, where they could see that they were an equal match for each other, and there was no advantage to further battle, so they both turned on Joe."

"And that's where you stepped in?"

"And that's where I learned to fight," she replied proudly. "But apart from that, I loved the way my younger brother was turning out. Ryan and Tom were just blokes, you know. They thought the biggest insult they could give a girl was to not want to sleep with them. And then one of them doesn't even have the sense to stay away from where the other has been."

"Mona?"

"Well, yes, actually," she said, and then looked at Gibson. Gibson hoped that she wasn't looking judgemental. "Well, at least Ryan had the gumption to see through her, but Tom, the big lump, literally ran around after her, for the first six months of their relationship, with his tongue hanging out. I kid you not, Nuala; he would walk behind her with his tongue over his bottom lip. At least she had the sense not to put him out of his misery, because he would have headed for the hills after the first encounter, but . . ."

"Yeah?" Gibson asked as Teresa broke into another of her wonderful smiles.

"Well, I hate to admit this, but Joe and I followed them one day down the fields and discovered how she was managing to string him along."

"Oh," Gibson said, biting the hook with all her might.

"We followed them down to the old ruin near the water; my dad had it done up and made it a dry shelter so he could store hay down there, closer to the cattle. Of course we all used it in our courting days, and I think we all spied on each other. Anyway, sure aren't they only talking away, more like two work colleagues than boyfriend and girlfriend, and eventually, without any kissing or preamble or anything, she drops to her knees, unzips him and treats him to a ninety-second Bee Jay. Afterwards they both tidied themselves up and continued talking away all the time as if they were in the office. Joe and I scampered off in stitches. Later Ryan confided to Joe that Bee Jaying was Mona's major at university."

"I wonder did she get her degree?" Gibson offered. Just as she was regretting this unguarded remark, Teresa broke into a fit of laughter.

"I can't believe you just said that."

"I can't either," Gibson admitted between fits of giggles. She hoped Starrett was out of ear range.

"I'll tell you, if only half of what Ryan said to Joe is true, she'd have her honours as well."

"Right, right," Gibson said once another fit of giggles had subsided. "We'd better get on with this."

Indiscreet Gibson felt she might have been, but on the professional side, she'd definitely made some kind of bond with Sweeney. Teresa had perked up and was now sitting even taller, willing Gibson to throw more questions at her.

"You were saying you were happy with the way your brother was turning out?"

"Yes, yes, I was," Teresa continued. "He really was a good guy. He was interested in the things we all wish we were interested in."

"Like?"

"He was interested in family values; he was interested in living off the land; he was interested in breeding a strong herd of cattle; he was interested in the upkeep and maintenance of this old, but wonderful, family home – he was always doing things around it, always upgrading or fixing things; he was interested in making sure my parents were all right. You know, we've all left the farm, so he's the only one here looking out for them, and he was always running around after them, taking them here and there to do this and that. He was very unselfish in his approach to life. Not anything that would make you want to puke or anything, but it was just . . . well, I suppose it was that he was growing into a great man."

"Like your dad?"

"Oh," she said shaking her head furiously, "it's hard to think of your father as a great man when he's continuously expressing his disappointment in you."

"You mean because you're gay?"

"You know," Teresa said, looking like she was trying to pick her words very carefully, "beneath it all, I don't really believe my mother and my father have anything against my being gay."

"Well, you're their only daughter. They're going to love you . . ."

"Whatever?"

"Yes, but because they're from a different generation, it's harder though, isn't it?"

"No, no, as I said, I really believe they are fine with me being gay . . ." Teresa began, sounding like she was about to say something she'd never shared with anyone before. "It's more that they have a hard time accepting my choice of partner. My theory is that if I'd come home with a Breda or a Maeve type of girl, or some pretty little thing like the girls our boys chase, then they'd have been fine. It's like: your brothers are fine with you bringing home girls simply because that's their sexual preference as well. But then, not only am I gay, but don't I only go and bring home a fecking truck driver as well."

Again Gibson couldn't help but bursting into another fit of giggles, which in turn started Teresa off again.

"Oh my goodness, we're never going to get to the end of this, are we?" Teresa said as they quietened down again.

"Yes, you're right, let's get back to Joe," Gibson said, giving herself a severe mental dressing down: "were you aware that he was in any trouble?"

"Enough trouble for someone to go and . . . to go and take his life?" Teresa asked, appearing to be also consciously keeping herself in check.

"Well yes, I suppose."

"Jeez," Teresa sighed, "like, maybe someone mistook him for someone else? Maybe he got into a fight helping someone out? Maybe he found out something he shouldn't have. Maybe . . . oh I don't know, why do people kill other people?"

"Usually it's related to money?"

"Joe wasn't really preoccupied with money; he wasn't the kind of boy who spent his every waking minute trying to work out ways of getting richer. Having said that, word had come out that the auld man was passing the farm on to Joe, so maybe someone out there figured he was a lot richer than he actually was. But it's like my father always used to say when we were growing up, 'Show me a rich farmer and I'll show you an idle one.'"

"What do you know yourself about this independent distribution network Joe was setting up?"

"Well, only that it seemed to be working well for him," she replied, appearing as though her mind wasn't really on her answer. "You know he was giving each of us – Ryan, Tom and me – a piece of it?"

"Yes, how did youse all feel about it?"

"Well, there are definitely two points of view on that one in the family. Supposedly, according to Mona, the farmland itself is worth millions and would have set us all up well for life. Then there are those who think Joe was on the farm, working the farm, the farm has been in the family for generations and Joe had found a way, he thought, to keep history, our father and the rest of us happy."

"So, was Mona really upset about the new plan?"

"Ah yes, it was like, in her own head, she'd already sold the land."

"How did Tom and Ryan feel about it?"

"Tom didn't have a choice about how he felt about it, and I believe Ryan had mixed feelings about it."

"And yourself?" Gibson asked, a question which didn't seem to go down too well with the only Sweeney sister.

"Oh me, I've always sided with Joe, and he me."

"And Sheila?"

"Sheila's fairly pragmatic about these things. She's always saying we can always do with more money."

"So, she was happy Joe was giving you a share of the farm produce company?" Gibson asked.

"You better believe it."

"OK, so maybe we have to rule out money. Do you know if Joe was the type who would fool around with a married woman?"

"You've got to be kidding, Nuala. We had to take him by the nose and lead him into Breda's arms."

"How did they hook up?"

"My brother was well on his way to becoming another bachelor country farmer. He was so preoccupied with the farm that he was going to wake up one morning forty years old and alone. One of the things that seems to have been lost between my grandfather's generation and my father's is the ability for the elders to matchmake. Some of the matches were downright disasters, but at least a man and a woman who would otherwise have ended up alone had some kind of life and a family together. But Joe had missed out on my father leaning across the fence with the farmer next door and discussing their respective son or daughter. I decided, with a few of my friends, that I had to take matters into my own hands, so we set him up with young Breda, who some of us knew. She's a pretty little thing, isn't she? In the beginning she thought she was one of the gang, but she wasn't really; it was just the lifestyle she liked. But she was an OK kid. So we set them up, but we had to keep fanning the flames."

"And they were getting on OK?"

"Yeah, they appeared to be. I can't really tell you to be honest, because since she took up with Joe I was no longer in her confidence."

"How long had they been dating?" Gibson asked.

"Long enough for both of them to see themselves as a couple – say fifteen months or so."

"What do you do for work, Teresa?"

"I don't work."

"What . . . you're studying or something?" Gibson asked, looking again at Teresa's bloodshot eyes.

"No, I'm well done with my studying days. Sheila won't let me work. We're a very traditional couple in that I stay at home and run the house and she goes out to work to, as she puts it, 'put the food on the table.'"

"Where do youse live?"

"We've a wee ugly pink bungalow just off the Golf Course Road, on the way to Letterkenny."

"What does Sheila do?"

"Nuala, I wasn't kidding. She's a truck driver."

"Noooo?"

"Well, not a truck driver, more a van driver; she has her own haulage company called Fit 2 Flit."

Gibson smiled. "How does she do?"

"All I can tell you is, she *keeps* putting food on the table."

"Difficult one this, but what were you doing between the hours of 1.00 A.M. and 5.00 A.M. yesterday morning?"

"Easy one that. One of our gang, Anita Pickering, is moving to New York, lucky cow, and we threw one of our famous midnight soirées for her."

"What time did it start and finish?" Gibson asked.

"I'd say the really boring people got there around about 11.30, and when I crashed out at 04.30 there was still a good crowd there."

"When you get a chance, maybe you could do me up the guest list for the party?"

"You want to know the names and addresses of the gang, do you?" Teresa replied, her eyes opening wide in an apparent new interest.

"No, no . . ." Gibson stammered, "I mean . . . yes, but I need it just to check your alibi."

"Oh right," Teresa said as she smiled. "I see."

Garda Nuala Gibson couldn't be sure, but she thought a self-confessed lesbian had just been flirting with her.

Chapter Twenty-One

Starrett was keen to get off the farm.

As much as he'd enjoyed his early morning dander, all those people – some mourning, some not, but all of them in a confined space – were overwhelming him.

He went to find Liam, who seemed to have regained his composure, and they both boarded the inspector's BMW and set the dials for Letterkenny General Hospital.

Liam seemed happy to remain silent, and Starrett was happy to leave him to his thoughts, but as they drove down the steep incline of the Gortlee Road, he started to quiz Starrett about what state they might find his son's body in.

"Ach now, Liam, don't you worry," Starrett began, regretting that he'd not phoned Dr Aljoe to tip her off about their impending visit. "They'll have him ready for us."

"Jeez, Starrett, this is a weird thing for a human to make a living at."

"Who, me or the doctor?"

"Why, the both of youse of course," Liam replied as they negotiated the heavy traffic at the Oatfield Sweets Factory roundabout.

"You know, Liam, sometimes I ponder exactly that same thing, and I wonder how I've ended up doing this," Starrett offered, trying very hard to draw the conversation to a more general level.

"But how *did* you end up doing it, Starrett, being in the gardaí?"

"The short version of that," Starrett continued, noticing they were reaching the top of De Valera Road and closing in on the Town

Park roundabout, "is ninety lectures, three exams, marching on the square, physical training in the gym, swimming in the pool, six months of rising every morning at 7.00 o'clock for porridge and two hard boiled eggs *and* having to have your hair cut twice a week."

"Fair play to you, Starrett, you've got me here without me ever thinking about the mortuary," the grieving farmer said as they drove up High Road and spotted the hospital rising regally to their left.

As they walked through the sliding front doors, Starrett leaned over and whispered, "Aye, Liam, I have a confession to make: I can't abide being in hospitals or going to doctors either, so it was really you who was distracting me."

"I've a few of those meself," Liam said to the ground as he side-tracked into the shop.

"What, distractions or confessions?" Starrett asked, worrying for a split second that Liam was going to buy flowers for his son. Starrett accepted that it would be, in a way, a perfectly normal reaction, but given the circumstances surely a wee bit bizarre.

"Confessions," Liam replied, digging deep in his pockets for change, "I'm addicted to these," he continued, picking up a fistful, four bars, of Cadbury's Milk Chocolate Tiffin bars. "They're my between meals fix of sugar. Right, let's do this."

Dr Aljoe wasn't quite ready for them. She sent word via her assistant, Adhemar, that she'd like to see Starrett first, and Adhemar was to remain with Liam Sweeney and furnish him with tea and sympathy.

Starrett then proceeded along his worst nightmare: visiting a corpse on the autopsy table.

"Ach, Gawd," he sighed, as he walked along the heavily disin-fectant-scented corridors.

"Follow the green line and you'll find me," was the message Aljoe gave to all who came to visit her. *And which colour line should I follow to find my way out of here?* he asked himself as he remem-bered her chant.

Even though Starrett knew full well the procedure of the autop-sy, he still wasn't expecting the impact the remains of Joe Sweeney would have on him as he walked into Dr Aljoe's examination room. The body was naked, save for a white cloth, which strategically covered his privates. Apart from the large incisions Aljoe had made to the body to facilitate her examination, Starrett noticed several marks and scars which could, in their own way, tell the story of Joe's life.

There was a large older scar, which cut straight across his right knee. He'd lost the top quarter of his left-hand index finger altogether. There was an appendectomy scar on his left side, just visible above his vanity cloth. The shin of his left leg was badly disfigured, as if he'd smashed something badly and then left it to heal the country way: through time. His hair was pulled up over his crown, and Starrett noticed his eyebrow was split in two by a small narrow band of healed, white and curled skin. The big toe on his right foot was bent back toward the shin at a severe angle. Starrett wondered was that post-death or pre-death. If it had happened just before death, what could have caused it? Being in an enclosed space? Lying face down? But then surely there would still need to have been some external pressure applied for the toe to be at such an acute angle to the body? Maybe it was just one of his unique oddities?

Starrett knew that Colette most probably knew each and every one of these blemishes. Come to think of it, she probably knew all of his personality blemishes as well. *The thing about mothers,* Starrett thought, *is that they know everything about their children, even things that they might not admit to themselves.* They are one of a very select group of people, maybe even the only people, who will have witnessed both the best in you and the worst in you. Your mother is definitely the only member of that group who will accept both without passing judgement. Mothers will love their children unconditionally, no matter what. Mothers, and mothers alone, possess this rare, if somewhat blind, quality.

What did Colette Sweeney know about her son that might help Starrett?

Perhaps within those secrets would lie her dilemma? If there was such a secret, a secret so important it could be the genesis of his demise, would the mother wish to protect her son's reputation beyond the grave by keeping her own counsel? Or would she risk posthumously damaging his reputation by her full revelation in the hope it would help Starrett to apprehend and bring to justice the perpetrator of the vilest of crimes?

Aljoe nodded to Starrett to come closer to the body. Reluctantly he did as he was bid.

The closer he came to the corpse, the more he was overcome by the powerful smell. The normal smell of death – akin to the smell of rotting apples – was in this instance augmented by incredibly fetid smells from the recently exposed interior of the remains.

Starrett felt his stomach heave. He didn't want to be sick; it felt so disrespectful.

"Starrett, I found water in his lungs . . ." Aljoe began, sounding like she wanted Starrett to finish her sentence. Maybe she sensed he was experiencing a queasy moment.

"Which means he wasn't dead when he was put in the water?"

"Exactly."

"What else can you tell me?" Starrett asked.

"I can tell you he didn't drown in bath water," she continued, as she walked around the body. Starrett had never had the opportunity to observe her do her work in the morgue before. She was dressed top to toe in blue, with her wild mane somehow defying gravity by remaining tucked up into a preposterously small skull cap. She wore a matching pair of blue gutties, which enabled her to move around the examination table silently and swiftly. Starrett witnessed a side of her he'd never seen before. Samantha Aljoe appeared to have a powerful compassion and respect for the dead body. She was so reverential towards her "patient" she reminded Starrett of Florence Nightingale attending her patients from the battlefield.

"Mmmm," Starrett said, distracted by his thoughts.

"I took some samples from the Leannan when I was down there. It's unusually clean for a river. Hopefully I'll be able to have a match for you later today, but I'd bet that's where Joe met his sad end."

"Anything else?" Starrett asked, taking great trouble to keep his focus on his investigation and away from the corpse.

"Yes," she said, going to her worktop, which was about a metre away from Joe Sweeney's head. She opened a manila file and appeared to study the contents before continuing, "We found traces of Rohypnol in his blood."

"The date-rape drug?" Starrett offered, the information snapping him out of his distraction.

"Yes, some say. But it's also used as a sedative, to calm people down or to help them sleep."

"Right, anything else you need to tell me before we bring Liam in?"

"Do you really have to?"

"Sam, I think he needs to, for his own sake as much as his wife's. It will help them deal with this. The last image of their son is as a lad full of life, laughing, smiling, talking and having fun. He needs to see the boy. He needs to acknowledge the death and then help his wife through this very troubled time."

"You're right, Starrett. Just give me a few more minutes to get the body covered and then bring him in."

Starrett was equally happy to have an excuse to leave the morgue. He reversed out like an actor trying to leave the stage without making too much fuss, but at the same time being careful not to bump into anything.

According to the large, loudly clicking clock high on the wall just outside the morgue, it was four minutes and forty-four seconds later when Starrett re-entered the morgue, this time with the deceased's father.

Dr Aljoe had packed up all of her instruments, covered the body up to the neck with a clean white sheet and dimmed the lights to soften the harshness of her workspace. Starrett wondered if Liam Sweeney noticed that the folds in the shroud covering his son formed a cross, the intersection of which would have been, as near as the detective could guess, directly above the idle heart.

If the father spotted this he made no acknowledgement of the fact. He stood in silence at the foot of the table by his son's covered feet.

Starrett and Aljoe stood back from the examination table and slowly manoeuvred themselves to the other side of the large room. Starrett was standing so close he could smell her distinctive rich blend of scents. Starrett loved the bouquet of manufactured perfumes combined with the natural aromas of a woman. He figured if men paid better attention, they could surely tell all they needed to know about a woman from her scent. She swayed slightly in his direction, and her hip briefly touched his. He hoped it was accidental.

Liam Sweeney, dressed in his checked shirt and brown corduroy trousers held up with a four-inch thick worn leather belt, was swaying backwards and forwards by his son's feet. He twisted his black cloth cap around and round in his fingers. He didn't look as Starrett remembered him when he was growing up. No, Liam had always been Farmer Sweeney, a friend of his father's and as solid and strong as the grey Massey Ferguson tractor he was permanently attached to. Now his shoulders seemed ferociously drawn down towards the earth's unforgiving magnet. Even his trusted tractor had deserted him. Starrett actually had a flash of Sweeney perched on his tractor, engine still rattling, using his tattered checked work hat to scratch his brow as he surveyed his laid out son from on high.

Something had changed in Liam Sweeney. Not just since Starrett's youth, but since earlier that morning, where he was behaving so vulnerably in the company of his wife. Starrett admitted to himself that it wasn't a *slight* change. Something bigger had happened to Liam's mood. He'd even changed drastically since their solemn drive in from Ramelton.

Was it the sight of his son – his chosen heir – and the confirmation that all of their hopes and dreams now lay withering slowly away amongst the decaying mass before him?

Sweeney moved clumsily along the length of table, his forefinger carelessly tracing a line along his son's body as he travelled. He seemed fine when his finger was moving along the top of the sheet, but when he reached the bare skin of his neck, something, maybe the coldness of the skin, seemed to send an electric shock through his fingers, and his arm instantly and instinctively recoiled, almost as if in self-protection. He seemed totally lost for a few seconds, then grew self-conscious and ended his journey by carelessly brushing his calloused fingers through his son's hair.

Chapter Twenty-Two

As Starrett and Liam Sweeney were driving back to the farm in silence, Garda Francis Casey was sitting down in the sitting room of the farm wondering what Ryan Sweeney's girlfriend Maeve Boyce might reveal to him.

Of all the Sweeney women (by blood and relationships), Maeve wasn't the one with the most natural beauty, but she was certainly the one who spent most energy on her presentation. The result was that, at least to Casey's eyes, she was by far the most beautiful. He'd always found himself attracted to women with long straight hair. He loved nothing more than clocking Nuala Gibson off duty and releasing her long hair from her complex system of hair clips. Maeve, in addition, had a perfectly trimmed thick fringe. She didn't exactly flaunt her near perfect figure, but neither did she hide it. Casey wondered why Ryan would have been attracted to Mona when it was quite obvious that Maeve was far more his type. Maybe the years, and two children, hadn't been kind to Mona, but as far as the young garda was concerned, Maeve Boyce and Nuala Gibson were built for pleasure, while Mona . . . well, Mona's body, not that it was overweight or anything, but it seemed to be a single mass. Even the way she walked displayed no sexual or physical pride. Her body was purely a functional support system for her brain. As he heard footsteps out in the hallway, Casey congratulated himself for putting his finger on what had been bugging him about Mona. Everything about her was functional. She lacked any sensuality. He was mentally chastising himself for having sexual thoughts about witnesses when the door opened and in walked Maeve Boyce.

Now Maeve's body moved as smooth as silk and as quiet as smoke. Casey hoped she hadn't spotted his jaw on the floor as he rose to greet her.

"Can I get you a cup of tea or anything?" he offered, giving himself a chance to get over her entrance.

"No, I'm perfectly fine, thank you," she said as she smiled naturally and confidently at him. "They wouldn't let us out of the house up at Frewin until they'd set us up for the day. I didn't think I'd the stomach for it, but when I smelt the bacon, I remembered I hadn't eaten since yesterday lunchtime. Then when we arrived back here on the farm, didn't Liam only insist we all sit down to a family breakfast together. I tried to nibble a bit more, but even Ryan, who usually has a big appetite, couldn't take more than tea and a bit of toasted wheaten."

She patted her very firm stomach before adding, "I'm going to need an extra half an hour in the gym when we get back down to Belfast."

"Oh, it looks perfect to me," Casey spluttered, unable to stop his words betraying his private thoughts. "I mean, I mean, I didn't mean . . ." he continued digging himself into an even deeper hole.

"I know exactly what you meant, Garda, and I'm very flattered. Fortunately my boyfriend feels the same way, but we'll leave it there, shall we?"

"Yes, yes, of course. But I didn't mean . . . I wasn't suggesting . . ."

She patted him on the knee and smiled at him. "Please don't give it another thought, Francis, but let me just say this, no matter what some girls say these days, we *do* like to be noticed, and there is certainly no harm in looking."

Start the questions, start the fecking questions, a wee voice in the back of Casey's head kept repeating. He took his notebook from his top pocket.

"How well did you know Joe?"

In one tick of the grandfather clock that stood guard to the left of the door, the garda's question totally changed the mood from a slightly flirty one to a more solemn tone.

"Well, I've known Ryan for ten years – although we've only been dating for half that time – and Jeez, I've probably known Joe since he was in short trousers. We get, sorry, we *got* on well with him. Ryan liked Joe and Joe liked Ryan. I've never heard them utter a cross word about one another. Joe and Teresa are . . . sorry, I mean were, probably better buddies though when they were growing up."

"You didn't have a personal friendship with Joe then?"

"No, not really. You know, as a couple, people have a tendency to develop friendships with other couples mostly. My individual friends are all friends I had before I started dating Ryan."

"But you were a friend of Ryan's before you and he became a couple?"

"Yes indeed, very good point."

"So, some of your friends might be friends you made in the early years when you were . . . friends with Ryan."

She smiled, "You mean when we were *just* good friends?"

"Well, yes."

"Surprisingly not," she replied, rubbing her black nylon covered knees with both hands. "When I first met Ryan at Queen's, we were both dating other people. And if I was perfectly honest, I'd have liked it if we had been more than just good friends. But sometimes, Francis, you have to take what you can get, don't you? And having said that, Ryan was a *brilliant* friend, and if I continue my line of being perfectly honest with you, the reason we're still together today is simply because we became good friends before we became . . ." she hesitated for a single breath, until she made eye contact with him, ". . . lovers."

Starrett was always telling Casey, and the rest of his team, that while in the process of questioning you'd always get more from people if you followed the natural line of the conversation. Of course, there were key points you needed to cover, but it was always a much more rewarding interview if you followed those natural lines.

"So were you and Ryan both in relationships for five years with other partners and then you got together when those relationships broke up?"

"Wow!" she exclaimed. "My goodness, I haven't been down this country lane for ages. Let's see: I was in a long relationship for, say, four of those years, and Ryan was preoccupied with his studies for about one year, a wee girl from Magherafelt for another year, drinking in the Student's Union bar for yet another year, Mona for less than a year and a series of one-night stands for the last year."

"When you say you were in a relationship for about four years, do you mean it might have been a bit longer or a bit shorter?"

"What I meant was, that particular relationship was for four years, give or take a couple of relapses."

"You broke up a couple of times?"

"Not exactly," she said, grimacing and looking slightly embarrassed.

"You cheated?" Casey said, with the enthusiasm of a conversation with someone he was a lot more familiar with.

His enthusiasm for this subject was clearly infectious, because she dropped to a near whisper as she continued, "Yeesss!"

"Oh my goodness." Casey couldn't help himself now. He was so involved in the conversation that he was in danger of breaking one of Starrett's golden rules: never become the witness's best friend while on the gardaí's euro. "With different people?"

"The same person," she said, then dropped to a whisper again. "Look, I might as well tell you, it's totally harmless, but I contributed two of the nights on Ryan's year of one-night stands."

"Did your boyfriend find out?" Casey asked, wondering if perhaps, in a case of mistaken identity, the wrong brother had been murdered.

"No, of course not," she protested.

"Ever?"

"No, no one knows," she replied very quickly and very positively. "I don't even know why I'm telling you, aside from the fact I'm trying to be truthful."

"So, this happened a couple of times?"

"Yes, a few," she replied as she grimaced again, "ehm . . . does four qualify as a few?"

"Ah, no," Casey replied; "four now, that would be considered a steady relationship these days."

"Cutting, but probably deservedly so," she said, appearing as though she wanted to draw a line under this topic.

"So, tell me, Miss Boyce . . ."

"Oh, Francis; Maeve, please. After what I've just admitted to you, you must call me Maeve."

"OK, Maeve: these four one-night stands, how do they fit into the Ryan-dating-Mona time-frame?"

"I believe she was somewhere there or thereabouts during one of the indiscretions, but I don't think Ryan even considered that he and Mona were anything other than . . . well let's just be polite and say they were never a serious item."

"How do you get on with Mona?"

"I don't," Maeve replied, very firmly.

"Do you think she thinks you stole Ryan from her?"

"I don't really care *what* she thinks. She's not a nice piece of work, I can tell you. If you dig around enough, you'll soon discover she wears the trousers in that house. She's a schemer; she's always scheming. She's the kind of person who never enjoys today because she's already used up tomorrow – might even be in the middle of next week. But look, in case you're thinking otherwise, I've got no feud going on with Mona. I leave her alone, and she leaves me alone. The only problem I have with Mona is that Bernadette and Finula are nice wee girls, both of them, but I fear they'll grow up to be just like their mum, and that would be sad. Ryan reckons Mona is exactly the same as her mum, a mum she grew up hating."

"What about Mona and Joe? How did they get on?"

Maeve Boyce looked at Francis Casey and remained silent.

"What?" Casey said, breaking into an embarrassed smile, and when Maeve still remained silent he continued, "Am I missing something here?"

"Mona hated Joe's guts."

"Why, what happened?"

"Well, only that she hitched her wagon to the wrong son."

"Sorry?"

"OK, this is not based in any fact, but my theory on the matter is this. Mona dated Ryan and she got to spend time up here in this gorgeous house. She saw how prosperous the farm was. When Ryan dumped her, she realised what a golden opportunity she'd just let slip through her wallet, so she honed in on Thomas because (a) he was malleable and, with her favours, she could wrap him around her little finger and (b) because he was the eldest and, with her legal training, she figured the farm would be passed on to Thomas."

"But Liam broke with tradition?"

"But Liam broke with tradition and was giving the farm to the son who loved farming rather than the son with the wife who saw it first and foremost as a development opportunity."

"Was Mona openly hostile towards Joe?"

"That wasn't Mona's style; all of her communications were issued through either her husband or her solicitor. To your face she was always sweet as . . . my oh my, I'm really digging up the dirt for you here. This is so unlike me."

"What can you tell me about Breda?" Casey asked, fancying his roll was about to end.

"I don't really know her all that well. She seems quite tight with Teresa and Sheila. I think one, or all of them, were friends before she met Joe."

"You don't sound like you've got a Donegal accent there?"

"Actually my family are more Donegal than most. My father, if he were still alive, could give you the complete lineage and lecture on how his family moved over here from England as a reward for services for the Crown. My mother was from Kent, but my parents spent quite a bit of time in Kenya, so my accent is more from my teachers than it is from the land."

"What did your dad do?"

"You know, I never really worked that out. I think we were what was called 'old money.'"

"Did you never ask your dad?" Casey asked, his disbelief apparent.

"I never had that kind of relationship with my father. I needed to make an appointment to talk with him. My nanny brought me up."

"No brothers or sisters?"

"No. I think my mother had to use all her powers of negotiation to get me. My father *was sixty years old* when I was born, so he wasn't predisposed to having his retirement disturbed by a litter of children."

"Where's your home in Donegal then?"

"The family home is down near Donegal town, overlooking Lough Eske."

"Who owns it now?"

"I do."

"But you don't live there?" Casey asked, now feeling completely out of his depth with this woman.

"No, it's rented to some big shot American film producer who likes to pretend it's his country pile. I live with Ryan down in Belfast."

"And where do you work?"

"I'm the box office manager at the Waterfront Hall."

Casey thought about the "pile" near Donegal town, and again his lips beat his brain to the words, "But . . . why . . . surely you don't need . . . sorry."

"Actually, I do need to work, if only for my sanity. Human beings need to occupy themselves physically and mentally. Ryan reckoned the real reason Liam wanted Joe to have the farm was because Joe would never have sold it and therefore, in retirement, Liam would always have had something to fill his days around the farm. I enjoy my work. There's something very exciting about being involved, albeit indirectly, in the entertainment business. It's always fascinating seeing who is selling tickets and who is not."

"Let's get back to Joe," Casey said, resisting inquiring about who could and couldn't sell tickets. "Are you aware of anyone who had a grudge against him, anyone who'd want to do him harm?"

"As much harm as *murdering* him? No, I don't believe I've ever come across such a person in my life. Mona, as I say, was pretty pissed at him, but I can't see her *murdering* her husband's brother, can you?"

"Inspector Starrett's always telling us never to rule anyone out until the murderer is locked up."

"Maybe he's just been doing his job for too long," she offered.

"Or maybe he's witnessed, just a wee bit too close, exactly what humans are capable of doing to each other," Casey said, as much to himself as to Maeve Boyce. "Tell me, Miss B . . . I mean Maeve, what were you doing between the hours of 01.00 A.M. and 07.00 A.M. on Monday morning?"

"I was asleep in our apartment in Belfast. If you know Belfast, we live in Brandon Parade, which is just off Connsbrook Avenue. It's quite close to Victoria Park and not a million miles from the Waterfront Hall."

"I'm assuming Ryan was with you?" Casey said, as he started to return the notebook to his pocket.

"Actually no, I'm a very light sleeper. I need my nine hours sleep every night, so whenever Ryan is on a late one, like out at a concert or something, he always sleeps in the spare room when he comes in. Believe me, Francis, you don't want to be waking me up in the middle of the night."

The words of Maeve Boyce's final sentence burned their way into Casey's brain and stayed there for the next few minutes. Then he saw Nuala Gibson out in the kitchen, and one look, just one look, was all it took for him to realise it wasn't down to the fear of Miss Boyce that he wouldn't risk waking her in the middle of the night. No, it was the love of another good woman which ruled his heart, not the fear or temptation of another.

Chapter Twenty-Three

When Starrett dropped Liam Sweeney off at the farm, he seemed to have totally withdrawn into himself. Starrett couldn't put his finger on it, but the farmer's persona was worrying him.

He told Gibson to take Casey and Robinson back to Tower House and start the trace on F&V Distribution Ltd – who appeared to be losing out big time thanks to Joe taking over the distribution of his own and his neighbours' farm produce – and the Sweeney cousins Dave, Lawrence and Adam Sweeney and their married sister, Beatrice Hewson. The cousins might have seen Joe as a target for their frustration at being deprived of part of the Sweeney farmland.

Slim pickings, Starrett knew, for getting towards what was the end of day two of his investigation.

Starrett and his trusted Packie Garvey headed back down to the waterfront and the scene of . . . well, not so much crime but more, at this stage, the scene of the discovery of the body.

It was a stunningly beautiful Donegal day. The rich, green and varied Donegal landscape loved the sun and always used the bonus of the dazzling light to show off its treasures in a "I'm ready for my close up" moment with its director, God.

"So, how'd the game go on Sunday?" Starrett asked Garvey, one of An Garda Síochána's *and* Donegal's favourite, not to mention finest, hurling players.

"I'd say it was an even match."

"Yeah?"

"Yeah, the first half was even and the second half was even worse," Garvey replied as Starrett did his vocal impression of a snare drum roll, followed by a crash of a cymbal.

"Not your best moment then?" Starrett asked.

"Not by a long chalk, but I'll tell you this, on Saturday I was up at Bowls Goals to see my brother's kids play, and I spotted two fine football players, brothers in fact, Oisín and Darragh Toal. Aye, don't be surprised if you see those two names on a Liverpool or Celtic team sheet in a few years' time."

Starrett was getting fidgety. Garvey knew he wasn't interested in football. Starrett wasn't interested in sport full stop actually, apart, that was, from Formula One, and that was only because that particular sport involved his beloved cars. No, Garvey knew full well Starrett's fidgety moments were the start of his dance, a dance that always ended up in Starrett blagging one of his stash of cigarettes. The inspector hated the act of smoking. It was dirty. Filthy in fact, he thought; it was also smelly, and it was impossible to get the smell out of his clothes. Not to mention the fact that smokers were now society's outcasts. But Starrett also reckoned smokers were a wee bit like Billy the Kid and all the other cowboys who wore black hats, in that they were not as abhorred as the spin doctors may have wished. That's because there was always something appealing about the outlaws, wasn't there? Starrett was even starting to hear tales of boys actually going to the trouble of taking up smoking just so they'd have an excuse to go out to the smoking areas and chat up all the girl smokers.

"When did I have my last ciggy, Packie?" Starrett asked, right on cue.

"That would have been yesterday evening, Inspector."

"Must be nearly time for another one, don't you think?" Starrett asked, sounding as if he felt he needed Garvey's blessing to indulge.

"I thought we were down to one every other day now, Inspector."

"No, no, my understanding was that we'd compromised, and I would only have a ciggy on every day that ended with a 'y.'"

Garvey and Starrett knew perfectly well that this conversation was only going one way until Garvey played dirty and announced, "I think you'll find that Maggie Keane believes you've stopped smoking altogether, sir."

At this point they were driving down Pound Street towards the quay, and Starrett was convinced he could have driven straight down the hill and into the Leannan if it hadn't been for the couple of remaining garda vehicles.

Starrett parked his clapped-out BMW by the Heritage Centre, a few yards from the *Hanging Gale* courtyard, and as they exited the car, he shot Garvey a look, a look with the desired effect of Garvey producing the contraband. Starrett immediately lit up. Yes, ciggies were dirty, filthy even, and yes, they were also smelly, but Starrett just loved what they did when the nicotine hit his bloodstream. If Maggie Keane walked naked along the quayside just now, he'd have a hard choice to make between her charms and the hit of this addictive drug. Well, on second thoughts, maybe not. To prove the point, to himself at least, he took another quick drag, threw the cigarette down to the ground in disgust and stamped it out violently under the toe of his black leather shoe. Point made, he looked the quayside up and down several times, but surprise, surprise, Maggie Keane was nowhere in sight.

"What do you have when you have a puzzle?" Starrett asked himself as much as Packie. They had entered the courtyard to the warehouses where Joe's body had been discovered just over twenty-four hours ago.

"Well, you look for all the pieces of the puzzle so that you can fit it all together properly."

"True, Packie my lad. But even *before* you address the issue of the puzzle, what does the fact you actually have a puzzle before you tell you?"

By this time Garda Gibson had joined them in Owen Bonner's courtyard. The three of them stood in silence, looking around while the scene of crime lads and lasses busily went about their work.

"The presence of a puzzle suggests someone is trying to deceive you," Nuala Gibson eventually offered, as she continued to stare intently at the iron sphere.

"Exactly!" Starrett replied as he wandered over towards the sphere.

A few minutes later, Starrett called both of them over.

"Here," he said as he grabbed one side of the sphere-shaped iron framework, "help me lift it over here."

It wasn't as heavy as it looked. Gibson suggested they use its shape to their advantage and roll it. As they were rolling it toward the low-back, floorless trailer, Starrett said, "Do you know how Marilyn Monroe achieved her world-famous wiggle?"

"An extra pint of Guinness?" Garvey suggested.

"No," Starrett replied humourlessly. "She had her cobbler shave off about half an inch from one of her heels."

"And the relevance?" Gibson asked, as she raised the sphere up and on to the trailer. Starrett urged them to continue rotating it until three protruding bolts on one end of it slotted into three corresponding holes on an iron plate soldered on above the middle of the axle. Starrett, once he was sure that the sphere was secure, tried to spin it around in its new position. It only moved about half an inch either way.

"The relevance . . ." Starrett said, as he dry washed his hands and then had Garvey help him take the trailer hitch. They heaved and heaved until eventually the trailer moved, and as it did, the sphere turned around automatically. ". . . is that there's a reason for everything."

"OK, and?" Gibson asked hesitantly.

"And I need you to discover what this is used for."

Starrett then looked at Gibson and seemed suddenly surprised to see her.

"I thought you were checking out the distribution company and the cousins?"

"I was, Inspector," Gibson replied, looking as if she'd suddenly remembered why she was down in the courtyard. "Major Newton Cunningham sent me down to fetch you. He said under no circumstances was I to accept any excuses from you because he wouldn't accept any from me."

"And I bet he told you to tell me that too."

"He did actually, now you come to mention it."

"Right then," Starrett replied, dusting off his hands some more, "in this instance I think we should follow rule number 99."

"OK, I'm biting," Gibson said as she and Starrett strolled towards the gate of the courtyard: "what's rule number 99?"

"Never keep an old major waiting; he just may keel over and die before imparting his knowledge to you."

"Inspector Starrett, really!" Gibson said, fighting, in vain, to hold back a chuckle.

The aforementioned Major Newton Cunningham was not, at present, as predisposed to appreciate Starrett's attempts at humour as Gibson was.

When Gibson and Starrett walked around the corner of Tower House, there he was, sitting on the railing at the top of the steps leading to the door. If looks could kill, well then Starrett in his next life might already be running in the Grand National.

"Ah, Inspector Starrett," the major said, his fine tenor voice and clipped tones booming around Gamble Square for all to hear, "I hear you've been detained on an investigation of a crime. Let's you and me take a walk along the clear Leannan here, and you can get me up to speed. Apart from which, I've another pressing matter to discuss with you."

Before Starrett and the major embarked on their journey, Starrett asked Gibson to resume her search for the Sweeney cousins and to locate the original distributor of the Sweeney farm's produce.

"Bean Garda Gibson seems to be working well with you, Starrett," the major said, some ten seconds later as they reached the end of their walk at the opposite, river side of the road. The major found his usual, well-worn and comfortable stone seat on the wall and rested his weary limbs thereon. Physically the major was a bit of a wreck, what with all of his war wounds and his advancing years, but his mind was still as sharp as a pin, and he had a memory to make you blush. "How's this Sweeney investigation of yours coming along?"

"Well, it's early days yet, and we're just collecting information . . ."

". . . and you don't like to be drawn until you've all the information in," the major finished.

"No, it's more that I'm getting a very bad feeling about this one."

"How so?"

"I'm not sure, there's just something about it that's already giving me the shivers."

"Is that sixth sense starting to get overactive again," the major asked, "or have you been rereading your Arthur Conan Doyle classics?"

"If only it were as simple as that, sir, if only. Everyone has a secret, Major, we just need to discover what the secret is in this case, whose it is and then we have to figure out if the secret is relevant to our investigation."

"Quite so, Starrett, quite so," the major replied dismissively. "Now, Starrett, tell me this, am I wrong or is young Browne a total pranny?"

"I'm sorry to say you're not wrong, sir."

"Hmmm," the major offered with a faraway look in his eyes, which were looking no further than the water flowing ten feet below them, "I was afraid of that. Obviously I put him on your team because of my fears."

Starrett looked very disappointed by his superior.

"Come on, Inspector, can you imagine what kind of garda he could turn into under the incorrect influence? I just need you to know, I really do owe his grandfather a big favour. Also, you know, we have to take into consideration that it can't be easy if your father dies when you are young and your mother brings another man into the house, who in turn leaves . . ."

"Really?"

"Oh, a nightmare, Starrett, an absolute total bloody nightmare.

Don't get me started, but his mother . . . well, let's just say has always been too generous with favours for her own, not to mention her son's, good." The major raised his eyes to the dramatic Donegal clouds before continuing, "And that was even when poor Allen was still alive. Oh, my goodness, Starrett, you wouldn't believe it. I'll discuss it further with you one night over a glass of poteen, but in the meantime, what are we going to do about Romany?"

Starrett was lost; he really didn't want to think about Romany Browne when his mind was so full of all the people around the dinner table at the Sweeney farm.

"Well, to start," the major said, filling Starrett's gap, "we need to find him and set him a task, and a task where no people skills are required, because from what I hear from Bean Garda Gibson, he's certainly lacking in that department."

Starrett had completely forgotten about where he'd deposited Browne. He realised he was about to be in bigger trouble than even Browne was capable of landing himself in.

"Tell you what I'll do, Starrett: I can see you're really up to your eyeballs in this one, so what say you that I supervise, as in babysit, our novice garda, and let's see if we can't set him a few tasks to ascertain if he picked up anything at all at our esteemed Garda College of knowledge in Templemore?"

"Right, Major, good idea. Bejeepers, a great idea in fact," Starrett said, just a wee bit too quickly. "We need someone chasing up these two leads: first, the Sweeney cousins. A few years ago their share of the farm was sold out from under their feet at a peppercorn rate on a deal their father David, Liam's uncle, had done some years previously . . ."

"David Sweeney; yes, I remember David."

"What happened to him?"

The major looked down the river again in the direction of the warehouses. "They say he lost his life, but I doubt anyone so clever would have been so careless as to misplace something as precious as life."

They both sat in silence for a moment. The thing Starrett loved about town life was there was always something going on to distract you. Scenarios started, you were distracted by something else, by which time the original scenario had developed into something else and caught your attention again. For instance, when the major and Starrett has first moved over to the wall for their chat, Starrett had noticed the newly-weds, First Minister Ivan Morrison and Betsy Bell – a woman who as a girl had caught the major's eye – get out of their car, a racing green Jaguar S type, a vehicle not common around these parts, and go into Liam Greer's design studio cum clothes cum art shop. A few minutes later they emerged into the sunlight a few bags the heavier. Betsy had spotted Starrett and the major and had seemed anxious to come over and say hello. Morrison, however, seemed reluctant, which might have had something to do with Starrett's investigation into the death of his wife, Dorothy, several months previously. Betsy had obviously instructed her new husband to stay where he was if he wished, but she was going to say hello to her friends. The first minister of the Second Federation Church had remained on the pavement outside Gambles' shop cum general store as Betsy swaggered across the square. By the time she reached the middle of the square and caught Starrett's eye, Morrison started, reluctantly, to waddle after her. All of this was developing behind the major's back.

"Ah, Betsy," Starrett said, sensing a life-saving opportunity, "it's so great to see you, and a belated congratulations."

"We did send you an invite, didn't we, Ivan?" she sang out in her beautiful soprano voice.

As Morrison was turning every shade of beetroot known to mankind, the major suddenly twigged the owner of the voice behind him. He nearly did himself an injury trying to swing around to catch a full view of Betsy.

"We sent you *both* invites, and neither of you turned up."

"I doubt I would have missed a chance to see you in all your splendour," the major said, hopping off the wall in a manner fitting a man half his age, all for Betsy's benefit.

Then Morrison joined the trio, his eyes pleading with Starrett.

"No, Major, remember we had to go down to Dublin," Starrett said. "Betsy, great to see you again. Unfortunately I've got to nip into the station now; there are a few things needing my urgent attention."

He kissed the presented air beside both her cheeks as she pouted and imitated kissing sounds on each side. She smelled of heather and flowers and, strangely enough, bananas.

"Betsy, how are you settling into the Manse?" the major asked, as he too went through the kissing ritual and Starrett nipped deftly across the road.

Five minutes later, Starrett appeared on the steps of Tower House with the aforementioned and severely warned off (by Starrett) novice Garda Romany Browne, who Betsy Morrison, formerly Bell, positively swooned over once she was introduced.

Three gardaí were just too many for Ivan Morrison, and so he reminded Betsy of American guests due to arrive at the Manse shortly and, amid her protests that the guests in question were not due until the following day, busied her back across the road again in the direction of their car.

Despite his warning to the contrary, Browne's opening line to the major was, "Thanks, Newton, for rescuing me from the dungeon. It's so dank down there."

"Major Cunningham to you, young man, and if I had my way, you'd still be down there. You've only Inspector Starrett here to thank for not having to spend another night down there."

Starrett smiled. The major had made his point about the error in the ways of both his juniors.

"Right, Starrett, we're in your hands entirely. What would you like us to do?"

Browne glared from the major to Starrett. He looked as sick as the proverbial pig. *Sick pigs are not a pleasant sight,* Starrett thought as he said, "Well, I could get Gibson started on all the paperwork we discovered on Joe Sweeney's desk, Casey could look into the Sweeney cousins, and Garvey could write up their reports for the

day, if youse two could find out as much as you can about the people who used to distribute the farm produce. At this stage, both
these parties certainly had a vested interest in young Joe Sweeney.
We really need to know how big a loss the original distribution company suffered, and we need to know if Liam's cousins still harboured
any discontent over losing their windfall."

"Right, Garda Browne," the major said, as they made their way
back to the station house, "let me instruct you in the ways of good
old-fashioned detective work."

"I'd rather go home and have a bath," came the ungrateful reply.

Starrett, who was walking in front of the others, couldn't be
sure, but he thought the sound he heard next was that of the major
clipping Browne about the ear.

Chapter Twenty-Four

Starrett informed Gibson and Casey of the change of plans and set them to work on their new assignments. He then returned to his office and started to write up the details gathered on the Sweeney murder so far into his black leather-bound crime book.

The first thing he did, and using information picked up by Garvey, was to draw a plan of the Sweeney dinner table with all the family seated as they were at the time Kennedy had arrived at the farm house.

He included various other notes to himself, which would ensure the names on the page were, in his head at least, more than just names on the page. He immediately photocopied this page several times, each time enlarging it until it was eventually double foolscap size. Starrett carefully blue-tacked it to the wall beside his favourite poster, a poster he'd enjoyed for a good twenty years now, first in his pervious office above the Kensington Classic Cars show room in one of the most expensive boroughs of London and now here in downtown Ramelton. The poster – of a 1959 green Jaguar Mark II driving through beautiful English countryside – always distracted him, and he found he often used it as a springboard for his thoughts while working on a case.

This time though he forced himself to focus on the people sitting around the dinner table. He tried to imagine the conversations that might have been going on around the table. He now had a sense that the undercurrent at the table would have been the family's preoccupation with the farm and, more importantly, where the precious land was going. From there, it was a short step to what motivated people, particularly this group of people. Could greed be the sole motivation behind this crime? Greed. Starrett honed in on that word. Taking greed as the genesis, who had most to gain by the removal of the youngest of the Sweeney clan?

Of the Sweeney clan itself, Tom had the least in common, physically speaking, with his father. As the eldest, he was certainly the one who should have been most aggrieved at the farm going to his youngest brother.

Again Starrett returned to his most recurring question on the case. Now that Joe was dead, who would inherit the farm? He had tried, several times, to bring this question up with Liam, but each time, for one reason or another, his efforts had been thwarted.

He made a note of it again in his notebook and turned his attention once again to Tom.

Thomas Sweeney certainly seemed to have the most ambitious partner. In fact, if talk gathered in questioning were to be believed, the main reason Mona was with him was down to how valuable the Sweeney family farm was. She'd admitted she had a client who was prepared to pay €11.8 million for the farm. That's a hell of a lot of motivation for murder. Tom and Mona were both solicitors and both, you'd have to think, would have considered such things as where the farm would go if Joe were to die. If the farm were to go to Tom in the instance of Joe's demise, then surely Tom would move to top of the suspect list. Even if the farm were to be split amongst the surviving heirs, then one third of €11.8 million or €3.9333 (3, repeating) million, even though it was only the lowly digit 3 that was repeating, was still a good few bob in anyone's book.

Next thought, surely if Tom was the murderer, it would be just too obvious, and he and Mona (were she to be involved) would have been at the top of *everyone's* suspect list. Did he, and/or they, factor this into the murder?

Who might the next likely murderer *around the dinner table be?* Starrett immediately flashed on Sheila Kelly, but then he chastised himself severely, knowing he was guilty of stereotyping someone just because of her looks (*quite definitely,* he conceded) and her sexual preference (*certainly not,* he assured himself).

After that he was struggling though.

Ryan Sweeney didn't, on the surface at least, seem to have anything to gain, and he seemed happy enough in his life.

What about his glamorous and ever-smiling girlfriend Maeve Boyce? Starrett couldn't see any reason there.

By all accounts Teresa Sweeney was the closest of the family to Joe, and he to her. She wouldn't have wanted the farm anyway, at least not from the running side. But then, €4 million, near as damn it, would certainly have put a lot of food on her and Sheila's table.

But for a brother or a sister to murder one of their siblings – Starrett was having a lot of trouble over that one. At the end of the day, you'd have to face your father and your mother. Starrett reckoned the look of rebuke you'd have received from Colette Sweeney, and the knowledge of what you were doing to her, together with the fact that Liam, most certainly, would tear your head off your shoulders, would prove a powerful deterrent. Liam looked to Starrett easily strong enough for such an action.

Breda Roche, what about her? Starrett decided he needed to know a lot more about Joe's girlfriend. Then he decided he needed to know a lot more about *everyone* and that he was guilty of breaking the golden rule he was always preaching to his team: never select a suspect before your evidence does.

He had to admit to himself, however, that the Sweeney cousins, or the original farm produce distributors, or person or persons unknown were starting to look very, very appealing as suspects.

Chapter Twenty-Five

S tarrett left Garvey, Gibson, the major and Romany Browne busy at work in Tower House and headed down to the Bridge Bar just after nine o'clock. He'd another bit of detective work he wanted to do that evening, but he didn't want to risk any of his colleagues discovering what other mystery, apart from the strange death of Joseph Sweeney, was occupying his mind on that fine August evening.

Thankfully none of his drinking buddies, namely local impresario John McIvor and local raconteur James McDaid, were in attendance, so he ordered up a pint of Guinness, found a quiet corner and took out his notebook from his windcheater, before placing the jacket over the back of a precariously high barstool.

He took a gentle sip of his life-affirming brew, savouring the delicious, but acquired taste, and opened his notebook to the words he thought Maggie had whispered to him on the previous evening.

He mouthed the words soundlessly:

"You have take men's (something – a short word) four we can move Ron."

He took out his pen and wrote it down again underneath the original – trying to see if anything sprang to mind. He started to doodle with it a bit. He scored out "take" and replaced it with "make." But why did "we" – assuming we to be he and Maggie – need to move Ron? Maybe there was another man in her life called Ron.

Who the feck was Ron?

And who was Starrett to have the nerve to think a woman as

beautiful as Maggie Keane *wouldn't* have other male admirers? Starrett encouraged himself with the thought that, as she was kissing him (Starrett, and not this Ron geezer), she was maybe feeling guilty about a friend without benefits whom she felt she owed it to to resolve the situation with before she became further involved with Starrett. Yes, he thought, that sounded a much more likely scenario, and, he reminded himself as he took another sip of his Guinness, she hadn't been wearing too many clothes at the time of her declaration.

He repeated the words again, not realising he was now talking at an audible level.

"The first sign of madness, you know?"

"Sorry?" Starrett replied automatically, as he turned around.

"Talking to yourself. You know, it's the first sign of madness."

"Dr Aljoe, hi, how are you?" Starrett said, doing a chicken-head impression around the Bridge Bar.

"Dr Aljoe, is it?" she hissed. "After what we did together on Rathmullan beach, it's still *Dr* Aljoe, is it?"

"Samantha!" Starrett declared loudly.

"That's much better," she said happily. "Now you'll be rewarded with total forgiveness if you just go and fetch me one of those beautiful pints of Guinness."

Starrett wandered over to the bar and leant against it as he ordered up, happy for the respite. Wouldn't it be just his luck if Maggie Keane happened to drop into the Bridge Bar on her way to or from somewhere? He wondered if the mysterious "Ron" would be in too. Perhaps she'd made a monumental decision about Starrett and decided that the best way forward was to invite Ron out for a quick drink and say, "Look, this isn't going anywhere; let's call it quits," thereby leaving the way clear for her and Starrett. This brought a smile to Starrett's face, and he continued smiling until the first part of Samantha's pint settled enough for the remainder to be poured. In the Bridge Bar, the pulling of pints of Guinness was a deeply serious, considered, if not religious, ritual.

Aljoe purred an "Aah" of absolute satisfaction as she came up for air following her first taste. She slowly, sensually removed the creamy moustache with her tongue and shook her upper torso and wild blonde mane vigorously.

"Who needs men?"

"Tell me this, Dr . . . Samantha," Starrett began, "if a person was trying to drown someone intentionally, then you'd have to imagine the victim would put up a bit of a fight."

"Oh, you old spoilsport you, how dare you not rise to my bait?"

"Down, woman, down," Starrett replied, trying hard to laugh it off.

"But, Starrett, I'm sooo in the mood," she whispered. She was so close to his ear she was able to feather his ear lobe with her tongue without anyone noticing.

"Jeez, woman, with the mood you appear to be in, I imagine I'd be surplus to your requirements anyway," Starrett protested.

"Maybe . . . okay, just get me started then . . ."

"Samantha, please, I've got something important to talk to you about," he said, genuinely pleading.

Her return look was worth a million words, all around the general theme of, "You *@?!ing piece of shit, how dare you treat me like this!"

The words she said were, "Inspector, please forgive me. Sorry, what was your question?"

Starrett nodded, hoping the moment had passed. "I was talking about drowning . . ."

"I know the feeling . . ." she said and then obviously thought better of it, "I'm sorry, Starrett, I am, really, it's just the . . ."

". . . Guinness," Starrett offered hopefully.

"Yeah. You now know what I think about every time I have a pint of Guinness."

Starrett's mind wandered back to their infamous night together on Rathmullan beach when, as far as he could recall, she'd also had a drop of Guinness. Not that anything regrettable had happened; they'd gotten close, very close, but on that single occasion she'd been the one who'd pulled back at the last possible moment. It was around that time, actually a matter of six hours later in fact, that Maggie

Keane had come back into his life. He was determined not to mess things up again with Maggie, as he had twenty odd years earlier.

"I'm really, really sorry Samantha, I really am."

"I know, Starrett," she said as she patted his arm. "You're such a gorgeous man, and all of this wanting to save yourself for a childhood sweetheart, don't you see, that just makes you all the more adorable."

"Now you see that line *is* working," he replied, extremely happy they were moving back to their friendly zone. "That's unfair."

"OK, OK," she sighed, trying in vain to pull the blue material of her ridiculously short skirt closer to her knees. "Not waving but drowning, that's what you want to talk about, right?"

Starrett nodded.

She paused for another generous and sensuous drink of Guinness before saying, "You want to know why, if Joe Sweeney was drowned against his wishes, weren't there marks and bruises of resistance about his body?"

"Bejeepers, you hit it in one, Samantha."

"OK, one of two things happen when you're drowning. Either you're unconscious and you don't know what's happening to you, or you're conscious and you suffer a violent traumatic asphyxiation. Basically, you're deprived of oxygen, and the more you're deprived, the more you open your mouth seeking oxygen, but the net result is that you take in even more water, depriving yourself of even more oxygen."

"So there would be lots of kicking, fighting, Joe Cocker arms and general splashing around?"

"Well," she said, drawing out the word, "perhaps the roofies would have subdued those movements somewhat, but even then your instinct for survival is going to kick in to some degree. By the way, the water in his lungs matched the sample we took from the River Leannan."

"Right," Starrett noted and filed the information away in some part of his brain, "but can we get back to the drowning issue for another moment? Why no marks or bruising? There were no marks on his wrists or ankles, so he wasn't restrained that way either."

Dr Samantha Aljoe started back on her Guinness; this time she stopped mid-sip and wiped her lips with the back of her hand.

"I think I must just have died and now I'm in heaven," she said, keeping her eyes fixed intently on a spot over Starrett's right shoulder. "You're off the hook, Starrett."

"Can we get you a drink?" Francis Casey asked the doctor and the inspector.

Starrett swivelled around to find Francis Casey and Romany Browne. They'd obviously just come from Tower House, but they'd the sense to leave their jackets behind and looked like navy cadets on shore leave in their black uniform trousers and blue shirts open at the neck. Browne has also rolled up his sleeves, revealing toned, tanned skin and bulging muscles. He couldn't keep his eyes off Aljoe's legs. She couldn't keep her eyes off him, all of him. Starrett had been so busy observing this interaction that he hadn't noticed Nuala Gibson accompanying the two boys. Gibson too seemed to be transfixed by Aljoe's legs, or maybe, Starrett feared, by how dangerously close those same legs were to Starrett's person.

There was a lot of looking going on and not a lot of talking. Aljoe broke the deadlock by looking Browne straight in his baby blue eyes and saying, "I'd absolutely love another pint of Guinness."

"And yourself, Inspector?" Browne asked, still not taking his eyes off Aljoe.

"I'm fine, thanks," Starrett replied, a little amused and a little disconcerted at how short a time it had taken Aljoe to move on.

"Francis, that'll be just two pints of Guinness and whatever you and Nuala are having," Browne ordered, all matey-like, perhaps to show Starrett how well he was mixing.

Nuala and Francis made their way to the bar. Aljoe sat upright on her bar stool. *She's actually preening herself for Browne,* Starrett thought. He had to admit it was a magnificent sight.

"Actually, I don't believe youse two have met," Starrett said.

"Perhaps in another life," Browne replied, taking her hand and looking deep into her eyes.

Starrett wanted to puke. But the most annoying thing was that the major's prodigy was getting away with it.

"Dr Sam . . . antha Aljoe, this is *novice* Garda Romany Browne."

"Absolutely delighted to meet you, Romany," she purred. Starrett comforted himself (slightly) in thinking that this whole act was for his benefit. The more they ignored him, however, the less he thought this to be actually true.

"The pleasure's all mine," he replied, pulling a spare stool up close to her. She had to turn away slightly from Starrett to talk to him.

Starrett couldn't be sure, but he thought he heard Browne excusing his look by claiming that he'd been working undercover, mixing with criminals, during the previous night. Then he'd been working on a murder investigation all day long. Starrett scratched his head like Stan Laurel. Aljoe looked like everything Browne was saying was going in one ear and out the other. Occasionally, she'd smile or touch his knee and offer some kind of remark of her own, all of it out of Starrett's hearing range. She seemed totally transfixed by this young man's perfectly chiselled looks. His jaw line looked like it had been copied from one of Michelangelo's sculptures. Starrett felt his own jaw line with his bent finger. It felt as though his jaw had been copied from Jed Clampet's profile.

Gibson and Casey arrived back with their two pints of Guinness each. Francis searched in vain for a couple more seats. Browne didn't offer his seat to Gibson, so Starrett did, which didn't gain a single protest from Browne.

"I'm off now anyway," Starrett said.

Aljoe hopped discreetly from her chair as well and gave Starrett a hug and peck on each cheek in farewell.

"What happened to your thirteen-month rule?" Starrett whispered in her ear.

"Oh, that only happens if I think I'm going to like the fella; this garda of yours, well, he's not exactly marriage material now, is he, but he does look like he might be fit for a . . ."

"OK. OK, no need for sketches. There are senior citizens present," Starrett protested.

"I know, Starrett; is it time for your cocoa yet?"

At this point, Browne raised his pint to his lips and downed it in one.

"What a waste," Starrett said quietly under his breath, so only Aljoe could hear.

"Yes," she replied in a stage whisper. "If only he had the brain to go with the body, he'd be the perfect human. Mmm, I wonder does he come with an off-switch for his mouth."

"Right," Browne sighed, catching his breath and now looking directly at Aljoe. He used the excuse that she was on her feet to say, "I'm off too. Can you drop me somewhere?"

Starrett rolled his eyes. At least it was marginally better than racing driver Eddie Irvine's famous chat-up line, "You've pulled; get your coat."

Francis and Nuala both looked very amused by the turn of events.

Francis was maybe relieved that Browne wouldn't be hitting on his girlfriend, and Nuala looking very happy that her friend Maggie Keane's only competition had disappeared in the time it took to drink a pint of Guinness.

Dr Aljoe turned back to her seat, finished her fresh pint of Guinness and started to stoop to pick up her handbag. Browne offered to get it for her, and there was a moment when they were both hunkered on the floor below Starrett's feet. She seemed to whisper something in his ear, and as they rose she said to all of them, "That's it for me too, I'm afraid. The Guinness did me in, and I've got an early start in the morgue. Great to meet you, Romany. Francis and Nuala, thanks for the drink. Starrett, as you're going, would you mind walking me to my car please?"

Chapter Twenty-Six

Thursday: 28 August 2008

Day three in the investigation into the death of Joe Sweeney, and Starrett woke up with a single question burning its way through his brain: "Who the feck gets the Sweeney farm now that Joe is dead?"

When Starrett had walked Samantha Aljoe to her car the night before, their conversation had remained light, the kind of conversation only friends can enjoy. His suspicions though were based on a momentary few seconds Aljoe and Browne hunkered on the ground together before Aljoe left the Bridge Bar. Had she said words to the effect of, "Look, we work together, so let's be discreet about this. Why don't we meet later?" and picked a rendezvous point later? Still, that wasn't really the question preoccupying Starrett this morning.

He went downstairs and made himself breakfast – orange juice, scrambled eggs and toasted wheaten bread – as he pondered. Once he'd polished off the eggs, he took out his notebook and wrote his question at the head of the page.

He also wrote down the list of people he and his team needed to have another chat with:

Liam Sweeney

Colette Sweeney
Tom Sweeney
Mona Sweeney
Bernadette Sweeney
Ryan Sweeney
Teresa Sweeney
Sheila Kelly
Maeve Boyce
Breda Roche

He considered his list and wondered if it would be safe to remove any of the names from the list.

He could think of only one.

Starrett also needed to chat with Major Newton Cunningham and see how he and Browne got on with their investigation into the distribution company and hear how Casey was getting on with tracking down the Sweeney cousins. Realistically it was probably too soon for any developments on both those fronts.

It was still only six o'clock in the morning. He didn't expect anyone in Tower House before seven, but he decided he would go in anyway and spend time reading up the reports of yesterday's interviews, just so he was totally up to date before his day's work started.

An hour and a half later, he was sitting in Steve's Café for a cup of tea and some more toast, catching up on the town gossip and catching his breath. He'd not picked up anything strange or startling in the reports. Sergeant Packie Garvey arrived about ten minutes later and ordered a full brekkie at the counter before sitting down beside Starrett.

About halfway through Garvey's meal, Starrett started to grow agitated.

"Ciggy attack?"

"No, I'm just realising how little we know and how much more we need to know."

"OK, where to first?" Packie asked, finishing his breakfast, washing it down with a gulp of tea and cleaning around his lips with the paper napkin.

"Back out to the Sweeney farm. I want to talk to Liam and Colette again. This time I think it's vital I interview them separately."

When Garvey and Starrett arrived out at the farm ten minutes later, everyone had left to return to their own homes. Starrett knew what they'd be feeling; he'd witnessed it often enough. Just like an echo that never really stopped, this surreal but at the same time strangely physical feeling was hard to escape.

Liam seemed more reluctant for Starrett to conduct his interviews individually than his wife did.

Liam Sweeney was a strong man, and strong men seem to feel a need to show their strength. Starrett thought sometimes that could perhaps be a strong man's greatest weakness. Liam wouldn't even consider leaving his wife's side, particularly when she was going to be interviewed by the gardaí. When Starrett made it very clear he needed to talk to them separately, the farmer, persuaded mainly by his wife, eventually agreed. Her winning argument was that she felt they needed to do all they could to help Starrett find the person who had murdered their youngest son.

So, once again, Starrett found himself in the Sweeneys' good room, this time accompanied by both Liam and Packie Garvey. He walked over to the sideboard again and picked up a duck, which was carved out of wood; it was varnished and polished so much it reflected every spare piece of sunlight in the room. Starrett wondered what stories the duck could tell. He set it back down and delivered his first question.

"Liam, what happens to the farm now that Joe's passed away?"

Liam Sweeney was sitting in his favourite easy chair, beside the unlit fireplace. He had sunk into the chair like a discarded puppet, staring deep into the blackness of the fireplace. He looked different from yesterday. Starrett thought the saying "the lights are on, but no one's at home" applied perfectly to Sweeney in his current state.

"Liam?" Starrett prompted.

"Sorry, Starrett, I was thinking about that. I can't really think about it now. What should I do? What's to happen to the farm? Who should I ask?"

"So there's nothing already set in place then?"

"No, what's the law of the land?"

"I think it would be divided equally."

"So Thomas wouldn't get it?" Liam asked Starrett, appearing as thought he didn't have a clue about what would happen.

"No, I'd say not. Without a will, it would definitely be split up between your heirs. But there's no provision in your will, you say?"

"No, no. I've a few bob set aside. I'd already made sure that Colette will be well looked after, and I was giving the farm to Joe, as you know, and then he was in the process of doing up this deal whereby he was giving all of his siblings a share of the profits from the farm produce. See, Starrett, that was Joe for you. I don't think any of the others would have done that . . . maybe Ryan, but most definitely not Thomas or Teresa. Have you any kids, Starrett? You don't, do you?"

"I never married, Liam."

"No, I didn't think so. Yes, I remember your father said something very traumatic happened to you when you first moved away from Ramelton. Where did you go, Starrett?"

"I went to Armagh to study to be a priest, Liam."

"And why did you not stick with it?" the farmer asked.

"Ach, you know, Liam," Starrett said, without saying anything.

"What, you were too fond of the girls?" Liam asked, obviously not going to let it go.

"Sure, it wasn't that at all, but I found that pretty strange all right having to be prepared to forgo a normal family life in order to join the Church. No, I think I was expecting something more spiritual to happen during my instruction. I wanted to believe, you know, but all I discovered were people who didn't. But you know, we all can't be priests, can we?"

"Times like this, the safest person to be."

Starrett couldn't work out if the farmer was referring to the death of his son or the troubled times we live in. He needed to get the conversation back on an information trail.

"Who's your solicitor?" he asked, wondering if it might be his son, Tom.

"Russell Leslie and Co.; they're down in Derry. We've used them for ever."

"Do you think I could see the will?"

"Of course, it's here somewhere." Liam walked over to the cupboard, hunkered down stiffly and opened the bottom right-hand door, fiddling amongst various files and paperwork before producing an official-looking document and passing it on to Starrett.

Starrett flicked through it quickly, not picking up anything. "Do you mind if I read this later?"

"No problem, as long as it doesn't leave the farm."

Starrett set it down on the sofa beside him.

"Do you know much about this alternate distribution circuit he set up?"

"Only that it seemed to be working and he was spending a lot of time setting it up," Sweeney replied. He was slumped back in his chair now and was making the questioning hard work. He looked distracted, as if he were totally preoccupied by something.

"Do you know the mechanics of it?"

"Not really."

"Did he have anyone else helping him on it?" Starrett asked.

"Other local farms were included in the system, and some of them were helping him out on the administration side. Like calling the shops, seeing what they needed, delivering and dealing with complaints. Joe explained to me that for this system to work, to convince the shops to keep working directly with him, he needed it to be flawless. No hiccups, no late deliveries, no bad produce. The customer, or in his case the shop, was always right. They got the best, and if they didn't get the best, they enjoyed more than a full refund. He felt we had to gain their trust. He knew the old distributor would be putting the screws on the shops to try and force them not to take Joe's produce."

"I can imagine," Starrett said absentmindedly as he focused once again on this as a motive.

"What Joe discovered was that the majority of the shops were desperate to find an alternative system from the old distributor.

Monopolies just don't work, Starrett," Liam said as he scratched his beard.

"It's difficult, isn't it? People always start off with the best of intentions, don't they?"

"Joe's way around it was to make it clear to the rest of the farmers that he didn't want this distribution to grow into a commercial company. He said he felt it was important they all accepted that it was nothing more than a back-up service for their farms. I think he felt it was important he convince me of this fact so I wouldn't worry about him neglecting the farm because the distribution company was so successful."

"Were you worried about that?"

"Starrett, there comes a time in every mother and father's life when you have to step back and give your wains the limelight. If you're not prepared to do that, well then, that's when your real problems begin."

"So you're saying, even if you were worried about such an outcome, you wouldn't do anything about it, because you'd already passed the reins over to Joe."

"Yeah, it's like they say. Mistakes have to be your own mistakes before they are of any use to you."

"Bejeepers, Liam, you're not quoting beer-mat wisdom to me, are you?"

"You're right, sorry. What's your next question?"

"Would there be any farmers Joe fell out with over this?"

"Fell out how?"

"Oh, you know, maybe Joe for one reason or another didn't include them in his distribution set-up, or . . ." Starrett had a flash. "Do you know if there were any farmers that Joe threw out of his distribution set-up?"

"He kept all the wheeling and dealing with the farmers to himself, Starrett, but surely there must be a paper trail somewhere?"

"Well, we took all of Joe's paperwork from his room away for examination," Starrett said, still distracted with the thought of potential outlaw farmers. "OK, I want to go back to Monday . . ."

"Yes, I told you, the last time I saw Joe was lunchtime," Liam replied half-heartedly.

"Yes, I remember, but I want to concentrate on your day."

"*My* day?"

"Yes, what did you do?"

"What's that got to do with Joe's drowning?"

"Well, you see, that's the thing, Liam. We don't know, we just don't know. If we just talked through your day, we might discover something, which at the time didn't catch your attention, but now, because of how things have transpired, might be of significance."

"Right then. I got up as usual around 5.30. I started milking around 5.55. I like to get the milking started then, come back and have a wee cup of tea and some toast and listen to the news on Highland Radio."

"What do you mean exactly by getting the milking started? Who's involved in that process?" Starrett asked, happy to be started back up again.

"OK, let's see: who would have been on the milking on Monday morning? John Lea was off down in Dublin for a long weekend, so it would have been Elvis."

"Elvis?"

"Yes, Elvis, Elvis Patrick Quinn," Liam replied, as though it was the most natural name for a Donegal farmhand.

Starrett shook his head, a faint smile on his face.

"OK, Elvis Quinn, what can you tell me about him? How long has he worked for you?"

"He must be here a good ten years now. He's a good man, a hard worker – a quiet man, just works away by himself and bothers no one."

"No problems with him?" Starrett said, as he wrote the name down in his notebook.

"Nah, nah, nothing wrong with Elvis, and he worships the ground our Joe walked on; thought he was a great fella."

"OK, that's Elvis. Who else would have been at the milking?"

"It would have been just me, Joe, Elvis and Mrs Sweeney."

"And everything seemed fine with Joe at that point?" Starrett asked, thinking that "Mrs" was a strange way to refer to your wife. Perhaps that was the way Colette was addressed by the farmhands and Liam out of respect.

"Oh, yes," Liam exclaimed enthusiastically. "Then me wife would have come in here around seven and we'd all have sat down to breakfast at eight. Aye, Colette's breakfast fair sets us up for the day. We're still in Monday, aren't we? Joe went off to his bedroom to make a few calls and attend to the distribution business. Elvis and I would have taken the cows down to the field by the water. Then Elvis would have gone off to do his chores; there are always things needing repairs and preparing and what have you."

"Do you know what exactly he would have been doing on Monday morning?"

"Haven't a clue, Starrett. We all do a few bits together, and then we go off to attend to our individual chores. Don't forget we were one short on Monday with John Lea out. The next time we would have met up would have been lunchtime."

"And how did Joe seem then?"

"The same as normal, nothing out of the ordinary. As usual he'd invoices and paperwork with him at the table. His mother didn't like that, said it didn't help with his digestion to be doing anything at the table other than eat. She usually packed them away, but I seem to remember he was at them the whole way through lunchtime."

"So, maybe it was a wee bit out of the ordinary that Joe worked the whole way through his lunch, even though his mum didn't like him doing so?"

"I suppose, but, Starrett, it really was just another day."

"OK. Let's move on. How long would lunch usually have taken?"

"Around half an hour."

"Did youse talk about anything in particular?"

"Ach, usual craic, you know, something and nothing. I think we were ribbing Elvis about his never-ending search for a woman. Aye,

Elvis doesn't have much luck with the girls. He's worn out three bicycles trying to find a girlfriend."

"And after lunch what happened?" Starrett asked, chuckling at the image.

"Ah, Joe was off to meet some of the shops he was supplying."

"Do you know which ones?"

"I wouldn't have a clue. He could have gone to Harrods for all I would have known."

"What did he drive?"

"A BMW, similar to your own, maybe a wee bit newer."

"I don't think that'd be difficult. I think the only other models around when mine came out would have been the Ford Model T," Starrett said, but then returned quickly to the matter at hand, "So where's his car now?"

"You know, I haven't a clue, but is that the kind of fact that you were after, is it?"

"Maybe," Starrett replied, wondering why he and his team hadn't picked up on this before. "There were no car keys found on him. Do you know his registration number?"

"No, but his mother definitely will."

"OK, after he left, what did you do?"

"I spent the rest of Monday raking out the cowshed. Elvis helped me on that chore. Then I fixed the gate down by the grazing fields and brought the cows back up at the end of the day. Elvis left around seven, and I'd my dinner at 8.30, read the papers and went to bed around 10.30."

"Tell me about this other farmhand, John Lea."

"John Lea, aye, he's not much younger than myself. He worked the farm with my father as well. John knows the land and farming inside out. Joe worked with him quite closely when he was building up the herd again. That's his wee cottage by the other side of the gate on the way in. He's quite a character, has lots of stories and likes his pint every Friday and Saturday down at Tootie's in Ramelton. He never married, and sadly he's going to be the last of the Lea line."

"What did he go to Dublin for?"

Liam looked at Starrett, acting like he'd been caught out.

"Damn, your father was right, you are good at this," Liam replied, seeming to forget what had been troubling him earlier. "I can't remember the last time he spent a day off the farm, winter or summer, Easter or Christmas, and then he ups and says he needs a day off because he was going down to Dublin for the weekend."

"Do you know how he got down?"

"I dropped him into the bus station on Saturday morning in Letterkenny, and he caught the 32 bus; it left at 9.20. He told me it would put him into Busáras at twenty past one."

"And he didn't say what he was going down for?"

"Not a word, Starrett; treated it like it was a weekly occurrence."

"And when did he get back?"

"When I took him down to the station, he said he was catching the 10.45 bus back on Monday night. Since it wasn't scheduled to reach Letterkenny until just before 3.00 A.M. and that was well after my bedtime, he insisted he would catch a taxi back to his cottage."

"And the next time you saw him?"

"That would have been at the milking on Tuesday morning," Liam replied, pausing for a few moments' consideration and then seeming to drop back into his earlier mood. He did quietly add, "And no, he didn't say anything about his trip to Dublin then either."

The interview over, Starrett tried, in vain, to coax Liam out of his mood, telling him that Colette and the rest of the family need-ed him to be strong. He seemed to react positively to the mention of his wife, but when Starrett said "family," Liam's eyes betrayed a look somewhere between hurt and disappointment.

Before Starrett started his interview with Colette Sweeney, he asked her for the registration number for Joe's car and had Garvey radio in to Tower House for them to start a search immediately for it.

Chapter Twenty-Seven

Colette Sweeney seemed to have regained some of her composure since yesterday. She was dressed in a black, high-collar, satin dress. For a farmer's wife, her hair looked like it needed and received a lot of attention. Her hair was off-blonde and fashioned in a French bob. Starrett figured if you were walking down the street behind Colette Sweeney, you'd take her to be a much younger woman. She was a slim, five-foot nine or ten. She had arrived for her interview with a tray of tea, to be served in her finest china, accompanied by sandwiches and biscuits.

"Your mother says you don't eat enough, Starrett."

Starrett had to smile to himself. Here he was, in his mid-forties, a grown man, left home a good twenty-five years since, and his mother still talked about him behind his back as if he were still a wee lad running around the streets of Ramelton.

Starrett cleared a space on the old pine coffee table and helped Colette rest the tray there. Starrett liked Mrs Sweeney. From when he was no age, he could remember her coming around to his house for elevenses with his mum every Friday after the country market in the Town Hall. He couldn't remember coming up to the farm much though. He'd always known her as *Mrs* Sweeney, and so that's how he addressed her.

"Mrs Sweeney, this is very good of you, but you know, with all of this, this trouble, you shouldn't have bothered."

"Thank you for thinking of my feelings," she said as she started to pour the tea, "but as I said to Liam, we have to do our grieving as a family. In the meantime, we have to do everything we can to help you in your work, so you can bring this evil person to justice."

"Yes," Starrett said, firstly to her statement, but also to the milk and sugar she was offering him.

"Do you think people are born evil or become evil?"

"Sadly, Mrs Sweeney, I think that these days people are more opportunistic. I think society hasn't encouraged us to respect human life anywhere near as much as we should, or to know the difference between right and wrong. I remember at the time I was growing up, if someone in the town died, it was a major event. The whole town grieved. We grew up believing all life, even an old person's life, was precious. Sadly these days, people don't have the same respect. I also remember that if a member of a family committed a crime, the entire family was shamed in the town and everyone was talking about it for ages. Bejeepers, sure there's a criminal in most families these days, and it's treated pretty much as nothing unusual. Heck, they're maybe even afforded a wee bit of a celebrity status."

"Yes, Starrett, sadly you might be right, but it is what it is, and we all have to deal with it," she said, settling back down into the sofa beside Starrett. They were both sitting at a forty-five degree angle so they were almost facing each other, with the length of the sofa separating them. "Thank goodness we have people like you in the gardaí. Everyone tells me you're very good at your work. I'll try my best to answer your questions, but I have to warn you I'm finding all of this very tiring; I mean physically, I quite simply can't find the energy. I've given myself a good talking to, of course. I know I need to be there for the family and for Liam, but for the first time in my life, I'm finding I'd just as soon stay in bed. Someone would probably say I'm just refusing to deal with it. But deal with it I must, Starrett. Joe . . ." and here her poise faltered for the first time, and she stammered to a halt, concentrating on drinking her tea. She used her napkin to pat, not rub, around her eyes.

"Sorry, Starrett, forgive me."

"It's perfectly fine, Mrs Sweeney."

Then she started to laugh.

"I've known you all your life," she said, somewhere between a fit of giggles and sobbing. "I do believe we've reached the point now where you can call me Colette. I'd much prefer it."

"Of course, Colette." But Starrett still had an overwhelming feeling that it just wasn't proper to call one of his mother's best friends by her Christian name.

"At least I can now claim these are tears of laughter," she said as she put the longest finger of each hand into the outer corner of her eyes to catch a couple of idle tears before they cut a trickle through her make-up.

She put her cup down on the coffee table and, looking Starrett straight in the eyes, said, "Oh Starrett, I'm so sick and tired of being sick and tired."

Her body started convulsing gently as the sobbing returned.

Starrett put his tea down and awkwardly moved across the sofa and put his arm around her and held her. She clung on to him so forcefully he felt he might suffer a broken rib or two. Neither spoke. He just rocked her back and forth gently the way you would with a child who is scared of the unknown world of darkness.

After a couple of minutes he could feel her gather her strength again and rise up a bit in his arms. She didn't let go, she continued to hold him tightly, but it felt, to Starrett, like she was summoning her energy for the next round.

"Now, what's this I hear about you and Maggie Keane seeing each other again?" she said, as she broke free, rose from the sofa and went over to the mirror above the fireplace to doctor her make-up with her napkin again.

Not what Starrett had been expecting at all. *Perhaps she was merely distracting herself from the thought of her son's murder for a few moments.*

"Well, yes, Mrs . . . sorry, Colette. I'm . . . I mean, I've met up with her again after a long time and . . ."

"She's a good woman, Starrett; you should never have let her slip through your fingers. You two always seemed so happy together. Did youse have a big fight or something before you left?"

It wasn't a topic he was altogether happy discussing. In fact, he'd never ever discussed it with anyone before, but first off she'd asked him a direct question on the subject, and no one had ever done that before; and secondly, if he expected Mrs Sweeney to tell him the truth, then the least he could do would be to return the compliment.

"No, we never fought, Colette. I was a young fool is the only answer I can offer."

"But why did she not put up a fight for you?"

"Well, I don't know if my mother ever told you this, but I thought, I felt I had a spiritual calling, you know, to the priesthood, and at the time it was the most overpowering thing in my life."

"But then why not come back here again and seek Maggie's forgiveness?"

Ah, Jeez, Starrett thought, this hole he currently found himself in was getting deeper with every word. Each time he was finding himself avoiding lies but only by delivering half-truths, which in turn only gave rise to other questions.

"Well, in my defence, the only thing I can offer is that I was young and I felt a failure, and in a small town like Ramelton, well, let's just say, it took a long, long time before I could pick up the courage to come back here."

"And by then Maggie was married and had three kids?"

"Yes, although by the time I met up with her again, Niall had sadly passed away."

"That was so, so sad, wasn't it? Poor Maggie was a saint during Niall's illness. I don't know how she did it, I really don't. I mean, she'd three young kids to bring up. If mine weren't all old enough to look after themselves now, I don't think I would be capable of getting through this. I just feel empty, totally and utterly empty: empty of feelings, empty of memories, empty of emotions, empty of hunger, empty of caring and, the most devastating for me, empty of love. I feel like I'm falling through a void."

Starrett considered her words carefully. They had been so powerful they'd taken him completely by surprise, and he had nothing, absolutely nothing, he could offer her in comfort.

"The echo?" Starrett suggested.

He could see her snap away from something by violently shaking her head.

"Is that what they call it?" she asked herself as much as Starrett. Starrett nodded yes.

"Starrett," she said after a few more moments of silence, "you're definitely your mother's son. Anyone I've ever met apart from you and your mum would have just said to me, 'Oh, don't worry, Colette, it'll get better with the passing of time.' Or, 'There, there, Colette, just let it all out.' You know, in a way belittling your feelings by saying essentially, 'Oh, don't worry about it; it'll get better soon.' But your silence has ended up being a great comfort to me."

Starrett still couldn't find anything to say. He just took hold of her hand and squeezed it.

"Now, let's refresh our tea, shall we? You better get stuck into those sandwiches or your mum will give me a kick up the backside next time we meet."

"Bejeepers, we wouldn't want that now would we?" Starrett replied, as he lifted and took a generous bite out of one of the egg sandwiches. He tried to get her to eat too, but although she looked like she was running on empty, she refused. Crumbs showed up something awful on black, she said, as she brushed away some imaginary spots on her dress.

"If you're sure you're OK, I'd like to ask you a few questions now."

"Yes," she replied, hiking up her shoulders. "Yes, let's start."

"When was the last time you saw Joe?"

"It would have been just after lunchtime on Monday," she said after a few moments. "Joe and his father had their lunch. Liam went back out again, and Joe disappeared upstairs to his room, which doubles as his office. He was up there for, say, twenty minutes. He came down with his mobile stuck to his ear and waved goodbye to me as he headed off."

"You don't know where he was going?"

"No, he didn't say. I can't believe it was the last time I saw him.

I know it's pathetic and all that carry-on, but if I'd have known it was the last time I was going to see him . . ." she said and stopped for no more than a second. "It's OK, Starrett, I'm fine. For some reason I'm fine talking to you about it, but when Liam and I are alone and we try to talk . . . we just start blubbering like babies. But as I was saying, if I'd known it was the last time I was to see him, I'd have dealt with it differently, wouldn't I?"

"You wouldn't have let him out of the house," Starrett said, thinking his sentiment sounded much better than his actual words.

"Oh, Starrett, you have to stand back and let your children live their lives. Most of the time it's actually breaking your heart, but you have to keep a smile on your face, otherwise you get alienated and that's probably worse – well, I know it's worse. Teresa and I, well now, we haven't had a civil word to say to each other in years."

Starrett's look said everything.

"No, no, it's not because she thinks she's gay; it's because of that auld hoor she's picked up with. I'd be happy if she never darkened our door again, but Liam says barring her from the farm is the sure way to lose our daughter. They used to be a lot closer, but Liam had sort of given up on her. He always tried to be civil, but they were never as close as when she was still living here."

Starrett needed to go down this road even though it might be nothing more than a dead end. The problem with dead ends in Donegal, however, was that first you start out on a grand road, and then, at a wrong turn, the grand road tended to narrow down a bit but was still solid enough, and then as you continued along didn't you only notice that the odd bit of grass was growing here and there in the middle of the road, and next the tarmac gave way to solid scree, then more solid chunks of grass in the middle where wheels had feared to tread, and then a solid dirt track. Next the branches of the trees and bushes started to bear down on you more and more, and then a few pot holes, and then before you knew it you were in a soft mud track where only a Massey Ferguson would be safe. By then it was too late. You found yourself stuck and about to have a very difficult time getting back to solid ground. But all the time you were travelling down this road, you kept hoping, thinking, praying that a better, more solid track lay around the next corner.

"How long have Teresa and Sheila Kelly been together?" Starrett enquired, hoping he wasn't heading down a muddy lane.

"Oh, much too long, far too long. Our Teresa can't see it, but everyone else can. Sheila Kelly has been with everything in the county, man and woman. She's even trying to confuse wee Breda Roche with her auld carry-on. I told our Joe that if he was serious about Breda, to keep her well away from Sheila Kelly. But Teresa won't hear a word against her. Then you've got the two of them living up there, pretending to be man and wife, proud as punch, if you don't mind, and shaming our Liam. Aye, if it wasn't for the fact that it would have destroyed Liam completely, I'd have had the gardaí up there to see what exactly was going on at their druggie parties."

"Really? No!" Starrett said incredulously.

"Oh, yes."

"How do you know that?"

"Well, on the rare family occasion where they have to stay here, guess who has to clean up the room and their funny smelling cigarettes after them? Disgusting it is, I can tell you."

"But surely not Teresa?"

"Starrett, as a mother I hate to admit this, but I can see it in her eyes, her sleeping-in late in the morning and her behaving like a zombie until after lunchtime. I'll bet you our Teresa is at that auld carry-on too. But listen to me now for a minute, now that our Joe is gone, I'll go to my grave rather than lose another of my children. I've warned Sheila Kelly."

"How did she react?"

"She laughed; she ignored me and kept saying nice things about Joe so Teresa wouldn't see her true colours."

This all happened after Joe's death, Starrett thought, so nothing could be taken from it, unless of course Joe was equally aware of what was going on with his favourite sibling and Sheila Kelly. What if Joe had also threatened to expose her? Starrett turned to what he hoped would be a more solid roadway.

"Were you aware of the meeting between Joe, Sheila, Ryan and Thomas?"

"Yes, of course. Liam and I discuss everything."

"How did it seem to go?"

"Apparently everyone was happy apart from Mona."

"Because she felt the farm should have gone to her husband as the eldest of the family?"

Colette nodded a "yes," but then floored him with, "Look, I'd been telling our Thomas for years that he was never going to get the farm, or even a piece of it. Sure he's not even Liam's son."

Here was Starrett having tea, sandwiches and bickies with his mother's best friend, who first tells him to address her by her Christian name, then she informs him she thinks her daughter is doing drugs, and now she's just admitted one of her children had been fathered by another man.

"Who's Thomas's father?" was the first question in the multitude circling Starrett's head that he could put words to.

"Oh, one of those older blow-ins who proved he wasn't in love with a country girl as much as he was turned on by the mystery of another woman's body. I've been trying to tell my children, boys and girl both, for years, that the treasures of familiarity far, far outweighs the novelty of newness."

"Are you OK talking about this?"

"I'll talk about anything if it helps bring Joe's murderers to justice."

Starrett looked at her.

"OK, I was eighteen; I was living with my parents in Clonakilty in County Cork. This man, this Englishman, came to town. All my friends and I thought he was charming, a wee bit handsome even, and he had this fine distinguished accent. Lenny Rankin was his name. He was thirty-six. He claimed to be thirty-six, but I always thought he was older. I thought he'd an older body. He'd a boat. He dressed well and he'd an eye for the ladies. In particular he'd an eye for me, and I was very, very flattered. The local spotty boys had never interested me, and I knew from all the stares I was receiving from my mother's friends' husbands that something exciting had happened to my body over the previous summer. I would admit I liked the attention I was getting. It made me feel good. Lenny picked up on this, and he was smooth, very smooth. He knew how to make me feel good. He never rushed me, but eventually the inevitable happened and . . . and I enjoyed it."

Starrett could feel himself blushing. It was like your mother confessing to you about the first time she'd made love.

"He made me feel good all summer, and then he left and I discovered I was pregnant, and I didn't even know how to get hold of him. By then I wasn't really interested in him. Great and all as the summer had been, I realised he was a ladies' man. Well, he'd admitted it to me. I'd asked him why he hadn't married, and he'd told me that for him the thing that kept him going was not finding one girl and settling down, but the joy and bliss of the next girl. The funny thing was I didn't feel bad about it. I was happy that he had been my first man. I'd much rather his experience than the usual teenage fumbling with someone who hadn't a clue about their own pleasure, let alone their partner's."

"How did you meet Liam?"

"Well, to save the family blushes around the streets of Clonakilty, I was immediately dispatched to my aunt's house here in Donegal. She had never married. She looked after my grandfather until he died, by which point she was too old to marry herself, but she got the house up at Carrigart, a bit of land and all his money for all of her troubles. So my aunt was well off, and I think the guilt that my father was the only family member who hadn't been left anything in the will made her take me in. Anyway," Colette Sweeney continued with a large sigh, "she was very, very good to me, and to Thomas when he was born. When Thomas was two I met Liam. I met him at an old-time dance my aunt had taken me to in Letterkenny in the Fiesta Ballroom. I felt I was young enough to have been the daughter of the youngest person there, but Liam was also there, to meet a cousin of his. Anyway, as the youngest people in the hall – I was twenty-one and he was twenty-six – we met up, and it really was love at first sight for both of us. Goodness, he was a handsome man, so big and so strong, and he had such lovely kind eyes. The only thing I didn't like about him was his beard. I've spent the rest of our lives together trying to get him to get rid of it."

"How long was it before you married?"

"I didn't tell him about Thomas until our tenth date. My aunt kept warning me that I'd scare him off if he knew about Thomas. She really was getting preposterous about it. One of her more bizarre ideas was for me to tell Liam that Thomas was in fact my brother and that I had to look after him as my parents had died. But by this time I was quite sure about Liam. We'd kissed and not much else. Because of Lenny, I swore to myself I'd never sleep with another man until I was married. I told Liam about Thomas and, being Liam, he took it in his stride; he declared his love for me the same day. We were down here on the farm. We were married six months later and never looked back. He officially adopted Thomas and made it legal and all. He treated Thomas like his own, but in a way when you treat someone as your own, you're admitting they're not. Do you know what I mean? It's like he never had to *treat* Joe or Ryan or Teresa as his own because they were."

"Did Ryan, Joe and Teresa know that Thomas wasn't a full brother?" Starrett asked.

"Yes, of course. But I don't believe it was an issue. Also, in fairness, we never publicised the fact outside the farm – you know how cruel children can sometimes be at school – but I think to them he was always just their big brother. I mean, you've met Thomas. He's not like Lenny at all you know. People don't like Mona, and she doesn't do herself any favours in the popularity stakes, but, in fairness to Mona, Thomas is the type of man who needs a Mona in his life. Do you know what I mean?"

"Yes, I think I do," Starrett replied. "But you felt because of this, because Thomas was another man's son, he was never going to get the farm."

"If I'm being brutally honest, then yes. I believe that to be a fact. Liam is very much into the farmland and the history of the farm and all of that, and for obvious reasons he wouldn't view Thomas as a true Sweeney. But having said that, Thomas, by his own admission, has never shown any genuine interest in farming anyway. Yes, when he was growing up on the farm, he most certainly pulled his weight, but farming was never a vocation for him. Joseph, on the other hand, well he was a different matter altogether. From when Joe was no age, we all knew he was going to farm for the rest of his life."

Colette Sweeney stopped talking as the impact of her last sentence sank in.

"It's strange to think I'll never see him wander over the fields again," she said as she looked out the window far over the fields as though perhaps recalling the times she used to sit on this very sofa watching her son. "He'd stroll along, always walking, always moving, checking his cattle, shaking a fence to see if it was secure enough, kicking a gate to check if it needed fixing, and then when he'd go down into the backyard, he'd scrape the dirt from his boots at the back door with a bit of rock he'd come across. The rock is still at the back door. I haven't the heart to throw it away, and I know it would be silly to bring it into the house. Sure, wouldn't Liam throw me out if he caught me at that auld carry-on?"

"Never be scared of collecting your treasures, Mrs Sweeney."

This time she didn't correct him. She said, "I used to feel sorry for people when they died, but now it's the survivors I feel for. I keep expecting Joe to come through the back door or even stick his head around the door just there. I can't get used to him no longer being here. I see someone around the farm who looks like Joe, and then I realise it's not him, and then . . ."

Starrett found himself thinking of his mother. What she would do?

"You know, earlier there when you put your arm around me and helped me through that bad moment, I got such a charge of life from you. I have no other words for it. It was as if you were giving me your energy. Your mother used to have that gift as well, Starrett."

"My mother is a good woman."

"Tell her that sometimes, Starrett; we all like to hear it. And don't you keep Maggie Keane hanging around for ever this time."

Then a head did pop around the door of the sitting room. It was Liam. He seemed relieved to see his wife's mood had changed to a lighter one.

"Are youse two nearly done or what?" he said.

Starrett would usually have asked, "What were you doing around the time of . . ." But he knew he'd found the second person in this investigation he didn't need to ask that question.

"No, Liam, we're good for now," Starrett said as he stood up and returned his notebook to his jacket pocket.

Chapter Twenty-Eight

Meanwhile, back at the fort, a.k.a. Tower House, Francis Casey was doing what he does best: desktop detective work. He'd retrieved Joe Sweeney's mobile phone records, and he'd discovered that on Monday, the deceased had made and received the following calls:

1. 09.20 to McGinleys' farm
2. 09.47 to the Toals' farm
3. 09.50 from his sister
4. 09.56 to Harvey's Point Hotel
5. 11.01 from Breda Roche
6. 11.03 to Breda Roche
7. 11.20 to the newspaper, *The Donegal News*
8. 11.23 to Highland Radio
9. 12.47 to his sister, Teresa
10. 14.04 to Whoriskey's in Ramelton
11. 14.07 to Rathmullan House Hotel
12. 14.09 to Frewin Guest House
13. 14.15 from the Sweeney farm
14. 16.06 from Breda Roche
15. 16.09 from *The Donegal News*
16. 16.11 from the Toals' farm
17. 16.17 from Breda Roche
18. 16.21 from the McGinleys' farm
19. 16.22 from the Flynns' farm
20. 16.27 from Breda Roche

21. 16.43 from the McKeons' farm

22. 16.51 from Highland Radio

23. 17.08 from Breda Roche

and then nothing, until the early hours of the following morning when the final call logged in his records was:

24. 02.43 from his sister, Teresa

Two dozen calls on the last day of his life. Casey noted that Joe made no calls on his mobile after the 14.09 call to the Frewin Guest House.

He offered to split the list with novice Romany Browne, who claimed that traditional desk work was too boring and he had a more modern lead of his own to follow, not to mention a very important trip somewhere or other with the major. Casey noted Browne seemed in a particularly bad mood and hoped the novice's mysterious "lead" wasn't after his girlfriend, Nuala Gibson, who seemed quite taken by Browne's looks.

Casey printed out a sheet with all the names and numbers and started his calling.

Chapter Twenty-Nine

Starrett found John Lea sitting outside his cottage at the top of the lane from the Fortstewart Road to Sweeneys' farm. He was a wee man, quite stocky, and his shoulders were permanently hunched, forcing him to carry his arms slightly to the front of the pockets of his trousers. Starrett imagined that should the horses tire while ploughing the land, then John Lea was the kind of farmhand who would have no trouble stepping into the harness and finishing the job off himself. Yes, he looked strong, very strong, but at the same time, he looked awkward. He looked as if he could do with a serious bit of massage work to relieve the fusions of his tense body.

Starrett reckoned John Lea could easily have munched a carrot through a letterbox. He had a curtain of what looked like dyed brown hair dropping from each side of his black pork pie hat. His patchy pallor was showing signs of the beginnings of a red flush, and he was freshly shaven. He wore a clean, white shirt, a colourful sleeveless Fair Isle sweater, a newish pair of brown corduroy trousers and a spanking new pair of black leather ankle boots.

He raised his hat ever so slightly to Starrett and Garvey.

"Rum do up at the farm, Inspector Starrett," John Lea offered by way of a greeting. He spoke very quickly, and his green eyes darted all over the place, but rarely at his subject.

"Aye, it was that," Starrett began, extending his hand. "This is Sergeant Packie Garvey."

"Ach, sure, don't the whole county know Packie," John Lea spat, with a bemused, "you've got to be kidding" look. He took first Starrett's, then Packie's hand in a vice-like grip. Starrett was convinced he could actually hear his bones cracking. The man obviously didn't know his own strength.

"I know what you lads could do with."

At John Lea's speed of delivery it sounded more like, "Iknowwauladscuddeewee."

"Wait here," he ordered as he disappeared through the front door of his whitewashed, rose-covered cottage.

Starrett looked at Packie, raised his eyebrows and smiled. Packie mimed hitting a sliotar with a hurling stick. For Starrett it was a wee bit similar to watching air-golfers, but it looked ever so much more energetic.

A few minutes later John Lea returned with a red metallic tray bearing a bottle of McDaid's Pineappleaide, three mismatched glasses and an unopened packet of Jacob's Mikado biscuits.

"Just outta the fridge, lads," John Lea spat. "This'll set ye up."

Starrett found if he didn't try and focus on specific words, it was easier to pick up John Lea's overall drift.

John Lea sat back down on his iron seat again. Although it was a double seat, he set the tray beside him, leaving no room for either Starrett or Packie. As he poured three generous glasses of the thirst-quenching Pineappleaide, he noticed the members of the gardaí looked like spare roosters at a hen's wedding. He darted back inside his cottage and returned, quick as a flash, with two three-legged wooden stools. The gardaí safely seated, John Lea futtered around for a few seconds with the cellophane protecting the precious Mikados. Eventually he grew so frustrated that he used his protruding molars to rip open the pack. He looked and acted as if he were short in patience and did everything in his life at a full-on speed. He shovelled two of the biscuits into his mouth and washed them down with at least half a glass of the fizzy drink. Starrett noticed the farmhand's Adam's apple doing a peculiar dance as he gulped away. John Lea let out a long and loud sigh when he finally came up for air.

"Right lads, how can I help ye?"

A matter of minutes and small chat later – mostly to do with the weather and how delicious Jacob's Mikado biscuits are – Starrett got around to his first question.

"So, we hear you had a trip down to the big smoke?"

"You heard right, man," was John Lea's snappy reply.

Starrett reckoned it was best to conduct the interview with John Lea aware he had this piece of knowledge of indeterminable value.

"You went down by yourself?"

"I did, aye. Sure, I'm a grown man; I didn't need anyone to hold me hand."

"You caught the bus," Starrett continued, laying another of his cards on the table.

"Yep, Mr Sweeney took me into the bus station in Letterkenny."

"Have you relations down in Dublin?"

"No, sure, I've no blood relations on this earth. Not many people can say that these days, can they?"

"You're right there, John Lea, and quite a few of the ones who can make such a claim reside on this island. Tell me this, John Lea, would you go down to Dublin often?"

"Twenty-two years since," John Lea boasted proudly. "It's another city altogether these days, I can tell you."

"Where'd you stay?"

"I stayed in the Shelbourne Hotel, up on Stephen's Green, same place I stayed the last time I was in Dublin."

"How'd you find it?"

"Ach, sure, didn't they go and bollix me bacon and eggs. I'll tell you, Starrett, I'm fit to be tied when I don't get me breakfast, fit to be tied. It's the most important meal of the day for me. But sure, now it's no longer an Irish hotel, they wouldn't know the importance of the auld breakfast, would they? I'll never darken their doors again, I can tell you."

"John Lea, what would a man of your age want to be off gallivanting in Dublin for anyway?"

"Aye, well, I'd a bit of business to do down there."

"Right so, and what would that business have been?"

"Me own, aye, me own business, Inspector."

"So you're not going to tell me?" Starrett asked, amused with the turn in the proceedings.

John Lea looked at Inspector Starrett, and then he looked at Sergeant Packie Garvey.

"Look, Starrett, I don't believe this is any of your business. I really don't, but equally I realise that in your investigation it might send out the wrong signal if I don't tell you what I was doing, so I'll tell you what I was doing, but only on condition it remains between the three of us, well four of us really."

"Who else knows?" Garvey asked.

"I'm not telling you that either, so do we have a deal?"

"Were you doing something illegal, John Lea?"

"Ehmm, in some people's eyes . . . perhaps, but not in mine."

Starrett looked up to the cloudy heavens. The lemonade was done, the biscuits were done, and Starrett was miffed he'd only got two of them, and if he wasn't careful, the interview looked like it might come up short as well. John Lea had that country martyr stubbornness off to perfection; he looked as though he'd be prepared, regardless of consequences, to derail the interview entirely rather than give up his precious information.

"So, you're saying you want us to ignore some incriminating evidence that may or may not clear you in our current investigation?"

"Aye, that's about the height of it, Starrett. On *Law and Order* they call it immunity, don't they?"

Starrett smiled at John Lea and raised his eyebrows to Garvey.

"Go on then, but first let me tell you this. If something on this trip has anything whatsoever to do with Joe's death, then all bets are off, OK?"

"Deal," John Lea said, shaking hands with both gardaí. "This is not my cottage; the cottage and the majority of the contents are owned by the Sweeneys. I've lived here most of my working life, so in a way I suppose I must have some rights. I wouldn't have been confident enough to take it up legally with Mona or Thomas though. Anyway, to cut a long story short, I was watching *The Antiques Roadshow* one night, and didn't I notice a wee item – an item like one that had hung on the kitchen wall here since I moved in. And then didn't the expert only go and value it at fifteen thousand sterling, and sure didn't I nearly fall off my chair."

"What was the wee item, John Lea?" Starrett asked.

"Aye, sure, wasn't it a quadrant."

Starrett felt the item John Lea was referring to must be something naval, but beyond that he hadn't a clue.

John Lea broke into a knowing smile, displaying his buck-teeth in all their glory.

"You've haven't a clue, have you?"

"Isn't it an instrument used to help sailors navigate in the auld days?" Garvey volunteered, taking the wind out of John Lea's sails.

"The auld days, I'll say," John Lean chuckled; "from the eighteenth century, I believe somewhere around 1730 no less. Anyway, it had been in this cottage gathering dirt since the year dot, but after your man put the £15,000 tag on it, I did a bit of research. Mine was made of . . ."

Starrett tilted his head and smiled a "come on now, John Lea" look.

"OK," John Lea conceded. "Liam Sweeney's model was made out of ewe wood. It was about two foot tall and one foot wide – I don't do metric – in a triangular frame. It had a dirty brass plaque with numbers etched on them to calibrate the measurements. And then at the bottom it had an ivory plaque with the name 'Charles Adam' engraved, but barely decipherable."

"Fifteen grand, that's a lot of change, John Lea," Garvey said.

"Not as much as it used to be. But anyways, I'm not done with my story yet; it gets better. I head down to Dublin and go and visit Adam's (no relation I was assured) up on St Stephen's Green. Didn't they want to pay me twenty-two thousand euro on the spot? I said no, I wanted to take it around and get more opinions about its value. The chap said he'd go to twenty-five thousand euro at a push. I nip out, have lunch and go back to the same chap at Adam's, pretend I've been walking around ever since and say I got an offer of thirty thousand euro elsewhere, and if he matched it, it was his. We did the deal there and then."

"Did Joe know why you were going down to Dublin?" Starrett asked, kind of regretting he'd agreed the deal with John Lea.

"He knew not a dickey bird about it, Starrett. You have to believe me."

"So who did? Who's the fourth member of our cosy quartet?"

"I'm not saying, Starrett, but you can take it from me there was no one more shocked than me when I returned from Dublin to discover someone had killed Joe."

"Any ideas, John Lea, about who'd want Joe Sweeney dead?"

"I've been thinking of little else since I got back, Starrett. All I've come up with is the farm; there were a few far from happy Liam was passing the farm on to Joe. And maybe a few people would have been upset at us for setting up our own distribution. But I'll tell you this for nothing, Inspector: you won't find a single untoward thing other than that in that boy's life. He made no enemies in his life."

"What about any of the farmers in Joe's distribution set-up?"

"Nah, they were all sound as a bell with Joe, sound as a bell," John Lea replied confidently.

"Did Joe ever have reason to throw anyone out of his distribution co-operative?"

"Sure, they were all making more money with Joe's system, so none of them was going to rock the boat, now were they?"

"Did youse two ever row?" Starrett asked, still trying to come to terms with John Lea's blatant heist.

John Lea looked genuinely upset as he said, "Joe wasn't the rowing or the bossy type. I enjoy working on this farm. Joe and Liam both made me feel part of what was going on here and not just an employee."

"You say that, John Lea, yet you still steal one of their heirlooms and run off to Dublin and sell it." Starrett had chosen his words carefully, and they had the effect of a perfectly aimed kick in the goolies by the look on John Lea's face.

"Look, Starrett, they'd probably even forgotten it was here. You know, it was probably passed on to Joe's grandfather. Maybe he even got it in that clever deal he did with the man who owned the house. That was pretty cute, wasn't it?"

"But it wasn't *stealing*, John Lea."

"Well, you know what, Starrett, I can live with it. Think of it as a little perk, and who knows what's going to happen to the farm now. I just might need the thirty grand. Has anyone told you what's going to happen with the farm?"

John Lea, who didn't seem to be a particularly bad person and who seemed extremely upset about the injustice of what had happened to Joe, could justify to himself that it was still OK for him to steal. He showed by his actions just how easy it was to cross the line between right and wrong. But from Starrett's point of view, the important question was: now that John Lea had crossed the line, how far would he have been prepared to go to protect his liberty?

Chapter Thirty

Major Newton Cunningham and novice Garda Romany Browne were not exactly Morse and Lewis, Kennedy and Irvine, Holmes and Watson – or even Starrett and Garvey for that matter. The major realised that unless he took Browne in hand, the novice was going to land up taking short cuts, which would end up being a short cut out of Starrett's team. There was only so much Starrett, who took great pains to handpick his officers, would do to help his senior before ejecting any bad apples from his team. He'd never take on older members of the force, because, and the major sadly had to agree with Starrett on this one, they were likely to have amassed years of bad habits. Starrett was desperate to keep his team away from these unprofessional methods of detective work. Never let the suspect dictate the investigation; always let your investigation dictate the suspect: Starrett's words, but the major agreed with them wholeheartedly. So, rather than risk his friend's grandson ending up with the old gardaí, the major felt it was best to dedicate a few weeks to instructing him in Starrett's approach to garda work.

Browne, on the other hand, felt he was fast-tracking the system, and he was happy to fast-track any system that had deprived him of growing up in the company of his father. In the better times, he'd always put his bad feelings down to the fact he felt sorry for his mother not being able to spend the rest of her days in the company of the man she'd loved all her life. In the black dog days, he knew his feelings came from the fact he begrudged feeling totally lost in the world without his father; a father – he had only started to realise – who had been a great man and a man he would have enjoyed becoming friends with. Yes, the untimely death of his father had dictated the path Romany Browne's life had taken, and now this path had taken him under the protection of one of the Donegal gardaí's main men, and he was damned if he wasn't going to milk that for all it was worth.

What he hadn't reckoned on was the presence and power of the man he was intending to coat-tail.

"Watch and listen, Garda Browne," the major said. "Just observe and take notes. Don't take any part in the conversation."

They were in the forecourt of F&V Distribution Ltd, a big modern metallic warehouse building on the Letterkenny side of Kilmacrennan. The location had been chosen, no doubt, for its close proximity to Letterkenny, the capital of the county, and also because it was quite well located to service the North-West generally.

All members of staff were dressed in company blue wellingtons, blue baseball caps and overalls, and long, dark green aprons. Both the aprons and the caps had the F&V logo, a combination of the initials above a carrot crossed with a banana and topped and tailed with a red apple and an orange.

The major flashed his warrant card to a young staff member, who offered to take them to the general manager's office. They were led into an office high up on a gantry at one end of the warehouse, which afforded the owner a clear view of all his workers below him.

"Good morning, Major. I'm Paddy Bryson, the general manager. How can I help you?"

The major guessed Bryson to be in his fifties. He wore a dark blue suit, and if the lack of creases was anything to go by, the major reckoned Bryson had taken the trouble to put his jacket on to greet them. A blue golf club tie perfectly complemented his dazzling white shirt. The major, whose eyes were no longer the best, couldn't decipher the logo on the tie.

"Well, you could tell me what club you play at and what your handicap is," the major replied.

Bryson visibly relaxed and invited the major and the young novice to take the two seats opposite his busy, but tidy, desk.

"Can I offer youse some tea?"

"Maybe a mineral water?" the major replied, trying to find a comfortable position in the seat.

"Tell you what, let me get a pitcher of our orange juice. We make it ourselves, and if I do say so myself, it's delicious – life-preserving perhaps."

"Now how could we say no to that, eh, Garda Browne?"

Browne mumbled a bored grunt as Bryson pressed a button on some antique intercom contraption and ordered up the refreshments.

"I have to admit," Bryson started, nodding his head in time to his words, "I do love my golf. I play up at Rosapenna Club, and I play off a handicap of eleven. I've never been able to reach the single digit."

"Do you now?" The major, visibly impressed, temporarily forgot his backache. "I do prefer the old course – the one Tom Moore designed at Rosapenna – but these days, what with all the bishops and politicians, I find it hard to get a round in up there. Occasionally I play at the Royal in Portrush."

"Much too windy for me," Bryson admitted.

"Well, that's my excuse for my seventeen handicap. In my younger days I was as low as four, but these days a successful golf round for me is being able to recall what I used to be able to do with the ball."

"The fish that got away?" Bryson said with a smile, as a young girl arrived with a large pitcher of orange juice and three tall glasses on an F&V company tray. Browne was like a rat up a drainpipe. He was so quick off the mark he probably didn't even realise what he was doing; he just saw a beautiful girl and sprang into action.

Bryson said, standing up to help find a space on his desk for the tray, "Can I introduce you both to my daughter, Ann."

"Daaaad-dd," she moaned.

"Sorry," Bryson offered humbly, "I'm not allowed to tell anyone that she's my daughter."

"Ann, a real pleasure to meet you," the major said, rising clum-sily and rescuing her hand from Browne's, "and don't be hard on your father. There's nothing wrong with a bit of nepotism."

"I don't mind nepotism," she replied sweetly. "It's just I think it's unprofessional that people outside the family should know."

"I doubt you'll depend on family favours much longer."

"You better believe it, Major," Bryson said proudly. "She'll be running this place long before I'm ready to retire."

Browne took the first glass of orange juice Bryson poured and offered it to the major, who reluctantly released Ann's hand to take his first sip of the juice.

"Oh, my goodness," he exclaimed, "you were right, Mr Bryson. This surely blows the cobwebs away. Drink up there, Romany; this'll do you a lot of good."

"Would you like a wee stiffener in there, Major?"

"Heavens no, I never consume alcohol before sundown."

"Now, gentlemen," Bryson continued, "I'm sure you're not here just to discuss golf, drink our orange juice or," and addressing only Browne, "admire my daughter."

"Dad-dy!"

"Yes, Mr Bryson . . ." the major started reflectively.

"Please. Call me Paddy."

"Thanks, Paddy. Yes, we're investigating the mysterious death of Joe Sweeney. A sad affair, a very sad affair."

Ann put her hand straight to her mouth. She'd taken a seat on her father's side of the desk.

"You knew him?" the major asked.

"Well, I knew his girlfriend, Breda Roche; she's from Milford, where we live."

"And how can we be of service to you, Major?" Bryson asked.

"We understand Joe Sweeney and some of his local farmer friends had been setting up a system that was regarded as competi-tion to F&V," the major replied.

Paddy Bryson laughed. "Ann, would you tell the major here how many staff we employ?"

"We currently have twenty-three full-time staff at the warehouse and another six permanently on the road delivering. On top of that, we have access to another twenty-eight part-time staff, depending on the volume of product."

"Thanks, Ann," Bryson said proudly. "You see, the thing with us, Major, is that we're dealing exclusively in perishable goods. We have to turn our product around quickly or we have to dump it. We import from as far away as Cyprus, and we're supplying our customers with a lot of exclusive items. The farmers' co-operative weren't really competition for us. In fact, if anything, they were proving to be quite an effective advertisement for us."

"How so?"

"Well, as Ann has just said, we have a staff of fifty-nine people including ourselves and part-timers; Joe had himself, John Lea and, now and again, a couple of his farmers would muck in and help him. Yes, naturally enough, some of the local stores were all on for making a bit of a thing of buying locally, supporting their local farmers and all that kind of stuff, but time and time again they were being let down with late, or, even sometimes, no deliveries at all. There were also questions over quality control, and, sometimes, even the simple lack of product. They'd be on the phone to me to help them out with orders that the farmers' co-operative were not fulfilling."

"So you weren't trying to squeeze them out?" was Browne's opening gambit.

"You've got to forgive my novice; he seems to have forgotten his manners," the major said, reaching deep into his pockets. "Here, Garda Browne, take this twenty euro and go downstairs and buy a bag of fruit for the Tower House team. You can wait for me by the car."

"Ann will show you where to go," Bryson said. Browne's mutinous glare changed quickly into a beaming smile.

"It would be funny if it wasn't so sad," Bryson offered after Browne and his daughter had left the office. "You know, I admired what young Sweeney was trying to do, I really did. They're a great farming family, and yes, they did make sure we kept on our toes. He had a couple of great ideas on the presentation or product side of things, and I will admit we have nicked some of their better ideas."

"Like?" the major asked.

"Let's see: shrink wrapping four large pre-washed potatoes – no waste, mothers love it. Then we fixed ridges in the apple boxes so the tray rests on the ridge and not on the tray of apples below. That cuts your waste way, way down. I mean we're always on for trying to take the product straight from the fields to the shops and hopefully on to the dinner table. Before Joe Sweeney, maybe we didn't work as hard to achieve this as we did when he came along."

"So no agricultural espionage?" the major offered, only half joking.

"Listen, I'll gladly give you the names of some of the farmers in the co-operative who were back on with us, pleading to supply F&V again."

"That would be very helpful. But what were their main gripes?"

"Bulk, mainly," Bryson replied. "Joe wasn't able to take anywhere near as much produce from his farmers as we can. I'll get you their names."

Bryson hit a button on the intercom unit on his desk and pretty soon his voice was booming around the warehouse below them.

"Would Ann Bryson please come to the office," he said. He let go of the button with such flourish that Newton Cunningham felt Bryson was extremely pleased to have the opportunity to rescue his daughter from Romany Browne.

Chapter Thirty-One

In his imagination, Elvis Quinn might have hoped for more than a passing resemblance to *the* original owner of his Christian name. Only in his imagination, however, could that have been considered remotely accurate – well, excepting for his waistline and hairline of course. Maybe this is how Elvis Presley might have looked had he worked in all weathers on a County Donegal farm and generously sampled the delights of Colette's home cooking.

From the squint in his bullfrog eyes, Elvis looked like he'd been expecting a visit from Donegal's finest. As Liam had told them, Elvis lived in Ramelton in Castle Street in a small, extremely clean, terraced house.

He shook their hands firmly and showed them through to the living room. As they walked through the narrow hallway, he spoke behind them.

"Mrs Bee, she's giving me so much jip at the moment you wouldn't believe it. Last night she ran out on me, and I haven't seen her since."

Starrett feared Elvis was going to be too preoccupied with his missing wife/lover/partner to concentrate on the gardaí's questions. From the name, Mrs Bee, he was assuming that "lover" would be the box that Elvis would tick on a missing person's report.

"Oh," Starrett said.

"Yes, last night she ran out into our garden – she knows she's allowed to do that – but then she crawled through a hole she found in the hedge into the neighbour's garden. She knows very well she's *not* allowed to do that. Mrs Bee is a bad cat."

Starrett was relieved.

"Anyway, I couldn't go in there and get her. But let me tell you, there's worse to come . . ."

"No!" Garvey said, mocking it up but only slightly.

"Yes! She stayed out all night. She needn't think I don't know what's going on. I've clocked who's been hanging around making a racket. That auld tom's got all the decent cats in the area into trouble, and I bet you a lot of his litters have ended up in sacks in the Leannan, and well, I just felt let down. Do you believe in reincarnation, Inspector?"

"Ah bejeepers, Elvis, to be honest with you, I've got a bit of a hard time with that particular concept."

"Well, let me tell you, I do. And I believe Mrs Bee in one of her previous lives used to be a fine lady. I thought that from the first moment I set eyes on her. Mrs Bee was the name that immediately sprang to my mind, and she's been Mrs Bee every since. But I feel very let down, Inspector, very let down."

"Right," Starrett said, hoping they were drawing a line under this particular feline tale.

"My sister wants to go to London to do social work; you don't know where she could start do you?"

At that moment Starrett was distracted from Elvis's Donegal lilt. He realised why, from the moment they'd walked into the house, he'd had this overwhelming sense of how clean the house was. Dettol. Yes the house was clean and dust free to the eye, but the overpowering smell of Dettol made the nostrils assume the house was also clean *under* the carpets and *behind* his mismatching, gaudy three-piece suite.

"I'd have her head straight to Westminster," Starrett replied and immediately moved subjects with, "Now then, Mr Quinn . . ."

"Elvis, call me Elvis," Quinn said, combing his heavily Brylcreamed quiff and DA lovingly into place.

"Is that your real name?" Starrett asked. An Elvis in Ireland was as rare as a clock on the wall of a Las Vegas casino.

Quick as a flash, Quinn popped over to a large pine dresser, hoaked around in a drawer for a few seconds and produced a laminated copy of his birth certificate which bore the legend: Elvis Patrick Quinn.

"Elvis, what's all this auld carry-on about you and John Lea helping yourselves to one of the Sweeneys' heirlooms?"

The look in Elvis Quinn's eye betrayed that, for a split second, he considered lying. It was all Starrett needed to convince himself that his hunch had been correct. At any other time in the interview, he probably wouldn't have gotten away with it, but Elvis's delaying tactic had, in the end, only served to distract him from the deed he was so desperate to hide.

"Well, you know," he started hesitantly, "there's such a thing as squatters' rights."

"Elvis, I'm here to tell you there's such a thing as prison. Now theft, as a crime, is something that can deliver you straight to one of those fine establishments PDQ."

"But I . . ."

"Let's cut to the chase. How much did you get from the proceeds?"

"Half of the sale, it was ten thousand euros."

Starrett and Garvey smiled at the same moment. Deception was another crime John Lea could add to his list.

"What I can't figure out, Elvis, is why John Lea needed you in the first place?"

"Knowledge, Starrett. He was paying for knowledge. It was my idea," Elvis admitted. "We were watching telly one Sunday night in John Lea's, and this thingamajig programme that I'd always liked came on. John Lea never spotted what has been under his nose for most of his life."

"Ten thousand euros is a lot of motive, Elvis, enough perhaps for murder."

"Ah, come on now, Inspectar," Elvis replied, giving Starrett's title the local hard ending, "ye don't really think we're involved in that, do you?"

"Come on yourself, Elvis. Think about it. Joe discovered what you and John Lea were up to. John Lea is down in Dublin doing the evil deed, and it's left to you to get rid of Joe . . ."

"Ah, stop, Starrett; please stop your messing, will you?" Elvis pleaded.

"Seems like a good motive to me. What do you think, Packie?"

"If we're talking about motives, Inspectar, I'd look a lot closer to his home if I were you," Elvis replied, before Packie had a chance.

Good old-fashioned self-preservation: this is exactly what we want, Starrett thought.

"You've got our attention, Elvis. Pray tell us more?"

"All I'm saying is there's a few of his blood relatives who'd a lot more incentive to get rid of Joe than me and John Lea."

Starrett nodded an "and?" nod.

"Well, Joe worked the farm, that's for sure, but he wasn't the first born, he wasn't entitled to the farm."

"And?" This time Starrett left a tinge of disappointment hanging around the word.

"And you're the detective, Inspectar."

"And you've nothing more for me than that?"

"What more do you need than that?"

Starrett felt there were only slim pickings left with Elvis, who'd clearly do anything other than invent to get himself off the hook. The thing about innocent people, at least people innocent of the crime in question, is that they are really the only ones who know they are innocent of that crime, and sometimes as the detective you have to accept they act accordingly.

"Tell me, Elvis," Starrett began, staring deeply into Elvis Patrick Quinn's eyes, "what were you doing between the hours of nine o'clock and eleven o'clock on Tuesday morning?"

"That's easy," Elvis replied quickly, confidently and without flinching, "I was down in Dawson Bates' getting a tractor-load of feed. You can check with Seamus, the depot manager there. I was with him most of the time."

"Right so, we'll check with Seamus."

"You check with Seamus. He'll tell you exactly where I was," Elvis replied, as shaky as a foal rising to its legs for the first time, but like the foal he was gaining in confidence with every passing second.

Starrett was about to ask Elvis what he was doing at the correct time of the crime when he thought better of it. He knew the farm-hand was innocent of this crime, and it might not do any harm to have some confusion out there as to exact times.

"In the meantime, Elvis, if I was you, I'd check in with John Lea and see when he's going to come across with the other five thousand euros he owes you."

Starrett and Garvey watched as Elvis's newly found land legs wobbled ever so slightly under him. He looked a bit like *the* Mr Presley did in his younger days when his gyrating hips sent the young girls wild.

Chapter Thirty-Two

"What now?" Garvey asked as they walked down Castle Street to where they'd parked Starrett's BMW, midway between Tootie's bar and Bakersville.

"Let's you and me nip into Bakersville and have a wee cup of tea to discuss that very topic," Starrett said, veering to the right in the direction of the master bakers.

Starrett took his usual high seat by the window as Garvey went over to the always cheerful Veronica and ordered the usual: a cup of coffee for Starrett, a tea for himself and a couple of the little jam-filled Bakewells, which Starrett always mistakenly insisted on calling cheesecakes.

Starrett loved looking out over the square, more like a trapezium with a rectangle stuck on to it, where he could take in the comings and goings of this end of town. He was trying to work out how to get a lawnmower up on to the roof of Tooties when Garvey returned with their mid-morning treat. Starrett knew Garvey was happy because the delightful wee Bakewell would keep Starrett away from the cigarettes for at least another couple of hours. Starrett was happy because he knew he could add at least another two hours of nicotine-free time to that if he focused in on kissing Maggie Keane.

"What now?" Garvey repeated.

"OK, Packie, we need to have Nuala Gibson speak to Tom and Mona . . . and Bernadette Sweeney again. I think they're top of our list at this stage."

"You fancy Tom for this, do you?"

Starrett, mid-munch, just raised his eyebrows at Garvey.

"I know, I know," Packie replied good-humouredly: "too early to tell."

Starrett nodded as he savoured the cake.

"Tell me this, Packie," Starrett said as he finished his first bite of the Bakewell: "how long have we been coming here to have our coffee, tea and these wonderful raspberry-filled cheesecakes?"

"Since they opened here," Garvey replied, looking desperate to get stuck into his own. Every time he was about to take his inaugural bite, Starrett would ask another question. "Must be getting on for eighteen months."

"Fair play to you, Packie, fair play, I've always said you've a great memory," Starrett continued, halfing the remainder of his cheesecake, "but tell me this: in all of those eighteen months of cheesecakes, did you ever once taste the slightest hint of cheese in your cheesecake?"

"Can't say I did, Inspector, can't say I did."

"Right so, then why would they call these wee bleeders cheesecakes?" Starrett said as he smiled and washed down the final few crumbs with his coffee.

"Search me, sir. Although I think you might be the only one who does," Garvey replied, finally managing to sink his teeth into his cake. "I always thought they were just called wee *Bakewell* tarts."

"You know what, Sergeant," Starrett asked rhetorically, "I think, in the name of research of course, that I'm going to have to try another of those cakes to see if I can solve the puzzle of all puzzles and locate the cheese in a cheesecake."

And with that he was off up to the counter for their customary second round.

Joe Sweeney's girlfriend Breda Roche, although now twenty-four years old, still lived with her parents in their large, detached, pebble-dashed pink house on the outskirts of the hilly, once-elegant Milford on the road to Kerrykeel. The Roches needed a large house; five of the original eight of the clan still lived at home with their parents. The house was a lot more comfy, cosy and classy than Starrett had imagined it might be from the outside. It was obvious to Starrett the moment he met Breda's mother, Phyllis, where the daughter's good looks had come from. Although her mother offered to sit in with Breda during the interview, Breda declined. She thought she might feel inhibited if her mother accompanied her.

Starrett took this as a good sign, and the minute he and Garvey were left to themselves with her in the cluttered sitting room, he said, "How are you doing?"

"I don't really know. I don't know how to behave. Sometimes I feel guilty because I don't feel worse than I do, and other times I just break into an uncontrollable fit of crying. I'm probably doing a lot better now though than the last time you saw me."

"Do you feel OK to talk about Joe?" Starrett asked, feeling they'd left the second chat at least one day longer than they should have.

"Yes, of course. I'd want to help, if I can."

Starrett imagined that even when Breda Roche was happy, she still looked sad. Maggie Keane didn't really do happy either, but she could at least flash you her embarrassed smile and you'd know exactly where her heart was. With Maggie it was more about being self-conscious. Breda, Starrett believed, had settled on what she felt was a great look, and that was all she could do. Now he considered her close up, he thought again how much she seemed to have modelled her look on Sinead O'Conner in the *Nothing Compares to You* video. Vulnerability, as applied by L'Oréal. It didn't mean, Starrett thought, she wasn't a good-looking girl, but it was all about the look of her face, even down to the fact there was no framing of hair to distract you from her classic chiselled features. Starrett thought it might all be about her face, even to the extent that she might be ignoring the rest of her body.

"When was the last time you spoke to Joe?" Starrett asked.

"I spoke to him on the mobile around eleven o'clock on Monday morning."

"Where was he then?"

"I believe he was on the farm. I rang him when I started my eleven o'clock break."

"Where do you work?"

"In the planning office here in Milford."

Starrett grimaced as he had a flash of the warehouse conversion by the Leannan side.

"Nothing to do with me, Inspector, I'm only a secretary, but I can tell you, there's too few people working in the department to do the entire county."

"Sorry," Starrett said and meant it. "So, you'd a tea break and rang Joe?"

"Kinda," she replied. "I rang him, but he didn't pick up. I left a message, and he rang me back a few minutes later."

"How'd he sound?"

"He sounded good, in his work mode, if you know what I mean."

"Did you discuss anything out of the ordinary?" Starrett asked.

"No. We talked about his father's birthday dinner; we talked about going off to Castlebar for the bank holiday weekend. I was organising that. We'd booked into the Royal Theatre and Hotel and were also going to see a Neil Diamond concert when we were there."

"Bejeepers, is Neil Diamond really playing in Castlebar?"

"No, no, no," she protested in amused disbelief. "I think it's one of those tribute acts. Anyway, I'd been trying to get him to go somewhere with me all summer, but he didn't have the time . . ."

"Castlebar, eh?" Starrett said, not needing to add anything further.

"I know, I know . . ."

She stopped talking. Starrett didn't think she looked like she was upset. She looked as though she was considering something.

"Look, Inspector, we'd . . . ehm . . . reached that stage in our relationship, you know, where we had to either move on to the next level or let it go."

"Ri-ght," Starrett said, stretching the word into what he hoped sounded like, "I understand."

"And, look, this is very difficult for me . . ."

"We understand."

"I don't think you do. You see, I'd never been with a boy before," she said, mumbling something very quietly which sounded to Starrett like, "I still haven't been."

"And youse were thinking of splitting up?"

"Well, as I said, not necessarily. But we either had to shift gears or call it a day. Joe's not, sorry . . . Joe wasn't really into the dating thing. Really, Teresa fixed it all up. Well, actually, I think Sheila had Teresa fix me up with Joe so Shiela could have Teresa for herself."

"Sorry, I'm not sure I picked that up right."

"Maybe you did, Inspector. I knew Sheila – but not like that, she wasn't my type – and we both met Teresa at the same time. I fancied Teresa, but Sheila hijacked her for herself."

"Right," Starrett replied as Garvey scribbled away furiously in his notebook.

"Teresa and Joe were very tight, and whatever Teresa wanted, he'd do. But you know, don't get me wrong, Joe is a really nice lad, I found myself liking him. I found myself thinking, you know, maybe I could make my mum and dad happy. Joe's the kind of boy mothers like to see their daughters bring home."

"Had you and Joe discussed this, you know, either moving the relationship up a gear or packing up?"

"A wee bit. He thought everything was OK. Then again, he'd no other relationship to compare it with. Joe had a chat with Teresa about what to do."

"He told you that?" Starrett asked.

"No. Teresa did. She said she told him to stop being a mammy's boy and get on with it. She said she didn't want Sheila knowing about it; she was worried if Sheila believed Joe and I were going to split up that I might be attracted to Teresa again."

"And would you have been?" Starrett asked, because he felt he must.

"Well, yes, of course. I told you why I was dating Joe in the first place. On top of which, I don't think Sheila and Teresa will last the course, do you?"

Starrett was flummoxed. Breda had obviously been thinking of little else since Joe died, wondering if she still stood a chance with the person she was really attracted to. It was Starrett's experience that the object of your desires always looks so much more appealing and attractive when, for one reason or another, you can't be with them. But more importantly, could Breda Roche's question raise the possibility that she had murdered Joe Sweeney, just so she could enter a relationship with his sister? Bernadette Sweeney had suggested the complexities of the various relationships on the first night of Starrett's investigation, and it had taken him a good couple of days to catch up.

"I'm sorry, Breda; I just don't know the couple well enough. But I suppose I thought that if you were in a relationship with Joe, then maybe . . . well . . . I . . . ."

"Maybe I wouldn't be interested in girls any more?" Breda offered, coming to Starrett's rescue.

"I suppose that was what I was trying to say."

"Inspector, I don't see love to be as black and white as that. I think you can fall in love with anyone, boy or girl, and once you realise who it is that you're in love with, well then you just deal with that situation."

"Did you tell Teresa that you'd . . ."

". . . be interested in her if I split up with Joe?"

"Well, yes, actually."

"I did mention it, yes. We had a glass of wine or three, and there was a little bit of flirting going on. But Teresa'd never cheat."

"So, your call from Joe after eleven, that was the last time you spoke to him?"

"Yes, I rang him two more times, early in the afternoon and late in the afternoon, after I'd finished work. I left a message saying I had a new shirt for him and to make sure he'd showered the smell of the cattle off him in time for his father's dinner party."

"Right, Breda, ehm, can you tell me what you were doing in the early hours of Tuesday morning between the hours of 1.00 A.M. and 5.00 A.M.?"

"Oh-my-God, is that when poor Joe was being murdered?" she asked, raising her hand to cover the shock her mouth had betrayed.

"We think so," Starrett replied, very, very quietly.

Breda appeared deep in thought. Eventually she composed herself and replied, "At that time, I'd have been asleep here, in my parents' house."

"Someone has broken the Sixth Commandment, Packie, and we're no closer to finding out who it was; it surely must be time for the first ciggy?" Starrett said, broaching the subject hopefully, as they made their way back along the tight winding roads towards Ramelton.

Chapter Thirty-Three

As Starrett and Garvey were leaving Breda with her dilemma, Garda Nuala Gibson and Garda Francis Casey were negotiating the borderlands and having a heck of a time finding Thomas and Mona Sweeney's house, which was, they were assured, just off the main road from Lifford to Strabane. Gibson was under the impression that not a lot, apart from an international border and the River Foyle, separated these two strangest of bedfellows. She'd been totally wrong, as locating the house in question proved. Apparently, their house was in Southern Ireland, and some of their outhouses were in the Wee North. The main reason why the gardaí kept missing it was probably because they were not expecting such a grand Georgian building with such perfectly manicured lawns.

Gibson had rung ahead and both Tom and Mona were in residence, so to speak. On her home turf, Mona was a totally different woman from the Mona on the Sweeney farm. Her demeanour made it abundantly clear she felt the garda presence was a chore she would tolerate (just) but with which she was far from happy.

On the other hand, Thomas Sweeney kept in character by appearing totally subservient to his wife in their home.

When they arrived, Mona was having a stand-up row with Bernadette about whether or not she could go for a sleepover. Bernadette's point, as far as Gibson could make out, was that just because her uncle had been murdered shouldn't mean she had to "lead the life of a nun."

Tom took Casey into the house while Gibson went off to act as mediator between mother and daughter.

"When you reach the point when both your children *and* your parents are high maintenance, you know you've reached middle age," Tom said with good humour as they walked into the opulent home.

Casey wasn't sure what additional information Starrett expected him to pick up on this visit. The only thing he knew for certain at this stage in the investigation was that Starrett wasn't sure either; he just wanted them digging around in hope of any sort of nugget.

"Have you had time to think any further about who might have been involved in your brother's death?" Casey asked when they were in the highly modernised kitchen.

"And how's your investigation going?" Thomas replied, totally ignoring his attempt at an opening question.

"We're still amassing information," Casey replied.

"Did you speak to the distribution company?"

"I believe two of my colleagues are working on that one right now," Casey said, taking a quick look in his notebook where he'd jotted down a few points Sergeant Packie Garvey had picked up in the first interview with Tom. "You mentioned women as being a possible motive. Did you have any further thoughts in that direction?"

"I believe I said that usually money or weemen are behind all murders."

"But you didn't mean women in this particular case?"

"Correct, I think this one's more likely to fall into the money category."

"Why are you so confident of that?"

"I know Joe. He barely had time for Breda, let alone trying to cheat on her with someone else," Tom replied curtly.

"OK, let's talk about the farm," Casey started.

"Oh, please, let's not talk about the farm again; I've been through all of this . . ."

"You and your wife were very keen to sell the farm to a developer," Casey persisted.

"And Joe was getting in the way of that?"

"Well, yes," Casey agreed.

"Two points, Garda; take a look around you. Mona and I are not exactly hurting (the practice does extremely well, thank you very much), and Mona's developer's generous offer would have helped out *all* of the family, not *just* us."

"Would it have been true to say that Ryan, Teresa, your wife and yourself all wanted the farm to be sold and that only Joe and your father didn't?"

Tom Sweeney considered this question for quite some time.

"OK, the selling the farm side were myself, Mona, Teresa and my mother, and on the not selling the farm side were Joe, my dad most definitely and perhaps Ryan."

"Ryan didn't want the farm sold?"

"Ryan certainly didn't need the money. He and Maeve Boyce will marry one day soon, and she, as the only remaining member of her family, has an extremely large trust fund, which will mature when she's thirty. I believe that's in about three years' time."

"Do you know how much is the trust?"

"No, neither Ryan nor Maeve will even talk about it. They act like it's not even there, but Mona did a bit of research, and the Boyce family have old money, real money, so we're talking millions, ten of millions probably, hundreds of millions possibly."

Casey scribbled away furiously in his notebook.

Tom smiled, looking pleased with himself that he'd let that particular cat out of the bag. Casey wondered if he realised he'd just possibly removed a name from the suspect list.

"But maybe that's not the reason Ryan wanted to save the farm. He has always been too eager to please. I always put it down to the fact that he was the child without a portfolio."

"Sorry?" Casey said, as he wrote the name "Colette" down at the top of his page.

"Well, when we were growing up, I was always the eldest, Teresa was always the only girl and Joe was always the youngest. Poor Ryan didn't perhaps experience the specialness the rest of us did, so he was always trying to make my mum and dad happy with him in order to get the attention he felt he was lacking."

"You say Ryan didn't need money, and as you've already said, with this great house and your practice, you aren't hurting, so who *did* need money?"

"Well, our Teresa's *always* needed money. She's one of those people who genuinely believe that the money you have in your pocket is for spending, but it must be spent *today*, it *must* be spent today, and she never thinks about how she's going to pay for what she needs tomorrow. Well, she does, I suppose," Tom laughed, "she's always gone running to my dad and he's always bailed her out."

"Bailed her out? You mean she's been in trouble?"

"Nah, nah, Garda, it's nothing as sinister as that; it's just her innocent inability to deal with basic economics. Tomorrow, left to its own devices, will never *ever* take care of itself; you have to be very careful and set aside funds to deal with tomorrow and, as you well know, tomorrow never comes, so you always have to have a reserve."

"Right," Casey said and looked at the name on the top of his page. "Your mum. You said your mum was up for selling the farm?"

"Ach, you know, I think my mum was just tired of it all, tired of all the bickering and all the family with all of our spouses, wives, partners, what have you, all with an opinion and all with an opinion they wanted to have heard. And this has been going on and on and around and around for ever. I think my mum thought that if the darned farm was just sold, we could all draw a line under this and move on with our lives. I'd watch her as she listened when Ryan and Maeve would talk about their travel plans: their trips here and there and the eventual plans to take a couple of years off and just visit all the places in the world they wanted to see. Obviously, we're talking post-fund-maturing time. But the look of envy was so transparent in my mum's eye, you could tell she'd had enough of the hardship of being a farmer's wife and sharing her husband with all the problems the farm threw up at them."

"So you think she'd quietly have wished for the farm to be sold even though it was against her husband's wishes?"

"My mother is not from a farming family. My father swept her off her feet at a time I believe she was very, very vulnerable. But I'd watch her flicking through her magazines with that faraway look in her eyes. I'd see the way she'd react to Maeve, interact with her and envy Maeve's dress sense and poise. No, Garda Casey, my mother had not been raised to wear wellingtons and to hide her hair under a scarf; she was totally in her element on the rare occasions we went to Dublin."

"Do you think any of your brothers or Teresa noticed this?" Casey asked.

"My mum and Teresa never really have had a lot of time for each other."

"Because Teresa's gay?"

"No," Tom said in consideration, "this was way before she even knew Teresa was gay. I mean, come on, they're mother and daughter. They didn't always fight, but Teresa was always the apple of her *father's* eye; well, until . . ."

"Until what?"

"Until she brought home her pantyhose truck driver."

"Ryan or Joe, would either of them have picked up on the fact your mum would have preferred to sell the farm?"

"Joe would most certainly *not* have. He was so in love with the farm and farming he wouldn't really have considered anybody would want to sell a farm that was as successful as the Sweeney farm. But as Mona said, we could have sold the farm, divvied up the money, and Joe could still have bought a perfectly adequate farm to keep himself occupied."

"What about Ryan?"

"You mean did he know my mum would like to have sold the farm?"

"Yes."

"Possibly. We never discussed it. Ryan tries really hard to be a good man. I'm not sure if it's a true social conscience he's nurtured or it's one he feels he needs to embrace, to compliment Maeve's trust fund."

Tom Sweeney obviously spotted the look of disdain in Casey's eyes.

Sweeney laughed, "Oh, it's easy for you and it's easy for Ryan. Try having a family, a house, three cars, an office building, not to mention a bunch of employees to support and be responsible for all of their salaries each month. Do all that and still have a social conscience, and I'll take my hat off to you. There are two of them on guaranteed salaries, with a wee car each thrown in. Liam helped buy Ryan the house up in Coylin Court, and the house or flat or apartment or whatever they call it in Belfast is probably Maeve's, or it was in her family, so they don't have any great exposure, or overheads, now do they?"

"What about Maeve, was she in favour of selling the farm?" Casey continued, as he considered Tom's obvious contradiction.

"Maeve, she has a mind of her own," Tom started his reply at a normal volume but then dropped as he continued, "which means she doesn't always do what Ryan does, and nor does she want Ryan to always do and say as she does. I haven't really discussed it with her, but I would imagine she would have tried to find a compromise where everyone would have been happy and there would have been no fighting, which was probably also my mother's priority."

"Like sell off *part* of the farm?"

"Like sell off part of the farm," Tom repeated quietly in agreement, looking at the door as if he'd just blasphemed.

Casey closed his notebook, signalling the interview had come to an end.

"Surely you have another question for me?" he said.

"Sorry?" Casey said, looking confused.

"You asked me if my brothers and Teresa knew my mother would have liked to sell the farm."

"Yes?"

"But you didn't ask me if my dad knew my mum would have liked to sell the farm?"

"And did he?" Casey asked, now intrigued.

"No, he didn't, and if he had, it would have been my mother and not my youngest brother who would have ended up dead."

Gibson had rescued Mona from Bernadette's tirade with a need for a private conversation.

Bernadette muttered something to the effect of, "I'm part of this family too. I'm also entitled to my basic human rights," as she sauntered off dialling furiously on her mobile.

"They grow out of it," Nuala Gibson said, in the hope of creating a consolatory bond.

She needn't have bothered.

"Do youse really?" Mona by name and moaner by nature replied.

Careful not to interrupt Casey and his ongoing interview with Tom in the house, Gibson suggested they, as it was such a beautiful day, enjoy the fresh air and go for a walk.

Surprisingly, Mona agreed.

"Youse all must be under a tremendous strain," Gibson offered, recalling how easy it had been to strike up a conversation with Teresa, indiscreet and all as it was. She wondered if perhaps Starrett would have had more success with this particular subject.

"You don't know the half of it. If my husband had only been more forceful, perhaps none of this would have happened."

Gibson was startled by how quickly the conversation had lost all undertones of aggro.

"How so?"

"Well, I have certainly found that, speaking as a solicitor, people want you to take charge. It's not that they want you to tell them what to do; it's more they *need* you to tell them what to do. So, when all of this started, if my husband had only laid it all out properly for them as I instructed, I'm sure we wouldn't be having all these problems."

"What problems?"

"You know, everybody and their brother *and* their truck driver having an opinion. Look, this is a no-brainer. Twelve million euros for the farm: that's half a million in interest alone each and every year."

"Who do you feel would have been most anxious for the security?" she asked, picking her words carefully.

"Well, Teresa and Sheila Kelly certainly have expensive habits."

"Really?" Gibson pushed, remembering the modest surroundings she'd interviewed Teresa in.

Mona looked like she'd realised she was on the verge of being indiscreet and pulled herself up short on her reply.

"You know how fathers always like to spoil their daughters. My father was exactly the same, fathers and daughters, mothers and sons; I mean, as a race, we're all so bloody predictable. It really is a crying shame."

"Did you get on well with your dad then?"

"Only when he saw that I'd a brain and that I was doing well in my studies. We'd a funny connection. I think he was happy he'd created someone in me who could carry on his work with his practice. But for goodness sake, I've still kept his name on the letterhead, the Dublin address as 'the head office,' which says more about me than it does about him."

"I suppose you could say Joe and you had that in common."

"What? What are you on about? I've already told Starrett I never dated Joe. Why do you all think that? I had a scene with Ryan," Mona said quietly as she looked around for fear Bernadette was in hearing range.

"No, no, I meant you both were carrying on your father's business."

Mona stopped walking. They'd reached the end of the perfectly manicured lawn, which was nearly the size of a football field. They were away from the road side of the house, and there was no noise apart from a couple of crows squawking aggressively at each other, which Gibson thought could probably be translated to, "Next worm's mine!" "No, mine!"

Mona looked as if she were considering Gibson's words for the first time.

"You see, the main difference is that Joe wasn't entitled; he wasn't the eldest. Tom was entitled."

"Are you the eldest in your family?"

"No, but I was the only one qualified."

"What happens now?" Nuala asked.

"To the farm?"

"To the farm."

"I've been considering this a lot recently. We can do one of two things. We can all sit around the table and sort this out like reasonable people, or we can all appoint our respective lawyers and we'll eventually reach the same settlement; the only difference is that if we take the second option, we'll all inevitably be at least a third poorer off."

"But surely another option would be that Liam would just carry on farming the farm."

"That'll never happen."

"Why?"

Mona Sweeney didn't have an answer to that question. She looked as if she hoped Liam would never consider such an eventuality. Her eyes darted around, not in panic but more in desperation. Gibson, for a split second, had a flash of someone who was thinking, *Has all of this been in vain?*

"Have you seen Liam recently? He's taking this a lot worse than the rest of us, even worse than Colette, if you ask me. He was strong enough for the first day or so, but when he returned from the morgue after seeing Joe, all the life had gone out of his eyes. He always looks lost now. Believe you me, he's not going to work that land any more. I think you'll find he's thinking it was the land and his selfish love of it that's the reason his son is no longer alive."

"Mrs Sweeney, could you please tell me what were you doing between the hours of 1.00 and 5.00 on Tuesday morning?" Gibson asked.

"That's easy, I was sitting in my study prepping for a case I had in court in Letterkenny later in the day. I find if I lock myself in there for at least three hours, with no distractions, then I can cram all the facts into my brain and (hopefully) get a shape on the case."

The crows stopped squawking and went off in opposite directions, choosing not to share their worms, but to source their own, far, far away from the competition.

When Gibson and Casey compared their notes, they had a number of interesting pieces of information: Maeve had a trust she would get in three years' time; Mona suggested that Teresa and Sheila had "expensive habits"; and Mona's alibi was different from Tom's, who said they were in bed together asleep at a time she claimed she was awake and alone in the study.

Chapter Thirty-Four

"OK," Starrett said with an exaggerated sigh, "where exactly are we with this?"

The team – Nuala Gibson, Packie Garvey, Francis Casey, Joey Robinson, Major Newton Cunningham and Romany Browne – were gathered with Starrett in the first-floor meeting room to update each other on their progress in the investigation.

On a smaller notice board, Starrett had the plan of the Sweeney clan around the dinner table.

Starrett talked them through all of those present at the table so they all knew each other's information.

On the main notice board he wrote the names:

John Lea

Elvis Patrick Quinn

He joined the names up with a seagull out of which he wrote, "antique Quadrant – Charles Adam."

"Did Joe find out what they were up to?"

"Even if he did," Nuala Gibson offered, "surely they wouldn't have felt a need to kill him over it."

"Oh, I don't know," Casey offered. "They could have ended up in Mountjoy Prison. Avoiding doing time can be a great reason to see off those who have evidence against you."

"But they liked him," Gibson, who thrived on these round-robin debates, persisted, "and from the little I've learnt about Joe Sweeney, I'm not sure he would have wanted to have them sent to prison."

"They're both just cowboys," Starrett began, as he drew a strike through both names, "but they're not murderers, and they confirm each other's stories. What did we find out about the distribution company?"

"Dead end," the major offered, only to be cut off by Browne.

"Maybe not," Browne boasted. "I discovered from the daughter of the general manager that one of the big investors in F&V is Owen Bonner."

This silenced the gang.

Starrett looked at the major and raised his eyebrows.

The major shot him back a "news to me" look.

"Isn't he a major crime baron or something?" Browne asked desperately, as the major glared into the back of his tanned neck.

"You're too late, Romany," Casey said. "He's gone legit, and all of his businesses are squeaky clean."

"I also did a bit of investigating unbeknownst to my former partner," the major continued, "and the names of all the farmers F&V claimed wanted to come back to them after their short time with the farmers' co-operative, all checked out positively."

"What if some of the farmers who went with Joe Sweeney wanted to go back to F&V and F&V wouldn't take them back, could that not be a good motive for one of them to have murdered the Sweeney boy?" Browne offered hopefully.

"Possibly," the major admitted, "apart from the fact that the F&V policy was to take back all of those who wanted to come back. Now, Romany, would you ever be a good fellow and share out that fruit you bought for the team at F&V. Hopefully Ann Bryson didn't serve you from the poisoned section of the shelves. On second thoughts, maybe you should check the merchandise out on everyone's behalf just in case."

"I think we're dismissing F&V too quickly," Browne protested, refusing to give up.

"I agree," Gibson ventured, much to the disdain of Casey and a bit of tutting from the major. "Maybe Owen Bonner has just been employing a better PR firm recently. Perhaps he saw Joe

Sweeney and his new farmers' co-operative distribution as more than just the 'friendly' competition F&V are claiming. At the very least this needs some more investigation; we just can't dismiss him as easily as that."

"And when we're on the subject of letting people go too quickly," Browne took up the thread seamlessly, and speaking as if Starrett weren't present, "I feel the inspector is dismissing Elvis and this John Lea character much too quickly as well. Down at Templemore, we were taught to do a full and meticulous investigation into suspects before we ruled them out."

"Well, we know that John Lea was down in Dublin at the time of the murder," Gibson said, raising a smile again from Casey, "so he's definitely out."

"Correct," Starrett said a few seconds later, following a mouthful of banana. "Browne, we'll leave you to do a full and meticulous investigation into Elvis Patrick Quinn, shall we? OK, moving right along, what else do we have?"

"You told us Tom Sweeney wasn't the real heir to the farm after all," Gibson offered, checking her notes. "Could that not be a good motive? He'd been deprived at birth, he'd taken Ryan's romantic cast-offs, and now he had been overlooked for the farm in favour of his younger brother?"

Starrett circled Tom Sweeney's name on the dinner table sketch.

"And," Gibson added, continuing to flick from page to page, checking her notes, "Tom Sweeney's alibi contradicts his wife's."

"Well, he could have thought she was in bed with him," Garvey offered.

"Thus speaks a bachelor," Gibson said, immediately realising what she was admitting and blushing.

"Perhaps he thought she was in bed with him," Casey said, coming as ever to her rescue, "but she didn't want to disturb him, so she crept out to her study to do her cramming?"

"Or he waited until she had left the bed, and then he snuck off down to Ramelton to murder Joe Sweeney," Garvey said.

"Or *she* snuck out of bed, went into her study, locked the door from the inside, climbed out the window and went into town and murdered Joe," Gibson offered, as Casey nodded positively.

"Hang on, hang on, we're getting a wee bit too far ahead of ourselves," Starrett said, replacing the chalk on its ledge at the base of the board and wiping the chalk from both his hands by playing cymbals with them. "You all make it sound like Joe Sweeney was hanging around Ramelton eagerly waiting for someone, anyone bejeepers, to come along and murder him. Let's deal with what we know."

The major grunted.

"What do we know?" Starrett asked, reluctantly picking up the chalk again.

No one replied, so he proceeded to list their facts as he wrote them on the board.

"Joe Sweeney drowned somewhere between the early hours of 1.00 o'clock to 5.00 o'clock on Tuesday morning.

"There were no marks on his body to suggest he'd been held under water.

"There were traces of Rohypnol found in his body.

"His hair was dry.

"All of his family were gathered together later that same Tuesday evening to celebrate Liam Sweeney, the father's, birthday.

"Joe was inheriting the farm.

"He was setting up a distribution system for his and other local farmers in direct competition to F&V."

"Owen Bonner has a share in F&V," Browne added.

"Owen Bonner has a share in F&V," Starrett agreed, before returning to his list. "Tom, Teresa and Ryan were being deprived of a division of a potential twelve million euro windfall from the suggested sale of the farm to developers.

"The Sweeneys' cousins had been deprived of what they thought was their father's rightful share of the farm.

"Ryan, it appears, didn't need the money.

"Teresa, it appears, couldn't get enough money.

"Tom seems well off, but he and his wife were the most proactive about trying to secure the sale of the farm to the developers.

"The last person we know Joe rang and spoke to on the phone was someone at Frewin Guest House. He was checking up to see if they had any additions to add to their order, due to be delivered on Wednesday morning.

"He left the farm for the last time just after two o'clock on Monday afternoon.

"Then his mother rang him from the farm to tell him his sister had rung looking for him.

"Twelve people tried to ring him after that, between 16.15 (message from his girlfriend Breda Roche) to 17.05 when he received another message from Breda.

"Then his mobile was inactive until 02.43, when he received another call from his sister Teresa.

"Francis, did you learn anything else from the phone calls?" Starrett asked.

"His sister said they were meant to meet up in the afternoon. They'd organised it that morning in their 09.50 call."

"Why did they need to meet up during his busy afternoon if he was going to see her the next evening at the party?" Gibson asked.

"She said they were planning something special for their father at the party, and, as usual, it had been left to her and Joe to find a suitable present. According to Teresa, Tom was boring and Ryan was busy and on his way up from Belfast," Francis continued, reading from his notes.

"And the late night call?" Starrett asked.

"She apologised for that one. She said by that time she was well wrecked, tired and emotional, at her midnight party. When she got to the farm the next day, everything seemed fine, and they were expecting Joe to arrive at any minute," Gibson replied.

"OK." Starrett returned to his chalk and commentary. "Back to what we know.

"Two trawlermen . . ." Starrett paused for a few seconds to retrieve their names from his book ". . . Janak Krawiec and Konrad Zajak, were casting off Ramelton quayside in the very early hours of Tuesday morning when they saw someone small(ish), dressed in yellow oilskins, on the quay, maybe fishing, maybe not. They couldn't tell as they only had a rear view.

"John Lea, one of the farmhands and a Sweeney peppercorn tenant, in cahoots with Elvis Quinn, steals from the cottage and sells in Dublin a valuable Sweeney family heirloom, the antique quadrant. John Lea cheats Quinn out of part of their spoils, but John Lea has a proven alibi for the time of the murder. He was still in Dublin. Elvis, on the other hand, was here in Ramelton in his Castle Street cottage and doesn't have any alibi for the time of death; equally he doesn't seem to know when the death took place."

Starrett circled Elvis Quinn's name several times and then wrote Browne's name beside it and circled it several times as well.

"What about Breda Roche?" Garvey asked.

"You really think so, Packie?" Starrett muttered, as much to himself as to his sergeant.

"Well, she admitted she still fancied her boyfriend's sister, and she doesn't have an alibi for the time of the murder either," Packie offered.

"You don't mean to suggest she expected Teresa Sweeney to run straight back into her arms after she killed her brother?" Gibson objected.

"And the majority of County Donegal won't have an alibi for the time of the murder," Casey added, as ever agreeing with Gibson.

"What about the rest of the family, Starrett?" the major asked.

"Well, Tom Sweeney, with or without his wife Mona Sweeney, would seem to have the best motive. They needed rid of Joe to unblock the selling of the farm to a developer for the princely sum of twelve million euros, give or take. Maybe, just maybe, he'd be the easiest to accept as the murderer of Joe. Tom was in effect being penalised for only being a half-brother," Starrett said, staring hard at the board.

"What a dysfunctional family," Browne said.

"It's just a good, old-fashioned, traditional family life," the major replied.

"I fancy the father, Liam," Browne volunteered.

"All the wee girls in Donegal are going to be very disappointed when that news breaks," the major said, without batting an eyelid.

Everyone laughed. The only person Browne chose to make eye contact with was Nuala Gibson, a fact not unnoticed by Francis Casey.

"Any reason in particular, Romany?" Starrett asked, intrigued.

"Just a hunch," Browne admitted. "I mean, he's changed totally since we first met him. It's like he's a different man altogether. To my eye he's behaving very suspiciously."

"Maybe he's just grieving for his son?" Gibson suggested, very sadly.

"It's more than that," Browne said. He was on the verge of grandstanding, but Starrett was pleased that he held back a bit, even admitting that some of Liam Sweeney's behaviour could be attributed to the untimely death of his son.

Starrett thought about his own father.

He wondered how anyone could suggest that a father had murdered his own son. How would another son, a daughter or a wife and mother react to such news if it were proved true? For Colette Sweeney, the death of her son was one thing, and certainly a monumental disaster that she would never, ever get over, but what if it were Liam who had killed him? Surely that would *totally* destroy her. Starrett had seen a woman destroyed in his last case, a woman who was not in the wrong, but who had been wronged, and who ended up taking the final solution.

"What about the developers? If they were prepared to pay twelve million, what must have been in it for them?" Gibson asked, stirring Starrett from his tangent.

"Yes," the major mused. "What's the loss of a life compared to twelve million euros. That's, of course, if we're to assume that they must be scheduled to make at least as much as they were laying out."

"At least," Starrett agreed.

"Who's the developer in question?" the major asked everyone in general, but he was eyeballing Starrett in particular.

"I'd put my money on Owen Bonner," Browne suggested.

"That would give him two solid reasons for murder."

"Right, Romany, add that to your list. Off you go and confirm the identity of the developer," Starrett said.

"I'm sorry, sir," Browne protested; "I'm working on another lead."

"I'd respectfully suggest, young man, that you change leads immediately," the major said, glaring at Browne.

"And how are we getting on with tracing the family of cousins?" the major inquired, turning his attention from the departing Browne to the grimacing Starrett.

Starrett looked to Casey, who'd been in charge of tracking down the green-eyed cousins. Casey continued writing in his notebook.

"Yes, ah sorry, that was my next task, Major. The trip to Letterkenny took longer than I expected. I'm on it."

"Starrett, I know you need a bigger team; that's why I'd been hoping . . ." and he looked towards the door through which Browne had just exited.

Casey, Gibson, Garvey and Robinson were looking up from their former preoccupations, keen to see how Starrett was going to react.

"You know, Major, as you used to frequently tell me, there are times when it's more important to a farmer to lose a bit of his load, just so he can make the market in time for the sale."

Definitely a net ball, Starrett felt, but he was very happy that it had enough momentum to carry on over the net and trickle on to the major's side of the court. He knew he didn't deserve to get away with it; he most certainly should have been on to the developers and the Sweeney cousins before now.

"Did I really say that, Starrett?" the major asked.

"I believe so, Major," Starrett bluffed. "I don't believe it could have come from younger lips."

For some extraordinary reason, the proper version of the late night words whispered by Maggie Keane that he'd been trying to decipher ever since suddenly flashed into Starrett's mind.

"We have to make amends before we can move on."

Chapter Thirty-Five

He'd finally figured it out. Those were the words Starrett was convinced Maggie Keane had whispered in his ear a few nights ago.

Make amends for what? Starrett wondered as he exited the garda station.

The moving on bit, however, now that did sound positive, didn't it? he said to himself as he hopped down the steps from Tower House, two at a time.

She was probably wondering why he hadn't picked up on the words and come back to her with proposals for restitution.

"Inspector, I've a message for you," a voice behind him called out, bringing him back down to earth. "You were out of there pretty sharpish."

He turned around.

"Ah, it's yourself," Starrett said to Nuala Gibson. They walked over towards the Fish House on the opposite side of Gamble Square from the garda station and sat down on the iron bench. The all-weather functional seat was one of two given by the Northern Bank Limited to celebrate the Leannan Festival in 1983. Starrett thought it amusing that, although the benches were still there, the bank wasn't.

"You know . . ." he said, intending to say, "You know Maggie Keane." Of course Garda Gibson knew Maggie. Gibson's mother was one of Maggie's old friends. In fact, Starrett, Maggie and Gibson's mum had all gone to school together. But Starrett lost his bottle and said instead, ". . . that this old garda station of ours would make a damned fine wine bar for some enterprising kind of chap."

"Right," Gibson said. "What do you think about Romany's hunches?"

Romany now, is it? Starrett thought as he said, "You know lions will eat their young, and do you know why?"

"Because they can?" Gibson ventured.

"No," Starrett laughed, physically itching for a cigarette; "because they're hungry."

"And this is connected to Romany how?"

"He wants to be a detective; he needs to detect. The male lion, given a choice, will leave his own offspring alone, providing of course there is something else equally appetising available for lunch. In time, Garda Browne too will be more selective in his choice of suspects."

"Hopefully," she added, which was what Starrett had been thinking too.

"You had a message for me," Starrett said, unable to find a way to bring up the topic of Maggie Keane.

"Oh yes, I almost forgot. Two things actually; I discovered what the iron sphere in the courtyard was originally used for: it was used as a float in the festival parade. There was a light inside and then it was covered by a canvas to make it look like a football and used to advertise the Football Special lemonade."

"Right," Starrett replied, appearing deep in thought about the subject. "That makes sense. And the second thing you needed to tell me?"

"I was speaking to Maggie Keane earlier today, and she said that if you'd nothing better to do, she would cook you a bit of supper tonight."

Starrett hesitated for only a heartbeat, but enough for Gibson to know what he'd been thinking.

"Don't worry," Gibson said with a smile, "I'm not going to cramp your style, sir. I'm not invited."

"Ach, look no, bejeepers, if you and her had something already organised, I'm not . . . I mean, I wouldn't want . . ."

"Don't sound so put out on my behalf," she said. "I've got my own man to keep happy tonight."

She put her hand to her mouth, "Sorry, sir, I didn't mean it to come out that way. I meant, of course, that I'm cooking a meal for Francis."

"I won't tell on you, if you don't tell on me."

"Deal! I'm outta here before I put my foot in it again."

Instead of hightailing it to Maggie Keane's cosy home, Starrett remained sitting on the bench. By this point, he thought, looking at his watch, the media pack, keen for developments on the death of Joe Sweeney, were probably enjoying their first pints over at the Bridge Bar. It was nine minutes past eight. Had he already missed dinner? Maggie didn't like her kids being up late. Still, he couldn't get off his seat. He was out of sorts with himself, probably to do with his lack of progress on the case.

Why had Joe been murdered? How had he been murdered? Had the person who'd committed the act sat on this very seat making plans? Had they walked the streets of Ramelton, perhaps even with a family dog, perfecting the murder? You see a man or a woman walking down the road, lost in their thoughts, and you just never knew what they were thinking about. Starrett would always pick people on the street and try and guess their thoughts. Were they thinging about lovers, mortgages, losing weight, doing something better with their hair, cars, sport, family or work when they were deep in thought? He wondered if someone really had walked these friendly streets figuring out how to rid the world of Joe Sweeney, a man who, from all reports, seemed to be one of your basically good guys.

Starrett watched as, one by one, his team left the building, some acknowledging him, some so preoccupied with their own thoughts they didn't even notice him. You could look through someone you knew, just because you'd never expect them to be in that particular place. He hopped into his car and headed off in the direction of someone he hoped very much would never be able to look through him.

Maggie Keane, in all her splendid beauty, was waiting for him at the front door.

Starrett didn't like to think of her as being "beautiful," because the word beauty itself suggested some degree of the cosmetic, or even surgical, process. No, Starrett acknowledged to himself, this was a very different bowl of cherries altogether. This was a bowl where no matter how often you dipped into this particular indulgence, you could never detract from the fullness. No, that ever-powerful first hit still had the ability to knock his multi-coloured socks clean off.

She looked clean; she always looks clean. Starrett didn't mean clean as in she didn't or couldn't have a smudge on her skin. He meant clean in a way that implied being naughty with her would be a non-stop-weekend event, as opposed to a furious and fast wobbly knee.

"I'm ever so sorry I'm late," Starrett apologised as he kissed her. He was aiming for her cheek, but she dodged and caught him on the mouth. "Hunger *always* means having to say you're sorry."

She rolled her eyes.

"You're off the hook, Starrett. Nuala rang to say she didn't have a chance to pass on my invitation until the end of the day. Come on in and say goodnight to the kids before they go upstairs. Joe's at university, but Moya is desperately keen to say goodnight to you."

None of Maggie's three kids had given Starrett a hard time when first he started seeing their mother again. He wasn't sure *exactly* what was going on himself, so how would they know or suspect anything. The slowest of the three, however, to come around to Starrett was Moya, and she was the one Starrett was most concerned about upsetting if things didn't work out. Maggie had informed Starrett that he had won her youngest daughter's undying devotion when he started to have serious conversations with her. The proud mother said no one had ever treated Moya seriously before. Starrett saw *so* much of Maggie in her it hurt.

Moya, as ever, started her conversation three questions ahead of her intended question.

"Starrett, how many people are there in the world?"

"Oh about 6,500 million," Starrett replied, not knowing where he'd plucked the figure from.

"Bejeepers, that's an awful lot of people."

"Indeed it is," Starrett replied with a smile.

"Tell me this, Starrett, please, out of all those people, how do you ever manage to find a friend, a real friend or a boyfriend or a girlfriend?"

Starrett thought Moya was too young to be feeling so down-hearted about this particular overwhelming subject.

"Look," he said, "we're all walking around this earth trying hard to live our lives and looking for a friend, a soul mate – a man, a woman, a boy or a girl. Now it's hard enough, if you think about it, firstly to find someone you will like 100 per cent, but then, if you are lucky enough to find such a person, the second big hurdle is that they need to like you at least an equal amount. So really, you can't be preoccupied about how big and impossible a task this search is going to be, because if you wander around looking defeated, dejected, sour or down in the dumps, then you're never going to be attractive and, therefore, you'll make the task all the more difficult."

"What you're saying is that you've got to get on with your life and live your life carefree and happy so the person you're looking for will be attracted to you."

"I suppose in a way that is what I'm saying."

"But, doesn't that mean if you're not *really* being yourself, there is a chance you'll attract the wrong person?"

"Right, exactly, so what I'm also saying is, you have to go to the stage beyond that – take the joys that are given to you, take satisfaction from your friends and your family's happiness."

"So what you're really saying is, just because you and Mum have found each other, not once but *twice*, I should accept that that is as close as I'm going to get to real happiness myself?"

"Ah, now, Moya . . ."

"And then there's that 'friends with benefits' thing. Can we discuss that, please?"

"OK, young lady, off to bed with you now," Maggie said, coming around the door to the rescue.

"Starrett," Moya continued, totally ignoring her mother, "what does 'friends with benefits' mean exactly?"

"Moya!" Maggie said.

"Starrett," Moya pleaded, "I'll be your best friend if you tell me, please."

"OK," Starrett replied, jumping into the deep end, "it's where you have a good friend, a very good friend . . ." Starrett could feel Maggie's eyes glaring down on him. ". . . and sometimes, you know, because they're a friend, you'll do favours for them."

Starrett could feel Maggie breathing a sigh of relief.

"What, favours like swapping iPod tunes?"

"Yeah," Starrett replied.

"And favours like loaning them your class notes?"

"Yeah, that as well."

"Favours like borrowing their DVDs?"

"Yes, Moya, friends with benefits would do that as well."

"And favours like, say, kissing?"

"Young lady!" Maggie looked like she didn't know whether to laugh at how Moya had played Starrett, or to be annoyed because of where this was going.

"That would only be *very* special friends," Starrett said, hoping that concluded tonight's quiz.

Moya was after a bigger fish than Starrett.

"Mum, are you and Starrett *special* friends with benefits?"

Moya winked at Starrett as her mother led her upstairs.

"It's all they talk about at school nowadays," Maggie said, by way of explanation when she returned.

Starrett went to kiss her. She dodged him totally but took his hand and led him through to the kitchen. Starrett got the feeling that Maggie, having just dealt with one of her children, was about to deal with another.

She removed the remainder of the shepherd's pie from the oven and shared it equally over two plates, poured two glasses of red wine and sat down beside Starrett.

"Eat," she ordered, as she held the hair back from her face with one hand and forked the cinnamon-flavoured food with the other.

"I'm famished," Starrett said, as the words *We have to make amends before we move on* swam around his head carelessly.

She looked at Starrett, and he was consoled with the look of tenderness in her eyes.

"Starrett, I hate to do this to you in the middle of a case and all, but there's something we just need to talk about. It's driving me crazy, and I can't hold it in any longer."

"OK," Starrett said as he thought, *I can deal with this; after all it's my fault.*

They were now both at the old kitchen table that had been in her husband's family for years.

"What can I tell you, Starrett? I suppose, what with you being a detective and all . . . I had hoped you would have worked all of this out before now."

In all the time he'd known Maggie Keane, he'd never seen her look so serious. His mind raced ahead with possibilities: she was going to take the family and emigrate to Australia, and she'd just come back into his life to spend time with him so he could see what it felt like to be the one left behind? She'd murdered Joe Sweeney? She was going to run away with the Reverend Ivan Morrison?

"Starrett, do you remember what we did that night all those years ago?"

"You mean . . ."

"Yes, Starrett, way back then when I'd allowed you to be the most important person in my life, more important than my family or even myself for that matter."

"Maggie, I've always wanted to explain."

She smiled her pathetic smile at him. This time, though, it was the most effective it had ever been. It cut him beyond the bone and way, way deep into his soul.

"But you could never find the words?" she said pointedly.

"Well, at the time, no . . . and then, when I wanted to, you'd met up with Niall and were happily married with your first baby, Joe, so I didn't think it was appropriate to even try to contact you, let alone discuss it."

"Tell me now then, Starrett. I really want to understand; I really need to understand."

"I decided that I had a calling."

"And how long exactly before you left had you decided you had this calling of yours?"

"I'd been thinking about it for most of my teenage years, Maggie."

"But you never once discussed it with me, although I knew you for each and every one of your teenage years, and a couple more as well?"

Starrett decided that now he'd started, it was best to plough on. He knew there was a good chance that she'd never talk to him again after this evening, so for his own good as well as hers, it was better he get this load off his chest. He was surprised this showdown had been so long in coming. This topic hadn't been raised even once during the pervious half a year. He'd convinced himself that she'd put all of this behind her and was prepared to move on. He reasoned that the death of Niall, the father of her children, had, for once and for ever, put Starrett and their teenage romance in its adolescent place.

"Maggie, I'm not proud of how I acted, but I felt the best way to deal with this, this calling I was feeling to become a priest, was to just go. I couldn't deal with it any other way."

"So you come to me on your last night, the night before you run away to take some oath, and you still don't tell me . . . Ach, Starrett, this is hurting more than I expected; more than I wanted it to. I wanted to deal with it rationally. I didn't want to get emotional. I really am over blaming you, Starrett. This is not what this is about. This is not what I need to discuss with you," she said, visibly hurting, but still managing to keep her tears at bay.

"Maggie, I deserve all your wrath, and I know now I was an idiot to ever think that we could put this behind us. I'll go if you want; I can't bear to see you hurt so much."

"No, Starrett, I promised myself I would deal with this and get it out; you need to know . . . you deserve to know."

"I deserve nothing, Maggie. My behaviour was unforgivable."

"Starrett, listen to me. That night, our last night, our only night, well . . . I could sense I was losing you. I felt all warm and tingly when we were together, but that night, at least at the start of the night, I could feel you were going from me. I thought it was to another girl; I never dreamed that it was to the Church. I acted immaturely; I felt there was one sure way to keep you."

"But . . ." Starrett started, and she cut him off immediately.

"Starrett, remember, I seduced *you.*"

Starrett's brain flashed back through two decades of memories to a fact, a very important fact, that he'd either forgotten or chosen to forget.

"So, that's why I contacted you; I accept part of the blame. We both did things that night we shouldn't be proud off. I made love to you, willingly, lovingly, and you ran away."

"Maggie . . ."

"I'm not finished yet, Starrett, please don't stop me or I'll never get this out. Starrett, what I've been trying to tell you for the last six months is that you are Joe's father."

Chapter Thirty-Six

"What? Your Joe?"

"*Our Joe,* Starrett," she said, with genuine love in her voice.

In that single moment, Starrett felt the power and compassion of her love and commitment to him.

In the distance he could hear the sounds of the siren of a garda car, then it was gone, and all they were left with was the silence of the late night kitchen and the sound of the clock ticking away on the wall.

Over the years, mostly while alone in London, Starrett had thought a lot about what had happened with Maggie. He had been in an idyllic relationship with her; he was madly in love with her and she in love with him. On the other hand, he felt he had no option but to follow this calling – a calling he was slightly embarrassed by and very secretive about. Of course, he had known it would demand a big break-up with Maggie and all the pain that entailed. He didn't want to hurt her, but, more importantly, as he later admitted to himself, he didn't want to hurt himself. So he just walked. One evening they went out together as they had done on most evenings of their young lives, and the next morning he left for Armagh.

It now turned out that from the other side of the relationship, Maggie had mistaken his distraction about spirituality as an attraction towards another girl, so she chose the often used route of getting closer in order to secure the mythical eternal bond.

Starrett had certainly been confused emotionally that they had made the ultimate connection on that fateful night. But with all his mixed emotions running under current, he hadn't bothered to stop and think about why he'd not stopped to say, "No." What he had said, in fact, was, "Bejeepers, *Maggie,* that was something else!"

"How do you feel about this, Starrett?" Maggie asked, ending the silence that was building between them like an imminent thunderstorm.

Starrett blew an exaggerated breath out the sides of his mouth.

"Maggie, I'm in turn elated, I'm very proud – Joe, and no thanks to me, is a very fine young man – and then I'm disgusted at myself for all the time I've not been here for you and for him."

"Well, do you know why I don't feel that way, Starrett?"

Starrett shook his head.

"If you and I had stayed together and we'd had Joe, well, then sadly I'd never have met Niall. If I'd never met Niall, then I'd never have had my two girls, and, Starrett, they are a joy to me and so much a part of me that I have to say I'm so glad we didn't stay together."

"But they might have been our girls, Maggie," Starrett said, not being able to help feeling more than slightly hurt.

"Yes, Starrett, we might have married and we may have had more kids, but who knows, we might have had boys rather than girls. Even if we had girls, we'd never ever have had Moya and Katie together. They're from somewhere else, Starrett, and I thank God each and every day of my life that they're mine."

Maybe Maggie could see the hurt in Starrett's eyes because she continued, "And equally, Starrett, Joe . . . to have Joe in my life, all the stuff you and I went through was a very, very small price to pay for bringing someone as magical as Joe into this world."

"And you really think you can forgive me for how I behaved?"

"I forgave you, Starrett, the moment Joe was born; I think the problem has been more that you've never forgiven yourself."

Starrett had started the evening feeling he was about to be dumped, and here was this magic woman, telling him she'd already forgiven him all those years ago.

234 • PAUL CHARLES

"If it makes you feel any better, I will admit I did take the occasional bit of pleasure from seeing and hearing that you were still giving yourself a hard time about it."

"Phew, so all that barbed wire in my underpants wasn't in vain after all."

"Ach, Starrett, that's just gross; get away with you." She punched him playfully in the arm. "But seriously, I really don't want to hurt you, but I feel I still need to say I was blissfully happy with Niall. He was a great husband and an amazing father."

"Did he know about Joe?" Starrett asked, noticing that she hadn't used the word "love" while describing her time with Niall.

"Well, he never called me Mary, so he knew it wasn't God's."

"Did he know I was the father?" Starrett said, ignoring her attempt to lighten his mood.

He was feeling very proud about being able to use the word "father" in a possessive manner for the first time in his life.

"Yes, he did," Maggie said very quietly, "but he brought Joe up as his own. There was never ever any difference between the children in his eyes. From my side, I would never have *dreamt* of wanting to do anything to get back in touch with you were it not for the fact . . ."

"I know, Maggie, I know," Starrett whispered. He didn't reach to comfort her; he didn't want to crowd her when her thoughts were with her dead husband.

She straightened up in her chair as if physically moving on.

"Right, Starrett," she said, getting up from the table and clearing away their cups, "I can't tell you what a weight that is off my mind. I fancy something a bit stronger to drink. Will you join me in some wine?"

"Bejeepers, Maggie, if you've enough to fill the auld bath, I'm game."

She gave him a tolerant tut as she passed behind him, ruffling her fingers through his hair, letting her arm trail behind her so it was touching his head until the last possible moment. She poured two generous glasses from an already opened bottle of Chianti Classico.

As they raised their glasses, Starrett said, "To your children, Maggie."

"Jeez, Starrett, never let them hear you call them that. Sure Joe's a fully grown man now."

"Maggie, I'm so sorry I wasn't around . . ."

"Starrett, listen to me, will you. This is very, very important. If we are to have any – and I do mean, any – chance, then there must not be a single regret on either side. It'll only serve to destroy us a second time."

"No regrets, Maggie," Starrett said, raising his glass to hers.

'No regrets, Starrett," she replied, nodding and accepting some degree of the contentment Starrett felt.

He was just about to wet his lips with his wine when his mobile went off.

She continued to stare at him in consideration as he took the call. Starrett looked back at her, feeling a connection that he'd never felt before. Something special had happened in their last thirty minutes together.

Pretty soon, though, he was distracted by Packie Garvey's words on the other end of the line: "Romany Browne has just arrested Liam Sweeney."

"The blundering eejit."

"Maybe not, Starrett," Packie responded. "Liam Sweeney has just confessed to the murder of his son."

Chapter Thirty-Seven

S tarrett left Maggie's house feeling greatly encouraged by her parting words: "I suppose I'm going to have to get used to this kind of situation, Starrett," which, Starrett reckoned, suggested some kind of a future.

He tried to hold that thought, but sadly it quickly disappeared the second he walked into the mayhem that was Tower House.

An obviously weary Major Newton Cunningham was waiting for Starrett in the reception area of Tower House.

"You've no doubt heard?" was the major's greeting.

"Yes, Packie told me."

"Seems we all misjudged him."

"Liam or Romany?"

"Why, Liam, of course," the major replied, looking as if he'd never, until that moment, considered the other option.

"Has he been charged yet?"

"No, but so keen was Browne in his endeavours, I had to have him pull up on the reins, otherwise he'd have tried, sentenced and hung Liam in the basement before sunlight."

"Where's he now?"

"Liam or Romany?" the major asked.

"Novice Garda Browne," Starrett replied distractedly, fearful everyone was putting the cart before the horse.

"He's upstairs with the rest of the team. I'm thinking I might need a couple of clean six-inch nails to attach his feet to the floor. Apparently he discovered a clue amongst the . . ."

"No, sorry, Major, I need to hear it from Garda Browne himself. I'll go upstairs and have a chat with him in my office before I do anything else."

"Bean Garda Nuala Gibson assures me it was all done by the book, Starrett."

"OK, at least that's something; look, would you feel more comfortable if you joined myself and Browne for our chat?"

"Yes, thanks, Starrett, I would like that."

"I'll meet you in my office in a few minutes then," Starrett said, as he left to find Browne.

Starrett found it interesting that the preoccupation of the station was not that a father had confessed to murdering his son, but that it had been novice Garda Romany Browne who had apprehended the suspect.

All things considered, Browne appeared totally grounded when Starrett spotted him deep in conversation with Nuala Gibson. He also noticed how visibly agitated Francis Casey was at this development. The conversation stopped as Starrett walked into the overcrowded, small and badly in need of decorating room.

Starrett strode up to Browne and shook his hand firmly. "Well done, Garda, very well done." The room seemed to breathe a collective sigh of relief.

"It was your notes, your power of observation, that did it, sir."

Starrett raised his eyebrows but didn't leave the opening very long for Browne. He didn't want to receive this vital information piecemeal, so he immediately continued, "Could you and Garda Gibson meet myself and the major down in my office in a couple of minutes so youse can bring me properly up to speed on this?"

Four minutes later, Ramelton's latest fab four were sitting around Starrett's desk – Starrett in his comfortable, cushion-laden, captain's swivel chair; the major sitting in his preferred location, on the corner of the desk with his back to Starrett, and Gibson and Browne sitting opposite them.

Gibson, being Gibson, had ensured they all had a mug of steaming coffee to kick-start the proceedings.

Browne didn't need any stimulant to kick his ticker into gear.

"So," he started unprompted, "as you know, right from the beginning I suspected it must be a member of the family. As I mentioned earlier, something was drawing me to suspecting the father. I'd read through your case notes earlier in the day, and something in them struck me as being odd. Not odd in itself, but odd that you would even mention or record it."

Starrett felt he was getting the fleshed-out version of events, and that perhaps Browne was preparing for his first media interview.

"Starrett's always very observant. You'd do well to follow his example," the major interjected. No one paid any attention to him.

"So, the point that caught my interest was the fact that Liam, in your company, had bought a fistful of Cadbury's Tiffin bars down in the shop in Letterkenny General Hospital. As I say, I thought it was an . . ." and here Browne hesitated as though he'd had second thoughts about what he had been about to say.

Eventually Browne continued, ". . . an *interesting* thing to record. Later in the day, I had occasion to be down at the crime scene. Once again I was trying to see if I could get any inspiration about how the crime had been committed. My instructor down in Templemore was always telling me that the crime scene can tell you so much, even beyond the hard evidence found there: 'It's all there; everything you need to know is at the crime scene. The important thing is how you read it.' So, I was walking around the area where the body was found, and didn't I only notice a crumpled-up wrapper of a Cadbury's Tiffin bar stuffed into a crack between the stones in the wall near where the body had been found. Obviously the SOC guys didn't find it because it wasn't on the ground. I remembered your notes, and it led me straight to Liam Sweeney."

Starrett waited and waited until eventually the major asked, "And then what happened?"

"Then I went out to the Sweeney farm with Garda Nuala Gibson to question the farmer further. He couldn't provide an alibi for the time of the murder, and then during our continued questioning, he broke down and confessed."

"Just like that, he confessed?" Starrett said.

"Well, obviously it wasn't *just* like that, was it, Garda Browne? Tell us how your questioning of the suspect went?" Newton Cunningham asked, a little concern now evident in his voice.

"Well, let's see," Browne said, a little flustered.

"OK," Gibson interrupted, saving Browne further discomfiture, "it was a little unusual, I'll grant you, but when we went down to the farm, we were told he'd been waiting for us, and he was sitting through in the sitting room. We went into the room. We chatted for a while. He seemed very distracted. We asked him what he was doing at the time of the murder; he said he couldn't remember. Then he stopped answering our questions; it was as if we weren't there."

"Yes, yes, that's it," Browne said, getting his flow back again. "He wouldn't answer us. He kept looking into the fire as though we weren't even there. I decided to push it a bit. I told him we'd proof that he'd been in the courtyard."

"Then," Gibson continued, "he seemed to snap out of his mood, and he said, 'Proof, what proof do you have?'"

"I told him that I found the chocolate wrapper stuffed into the wall. I also told a little fib," Browne admitted as the major raised his dark eyebrows. "Well, it wasn't so much of a fib as it was a bluff. I told him that his fingerprints had been found on the wrapper, so I asked him once again if he'd been down in the courtyard, previous to the discovery of the body, and he said," Browne at this point pulled out his notebook and quoted directly Liam Sweeney's words, "'Yes, Garda, I have been in the courtyard you speak about. I left my son's remains there.'"

"Those were his exact words?" the major asked. Starrett felt the question was more for his benefit than the major's.

"Yes," Browne continued. "I cautioned him and asked him if he had anything else he wanted to tell us, and he said," and Browne dropped to a much quieter voice as he read from his notes once more, "he said, 'Look no further, Garda Browne. You've found your man.' I wanted to take his full confession there and then, but Garda

Gibson very wisely advised me that we should bring him down here for further questioning and arrest. That's exactly what he said, Inspector Starrett: 'Look no further, Garda Browne. You've found your man.' Can I assist you in questioning, sir?"

"There'll be no further questioning tonight," Starrett said solemnly.

"But, sir, he's ready to give us a full confession," Browne protested.

"We don't want his solicitor claiming we got a confession under duress after the poor man has been without sleep since his son died."

The major nodded his approval.

"Garda Gibson, can you rustle the poor man up a bit of super; some sandwiches or something and a mug of tea?" Starrett asked, standing up to signify that the meeting was over. "We'll take this up again in the morning, but well done both of you," and here he was looking directly at Gibson. "You both conducted proceedings in the proper manner, thank you. Garda Browne, you and I will continue the questioning of the suspect at 9.00 in the morning. Please make sure his solicitor is present. Garda Gibson, will you please go up to the farm and reassure Colette Sweeney that Liam is with me and he's . . ."

"A suspect?" Browne ventured.

". . . he's helping me with the case," Starrett concluded, with such an air of finality that it was left there.

And then Casey interrupted to ask if he could have a moment with Starrett.

"I've managed to track down the cousins, sir," he began as soon as Browne, Gibson and the major had left Starrett's office. "Sorry it's taken so long."

"Not to worry, Francis; better late than never," Starrett replied, moving his brain into yet another gear.

"Well, maybe not," Casey replied, opening his file. "I'd left lots of messages for Beatrice Hewson – she's the sister in the Sweeney cousins."

"Yes?" Starrett nudged.

"She moved to Dublin in the eighties, married a member of a rock group who was a tax exile there at the time. They've since divorced, although she claims she did okay out of it. She married again, has one son, and she runs a wee bistro out in Dún Laoghaire. Anyway, she said she hasn't been to Donegal for over fifteen years. She claimed she has neither the time nor the inclination for a visit. Her brother Dave moved to America around the same time she moved to Dublin. She's been over to see him a few times, but he's never been back to Ireland. Lawrence was in some bizarre accident in London a few years ago, and he's been hospitalised ever since. Adam, now Adam is a different matter entirely."

"Y-e-s?" Starrett replied, his ears picking up for the first time in the conversation.

"It appears that Adam Sweeney is in Belfast . . ."

"Y-e-s?"

"*And* a member of the Police Force Northern Ireland."

Starrett was going through various possibilities, starting with, *Well, a member of the police force is hardly going to be involved in a murder.* Which gave way to, *Well, it wouldn't be totally out of the question.*

And Starrett was working on that arc when Casey interrupted his superior's thread and burst his balloon with, "And he was working on a case all Monday night through Tuesday morning."

As Starrett wandered around his house in the early hours of the morning, he tried to get a fix on things. He was much too wired to the moon for sleep. The thing keeping him awake, however, was not the most recent development in the Joe Sweeney case, but Maggie Keane's revelation. He wondered if this preoccupation was in fact the real reason why he'd decided to delay the questioning of Liam Sweeney until the morning.

He kept coming back to his immature actions of over two decades ago. Yes, Maggie claimed she'd forgiven him, said she'd moved on, citing as compensation the relationship with Niall and the children that relationship bore. But there was no way Starrett could ignore the fact that he'd most certainly behaved like a proper wee shit on that occasion. He clearly wasn't proud of his behaviour. Not having the guts to tell her he was leaving Ramelton to be instructed in the priesthood was one thing, but taking her virginity the night before he left? Well, if Moya was his daughter and someone behaved with her in such a manner, then Starrett knew at the very least he'd feel compelled to chin the culprit.

He hadn't wanted to make a fuss all those years ago just as he was about to leave. He wanted to keep everything rosy in their wee garden of bliss. Still, to make love with her, knowing that the following morning he was walking out of her life for ever, was way out of order and certainly out of character, he felt. Certainly, the very least you'd have to say is that, it wasn't the most perfect way to commence a spiritual calling.

She claimed she'd seduced him. That wasn't Starrett's memory, but then his memory was tainted with twenty years of guilt.

But even if she had instigated their sexual union, how could he have possibly allowed it to happen? He didn't consider himself to be a saint, but he did possess some morals, he felt. He couldn't remember sitting down and considering all of the facts of what was right and what was wrong before making those two monumental decisions. He'd decided that he was going to follow a calling and become a priest, so he made plans accordingly. No matter how it happened, when he was presented with an opportunity to take his relationship with a teenage Maggie to a more intimate level, he didn't think, *As I'm leaving in the morning, I shouldn't really be doing this.*

He wondered if right and wrong only come into consideration with hindsight. He wondered if we all, quite simply, behave as we want to behave, and then later there might, or might not, be consequences to pay? He fell asleep wondering how far down that particular slippery slope one had to slide before one broke the law or even, as with his current case, took someone's life.

That was part of the puzzle that had always troubled Starrett. How can one human possibly take another's life? It was probably the subject he thought of most. He felt if he could just understand the mind-set of murderers, then he might, just might, be better equipped for catching them.

As his mind closed down for the night, he wondered if that might be it; that murderers didn't have a line they crossed. The line didn't appear until later, when others, such as the gardaí, considered what was right and what was wrong. Perhaps, he pondered, we are all capable of doubtable deeds, and then afterwards someone had to decide if they were right or if they were wrong.

Friday: 29 August 2008

Chapter Thirty-Eight

Starrett was at his desk in Tower House by 7.00 A.M. He avoided thinking about Liam Sweeney and what he might or might not admit to when questioned later.

Instead, he cleared his head totally of the case by thinking about Joe Keane, who was really, in effect, Joe Starrett. He wondered about how their relationship might develop once Joe knew Starrett was his father. Would he resent him for his late teenage actions and want to have nothing more to do with him? Would he be too preoccupied with his own life to even think about Starrett, let alone consider a place for him in his busy life? And then, there were Maggie's two other daughters. How would they feel about Starrett? More importantly, how would they feel about the fact that Joe had turned out to be only their half-brother?

There is a lot to be said, Starrett thought, *for leaving things as they are.*

The problem with that, as Starrett well knew, was that nothing in this world stayed the same. If he could just accept this, he'd be able to enjoy his life better, instead of wishing for better, older times and fearing the road ahead. Starrett eased up on giving himself a hard time, because he knew that he, pretty much, had come around to enjoying living in the present. Yes, he'd like his parents to be around for longer than they were going to be, and he felt guilty about not spending more time with them. And yes, he'd like to avoid having to work with people like Romany Browne, because people like him had a habit of upsetting the equilibrium. But he knew, and was thankful for the fact, that he woke up each day hungry for the day and what curve balls it might throw at him.

While he was on the upswing, he considered Maggie Keane and how her revelation would affect their reviving relationship. Her admitting that Starrett was the father of her oldest child surely must put him in a position of – how was it Moya put it – a friend with benefits?

That brought a smile to his face, a smile that quickly disappeared the moment he thought of the other Joe currently on his radar – Joe Sweeney.

Then, in light of Maggie's news, he thought of Colette Sweeney. She too had brought another man's child into a marriage.

Starrett wondered why he was still considering Thomas Sweeney so intently. Surely there was no need to; Liam had admitted he had murdered his youngest son.

Maybe it was just the budding seeds of fatherhood, but Starrett was having a hard time with this fact.

He went upstairs to the crime room and looked at the notes and photos of the crime scene on the notice board. Joe Sweeney, even in the greyness of death, looked as though he'd met a peaceful end. Starrett unlocked the evidence cupboard and searched through the transparent evidence bags until he found the one containing the Cadbury's Tiffin wrapper. He examined it closely and discovered what looked like an individual number stamped on the back of the wrapping paper in the "Best before" box, which was located just below the bar code.

02 2009

_ 10072 (15

He checked and rechecked the series of numbers and eventually wrote them down in his notebook:

Starrett also took out the call log sheet for Joe Sweeney's mobile phone.

He studied them closely:

1. 09.20 to McGinleys' farm
2. 09.47 to Toals' farm
3. 09.50 from his sister
4. 09.56 to Harvey's Point Hotel
5. 11.01 from Breda Roche
6. 11.03 to Breda Roche
7. 11.20 to *The Donegal News*
8. 11.23 to Highland Radio
9. 12.47 to his sister
10. 14.04 to Whoriskey's in Ramelton
11. 14.07 to Rathmullan House Hotel
12. 14.09 to Frewin Guest House
13. 14.15 from the Sweeney farm
14. 16.06 from Breda Roche
15. 16.09 from *The Donegal News*
16. 16.11 from Toals' farm
17. 16.17 from Breda Roche
18. 16.21 from McGinleys' farm
19. 16.22 from Flynns' farm
20. 16.27 from Breda Roche
21. 16.43 from McKeons' farm
22. 16.51 from Highland Radio
23. 17.08 from Breda Roche
24. 02.43 from his sister

He noted the early morning call from Teresa to her brother on the day he died. Mona's claim that Joe and Teresa were very, very tight must have been true if she took the trouble to ring him at that time of the night, well more like morning, in the middle of her midnight party.

He noted the calls from Breda, Joe's girlfriend. Starrett didn't know about Joe's feelings towards his girlfriend, but he was quite convinced that Breda wasn't really in love with Joe. Was it just a relationship of convenience for her, or a way of getting closer to Teresa, whom she'd openly admitted to having feelings for? Or, could her attachment be more mercenary; i.e., yet another person hoping to make a connection to the Sweeney farm and all the precious land that went with it?

He returned the evidence to its cupboard, carefully locked the door and studied the notes on the notice board once again.

Mona Sweeney had pushed her husband about whether or not he had discussed something with his father. What had Tom Sweeney wanted to discuss with his father? Maeve Boyce had in turn asked Ryan if he'd had *his* chat with his dad. What had Ryan needed to talk to his father about that was so important even his girlfriend knew about it?

Was there a chance that either of these potential conversations had anything to do with Liam murdering his son?

There was that phrase again that was now troubling Starrett so much: "murdering his son"!

Starrett noted the time; it was 8.55, and it would soon be time for that particular mystery to be revealed.

Chapter Thirty-Nine

Novice Garda Romany Browne was chomping at the bit outside the basement interview room when Starrett strolled down on the dot of 9 o'clock. With him was Russell Leslie, the Sweeney family solicitor. Starrett nodded to Browne to fetch Sweeney from one of the three small holding cells near by. The cells were not particularly comfortable and tended to get overcrowded at the weekends.

"Starrett," Sweeney offered by way of greeting as he was led in to the interview room, which was close to being subterranean. The small windows along the top of the longest wall were eighteen inches deep at the most, and you could see only the wheels of cars, and the legs of dogs or people, up to their knees. Starrett's preference for viewing the gathering media pack was knee height at the very most. The room had been used mostly for storage in the early days, but when the garda authorities had insisted on "comfortable, ventilated, dedicated interview rooms," Starrett's predecessor had merely cleared all the contents into various cupboards around the station house (where much of it remained until this day), given it a lick of paint and used self-adhesive letters which spelt out, "INTERVIEW ROOM." Over the years the "R" had dropped off, only to be replaced by some bright spark writing two matching, size and style, letters in felt-tip pen. When it came to complying with the authorities' requirements of "comfortable, ventilated and dedicated interview room," then Tower House garda station qualified on only one account, i.e. the word "room." The replacement letters "GL" seemed to catch the mood of the location much better, so Starrett hadn't asked for them to be removed.

"Liam," Starrett said in an exchange greeting. Starrett knew in Donegal, particularly on farms, people could go for entire days uttering nothing but single word statements. Sometimes "Liam" would suffice for, "Hello, Liam, how are you doing?" Another time "Liam" could be translated as, "Liam, could you come over here and help me please," or "Liam, it's time to fetch the cows for milking." It all really depended on the time of the day, the tone of the delivery and the nod of the head.

Starrett hoped this wasn't going to be a monosyllabic interview.

Without any preamble, he nodded for Liam Sweeney, his solicitor and Romany Browne to take the dirty, grey plastic bucket seats on either side of the old wooden table; Sweeney sat on one side with his solicitor, and Browne and Starrett sat on the opposite side.

Starrett switched on the recorder and announced the date, time and the names of those present.

"Mr Sweeney, will you please tell the inspector here what you told me yesterday?" Browne started keenly.

"Hauld your horses, hauld your horses," Starrett declared. "Sure, the sleep is not long from our eyes; let's just backtrack a wee bit here. I think we need to warm up a little before we start racing away with ourselves."

Browne slumped back into the chair so far so that he nearly slid off it altogether.

"Right, Liam," Starrett started again in another gear, "let's go back to Monday past." Starrett took out his notebook and, leaning over the table, peered over the pages. "Right, here we are. When I first interviewed you on this sad affair, you told me the last time you saw Joe was at an early lunch on the Monday. You thought he'd been out and about on his rounds on the Tuesday morning before you'd a chance to see him."

Liam Sweeney grimaced and slid around uncomfortably in his chair.

"Yes, Starrett, I felt bad about lying to you."

"A lie, yes," Starrett declared. "Of course you realise that in my line of work people lie to me mostly for two reasons. The first reason for a lie is so a criminal can distract a detective from the truth. The second type of lie is told so the criminal can distance themselves from the crime."

"Starrett, look, I did it. Can we just stop this auld song and dance and get on with it?"

Sweeney's solicitor, who'd been mid-sip of his coffee, nearly choked at his client's declaration.

"OK, Liam, OK, there'll be time enough for all of that," Starrett sighed, "but for now, why don't we just start at the beginning?"

"Right so," Liam offered half-heartedly, "the beginning?"

"Yes, you know, in the first place, why did you feel the need to . . ."

"Well, with this co-operative thing Joe was setting up and all, sure, wasn't that just a communist's way of dividing up my grandfather's farm? I couldn't let that happen, Starrett."

"But I thought that was Joe's ingenious way of not only keeping the farm together, but also a way of keeping his brothers and sister involved at the same time."

"Well, that was the theory. At least the way it was described to me, but then I discovered that Mona was busy drawing up papers to make it all legal. But in those papers she was proposing that at any time a majority of the principals – Thomas, Ryan, Teresa and Joseph – could implement any changes they wanted."

"Including selling off parcels of land?" Browne prompted hopefully.

"Including selling off parcels, if not all, of the land," Liam Sweeney confirmed.

"And how exactly did you discover this vital piece of information?" Starrett asked.

"All I'll say is that one of my children told me."

Starrett reckoned that must have been what Ryan wanted to talk to his father about on the day of the birthday party.

"But surely Joe, who was after all in the driving seat, wouldn't have agreed to a change like that and would have knocked it back."

"Starrett, my youngest son," Sweeney began with a great swell of apparent pride, "was first and foremost a farmer. He didn't really have time for all of this legal mumbo jumbo, and he really just wanted this sorted. He wanted to get on with what he loved most, farming. He loved his mother and he didn't want her to witness all of her children squabbling all the time over the farm. A man will do a lot for his wi . . . for his mother, Starrett. But Joe didn't really want to run the distribution company – he was hoping one of the others would have taken over that side of stuff. He was still hoping we'd all be one big happy family again."

"I see what you're saying, but, Liam, they're all blood; surely one of them would have stepped up and pointed out to Joe what was going on."

Liam looked Starrett dead in the eye and said, "One of them told me, Starrett. As far as I was concerned, that was their way of stepping up and saving Joe."

Starrett thought, *But Ryan obviously failed.*

"So what did you do about this?"

"At lunch on Monday, I told Joe I needed to speak to him, but away from the farm. He had stuff he needed to do on the distribution side, so we agreed to meet up early on Monday evening."

"Where?"

"Sorry?"

"Where had you agreed to meet up with Joe, Liam?"

"At the warehouse?" Browne suggested hopefully.

"The gardaí are leading the witness," the solicitor said for the benefit of the recorder.

"Don't be daft, Leslie," Liam laughed. "We're not in court. He's only trying to be helpful, aren't you, lad?"

"Liam, you were about to tell us where you met up," Starrett said as he glared at Browne.

"We went for a drive," Liam offered, after a few moments, as though thinking back to the time. "I picked him up and we went for a drive along the Swilly."

"Had you made a decision at that time . . ." Starrett hesitated; there was no nice way to put what he wanted to say.

"Had I made a decision to kill my own son?" Sweeney said, woefully.

Starrett nodded slowly.

"Ach, my first reaction would be to say, 'No, I didn't.' But then I have to look back and consider my actions. I'd taken some of Teresa's prescription Flunitrazepam sleeping pills – she's so hyper she has trouble sleeping unless she takes them. There are always some of hers in our medicine chest. So even though I may not have admitted as much to myself, I had something in the back of my mind."

The fact that Liam had mentioned Flunitrazepam, also known as Rohypnol or roofies, was a big admission to Starrett. The fact that traces of the same had been discovered in Joe's blood wasn't public knowledge yet, even to the family. Starrett grew very depressed by Liam Sweeney's admission. Until that point, he'd figured Romany Browne had got it all wrong, and he'd figured he'd get to the bottom of the misunderstanding in his current questioning. He wondered how his father, a friend of Liam's, would take this drastic news. The media pack, desperate for something, anything really, would most certainly have a field day when this news broke. Starrett could feel himself slumping into his chair, which was, by the second, growing increasingly more uncomfortable.

Browne must have picked up on Starrett's uneasiness, because he seemed to grow in confidence again.

"So, you picked your son up," Starrett began again. "Where would that have been?"

"The end of our lane."

"Did you ring him on his mobile to organise it?" Starrett asked, half-heartedly working on a trap. He already knew that Joe hadn't received any calls on his mobile from his father.

"No, I just met him there. I was on the way out looking for him, and he was on the way back in to the farm. He parked up outside John Lea's cottage and hopped into my van and off we went."

"Did you stop anywhere?" Browne asked, taking up the thread again.

"No, we drove out by Whale Head. We both loved it out there. I took him out there a lot as a boy. We parked up. I told him I was aware of what was going on, you know, the paperwork Mona was drawing up for the farm, and do you know what he said?"

"What?" Browne felt compelled to ask.

"He said, 'Dad, you've had your day, and now it's time for the rest of us, and this is how we want to do it.' I told him that Mona still wanted to sell the farm and that he was gifting it to her. He said he was tired of all the fighting. He said, 'What's the use of having a family if all we're going to do is fight with each other?' I told him not to confuse conflict with greed. I told him Mona, like all solicitors, had a way of grinding people down to get exactly what she wanted in the end. He said he just wanted to have a peaceful life and be a farmer again. He said that was all he was interested in and that he and Teresa and Thomas and Ryan were in agreement. I told him they couldn't all be in agreement if one of them had tipped me off. He said he knew I was talking about Ryan and went on to explain that Ryan and Maeve had so much money it didn't matter to them. I tried to explain what the farm had meant to me and my father and my grandfather. I tried to explain to him that I just couldn't let Mona do what she wanted to do and sell off the farm. He said he wasn't like me, and he didn't have the patience for the politics of the farm, and that besides, it was too late, he'd already approved Mona's plans, but I wasn't to worry. She wouldn't allow the farm to be sold off either. I asked him if they were his last words on the matter. He said they were, and so after a few minutes had passed I very calmly and casually offered him a drink out of a small bottle of mineral water, which I'd already contaminated with Teresa's medication. She loved this particular medication because there was no smell or taste to it; she's too sensitive for her own good is our Teresa. We drove around for ages and eventually he passed out.

"It was getting quite late. I realised what I had to do, but I didn't know how to do it. I went through the various ways to end his life, and eventually I realised that drowning him was going to be the most humane for all concerned. So, around three o'clock in the morning, I placed him in the water down by Ball Green. It was quite difficult because the tide was out, so I had to carry him over the wetlands. Eventually I found a spot with a couple of feet of water, and I placed him in it face down, and I held on to his hand. There were a few violent spasms, but eventually he grew motionless and the bubbles stopped coming to the surface. I sat there with him in the water for another hour or so. I have no idea really when he stopped breathing; I lost all sense of time.

"I took him back to the van and drove around for a while, trying to figure out what to do with the body. It was like I'd solved one of my problems – the potential dissolution of the farm – but created several more in its place. I thought that when I'd fixed my main problem, I'd be able to enjoy peace again. But life's not like that, is it, Starrett? There's always something to bug you. Now I had a dead body. I had a wife who was soon going to be grieving the loss of her youngest. I'd have an actual stampede from Mona, Thomas, Teresa and Sheila as to who was now going to get the farm. I knew, for Colette's sake, I needed to place Joe's remains somewhere they could be found. It would destroy my wife if he just disappeared off the face of the earth. So I drove into town and placed him in the courtyard where he was found."

Liam hung his head as he stopped talking.

Romany Browne looked extremely pleased with himself.

Russell Leslie looked like he'd heard too many clients' confessions to be shocked at even one as bizarre as Liam's.

Starrett waited for Liam to continue, but the farmer remained silent.

"Then what did you do?" Starrett asked.

"Then what did I do? I drove back to the farm."

"You did nothing else?" Starrett continued, as both the solicitor and Browne looked at him like they were looking for a clue as to where he was going with this.

"I poured myself a stiff drink before I went to bed."

"You did nothing else in the courtyard before you left your son's remains?"

"Nothing," Liam replied confidently, but looking confused.

"Right," Starrett said, standing up, "we'll have your statement typed up and presented to you and your solicitor for signing. This interview is terminated at 10.23 on Friday, 29 August 2008."

Inspector Starrett left the interview room with a face like thunder and without acknowledging any of those present.

Chapter Forty

S tarrett returned to his office, made a few notes in his murder book and buzzed through to Sergeant Packie Garvey to meet him by his car in front of Tower House. He needed to go to Letterkenny, and he didn't trust himself to drive. On top of which, wasn't it nearly time for another of those precious cigarettes?

The thought of Maggie Keane's minty fresh white teeth was enough to help Starrett resist the temptation of a white coffin nail, well, at least that was until they'd passed the Silver Tassie hotel. Fortunately for Starrett, just as he was about to succumb to the temptation, he benefited from a different distraction.

A "*massive*" (as all the adverts on Highland Radio claim) Audi 4×4 pulled out into the right filter lane and overtook Starrett and Garvey at a fierce rate, very nearly driving straight into a packed Ford family car pulling out of the Silver Tassie in the direction of Ramelton. A matter of a split second later and the carelessnees of the Audi driver would have resulted in at least seven fatalities.

"Catch up with that eejit and pull him over," Starrett said, the pull of the nicotine wafting in their wake like a disintegrating Players' plume of smoke.

The smirk in a pinstripe suit who exited the Audi half a mile later charged straight in the direction of Garvey and accosted him before he'd been fully able to get out of his seat.

"What the fu . . ." he screeched, his face going a beetroot red to match his braces.

His face was just six inches from Garvey's chin when he

noticed the garda uniform. Starrett, by this time, had sprinted around to Garvey's aid and grabbed a fistful of red ear and tugged away with all of his might, leading the reckless driver to the hedge side of the car. Even while sheltered by the safety of his car, Starrett didn't let go of the ear. If anything, he tugged on it more fiercely, the memory of the hapless family in the other car fresh in his mind.

The offender was now nearly bent over double.

"What the fu . . ." he started, once again. Starrett tightened his grip. He now led him by his ear to the back of the Audi 4×4.

"I wasn't giving due cause," he protested.

"Well, unfortunately for you, this is not LA, and see this here," Starrett said in a very controlled voice, "your off-side brake light is not working. That's all the fecking *due cause* I need."

The driver stood up, Starrett loosened his grip a little, the driver kicked his car just under the malfunctioning light, and it miraculously sprang to life, glowing in a colour extremely close in colour to the driver's burning ear.

"Good trick," Starrett said, as he trailed his prisoner around to the front of his car. "Now perhaps you might want to try kicking the windscreen, just by the tax disc, and see if you can fix that as well by bringing it up to date."

Garvey wrote up the offence and led the driver off the dangerous main road and on to the forecourt of a petrol station just outside of Letterkenny. He confiscated his keys and waited until a taxi could be summoned to take him to his destination.

Much to Garvey's concern, Starrett now insisted on taking over the wheel of his own BMW. But apart from Starrett ranting on about, "These people need to be taken off the roads permanently," and "Of course Yoko Ono was responsible for the Beatles' split," the remainder of their journey to Letterkenny General Hospital was relatively sane.

"Ah, an inspector calls," Dr Samantha Aljoe declared as she caught sight of Starrett standing outside her office, both his hands the same length. "I hear that new novice of yours is turning out to be handy in more ways than one," she said, winking at Starrett.

Starrett hoped Garvey hadn't caught the wink.

"Adhemar," she said, calling into the adjoining office, "will you take Sergeant Garvey down with you to the canteen and fetch us four cups of coffee and a few Kit Kats, although none for me. I have to watch my figure," she added, sensuously patting her tummy.

Starrett was distracted by the very same perfect "10" figure as she led him into her office, closing the door behind them. The office was so small he had to squeeze past her to take her up on her offer of the seat beside her desk. Dr Aljoe appeared to enjoy Starrett's discomfort as he had to squeeze past her. She refused to step aside to let him past and said, "Starrett, we haven't been this close since our famous night down on Rathmullan beach."

"Bejeepers, Samantha, whatever will we do with you?"

"I've quite a few suggestions I'd like you to take into consideration," she said as she took a couple of successive bites out of her Granny Smith apple.

Starrett figured women never looked pretty when they were eating apples; they are, however, quite refined and genteel while nibbling on a bit of chocolate. Could this have anything to do with the fact that the apple is obviously healthy, so they don't have to worry about how they look as they munch away. Chocolate, on the other hand, is allegedly bad for the figure. So, perhaps while eating the latter they try to distract observers from their hit of sugar.

Starrett smiled at both his thought and her observation. "Sure, you'll have no need for me now with your new toy boy in tow," he offered.

"Could that be just the slightest hint of jealousy I'm picking up on, Starrett?" she said very seductively. "Besides, I'd go for experience over reckless enthusiasm any time."

Starrett knew it was just her way of getting through another day being involved with death. He sat down in the chair offered and she squeezed herself next to him. Starrett observed that with the shortness of her skirt and the fact that her hospital gown was opened, she'd just pulled off a near impossible feat in retaining her modesty at all times during the complicated manoeuvre, which, in spite of all of her flirting, said a lot about the real her to Starrett.

"How's Mrs Keane, Starrett?"

Starrett blew the breath of frustration through his lips very slowly and deliberately.

Where to start? If, indeed, to start at all?

"Well, you know, Samantha, the thing is this: a long, long time ago when we were younger, we both were in love. But now we're so much older, things are so very much more complicated," he said. These were not the words he started out to say, but he felt safer, not to mention most respectful of Maggie, to be more general than specific about their personal details.

"Does that mean it's not going to work out?" she said with genuine compassion and sadness.

"Maybe I made it sound that way. I assure you I didn't mean to. It's more that I really want it to work out, but I wonder if I've really got the proper experience to make it work."

"You know, Starrett, I think in these situations, sometimes you just have to forget all the baggage and consider, 'Is this what we both want?' and if the answer is yes, then you just have to get on with it and let all of the other stuff come out in the wash."

Starrett stopped to consider her advice.

"What if other people are involved?" he asked.

"You mean her children?"

"Yes, I suppose I do."

"How many children has she?"

"Three. There's Joe who's at Queen's, he's around twenty, and Moya and Katie, who are each ten, one just ten and the other nearly eleven."

"I'd say all the more reason for the mum to be happy. And what does Maggie say in all of this?"

"I think she seems to be OK with it, but it's hard to say."

"For goodness sake, Starrett, do you ever talk to the woman at all?"

"Well, yes."

"About this stuff?"

"Well, no, not really," Starrett confessed.

"Where's your head at, man? Talk to her. There are no short cuts to a woman's heart."

"Right, I will so," Starrett said, resolving to do that very thing the next time he met up with Maggie. He rose to leave as if he'd been attending a doctor's surgery and he'd been given his diagnosis and the necessary prescription.

"Ah, Starrett," Dr Aljoe said, raising her right eyebrow.

"Yes?"

"Can I assume you came to me for something other than advice on your love life?"

"Oh, bejeepers, you're right, Samantha," Starrett said through a wide smile as he sat down again. "What I came to see you about was Joe Sweeney."

"That makes me feel a lot more comfortable."

"Remember when we were in the courtyard with his remains. We discovered that although his clothes were still damp, it looked like his hair had been dried?"

"As if he'd just come out of the swimming pool?"

"Yes."

"Of course I remember."

"Well, when you examined the body back here, did you find any reason why that might have happened?" he asked hopefully.

"Yes, as it happens I did," she said, rising and leaning across Starrett to a cupboard above his left shoulder. It was at that moment that Packie Garvey and Adhemar McIvor entered, each with a cup of coffee in each hand and unable to knock on the door.

Starrett, startled, rose, and as he did so bumped into Aljoe, who had frozen in mid-air above him. They both collapsed in a heap into Starrett's chair.

"*Pour l'amour du ciel prenez une chambre,*" her assistant hissed dismissively under his breath.

Aljoe dusted herself off and smoothed out her skirt as she sat back in her seat again, but with the precious evidence bag she'd retrieved from the cupboard above Starrett's head. She took a large gulp of her coffee, told McIvor to return to his research, and said to Starrett and Garvey, "I found these in Joe Sweeney's hair."

Starrett examined several small, aqua-coloured particles closely through the transparent bag.

"What are these?" he asked as he passed the bag on to Garvey for a look.

"They're the particles from the towel which was used to dry his hair, Starrett."

Chapter Forty-One

"Time to visit a member of the Sweeney clan I think," Starrett said when they were back in his BMW.

"And which member would that be?" Packie asked as they headed up the steep hill of the Ramelton Road.

"Today, Mathew, I'm going to see Ryan Sweeney," Starrett said to the dashboard. Luckily enough, Packie's television show references were as bizarre as Starrett's, and he too was able to transpose the "see" to the original "be."

"Packie, tell me this . . . as you give me one of my remaining Players."

Garvey raised his eyebrows but knew better than to argue with his senior, particularly on the latter point.

"Yes?" he said.

"Have you ever noticed that innocent people always look nervous while in custody?"

"Well, kind of," Garvey replied, running through his memories.

"Why do you think that is, Packie?"

"People are scared of the gardaí," Garvey claimed, but then added, "but not as much as they used to be."

"That's a different kind of look, Packie; I'm thinking more that innocent people realise that with just the slightest twist of fate – not to mention bad luck – they may suffer the gravest miscarriage of justice and end up permanently in custody. Guilty people, on the other hand, don't share this look of frightened guilt."

"Are you suggesting Liam looks guilty, therefore he's innocent?"

"Lying, Packie, that's what we have to be very concerned about," Starrett said expansively as he lit up. He crunched his eyes up as the cigarette smoke made them water before adding in a strained voice, "Now what we have to examine is why do people lie."

"But we're not *usually* concerned about considering that people who confess might be lying."

"Could that be because perhaps we just want our lives to be easier?"

"Are you telling me you think Liam Sweeney, who has confessed to the murder of his son, is in fact lying?"

"I'm telling you it's too early to say. I'm telling you we haven't collected all the available evidence as of yet, and until such time as we do, we should be very careful about jumping to conclusions."

"Inspector, surely we could never be accused of jumping to conclusions when the person in question puts his hand up and says, 'I did it. It was me?'"

"Perhaps not, Packie, but nevertheless, we still owe it to the victim to conclude our investigation and produce evidence to back up Liam's confession."

They drove on in silence, Packie deep in thought and Starrett deeply inhaling.

The drive into Coylin Court reminded Starrett of how he'd imagined cavalry forts should have looked like when he was growing up playing cowboys and indians. He half-expected Randolph Scott, in his calf-leather boots and cavalry uniform, to step out of the first house by the fort's gates and greet him. The houses were as stylish as any modern house in the county and, at least for now, enjoyed enough breathing space from each other.

Ryan Sweeney and Maeve Boyce's house was the last one on the far right-hand side, which meant it was ideally positioned to enjoy beautiful panoramic views of Ramelton.

From the state of Ryan's garden and surrounding hedges and fences, Starrett concluded that Ryan's presence wasn't anywhere near as consistent as some of his neighbours'. The inside had a similarly unlived-in, holiday-home kind of feeling and smell. The house was new, so new in fact the snag list was still attached to the fridge door by a Wallace and Gromit magnet. They were already up to item 37: "Hot water power is very weak." Maeve was scooting around the house lighting scented candles as he and Garvey were greeted by an unshaven Ryan. Sweeney's pretty boy looks weren't suited to designer stubble. Starrett wondered where one would go to buy designer stubble; did some people make a living growing it for others? At one end of the airy, bright kitchen/dining area into which they were shown was the functional kitchen cum preparation area with its Ikea units and worktops and basic essential utensils, and at the other end was a circular pine table and six matching chairs. For all the newness, space and magnificent views, Starrett felt that neither Ryan nor Maeve embraced this house as their home.

Starrett reckoned Miss Boyce's come-to-bed eyes were working big time on Sergeant Garvey. Even though she and Ryan were just hanging around their house, she was perfectly made up and dressed to the nines.

Starrett noted that Ryan and Maeve were very comfortable with each other, although they didn't feel the need to be all over each other to prove that they were a couple. She ran her hand gently along Ryan's back as she passed him en route to the sink to fill up the kettle. She stood behind him massaging his shoulders in a very functional and non-sexual way as they talked and waited for the kettle to boil.

"Starrett, Maeve was down in Whoriskey's this morning, and this news we're hearing – it's all over town apparently –" Ryan said, "is that my old man's involved in this mess?"

Garvey, who was sitting opposite Starrett, looked directly at his superior, with a look on his craggy face, which seemed to say, *How are you going to get out of this one?*

Maeve, who'd started the ritual of tea preparation, came over to Ryan and put her arm around his shoulder, as if preparing for drastic news.

"The only thing I've ever learnt in the auld garda work, Ryan, is that it doesn't matter if you're in a hundred yard dash or a marathon, the only thing you never do is to stop running before you cross that finishing line."

"Don't flannel me; is my dad involved?"

"Ryan, the only thing I can tell you at this point with a 100 per cent certainty is that we don't know."

"But surely . . ."

"Listen to what I'm saying, Ryan: We don't know!"

"Is he a suspect?"

"Ryan, I'm here to ask you and Maeve some questions," Starrett said patiently.

"Meaning?" Ryan persisted, as Maeve returned her attention to the tea.

"Meaning exactly that, Ryan: we are still working on our investigation. Yes, I questioned your father, and we've also questioned your brother and your sister, and your sister-in-law and all the various partners. We will continue to do so until such time as we solve this crime. All I can tell you is that as of now, at . . ." Starrett paused to check the clock on the wall by a framed copy of a Paul Brady poster, ". . . 3.37 on Friday, the twenty-ninth of August, we have not yet solved this crime."

As Maeve delivered cups, tea things and a large, antique blue and white patterned plate with three wee Bakewells, several Penguins (the chocolate unfeathered species) and a couple of Kit Kats, she said, "You said you had some questions for us?"

"Yes," Starrett replied, momentarily distracted by the fact that if he were to be the perfect gentleman and let the others around the table choose first, then there was an even chance he was going to miss out on the Bakewells. "Ryan, on Tuesday, up at the farm when Maeve arrived, apparently she asked you if you'd spoken to your father yet?"

"Yes?" Ryan replied.

"What was it about?"

"Liam had been upset for a time . . ." Maeve started.

". . . and I thought it must have had something to do with the farm and all the squabbling about splitting it up," Ryan finished.

"So, Ryan had an idea, which we had discussed, and Ryan was going to put it to his dad."

"OK," Starrett said. Everyone had started their tea but no one had made their move on the contents of the plate. "And what was this idea?"

"Right," Ryan said, looking at Maeve. "We both thought it was sad that someone like my father would work his entire life on the farm, all the time trying to create something which would live on after him, and then his children would grow up and move on and appear totally unconcerned about it."

"Apart from Joe," Maeve added.

"Apart from Joe," Ryan continued, "who was as committed, if not as ambitious, as my father. You see, my father wanted to create something, but Joe just wanted to farm the land. Anyway, my father gives the farm to Joe. Tom, well Mona mainly, is up in arms at this, as is Teresa. She doesn't work, as you know, so she's got an obvious need for money. Joe's idea that he would keep the land, but what the land produced would be owned and shared by all of us in a co-operative had one basic flaw. When he was doing the divvying up, he forgot to include our father."

Starrett nodded.

"Well, Maeve and I discussed this and, well, we're doing OK. Maeve is an only child and her family . . . well . . ."

"What Ryan is trying to say, Inspector," Maeve continued on her partner's behalf as she passed the plate with the goodies around, "is that my family were very, very well off and so we're looked after."

"So," Ryan went on, taking one of the Bakewell tarts, "we decided to give my father my share of the co-op."

"This way he's involved again, and more importantly he has a casting vote," Maeve said as Garvey took the second of the Bakewells.

"Yes, so we wanted to discuss it with my father before we told Teresa, Joe and Tom."

"But you didn't get a chance to discuss it with him, did you?" Starrett asked as he signalled to Maeve to take the last remaining Bakewell tart.

"It's got your name on it, Inspector," she said, and smiled as Starrett showed he needed no further encouragement. She returned to the main thread of the conversation: "Sadly, we didn't get to discuss it with Liam. It's obviously of no consequence now, but we're sure he would have appreciated it."

"Were you aware that Mona was in the process of drawing up paperwork for the co-operative?" Starrett asked, delaying his first bite until his tea had cooled down enough so he could enjoy both together.

"News to us," Ryan replied immediately. "Where did you get this information from?"

"Your father told us," Starrett replied and added, "He believed she was going to set it up so that a majority vote could settle any disputes."

"Including the selling of the land?" Maeve asked.

"Liam thought so," Starrett said.

"And did Joe know this?" Ryan asked.

"I don't know, but your father thought Mona would either get it through or had already got it through because Joe was so preoccupied with other issues."

"Surely for Mona to make this binding she would have needed Ryan's approval and signature as well," Maeve offered.

"Bejeepers now, that's a good point," Starrett said, "a very good point."

"Yes, of course, Maeve's correct," Ryan added, "which means Mona hadn't got it through. Teresa probably would have signed, and Thomas wouldn't have had a choice. Joe wouldn't have knowingly signed."

"I thought Teresa and Joe were very tight?" Starrett said.

"Yeah, they were when they were growing up," Ryan agreed, "but that was then, and this is business."

"Do you get on well with your sister yourself?" Packie asked.

"No," Maeve said when her partner hadn't replied.

"That's unfair, Maeve," Ryan protested. "We hardly ever see her."

Starrett found himself wondering about Maggie Keane and her three children. Would her son – Starrett corrected himself, would *their* son – Joe, ever say he didn't get on with one of his sisters, just because he hardly ever saw her?

"Do you think," he said, letting the sentence form as he said it, "there is a chance that Mona could have, or would have, for that matter, forged Joe's or your signature, just to get the paperwork processed?"

Ryan thought hard for a time. Maeve kept staring at him as though she didn't know how he might answer.

"I know that Mona would fight tooth and nail to get what she felt she was entitled to. I think that in certain instances, she might bend the law, but I very much doubt that she would break it so blatantly."

Starrett and Garvey said their goodbyes to Maeve Boyce and Ryan Sweeney beside her Volkswagen. They were heading up to the Sweeney farm to comfort Colette, while Starrett and Garvey headed for the badlands of the borderlands and the home of Mr and Mrs Thomas Sweeney and their two daughters.

Chapter Forty-Two

"**M**ona, Hey Mona, Hey Mona," Starrett sang in a whisper as he and Sergeant Garvey walked up to the front door, "*please,* stay out of my dreams."

"Sorry?" Garvey said in disbelief.

"Just a wee tune we used to sing when we were growing up."

Starrett knew and accepted that each and every one of us has to deal with our shortcomings on a daily basis. We're too fat, too thin, too tall, too short, too bald, got bumps where bumps never ought to be, or got no bumps where bumps most definitely ought to be. We've got acne, bad eyesight, bad breath, troubled breathing, limps, twitches and bad habits for ever and a day. Yes, and we all have to find a way to accept our personal foibles and deal with them. But Mona Sweeney was, Starrett reckoned, the first person he'd ever come across who seemed to positively celebrate all of her flaws and expensively dress them up to draw others' attention to them.

"Inspector Starrett and Sergeant Garvey. My husband is not around at the moment; can I be of any help to you?"

"Actually, Mrs Sweeney, it's you we've come to talk to, you and your daughter Bernadette."

"Oh, please call me Mona," she insisted, in better humour than Starrett had witnessed before, "Mrs Sweeney – and there's no offence meant to Colette here – but it makes me sound old and decrepit."

Starrett thanked his God that he hadn't been drinking soup at that point, for if he had been, his crisp white shirt might have developed a speedy tie-dyed look.

She shooed them into her big house and told them to go through to the kitchen. Starrett followed the black and white cat, which had grabbed the opportunity to slip between Mona's legs and skip into the house, to navigate the complicated route into the kitchen; cats always go straight to the cosiest and warmest room of the house.

Starrett started immediately, "Is it true you were drawing up paperwork for the Sweeney farm co-operative?"

"Ah, Liam's been spilling his guts. I hear he's been detained at Tower House."

"Liam, like all of the family, Mrs Sweeney, is helping us with our enquiries."

"If I'd a euro for every time I heard that turn of phrase," Mona started.

"You'd probably have enough money to buy the Sweeney farm yourself," Starrett offered acerbically.

"We seem to have gotten off on the wrong foot once again."

Starrett saw Garvey raise his eyebrows, but he was confident that if he was to get any valuable information from this hardened solicitor and seasoned manipulator, he was going to have to get her riled up a bit; take her out of her comfort zone.

"I always find it difficult to get off on the right foot when someone is already standing on it."

She seemed genuinely surprised by his aggression towards her, but still she managed to force a smile. Starrett pushed onwards.

"Look, Mona, if my information is correct, you downright lied to me about your involvement in these affairs. The least I'm going to have you on is obstruction of justice. I'm sure we'll be able to look at your conflict of interest as well. If I don't get anywhere on that front, I'm sure the Law Association will be very interested in your dealings."

"How on this earth is my representing the family in some private business in any way involved in the death of one of the principals?"

"Motive, Mona, motive," Starrett spat. "Where did you ever get the gall to take a beautiful, generous gesture, like Joe Sweeney wanting to take financial care of his brothers and sister, as a back door opportunity to try and wrestle the farm away from him?"

Mona hopped to her feet and desperately fought for words, but she was so angry that none would come.

"I know, I know, Mona, you *resemble* that remark. But really, Mona, please tell me, where does that action come from? I'm serious; I really need to know? What happened to all your childhood dreams? Do you not realise that our wildest deeds live on?"

Mona eventually managed to vocalise a word. "Out!" she screeched in a rant that would have displaced all the banshees of the borderlands. "Out!"

Starrett wondered if perhaps he'd gone a little too far.

"What the feck do you know about me, Starrett? Sure you're nothing but a tinpot garda inspector in a tinpot village. I don't need to justify one fecking thing to you or your likes."

"Town, Mona, town."

"What?" she shouted at the top of her voice, annoyed she'd been frustrated in her efforts while only at the beginning of her rant.

"Ramelton is a town, Mona. It's not a village, it's a town, and the people down there get very annoyed when you call it a village."

"Starrett," she said her voice now cracking, "what are you on?"

"OK, Mona, here's the thing. You're a solicitor; you must know the consequences; why didn't you tell me about this plan of yours at the beginning? Ryan didn't even know about it."

With "Ryan," Starrett had hit the key word right on the head.

Mona Sweeney sat down again and started rubbing her temples furiously with the fingers of each hand.

"Ryan Sweeney. You want to know where all of this comes from, well look no further, Inspector."

And? Starrett thought.

"This family owes me a lot, Starrett, and it all starts with Ryan; sweet-talking me into bed when I still had my looks and getting me to do stuff gratis for his father. And for what? Then he dumps me; he dumps me when the heiress Miss Maeve Boyce appears on the scene. He was mine, Starrett; he was meant to be with me. There is meant to be honour in our actions. All agreements don't need to be documented as contracts. In my father's day, Ryan would have been tarred and feathered. So don't accuse me of taking advantage of the Sweeney family. I've put my time in with them. I've accepted the consolation prize. I will admit to you, when all this came up, I didn't realise my husband wasn't born a Sweeney. How was I to know he wasn't next in line to the farm? He didn't even admit it to me when Liam started talking about giving the farm to Joe. I confronted Liam about it. I claimed it should be Thomas, as the eldest, who should get the farm. Liam said to me, sarkey as you like, 'He's not my eldest, dear.' Then Tom admitted he'd been deceiving me all these years and that Liam wasn't his father. He admitted that his mother had always said he'd never get the farm. But it *should* have been ours."

Mona paused, as if to let all of this sink in with Starrett. Before he'd a chance to comment, she continued, "So all I'm looking for is what I'm entitled to. Listen to me carefully now, Starrett: I've never broken the law in my life. I never will, but I will admit in this instance to using it to my own benefit, and that's because I'm entitled."

"OK, Mona," Starrett said as she ran out of steam, "tell me about this plan of yours. Who knew about it?"

"It was simple really. I just drew up the paperwork for Joe's co-operative. Nothing wrong, Starrett; I was merely protecting my husband's interests."

"But how did you manage to do it without Ryan's signature?" Starrett asked.

"I didn't, is the simple answer. Tom was meant to ask his father to approve the paperwork and try and get Liam to encourage Ryan to sign it. He didn't get a chance to discuss it; he left the paperwork for his dad. I didn't think Liam had even bothered to look at it."

"And if he did read it, Liam was never going to sign it."

"There were a lot of pages, and there was a lot of small print. There was a good chance Liam and or Ryan or whoever would never even have read it. That's why I had Tom present it to them. If I had done so, then I would have been obliged to spell everything out in detail."

"So really, *since it hadn't been signed,* nothing had changed, and everything was still as it was. Joe got the farm and he divided up the profits of the sale of the farm's produce between his two brothers and one sister?"

"Exactly, Starrett, so maybe you'll get down off your high horse again."

"Where's your husband?"

"I encouraged him to go down to Ramelton to try and get in his mother's good books again," Mona replied.

Starrett couldn't believe this couple. They'd heard that Liam was being detained, maybe even (if Browne had anything to do with it) charged with the murder of his son, so Mona's legal brain had sprung swiftly into action once again. The father is incarcerated, so the mother is the acting head of the family. *Her* first-born son, Thomas, returns dutifully to the farm to take his place at the head of the queue again – well, maybe not at the head of the queue, but at least joining the queue once again.

Tom Sweeney, as a son and a father, was just a middleman.

Unbelievable was the word that kept floating around Starrett's head. Yes, unbelievable, but, as Mona had quite rightly pointed out, not illegal.

However, did Mona feel deceived enough to go beyond the law in her actions to get what she felt was Tom's, and subsequently her, due?

Desperate for some light relief, Starrett excused himself, left Mona giving an official statement to Sergeant Garvey and headed off in search of Bernadette.

Starrett could hear the sound of the two girls playing before he could see them. He headed down a lane in the direction of the voices, past a grazing goat, which raised his head to give Starrett a severe once over before returning to his tasty snack. The lane opened out into a small field of well-tended grass, with two horses and three foals grazing down close to the girls. The closer he got to the girls, the more attention he paid to the horses.

He clicked his tongue a few times and greeted the horses with, "Hello there, boys."

"They're both girls," Bernadette laughed, "and why do grown-ups always talk to horses and cattle?"

"Well, young lady, we're either scared of them or we want to keep our hand in, in the art of salutations."

Finula, dressed in sky-blue dungarees, kept quiet, and Starrett couldn't see her eyes because of the thick mop of black curls cascading around her head. She totally ignored Starrett.

"My sister gets very upset when my mother goes off on one of her tantrums," Bernadette offered by way of explanation. Bernadette, Starrett figured, was midway between the angular uncertainty of youth and the confident poise of a young adult. She was dressed in blue gutties, denim jeans and a long-sleeved Batman T-shirt.

"Listen, Bernadette, screaming and shouting is much cheaper than banging doors and breaking them or smashing dishes," Starrett declared, causing Finula to look up at him for the first time.

"Have you seen a lot of that?" Bernadette asked.

"Aye, a bit in my time," Starrett admitted.

"Have you ever been shot at?" Finula asked in a very small voice.

"Have I ever been shot at?" Starrett repeated, knowing exactly what his audience was after. "Bejeepers, I'll tell you better than that: I remember during the big war . . ."

"You're too young to have been in the war," Bernadette said, rolling her eyes.

Starrett winked at her as her sister turned her attention to the electronic game she'd been playing with.

"Anyway, I was in the war, and this submarine kept firing off at us, but we couldn't get at it because it was underwater."

"So what did you do?" Finula asked.

"Well, I swam out there to its periscope; do you know what a periscope is?"

"Of course we know; it's how personnel in submerged vessels monitor above-surface activity," Bernadette offered.

"Excellent, Bernadette, I couldn't have put it better myself. Anyway, I swam out to the periscope with a pot of green paint, and I painted the glass of the periscope green, so the next time the captain raised the periscope the crew just saw the green and thought they were still underwater, so they kept on rising and rising, and when they were twenty foot in the air, we shot them down."

"Oh, Inspector Starrett," Bernadette laughed, as she and her sister chuckled at the image.

"Have you arrested the man who killed Uncle Joe?" Finula asked in an even quieter voice.

"No, Finula, we're still looking."

"Aren't you scared he'll get away?"

"It's OK, Fin, my friend Katie Keane says he's a great detective and he'll catch the man."

Starrett basked in that glory for all of two seconds, when Finula said, "Well, he better hurry up or the killer will get away to Dublin, and Daddy says anyone could hide in Dublin for all of their lives and never be found."

"Auntie Sheila says that the murderer will never ever be found," Bernadette offered.

"What's wacky baccy, Mr Starrett?" Finula asked.

"*Inspector* Starrett – he's Inspector Starrett, Fin."

"Why do you ask that, Fin?"

"Finula, my name is Finula. Only my sister calls me Fin," she said very proudly. "What's wacky baccy, Inspector Starrett?" she said, sounding like she was trying out the words again for size.

"Well, you know sometimes grown-ups like to drink beer or whiskey?"

"Or wine? Our parents prefer wine. It's much more sophisticated," the elder sister replied, as Finula nodded eagerly in agreement.

"Yes, or wine," Starrett agreed, "and when grown-ups have had a wee bit too much to drink they . . ."

". . . fall down," Bernadette interrupted, and she and her sister broke into a hysterical fit of laugher.

"Yes, well, wacky baccy is a funny cigarette, which can give you that same giddy feeling."

"Like when you keep turning around and around?"

"Just like that, Finula," Starrett agreed with a smile, and then continued, "So how do you know about wacky baccy?"

"Well, my mum said that if Teresa and Sheila Kelly would only get off their backsides and stop smoking so much wacky baccy, they wouldn't be so broke and wouldn't always need to be borrowing money."

Chapter Forty-Three

As the two members of the gardaí were with members of the Thomas Sweeney family, Garda Nuala Gibson and Novice Garda Romany Browne were walking down towards Whoriskey's.

Gibson had in her possession the precious wrapper of the Cadbury's Dairy Milk Tiffin bar, and she was preoccupied with the message Starrett had wished to be passed on to Browne: "Find me your evidence to convict Liam Sweeney."

Browne himself was preoccupied with the fact that he was in the company of a female.

"So, what's the story with you and Francis Casey?"

"So, what's the story with you and Samantha Aljoe?"

"Ah, she just wanted to make Starrett jealous. Would you like to make Casey jealous?"

"Jealousy has no place in a healthy relationship," Nuala replied, and in a more considered tone asked, "Do you think there is anything going on between Starrett and Dr Aljoe?"

"I'd bet not," Browne admitted. "If Samantha had anything going with Starrett, she wouldn't be trying to make him jealous with his junior. But let's get back to me and you."

"Let's not."

Gibson was distracted by Headworks, the new shiny as a button unisex hairdresser salon at the bottom of the Tank, thinking she'd love to see a farmer in there. Looking at Browne, she admitted to herself she was tempted. Browne had the chiselled looks of a

Greek god, but the downside was that he had an ego and a hunger to match. Part of her knew that her saying "no" would only serve to intensify her attraction, so she wanted to be careful that Browne's unwanted, though flattering, attention did nothing to upset her budding relationship with Francis.

"Right, we're here, so," she said as they entered Whoriskey's.

Three young students, obviously intent on some post-exam results celebrations and dressed up in super heroes' costumes – Superman, Batman and Spiderman – were on a shopping spree. Batman took a case of lager up and plonked it down at the checkout counter.

"Can I check your ID, please?" the wee girl at the checkout asked without batting an eyelid.

"Batman doesn't need ID," the puny version of Batman replied.

"In here he does."

"In that case," Batman continued unperturbed, "could I have a big bag of sweeties, please?"

Even super cool Romany Browne smiled at the super heroes as Nuala went up to one of the floor managers.

"Good morning," she said, producing the Cadbury's wrapper. "I wonder if you have any way of knowing if this bar was purchased in here?"

"Most probably," the friendly manager said as he examined the wrapper carefully through the transparent evidence bag. "Let's see now. The Tiffin bar is one of our slowest sellers out of the forty-nine lines of Cadbury's we sell. It's usually our customers from the Wee North who buy these."

"Why?" Gibson asked.

"Oh, the flavour of Cadbury's processed in the South is much superior to the English blend sold in Northern Ireland. Ours is made in Kerry, and I've never met a man, woman or child yet who doesn't prefer our blend. I reckon it's all to do with the milk."

The manager then pointed out the numbers in the "Best Before" box on the back of the wrapper.

02 2009

_ 10072 (15

"So this is best used before February next year. That dash before the numbers on the bottom line is actually a misprinted 'L,' which indicates with the numbers after this 'Lot' were produced on the seventy-second day of this year. The 15 in a bracket – the end of the brackets is also missing, but again that's just a misprint – is the code number of the production line responsible for this batch, we'd have got the whole batch 15."

"Right so," Gibson said, wondering where to take this. "I don't suppose you'd have any idea when you sold this?"

"Normally not," the manager replied, "but we have to watch the 'Best Before' dates like hawks – Cadbury's won't take back out-of-date stock. We sell the majority of our chocolate over the weekend, but don't always get round to refilling the chocolate shelves until Tuesday. I think you'll find the bar that was once with this wrapper," and he dangled the evidence bag up for them to see, "was sold on Tuesday, sometime after 11.00 A.M."

He walked along the rows and rows of various Cadbury's chocolate bars, which were located by the till closest to the far wall of the popular shop. He put his hand directly to the several Tiffin bars and turned them around so that he, Gibson and Browne, could examine them at the same time.

"There you go, same sell-by-date, same date of manufacture and same production line code."

"And you're absolutely sure?"

"Come with me," he said as he walked up the aisle towards the back of the shop. They went up a few steps and crossed a courtyard into a large well-stocked storeroom. On the opposite side of the storeroom, they came upon a child's Cadbury heaven: boxes and boxes of every imaginable chocolate bar.

The manager eyed the neatly lined rows of boxes and eventually came upon what he was after.

"Here we are," he said, fetching an already opened carton from the pile. "These cartons have forty-eight bars in each. Did either of you clock the number of bars still out on the shelf in the shop?"

"Six," Browne offered.

"Eight," Gibson corrected.

"And I bet you'll find thirty-six left in this carton. That means we've only sold four since Tuesday. And all thirty-six wrappers will have matching numbers in the 'Best Before' box to your wrapper."

Again they checked, and again the manager was correct.

"Sorry I can't tell you who bought the bar," the manager said with a bit of a grin, as he brought them back through to the front of the shop. "Give me a week or so, mind you, and I'd have a pretty good idea."

"That won't be necessary, thanks," Gibson said as they bid farewell on the pavement. "You've been helpful enough as it is."

Gibson and Browne walked back down the street towards the garda station.

"Right, let's get this out in the open," Browne said as they crossed the Tank again. "Do you think I planted the Tiffin bar wrapper in the warehouse, after the fact, to try and incriminate Liam Sweeney?"

"Well, if you had planted the evidence, I doubt even you would have been dumb enough to come down with me to the shop for fear they spotted you as the purchaser."

"Right, then where does that leave us?" Browne asked, perking up considerably.

"Not to put too fine a point on it, the bar of chocolate in question was not purchased until the morning after Joe Sweeney was murdered," Gibson offered helpfully.

"And?"

"And that means that either someone planted the evidence to, as you say, incriminate Liam Sweeney . . ."

"Or?" Browne asked, sounding as if he feared he already knew the answer.

"Or, Liam Sweeney planted the evidence, after the fact, himself."

"Either way I'm f . . . . . ."

"Either way, Garda Browne, you're in *flipp*in' trouble."

Chapter Forty-Four

When Starrett returned to Tower House, there was a message in Nuala Gibson's tidy handwriting for him to ring Maggie Keane.

Starrett went down to the basement to see Liam Sweeney.

"Anything you want to tell me, Liam?" Starrett asked as he opened the door.

"What, you mean beyond my confession?"

"Yes, Liam?"

"No, I think we've about covered it."

"OK, you can go."

"But, Starrett, I've confessed."

"Yep, thanks for that, you can go now. We'll contact you when we need you."

"But shouldn't you be arresting me?"

"Look, Liam, Colette has lost her youngest son; I think you need to be with her just now. I imagine the press and TV crews will be all over the farm by now. You need to be with her and protect her from all of that auld carry-on."

"But what if I run away?"

"OK, Liam, will you give me your word you'll not set foot out-side County Donegal?"

"Yes," Liam Sweeney replied, looking very confused, "I give you my word. I won't leave."

"That's good enough for me," Starrett said, taking and shaking Liam's firm calloused hand.

Starrett brought the weary farmer up to the front door and had Nuala Gibson drive him back to the farm. No one in the garda station reception could decide whether to stare at Starrett or the disappearing marked car.

"Fancy a drink?" Starrett said a few minutes later to Sergeant Packie Garvey.

"Aye, go on then," Packie replied. "But I should warn you that I know you only want me for the contraband I'm carrying for you."

Chapter Forty-Five

Starrett and Garvey drove out past Rathmullan and ended up in a famous traditional musician's white-washed, thatched cottage, looking out on Lough Swilly and beyond to the Inishowen Peninsula. The incessant rain of the day had just stopped, and the sun was shining gloriously. The most incredible landscape to be found anywhere in the world was benefiting tremendously from the hue of the sinking sun. God had delivered yet another of his double rainbows to remind all of Donegal of his promise that no matter how much rain fell, they'd never suffer a flood.

Tell that to the ducks, Starrett thought, as he had to stoop to enter the back door of the cottage.

The craic was ninety, and the house was packed with the good and great of Donegal's music scene. Starrett found there was something infectious, even tribal, about the sound of a fiddle or a bodhrán or a set of pipes, or any combination of all three instruments. The sound set his heart alight as he and Garvey walked through the door.

"For what shall it profit a man if he shall gain the whole world and still not be able to get an after-hours drink," Starrett declared, as he led his sergeant straight into the thick of it. Word around the county was that Paul Brady had dropped in the previous night and raised the roof with a bunch of his new songs, plus an even longer than usual version of his time-honoured concert-set closer – the rousing 'Homes of Donegal'. Starrett felt he could hear the sound of Brady's dying chords still ringing around the walls of the small rooms. The cottage was packed with many who had come hoping for a repeat of the appearance they had missed. Starrett thought otherwise; lightning never strikes twice in the same place. He could hear, somewhere in one of the rooms, a lone voice start up with, *"I've just dropped in to see you all, I'll only stay a while."* But Starrett knew he wasn't hearing the legendary mountainous voice of Strabane's finest chanter.

Starrett eventually spotted the character he'd come to talk to. He'd also spotted Starrett and quickly scampered, ducking and diving feverishly through the crowd, out the permanently opened back door and into the waiting strong arm of the law that was Sergeant Packie Garvey.

"Ah, Moondance, great to see you again."

"Jeez, Starrett, not in here, please. These are my people."

"No, they're not, Moondance; they're mostly decent people here. You're just looking to hoover up the hangers-on you make your money from."

"Ah, please, Starrett; keep your voice down for God's sake, head," the man known as Moondance – a.k.a. Be Be, a.k.a. Brian Boyce, or to give him his professional DJ moniker, B. B. Boyice – pleaded.

"What are you working on these days, Moondance?"

"Jeez, Starrett, you won't believe what I've got. I found this young guy. He's a cross between Christy Moore and Jay Z. He's called Flanagan, just the one name, FLANAGAN: cool, huh? We've done a fecking ace rap version of "I Still Haven't Found What I'm Looking For." I've sent it off to McGuinness for approval. It'll only work if we can keep a sample of Bono's voice on the track. The other thing we're working on is Flanagan's rap version of the *1812 Overture*. Fecking mega, head, mega!"

"Ah, no, Moondance, I meant what are you working on these days in your other career?"

"Inspector, that's all behind me."

"So, if Packie here were to search you now, he wouldn't find you carrying, would he?"

"Please, Starrett, not here, not with my people," Moondance whined, as his hands automatically dived into both pockets of his white-flashed, electric-blue trousers. He'd a matching jacket with a high white collar zipped up to nearly his nose. He was topped with a snow-white Magic Johnson baseball cap, pushed well back on his shaved head so the peak added an extra four inches to his slight five-foot-four-inch and one-hundred and twenty pound frame. His matching white Nike trainers – with all their flashing lights – looked as if they might have cost more than Starrett's car, which was parked just behind them. As fitting the image Moondance was trying desperately hard to project, he was blinged up to the brown eyeballs of his acne-ridden face. For all his imperfections, in his current get up, he'd managed to shave at least fifteen from his forty-plus years.

"As I keep telling you, your people are not wanted in this county."

"Starrett, look, it's either me or those who come after me. I'm harmless; I'm just trying to finance a legit business. Once I break Flanagan big time, I'm totally legal, I tell you. The other boys will never change; save your wrath for them, Starrett. All they deal in is personal destruction; I'm really not interested in that."

"Bejeepers, Packie, my man, I do believe we've found ourselves a drug dealer with a heart. He just might be the only one in captivity."

"Here, Starrett, what are you on about? I'm not in captivity," Moondance whined again.

"I do believe the cent is dropping, Packie."

Moondance nodded to signify he was getting to the same page.

"Right, Moondance, you can forget calling your solicitor on your Blackberry, well at least for the moment," Starrett said.

"Right, man," Moondance said. "*Your* drug of choice is information. That's the game, isn't it?"

"Bejeepers, you're spot on, Moondance. Packie and I need our daily fix, and you're our man."

"OK, OK, I'm hip to that, but not here, right."

"Take a look around, Moondance; not a single person is paying attention to us. You're so paranoid you must be smoking too much of your own weed."

"Walls have ears, Inspector. I'll help, but only if we do it my way. I'm going back into the cottage. I'll hang around for half an hour or so and then make my excuses, say I've got to split for a meet with Flanagan, and then I'll meet up with you guys down on the end of Rathmullan pier."

And that was how Inspector Starrett and Sergeant Packie Garvey came to be standing on Rathmullan Pier in the fading light of late evening, Starrett eating a well-done Hawaiian Burger (no tomato) with chips and Garvey enthusiastically polishing off cod and chips, both meals purchased at the nearby Salt and Batter. Moondance joined them ten minutes later and nicked half a dozen of Garvey's chips. Try the same with Starrett, and he just might have lost a hand in the process.

"Jeez, you boys are bad for business," Moondance started, as they stood like the silhouettes of the three monkeys hopping from one foot to the other, clicking their heels and staring out over the Swilly. "OK, head, who exactly do you need information on?"

"Sheila Kelly. What can you tell us about Sheila Kelly?" Starrett asked.

"Sheila 'Fit 2 Spliff' Kelly – she makes Rod Stewart sound like a choir boy. She's a famous All Star."

"Sorry?" the inspector asked.

"An All Star. She does all drugs. Her girlfriend's got a fiercer habit though; she does love her atom bombs."

"Atom bombs?" This time Garvey asked the question on Starrett's eyebrows.

"A bit of African Black and a bit more Aunt Hazel."

"Bejeepers, Moondance, would you ever listen to yourself? Could you try that again for me, only this time in Gay Byrne English, please?"

"Right, that's hash and heroin taken together. The farmer's daughter used to love her battery acid; sorry, that's LSD. She took so many trips that Sheila's dealer ended up giving her frequent flyer points."

"But is she on heroin now?" Starrett asked in a whisper.

"Not all the time. She only takes it when she wants to slow down. You got to be careful of that shit, Starrett; heroin not only takes your soul, head, it *becomes* your soul. The word around town is that she was doing a lot of blow – sorry, coke, man. I meant to say cocaine."

"You got there, eventually," Starrett said. "Do you know the farmer's daughter's name?"

"Ye-ah," he whined, sounding upset that Starrett would think he wouldn't know who he was talking about, "like Teresa Sweeney, the farmer's daughter, just like I said, man."

"Who's her dealer?" Starrett asked.

"I really haven't a clue Starrett," he started, but taking his lead from Starrett's obvious look of disbelief: "No, man, I really don't, but Sheila travels a lot, so it could be some Dublin head, and you don't want to mess with them."

"Does Sheila do well, Moondance?"

"She couldn't be doing that well, man."

"What do you mean?"

"Well, let's just say, Teresa is so strung out that she can't hold down a job. 'She's creative.'" He used the two fingers from each hand around the word "creative" to illustrate the inverted commas. "You know what I mean; she's at home all the time, creating. Listen, I don't know this for a fact, but the word on the street is that Sheila does a bit of dealing on the side, you know, among her pink posse friends."

"Tell me, Moondance, has Teresa always been into drugs?" Starrett asked.

"Most definitely not, man – only since she took up with Fit 2 Spliff."

"Moondance, this word on the street that you keep referring to, what does it say about how much Sheila and Teresa are into their dealer for?"

"Big change, Starrett. *Big* change. There are even a few rumours that her brother was, you know . . .?"

"What?"

"You know . . . bumped off as a warning," Moondance said.

A shiver ran up Starrett's spine and, if looks were anything to go by, most probably the whole way down Garvey's.

"But you know the bro."

"The *bro?*"

"Sorry, Starrett, the brothers, the *dealers.* The dealers are not beyond taking advantage of a family bereavement to send a message the whole way around Ireland, to show that extended credit always offends."

"Bejeepers, lads, what the feck is going on underground in this beautiful county of ours?"

"Now you know why I want to go legit with Flanagan," Moondance said, changing gear and tones on a cent. "Talking about Flanagan, tell me this, Starrett: you know those garda balls youse have up in Letterkenny? Who is responsible for booking the entertainment for those events?"

"Moondance, would you ever feck right off."

"Sorry, Inspectar, only asking, no offence," Moondance added, sounding as good-humoured as he knew how to be. "Right, lads, if you're done with me, I've people to see, deals to do . . . *No,* Starrett, not *those* kinds of deals."

"Thanks, Moondance. We owe you," Starrett started, and as Moondance started to turn all gooey and warm inside, he added, "Pop into Tower House any time you want, and the tea and bickies are on me and the sergeant here."

"Ever thought of the stage, Starrett? You know, with me as your agent . . . OK, OK . . . maybe not."

"Moondance, sorry, just one more question. You know this drug, Rohypnol?"

"Yeah, man. Roofies, the wonder drug."

"Are there any circumstances where druggies might take it themselves?"

"Apart from the obvious?"

"Yes, Moondance, apart from the obvious," Starrett said slowly.

"Oh, yes. If you're doing a lot of gear, that would make you all hyper, and if you needed to chill for one reason or other, then Rohypnol would work for you big time. It gives a whole new meaning to the lost weekend though."

Chapter Forty-Six

Starrett could never recall a time when he wasn't aware of Maggie Keane. From way back in their school days, even when he wasn't meant to be interested in girls, he could remember thinking, "She's cool." He could remember the time Maggie and he became friendly, in a mates kind of way. It wasn't just that she was a tomboy; it was more that she was good fun. She'd a great sense of humour and an amazing outlook on life. But then, because they were "friends," he never really realised that she was morphing into a beautiful young girl. He first started to take note of the fact when his male mates started drooling over her. But because she didn't realise what was happening, she wasn't affected by this new attention and continued contentedly in her budding friendship with Starrett.

Then, before he knew it, she'd blossomed into this beautiful young woman. Her looks, for Starrett, were nothing short of breathtaking. She could always shatter her beauty, though, by breaking into one of her awkward smiles. This flaw, in a way, only served to make her human in Starrett's eyes.

He dropped Garvey off back at Tower House and drove straight to Maggie's house on the Shore Road. When she'd left a message for Starrett to call her, Starrett knew that she hadn't meant in person; but desperate times called for desperate actions. As he knocked gently on her back door, he could remember Dr Samantha Aljoe's advice: "Talk to her, Starrett, just talk to her."

Maggie Keane looked through her darkened window before unlocking and opening the door. She seemed happy to see him.

"Maggie, what do *you* want?"

When she looked at him with a confused look, he repeated his question.

"Maggie, what do you want, from us, from you and me?"

"OK, Starrett: yes, you can come into my kitchen at this time of the night, and yes, it's good to see you too. Now let's have a drink and chat a bit and try and work our way up to your big question. What would you like to drink?"

It was only then that Starrett noticed she was wearing the same bed gown she'd been wearing a few nights ago. He remembered how good it felt to feel her body so close to his as they communicated solely and chastely through a lingering kiss.

"Right," Starrett said, catching his breath, "I'll have a coffee, please."

Maggie Keane moved about her kitchen, quietly, efficiently and sensuously, and in a few minutes had a tray filled with two milky coffees, two glasses of tap water and a plate of goodies. She ordered Starrett to follow her through to the sitting room.

In her sitting room, her current book, Jodi Picoult's *Plain Truth,* remained open and face down straddling the arm of her sofa, the jacket illuminated by her reading light. The dying embers of the fire showed Starrett that this was where she had been when he came knocking on her door close to midnight. If she'd not been expecting him, she'd probably have already been tucked up in bed, reading away. He took great comfort in this deduction.

"Starrett, I want us to be together," she said, as he took his first sip.

"But?"

"No buts . . ."

"Except?" he pushed, because he knew there was still reservation there.

"Except . . . well, maybe I want us to be together for today, not as an idyllic continuation from a schoolboy and schoolgirl crush."

"Bejeepers, Maggie, it was a great deal more than that."

"Please hear me out, Starrett," she said, while she raised her coffee cup tenderly cradled in both her hands to her full lips. She'd gathered her legs up underneath her, so it looked like her head was sticking out the top of a light blue tepee. "I want us to be together because of who you and I are today, because of what we've become. I don't ever, ever want to look in your eyes and see some kind of misplaced pity because of something that happened between us over twenty years ago. I certainly have no regrets, Starrett, and if we are to have a chance, I need to believe you don't have any regrets either. I'm very comfortable with all of this because I see the way my girls are with you. I need to tell you that our son, Joe, is very, very disappointed in you."

"Oh my God, Maggie, did he really say that? Why?"

"He's a big fan of Bob Dylan, Starrett, and he finds it hard to believe that anyone from Dylan's generation, like yourself, could be totally indifferent to Dylan and his work. He says he's tried to chat with you about it, and your only observation on the subject was, 'Oh yes, he was a big fan of The Clancy Brothers and Tommy Makem, wasn't he?'"

"Bejeepers Maggie, I thought you were serious there for a moment."

Maggie smiled her awkward smile and added, "But I am, Starrett, I am serious. I suggest you get Nuala Gibson to help you brush up on your Dylan; that's a sure certain short cut to getting to know Joe. You should definitely use it."

"Well, she's got me up as far as The Beatles, so I'm sure Dylan won't be a giant step."

"I think you'll find that in our son's eyes and ears it is a major giant step," she said, returning her empty coffee cup to the small tray beside her side of the sofa. She used her freed hands to hug her legs.

"Does Joe know I'm his father?"

"When Joe was eleven years old, Niall and I sat him down and told him Niall was not his blood father. Don't ask me why I did it then, because I honestly don't know. Maybe I was scared he would hear it from elsewhere, and maybe I felt he was getting to an age where it might affect him if he heard from anyone else but me. Joe and Niall were always very close, and Joe was fine about it. I told him if he ever wanted to find out about his blood father to come to me and I'd tell him everything he wanted to know."

"And did he?"

"After I invited you to Joe's birthday party, he asked me if you were his father."

"Bejeepers, he's sharp enough, isn't he?"

Maggie smiled a contented smile, taking satisfaction in Starrett's obvious pride.

"And mature, Starrett," she continued. As far as pride and their son was concerned, she was equally guilty. "He told me that he hadn't mentioned it before because as long as Niall was alive he never felt the need to know. He felt Niall was his father."

She stopped talking and started to laugh, a laugh that developed into a sob.

"Maggie, what's wrong?"

"No, no, it's okay. It's just that I remember that he also asked me what my intentions were with you."

"Getaway."

"Yes. I told him that I liked you, I still had feelings for you, but I needed to take it slowly to see how things would develop between you and me and him and the girls. He said he understood and he would totally abide with whatever I wanted to do . . . but he was totally fine with it, with me having another man in my life."

Again Maggie started sobbing and laughing.

"Starrett, Joe encouraged me to 'go for it.' He said he'd be there for me in whatever I wanted to do," she said as she dried her eyes with the edge of her gown, regaining her composure again. "So, Starrett, he's totally okay about you and me, and this Dylan thing, well, it's . . ."

"OK, understood. What else do you want, Maggie?"

"That's it . . . well, just one more thing really. You see this?" she said shyly, nodding to the carpet along the front of the sofa.

"Sorry?"

"Do you notice anything about my carpet, Detective?"

"Well, I can see that it's worn down a lot more at the corner you're sitting at than it is along the rest of it."

"Very observant, Inspector Starrett, very observant. That's because I've been sitting here alone for all these nights, eating my dinner alone, watching my television alone, reading my book alone and wearing my corner of the carpet threadbare. It's not that I've wanted to share it with a man, any man. I've wanted to share it with you, Starrett."

Starrett made to move across from his seat by the fire to join her.

"No, Starrett, please, stay there for now or I'll start to cry again. When I made that call to you a few months ago to help my mother, it wasn't out of the blue. I'd been thinking of contacting you for at least a year before that, but I was nervous of doing so. I felt it was dangerous to mess with your memories, no matter how great they were."

Starrett was about to say that all the memories couldn't have been great, but then he remembered her saying that she needed him to have no regrets about what had happened between them all those years ago, so he merely said, "Maggie, I don't think there is a single day in my life that has gone by that I didn't think of you at least once."

"But I was still nervous when I did contact you," she continued, choosing to ignore him. "I was scared that I might not like the man you'd become, or you wouldn't like me any more, or there wouldn't be that attraction there between us any more. But I really love the man you've grown into, Starrett. You're still a good person – innocent and sometimes childlike – but I don't think they're bad qualities for a man. I needed to see how Moya and Katie took to you before I got to know you too well again. And then, I needed to be sure of my feelings for you before I could tell you about our son. I also needed to see you weren't just hanging around for . . ."

"OK," Starrett said, nodding furiously to save her the embarrassment of having to spell it out.

"But here you are. You didn't turn and run the first time it appeared it wasn't going to be plain sailing into my bed. We've managed to get to this point. But now, Starrett, it's your turn. You've got to tell me what you want."

His eyes betrayed him.

"I'm serious."

"Maggie, there was a time in my life when I found it nearly impossible to breathe just because you weren't around. When I moved away from Ramelton, there were lots of nights when I just wanted to hitch a lift back here to be with you. I'd no ideas or plans as to what I was going to do when I got here. But then something happened, something bad happened."

"What happened, Starrett?"

"I've never been able to find the words for it, Maggie. I've never even tried, to be honest. I just concentrated with all of my might to block it out of my mind. And I succeeded. Perhaps sometime I'll be able to talk to you about it, but not now."

"You shouldn't worry about what's gone before," she offered compassionately. "William Shakespeare says that all men are moulded from their faults."

"Aye, this long fellow of yours, Billy Shakespeare, he's not from these parts is he? Now Hugo Whoriskey, he is, and he says that farmers don't eat ice cream when it's raining."

"In other words?"

"In other words, there is a reason for everything. All the things that have happened to us up to this point in our lives are all the very same reasons why we're here together now."

"That's totally fine, Starrett. And you tell me about the other stuff when you're ready," she said gently. "You were about to tell me what you wanted."

"Maggie, I just want to be with you. Yes, we are older, different people, but luckily, the man and woman we've grown to be share the attraction we once enjoyed. Maggie, I've never *not* loved you. But it's no longer a memory that I love. I want to do all the things we need to do, to be together. I don't say that begrudgingly. I'm happy, no, I'm delighted, to embark on this adventure with Joe, Moya, Katie and you."

Starrett felt a wee bit self-conscious.

"But look, Maggie, it's very late. I'm just so happy we've discussed this. I should go."

"Here," she said, passing him a glass of water as she took a drink from her own.

"No, I'm fine with the coffee," he said.

She stared at him.

"Take a drink of the water, Starrett; it's quite foul kissing someone when they've just had a drink of coffee."

Starrett did as he was bid and thanked his God *and* Packie Garvey for distracting him from his Players for the majority of the day. He drank the entire glass of water in two gulps.

Maggie Keane walked across to him, took both his hands and looked deep into his eyes. He loved her eyes. He loved the love no longer hidden in her eyes.

She took him by the hand and led him, with the single forefinger of her free hand across her lips, very quietly up to her bedroom.

"Bejeepers, Maggie, that was something else," Starrett declared just over two hours later.

"All these years and you still haven't improved on your lines."

"Practice, Maggie; I'll be grateful for the practice."

"Starrett, can I ask you something?" she said, snuggling cosy into the nook of his arm and shoulder, as she had twenty years before.

"Of course."

"Earlier, downstairs, you looked different, you looked more confident."

"Define confident," Starrett said, pulling her tightly to him and gently rubbing her shoulder.

"Oh confident in a . . . let's say, in a romantic way," she said delicately.

"Romantic as in . . ."

"As in this," she said, as she took his free hand and placed it gently on her breast.

"Are you saying I was confident I was going to end up in bed with you?"

"Well, actually yes, in a kind of way," she said, disengaging from Starrett and supporting herself on one elbow, looking face down at him.

"OK, woman, there's no fooling you. I'll come clean. I knew we'd end up here tonight."

"Starrett!"

He grinned at her.

"How?"

"Do you really want to know?"

"Yes, and it better be good or you're in big trouble."

"OK, Maggie. Every single time I've come over here during the last several months, you always, but always, warned me that I was not staying the night; tonight for the first time you gave no such warning."

"So all that crap about it's late I should go . . ." Maggie started. "I need to keep reminding myself that first and foremost you're a detective. Right, you're still going to pay for that."

"I'm all yours."

Her "Bejeepers Starrett, I know," was partially lost in their kiss.

Chapter Forty-Seven

Saturday: 30 August 2008

Second thing Saturday morning, Starrett, on his way from Maggie's house to his own, stopped off at Tower House to make a call to the Drug Squad in Letterkenny.

Forty minutes later, as Starrett was writing up his Murder Book in time for an 8.00 A.M. meeting with his team, his telephone rang.

"Hello?"

"Hello yourself."

"Maggie."

"Ten points, or was it a lucky guess, Starrett? You left early."

"Aye, I've a bit to do here and I thought . . . the girls, you know."

"I love you for being considerate, but I'm not hiding my feelings for you from them."

"OK, good. Have you told them?"

"I have."

"What did you say?"

"I told them I loved you."

"Wow! What did they say?"

"They asked me if you loved me," she admitted.

"What did you say to that?"

"I told them to ask you themselves."

"Good answer, Maggie."

"Mind you, they're cute enough. You should have seen Katie's antenna rise to the ceiling any time Nuala and I were chatting about you. Did your ears ever burn, Starrett? They should have."

"Ach, you know," he said, puffing up his chest.

"It wasn't always good," she said, bringing him back to land again, "but listen, I've rung you for a favour."

"Anything."

"Be careful, Starrett, I might just ask for a blind date with Romany Browne."

"Aye, he's got a way with women all right. He's just not going to get away with mine."

She laughed.

"Well, my favour," she said, as she dropped her tone considerably, "and it really is OK if you don't want to do this . . ."

Starrett wondered what it could be.

"Ehm, you see, last night . . . well, truth is, you caught me unawares and ah . . . well, I wondered if you'd mind asking that doctor friend of yours, Dr Aljoe, if she could score a couple of morning-after pills for me?"

After Starrett set the phone down, a smile crossed his face. Maggie Keane was publicly staking her claim to her man. He absolutely loved her for it. He experienced such an incredibly warm feeling of belonging. The feeling lasted for, oh, all of a full minute, by which point he was trying to figure out how best to approach Dr Aljoe about this delicate subject.

Chapter Forty-Eight

"OK," Starrett started as everyone drifted towards the seats, "let's get started."

Novice Garda Romany Browne was first to speak.

"It would appear that the vital piece of evidence I uncovered had been *planted,*" he admitted.

Starrett had to give him credit for not being sheepish about admitting he'd been duped.

"The short version of the story is that the chocolate wrapper indicated the bar only went on sale to the public the morning after the murder actually took place. I can give you it chapter and verse if you really want it."

"That'll suffice, Browne. I appreciate it took a lot of guts to jump up right away and admit your mistake. I know I don't need to remind you that in future you must follow the evidence, not lead it."

Browne nodded and acknowledged that Starrett had done just what he said he wouldn't.

"OK, let's put all of that behind us," Starrett said as Major Newton Cunningham nodded agreement, "because we've other developments. In approximately another forty-seven minutes, the Letterkenny Drug Squad are going to raid Sheila Kelly and Teresa Sweeney's bungalow up on the Golf Course Road."

There was a bit of muttering around the room at this news.

"I want you two," Starrett said, looking directly at Garda Browne and Garda Casey, "in one car. And I want Garda Gibson and Garda Robinson in another, and I want you both parked at the end of their lane, in full view of the house. I want you to stay there all day. If Kelly or Teresa Sweeney drives off, either together or separately, I want them tailed, and I want them and anyone else they come into contact with to know they're being tailed.

"The major, Packie and myself will be down at the scene where the body was found and then up at the Sweeney farm, but please keep us up to date on any developments."

Chapter Forty-Nine

"OK, what do we know so far?" Starrett asked, as much to himself as to Sergeant Garvey and Major Cunningham. The major had found a relatively comfy seat on an upturned five-gallon oil can in the courtyard where Joe Sweeney's body had been discovered four days previously. The relief on the major's face was visible to all concerned. And Starrett *was* concerned. The major's ability to stand around for any period of time was now close to zero. However, as long as he kept moving or found somewhere to rest, he seemed to be OK.

"So," Starrett continued, "the body was found where, Packie?"

Packie pointed to the location in question. Even the grass and weeds that had once been flattened by the weight of the dampened corpse had now sprung back to life.

"Right so," Starrett said, as he used his bent forefinger and thumb to scratch his chin. He felt his stubble and was distracted by another thought. "And while I think of it, Sergeant, how many Players do I have left in my stash?"

"Six, sir," Packie replied dejectedly, without checking.

"Dump them immediately," Starrett said, as he enjoyed another flash of kissing Maggie Keane.

Garvey, neither getting nor seeking any further clarification, went straight to the water's edge and threw the remains of the packet of Players into a rubbish bin.

When he returned to his superior, Starrett said, "Thanks, Packie. Now, do me a favour and go and stand where Joe's body was found."

Garvey did as bid and stood by the wall close to the rusted spherical iron grid.

"Has everything else in here has been left as it was?" Starrett asked.

"Yes," Garvey replied immediately, "we've had someone on the gate here ever since the incident."

"Obviously the guard wouldn't have suspected Liam when he walked in and around the courtyard to plant his chocolate wrapper. We can file him as nothing worse than a grieving father. But we also need to look beyond that and think why would he do that?"

Starrett's eyes paced the distances from Garvey – in Joe Sweeney's resting place – to the rusty spherical iron grid. It was at most half a body's length. Then he paced out the distance from the sphere to the gate of the courtyard – at most twenty feet. He walked to the gate, then from the gate to the water's edge, about another twenty-five feet. Under scrutiny of Newton Cunningham and Garvey, he next paced that distance out from the water's edge, down past where the absent boat had been docked the day the body was found. To the ancient stone steps to and below the water level was another forty feet.

"Packie, do me one final favour, will you?" Starrett asked.

"Not a problem, sir," his faithful and enthusiastic sergeant replied.

"Would you ever climb into that monstrosity for me."

Packie Garvey tried every way he could. Some of his antics were extremely amusing to both the inspector and the major, but he couldn't gain access to the inside of the sphere. There were no gaps in the grid large enough to accommodate his lean physique.

"OK," Starrett said as he too went across to the sphere, "help me move it back here."

Before Garvey had a chance to lend his weight to the task, the sphere started rolling as a direct result of Starrett's sole efforts.

"Interesting," Starrett declared. "It's a lot lighter than I imagined it would be."

When he rolled it half a turn, they found that the rim the sphere had been resting on, the rim that was used to attach the sphere to the matching fixings on the nearby trailer, was indeed large enough – Starrett reckoned about twenty-four inches – for Garvey to enter the sphere through.

Garvey hopped in and out of the sphere via the ring with an agility and flourish that Houdini, in his prime, would have been proud of.

"We'll come back later," Starrett said as he led them out of the courtyard. "Maybe we'll bring a bit of an audience with us next time though."

Chapter Fifty

Packie Garvey then drove Starrett and the major in Starrett's car up to the Sweeney farm.

The farm had now grown strangely serene. Starrett thought it was like a beautiful woman who, having lost her lover, was desperately sad, lost and resigned to the fact that she would never take another. Like the woman, the farm, through lack of love and attention, would start to decay. The process would certainly be slow, but it had already started. As on the Wednesday morning, he was overcome by the beauty of the farmland that stretched out on all sides, with the magnificent house and all its history and memories at the centre.

The inspector took a long and deep breath, drinking in all the rich outdoor aromas. He could see why a man would want to enjoy this piece of land for a long, long time, maybe even as long as a lifetime. But, at the same time, he wondered why a man would get so preoccupied about *owning* this piece of land, *owning* any piece of land in fact. Men and women could certainly benefit, in numerous ways, from the land, but they could never ever really own it, he felt. As in the case of the Sweeney farm, and the mystery of their youngest's murder, therein lay the problem and the pain.

Although anxious to enter the house and get the unpleasant chat with the farmer behind him, Starrett excused himself from the major and Garvey for a few minutes, leaving them in the car, and forced himself to go for a walk so he could prepare himself by soaking up and enjoying the magic of this beautiful countryside.

As he walked down the leafy lane, away from the farmhouse, he had a flash of a happy, smiling, youthful and considerate Joe Sweeney driving around these fields, working the land he loved so much. He wished so much that he had had the opportunity to meet Joe Sweeney. He always found himself wondering what the victims in his cases had sounded like. He'd rarely been as distressed by the absence as he was on this occasion. By all accounts, Joe Sweeney was a good man, a fair man, and by his deeds, at least the ones Starrett had uncovered, a generous man.

Yes, Starrett thought, *Joe Sweeney was a good man, deprived of the chance of greatness by an evil deed.*

Starrett returned to the farm with a resolve he hadn't possessed before his short walk. He knew that to carry out his duty meant that he had to completely destroy a family. He took little comfort in the fact that it was the initial evil deed, and not his carrying out his duty, that was going to destroy the family.

Packie Garvey stayed with Colette Sweeney in the kitchen while Starrett, the major and Liam Sweeney went through to the sitting room.

"Liam," Starrett began as they each took seats around the fireplace, "we needed to talk to you one more time, because . . ."

"Starrett, I thank you for having this time to spend with Colette. If you've come to take me in, I'm fine with it. I'm ready to sign my confession and take my punishment."

"Have you mentioned anything about this to Mrs Sweeney yet?" the ever proper major asked.

"No, I haven't. But before you take me away, maybe I can have a few minutes with her?"

"Starrett is offering you a lifeline here, Liam. Stop this carry-on. We all know you didn't murder Joe. You couldn't have, even if you'd the need to."

Liam stood up and paced the room.

"No bleeding wonder the guards are in such a bad state," he declared. "A murderer comes up to them and says, 'It was me. I did it!' And all they can think of saying is, 'Oh, go you on back home, and we'll see if we can find anyone else.' Major, I can find an excuse for your man here – sure he even tried to be a priest, for heaven's sake – but yourself, with all your military background, surely law and order must be top of your agenda."

"Bejeepers, Liam, cut the crap," Starrett warned. "We know you didn't do it. We know you planted the chocolate wrapper. We know you entered the courtyard to pay your respects, and when the guard wasn't looking, you placed your incriminating wrapper in the wall so that we'd think you'd been there earlier, depositing the dead body of your son. Joe's car wasn't parked out by John Lea's cottage as you claimed; we eventually found it around behind the Town Hall. Ryan hadn't tipped you off as to what Mona was about. You said you had trouble taking Joe's body over the wetlands because of the low tide, when in point of fact, we all know, with the full moon, it was a very high tide that night. We've a witness who saw the murderer – just a silhouette, but most definitely a smaller person than you – on the water's edge by the warehouses."

"Liam, Colette has lost her youngest son. She doesn't need to lose her husband. She needs you now more than ever, man," the major pleaded.

"She won't be able to get through this without you, Liam," Starrett appealed, hoping the frustration wasn't showing in his voice.

"It's better than the alternative," Liam said, in little more than a whisper.

"I know, Liam," Starrett said.

Sweeney was shocked by Starrett's admission. They eyeballed each other for about thirty seconds, but it was enough time for Liam to see and accept that Starrett was serious. He did know.

"I owe it to Colette. Please, Starrett," the farmer said, his voice breaking.

"I owe it to Joe, Liam," Starrett countered.

"But he's already gone, Starrett; Colette will never get through this."

"No, Liam, you're wrong. What she'll never get through is the fact that you sacrificed yourself in place of the real murderer."

"Look, Starrett . . . please, Major . . ." Liam started, appearing not to know which one he should be pleading with, "I'm an old . . ."

"Phew," the major tutted, "I'll give you ten years any time you want, and you'll still never catch me up."

"Then you'll realise more than most how aging wreaks havoc on your body, not to mention your brain. The positive side though is that it removes your fear of death."

"For heaven's sake, man, who's talking about dying? No one's going to die. They dropped the death penalty years ago," Starrett insisted.

"But it's all relative, isn't it? My turn is going to come sooner . . ."

"And my turn will be sooner still, but I'm certainly not ready to give up," the major said.

"Aye, everyone wants to go to heaven, but no one wants to die," Starrett said, sing-song style. "Liam, let's cut the crap. I know you didn't murder your son. I know who did. It's my guess you also know who the real murderer is, and when you discovered who it was, you, with . . . with your misguided, but honourable, sense of duty, felt it was better you take the rap."

Liam Sweeney looked relieved, looked like he'd already had second thoughts about his planned course of action, but his honour wouldn't let him break his word, the word he'd given in his statement.

"I won't help you," Sweeney said sadly.

"All I need you to do, Liam, is withdraw your confession and go and give your wife the comfort she's going to need," Starrett said, as he rose out of his seat.

Liam Sweeney nodded obediently.

When they walked back into the kitchen, Colette saw the look on her husband's face. She was confused by his mixed signals, but sought and took comfort in his arms.

Chapter Fifty-One

After telling Garvey he would meet him up at Teresa and Sheila's bungalow in an hour, Starrett dropped the major and Garvey off at Tower House. He didn't tell him about the important visit he first needed to make to Letterkenny General Hospital, after which, hopefully, he'd still have time for a quick dash back to Maggie Keane's house on Shore Road.

Today was a day entirely about waiting around. Starrett figured the earliest time to bring Teresa and Sheila in for questioning would be first thing tomorrow morning. He hoped it would be after a sleepless, drug-free night. He figured that twenty-four hours without whatever their controlled substance of choice was would probably have a more severe effect on Teresa. Well, that was, of course, if Moondance's information was anything to go by.

Starrett didn't mind waiting about. He was a patient man.

He wondered how patient the stunning Dr Samantha Aljoe would be when she heard his request. He was still smiling fondly as he recalled Maggie Keane's requested "favour."

It felt good to be wanted. No, it felt absolutely wonderful to be wanted, and particularly to be wanted by the person he'd thought of, dreamt of and fantasised about for the previous twenty years. If nothing else showed his patience, then those painful twenty years did. Equally, for 99 per cent of that time, he'd never thought Maggie Keane would speak to him again, let alone willingly enter into a relationship with him.

His son Joe was probably the single, mitigating factor that had brought Maggie and himself back together again. On the flattering side, the memory of Maggie Keane's claim that she'd only decided to give it a try with Starrett again when she discovered she also liked the man he'd become made him sit upright in his BMW.

Starrett was enjoying his thoughts of Maggie and her family, but the closer he drove to Letterkenny, the more he became preoccupied with the fiery Dr Aljoe.

He knew there was no way out of this one. It was a test. He knew Maggie could, though perhaps not easily, have managed to pick up a morning-after pill. She might not have wanted to get a prescription and publicly troop into Murray's Pharmacy and purchase a wee box of the pills, but she could have gone up to Derry herself and popped into a chemist where she was unknown, *if she'd wanted to.* For that matter, Starrett could have asked Gibson to get them, but he knew if he did, he'd have failed the test. It might not have ended his renewed, still budding relationship with Maggie, but he knew she would certainly have been upset with him.

After the fact, Starrett realised, and accepted, that Maggie Keane, being Maggie Keane, would not have been on the pill. He also accepted that it was as much his responsibility to take precautions as hers. But in their very natural moments of gentle passion together, neither had thought to even pose the question.

He wondered how Dr Aljoe would react.

She was, outwardly at least, totally cool about it.

"So my recommendation of talking to the woman actually worked," was Aljoe's immediate reaction.

Starrett just gave an embarrassed shrug.

"Goodness, old man, if I'd known my advice was going to be so effective, so quickly, I should have taken it myself."

Starrett could do nothing but stand there in her very small office and look sheepish.

"And now Maggie Keane has sent you to me to pick up a morning-after pill. My, my . . . how I underestimated her. She's some woman, Starrett."

All things considered, Starrett thought, so far Dr Aljoe seemed to be taking the situation OK. It was time for him to say something.

"Samantha . . . I'm sorry."

"Don't be, Starrett; the most you and I would have had would have been a fling, a nice fling, but a fling nonetheless."

Starrett didn't feel that in Aljoe's magnanimous moment he should be churlish enough to say that he wasn't sorry about Maggie Keane.

"But I do like you, Starrett. I've grown very fond of you, and you put up with all of my flirting like a saint. I hope we'll stay mates. I know this is important to you, and it's obviously very important to Maggie. In fact, I'm flattered that she would even think she would need to make a mark on you so I could see it. Hopefully we'll all be friends . . . some day, but not some day too soon, eh?"

She reached below her desk, down past her shapely, tanned legs, to her handbag and dug her hand in deep and futtered around in there without looking at what she was doing, all the time keeping her eyes focused on Starrett. After a few seconds, she produced the wee magic box of Plan B, ECP pills.

"Take them all, Starrett. I'm not going to need them."

Starrett quickly read the instructions and tore off a strip of four.

"You should keep the rest, Samantha. You never know," he said as his mind flashed back to their night down on Rathmullan beach.

She took the remainder of the ECP pills, smiled and dropped them back in her bag.

"You know . . ." Starrett started and stumbled.

"Go on, Starrett, and get out of here," she said, fondly, "before it's too late."

"What?" Starrett replied in a panic. "Is there a time limit?"

"No, no, you're fine, Starrett," she laughed; "you've got seventy-two hours, from the time . . . you know . . . of . . ."

"Right, right. Bejeepers, I'll dash. Better safe than sorry, eh?"

"Too late for that, Starrett," she giggled. "Boom! Boom!"

She rose, pulled him towards her, pecked him on both cheeks and gave him a wee chaste hug.

Just as he was about to leave her office, she called out after him, "Oh, Starrett."

He turned back, "Yes?"

"Ehm, that Packie Garvey fellow, I hear he's got great legs and a lot of stamina. Is he . . . ah . . . I mean . . . is he seeing anyone?"

Chapter Fifty-Two

Maggie Keane's eyes lit up when Starrett walked straight into her kitchen and produced the strip of Plan B. Starrett only had time to explain the dosage and hug her and kiss her before he was off. She made him promise to return that night; she didn't care how late, she said, and she gave him a key to let himself in, just in case she'd gone to bed.

This thought entertained Starrett until he was pulling up at the lane off the main Letterkenny to Ramelton Road and on to the Golf Course Road.

What he was entering was like a scene from *CSI;* here there were more flashing lights than at the Beijing Olympics. Following his instructions, Starrett's team was on duty at the foot of the lane.

Nuala Gibson exited her car and strode over in the direction of Starrett.

"Any attempt at movement by Teresa or Sheila?"

"No, sir," Gibson replied, "but the Drug Squad and their tracker dogs must be having a very rewarding day. They've been in there for over two hours now, and they keep bringing stuff out and taking it away. Is there a chance they might arrest the girls?"

"No. That's part of the deal," Starrett said as he surveyed the scene. "They agreed to stand second in line as a return favour for the tip-off.

"Right, you and Packie head off for a break, and I'll stay here with the two boyos. How have they been getting on?" Starrett asked, referring to Romany Browne and Francis Casey.

"No fisticuffs so far," Nuala said through a generous smile. "In fact, if I'm not mistaken, there's been a considerable amount of laughing between the two of them. I don't know if I should be happy for Romany or worried about Francis."

She hopped in the car she was sharing with Garvey and sped off in the direction of the Silver Tassie Hotel and Restaurant back up the road towards Ramelton.

Starrett hung around the bottom of the lane, kicking his heels. At various times he could see Teresa and Sheila, both together and separately, come and take a look at him loitering at the end of their lane. This was exactly what Starrett wanted.

Eventually the detective in charge, an Inspector O'Rourke, originally from Dublin, now based in Letterkenny, wandered down the lane. He handed Starrett a large evidence bag containing an aqua-coloured towel.

"Is this what you're after?"

"The very same, Frank," Starrett said as he shook the detective's hand. He knew O'Rourke; he was a lot gentler than his physique suggested, but his reputation as an honest garda was second to none. "Are we all legit?" Starrett said, nodding in the direction of the evidence.

"Yes indeed, Starrett. It's officially evidence obtained while in the course of a search under this warrant. I've done a copy up for you."

Starrett checked his copy of the search warrant and said, "Thanks for this, Frank."

"You've got those girls up to high doh, now," he said, by way of explanation. "They seem to be ignoring my boys altogether, you've got them so agitated."

"Find much stuff, Frank?"

"No bulk, but lots of cocktails. The girls like their variety. The Sweeney girl looks like she's strung out, that's why we're still looking. She must have her serious stash hidden somewhere else."

"I reckon you're right, Frank," Starrett said, as both girls came running down the lane towards them.

Actually, that wasn't quite accurate, Starrett realised as they grew closer to him. Teresa Sweeney was running towards him. Sheila Kelly was trying to restrain her.

"Miss Sweeney, Miss Kelly," Starrett said as Teresa was finally pulled up and restrained, just three inches from his nose. Starrett nodded to O'Rourke that he was OK. O'Rourke clocked that he was and left to go back up the lane to the bungalow.

"*You're* behind this, aren't you?" Teresa cried out. "That's my towel. What are you doing with my towel?" and she started to tug at the evidence bag. Eventually she fell over, landing on her backside, showing her underwear to all and sundry.

Starrett felt very sad. She was the daughter of a very good friend of his father's. The detective took no pleasure in seeing her in such a state, a much worse state than Starrett had expected.

"Be careful, Inspector Starrett," Sheila said loudly in her permanently hoarse voice.

Starrett couldn't work out if she was trying to protect him from Teresa or if she was threatening him. Both were now talking, screaming and shouting over and under one another. All their attention and anger seemed to be focused on their towel. At one point, Teresa threatened to get Mona Sweeney – hardly her best friend in the world – to sue Starrett if he didn't return the towel immediately. Starrett kept totally quiet. Casey and Browne stepped out of their car and walked across to Starrett's aid. Starrett signalled them to keep their distance.

Inspector Starrett remained calm and silent and just stared at both girls as they ranted and raved. The girls were either bemused or unsettled by Starrett's calmness, but eventually they fell silent, and all that could be heard was the buzz of the activity up at the bungalow and the crows squawking loudly in the nearby trees.

Starrett continued looking at the girls for a minute that felt like it was an hour. Eventually, eyes still fixed intently on both girls, he said, "I know exactly what you did, and you're not going to get away with it."

At 4.45, just as the nation was settling down to view the day's football results, Inspector Frank O'Rourke and his resourceful team eventually discovered Teresa's and Sheila's stash of cocaine, heroin and grass. It was cleverly sealed in several airtight plastic bags and stuffed in a large bottle of Tommy Hilfiger perfume. The heavy scent of the perfume had confused the dogs. The fact that the bottle, although appearing well worn around the cap, was still completely full was what raised the interest of O'Rourke.

O'Rourke was happy that they'd found the stash, and Starrett was happy the drugs had been removed from the premises.

Starrett and his team took turns throughout the night to keep guard on Teresa and Sheila's bungalow so no fresh supplies would get through. The only other Saturday activity was that Starrett sent Nuala Gibson up to Letterkenny General Hospital with the aqua towel O'Rourke had confiscated from Teresa and Sheila's bathroom. The best Dr Aljoe could do was to say that the pieces of fabric discovered in Joe Sweeney's hair at the time of his death were *similar* in texture and colour to the towel Gibson had given her.

Starrett, on one of his breaks, dropped in on Maggie Keane to advise her he'd be on duty most of the night. She forced him to sit down at the table to share some supper with her and Moya and Katie. The girls were, as ever, very friendly with Starrett. This time, however, they both seemed either very pleased with themselves or very pleased with their mum. He found himself totally relaxing into this particular family life and enjoying very much the privilege of being warmly invited to do so.

Chapter Fifty-Three

Sunday: 31 August 2008

At exactly 7.20, just as the clouds opened for what would be the twenty-fourth day that month – a record of sorts even for Donegal – Starrett stepped up to the front door of Teresa and Sheila's ugly bungalow and knocked three times on the door. He barely had time to return his hand to his trouser pocket when the door was opened, and there stood the lady in black herself. All things considered, Sheila Kelly looked incredibly alert, remarkably well rested and more pleasant than anyone, or at least a garda inspector such as Starrett, might reasonably expect.

"We'd like you and Miss Sweeney," Starrett began on behalf of his colleagues, Guards Browne, Garvey, Casey, Gibson and Robinson, "to accompany us to Tower House."

"Would you really, Inspector?" she croaked. "I'm flattered, I really am, but . . . ehm, I don't know if anyone has ever mentioned this to you, but I'm gay and proud of it."

Novice Garda Romany Browne had a good chuckle at that one, but he stopped short immediately after Gibson elbowed him sharply in the ribs.

Pretty soon thereafter, a red-eyed, bedraggled Teresa Sweeney, in her Marks and Sparks two-tone jim-jams, arrived at the door. Starrett and the team had been expecting sparks to fly at this point, but Sweeney showed that at the very least, she had learned one of the golden rules of life in Donegal: never ever have the gardaí hanging around your doorstep. She invited them in, so she had time to make herself decent.

Starrett instructed Browne, Casey and Robinson to take Sheila Kelly back to Tower House, and he, Gibson and Garvey followed Sweeney into the bungalow.

"I hear you've cleared the auld man?" Teresa said, as she exited her bedroom five minutes later dressed in a pretty, butter-wouldn't-melt-in-my-mouth, blue and white polka dot dress. She sat down on one of the kitchen chairs and put on her white socks and a pair of dark blue Doc Martens. Starrett couldn't be sure, but he thought she was making sure either he or Garvey, or maybe even Gibson, was getting an eyeful as she crossed one leg over the other to tie her laces.

"Teresa, your father never needed clearing," was Starrett's only response.

"Funny that now, isn't it?"

"What's that, Teresa?" Starrett asked, deadpan. He was finding he didn't have much stomach for this.

"A man confesses to a murder. The same man has a very good friend, and that very good friend has a son, and the son in question is an inspector in the local gardaí, and, well, I'll be damned if the son doesn't go and clear the confessed murderer. I've never seen that one before, even on the telly, Starrett."

Starrett gave her a gentle, considered smile. He realised what was said and how it was said was vital and would be analysed and studied in greater detail in the months and possibly years ahead.

He decided to say nothing except, "It's bucketing down out there, Teresa. Do you want to put a coat or something on before we go?"

"I'm right as I am," she said, then added, "in more ways than one. Let's go."

Ten minutes later, Sheila Kelly was led into the interview room in Tower House. Two hours and forty-seven minutes later, she walked out of the interview room. In those one hundred and sixty-seven minutes, Sheila Kelly's only words, delivered in her painfully hoarse voice, were, "I've got no comment to make."

It took Teresa Sweeney merely one hundred and three minutes to cover the same territory, and her repeated "I've got no comment to make" was delivered in much more comfortable tones.

Shortly after noon, Starrett took a break. Starrett was sure that the tactic whereby a suspect says nothing, literally nothing, was probably pioneered by American lawyers. Suspects tune out each thing that is said to them. They let each accusation that is made to them and each bit of proof that is presented to them fly over their heads; they don't deny; they don't agree. At every possible pause, they repeat, like robots, in controlled, measured tones, "I have no comment to make." As long as they can find a way to remain Zen-like and above the repeated barrage from the detectives, they put the onus entirely on the detectives to come up with cast-iron proof that will convict them in front of a jury.

Starrett had no such proof. Hell, he wasn't even, at that stage, entirely sure which of them had committed the crime or, indeed, if it was both of them. He didn't have very much that te State's prosecutors could use to present to a jury of twelve men and/or women, good and true who would do their duty.

Yes, Starrett accepted that he didn't have much evidence, but he did have an idea. If he couldn't address the evidence issue – beyond the skimpy circumstantial bits he'd dug up – perhaps he could address the case from the jury's angle. He didn't have twelve people for his jury, but he knew of eight candidates – five women and three men – he could summon up for it.

Chapter Fifty-Four

So, at two o'clock that afternoon, as the clouds broke to reveal the bluest of skies and the sun shone and dried up everything within minutes, a nervous Inspector Starrett, an amused Major Newton Cunningham, an eager Garda Nuala Gibson, a fidgety Sergeant Packie Garvey, a novice Garda Romany Browne dressed up in a translucent blue SOC evidence-collecting overall, an envious Garda Francis Casey and an intrigued Russell Leslie, the family solicitor, all gathered in the warehouse courtyard where Joe Sweeney's body had been found.

Also in attendance were the two who could only loosely be described as suspects, Teresa Sweeney and Sheila Kelly, along with the members of Starrett's makeshift jury. The jury consisted of Liam and Colette Sweeney; the surviving sons Thomas and Ryan; Thomas's wife, Mona, and their daughter, Bernadette; Ryan's girlfriend, Maeve Boyce; and Joe's girlfriend, Breda Roche. It was the first time they were all gathered together in the same space since Tuesday night last. Again, regrettably, Joe was missing. Also missing from the original dinner party was Finula, Thomas and Mona's youngest daughter, who was too young, Starrett felt, to attend the proceedings. Bernadette, age wise, was borderline, but she was Starrett's wild card because a) she was honest, b) she had shown she had a keen eye for observation, and c) he hadn't worked out if having Liam Sweeney in the mix was going to be a positive or a negative.

He needn't have worried. The bearded farmer drew his line in the courtyard nearly immediately.

Teresa, unrestrained and able to wander around the courtyard at her will, observed the proceedings with a wry smile and said, "All we need now is for Perry Mason to arrive in his wheelchair. On second thoughts, Starrett, with all your wrinkles, you're more like Miss Marple."

"Shut up, Teresa. Will you ever just shut up and listen to someone for the first time in your life?" The farmer spat the words at his daughter with such venom, he hushed not just his daughter but all those in attendance.

The one who seemed to enjoy Liam's outburst most was Bernadette, who obviously agreed that Teresa's chastisement was long overdue.

Colette Sweeney refused to look her daughter in the eyes. Starrett wondered if Liam had discussed his suspicions with his wife.

"OK," Starrett said, as much to himself as to the others, "let's begin.

"On Monday of this week, Joe had lunch with you and your wife, Liam."

"That's correct," Colette offered. "That was the last time we saw him."

Starrett opened the folder he'd brought down with him.

"I have here the records of all the calls from and to Joe's mobile that day," Starrett continued, growing in confidence now he'd grown accustomed to hearing his own voice in front of his audience.

"At 09.50 the same morning, Teresa made a call to her brother on the mobile. The call lasted just under three minutes, so we have to assume you spoke with your brother, Teresa."

"I hate to get in the way of the revelation of the century, Starrett, but, duh, he was my brother. We did speak a lot on the phone."

"Yes, you did," Starrett agreed. He was happy the family had seemed finally to release Teresa from her incessant "I've got no comment to make" parrot call of earlier that morning. Starrett continued, "Indeed you did, but we'll get back to the other calls later.

"At 12.47 Joe made a call to his sister, no doubt to confirm or agree arrangements they had discussed in the earlier call."

"How can you say that? You weren't even there. How the f . . ." Teresa pulled herself up on her swear word and paused to look at her mother, who was still avoiding eye contact with her daughter. "How can you stand there and say that with such confidence?"

"Just bear with me, Teresa, please," Starrett said, in his very controlled and quiet tone.

"No, I will not," Teresa ranted. "Mr Leslie, are you taking my father's money just to listen to this crap? Mona, you're a solicitor; why are you allowing this? This is a travesty. I'm outta here."

"Try to walk out of here, and we'll be forced to arrest and restrain you with handcuffs," Starrett cautioned.

Teresa looked at her mother and made no further move.

At that stage, Breda Roche looked like the only one who felt sorry for Teresa.

Liam Sweeney nodded at Leslie to remain as he was.

"I'm interested to hear what he has to say, Teresa," Mona offered. "It'll have no bearing whatsoever in a court of law, but I would like to hear what he has to say now he's taken the trouble to get us all together."

"The last call Joe made on his mobile," Starrett continued, "was to Frewin Guest House. He made that call at 14.09. I've checked with the owner, Thomas Coyle, and Joe was on to them to see if he could encourage them to up their weekly order. At 14.15 he received a call from someone up on the farm. He didn't answer the call, and all future communications to his mobile went unanswered. Somewhere between 14.09 and 14.15, Joe dropped out of circulation.

"I believe he met up in the vicinity of the Town Hall with either his sister or his sister and Sheila Kelly," Starrett said, choosing his words carefully.

"Sheila, tell them it's just not true. Tell them we did not meet up with Joe that day," Teresa pleaded, growing visibly frustrated with the proceedings.

"I've got no comment to make," Sheila said, continuing with their earlier mantra. Starrett wondered if he could take any encouragement from the fact that Teresa and Sheila were no longer singing from the same hymn sheet.

Starrett returned the call sheet to his folder.

"Traces of Rohypnol were discovered in Joe's blood. I think we all know the drug by its other name, roofies." Starrett hesitated as his eyes fixed on the eleven-year-old Bernadette.

"I've heard roofies mentioned on television. It's the date-rape drug, isn't it?" Bernadette asked, as Liam's eyes also betrayed knowledge of the drug.

"Yes, Bernadette, but it is also used to sedate people, to . . ."

"To make them unconscious?" she offered helpfully.

Starrett nodded a yes to Bernadette before continuing. "So, sometime in the 14.09 to 14.15 window, Joe met up with his sister and, as I say, she might have been accompanied by her girlfriend. I'd bet they hightailed it back up to her bungalow. Either there or on the way there, she spiked whatever it was she gave Joe to drink. She also must have decommissioned his mobile, because within a few minutes he was no longer receiving calls."

"Ah, no," Tom protested, looking as if he wished to stop the proceedings. "No, no, our Teresa wouldn't."

"She always has a lot of pills, Dad," Bernadette remarked.

"Just listen, Tom. Just listen," his wife said, in very measured tones.

"But why, Mona?" Tom, who seemed vocally to be the only Sweeney family member siding with his sister, pleaded.

"I'll get to that later, but please bear with me," Starrett said in as reasonable a voice as he could find. "Joe's comatose body was then placed in the back of one of the Fit 2 Flit vans. The longer he lies there, the more the Rohypnol kicks in.

"Eventually, around about eleven o'clock, Teresa – now without Sheila . . ."

"Starrett, just listen to yourself, will you? Where are you getting all of this from?"

"Well, there was actually a witness who saw someone smaller than Sheila dressed in waterproofs. They thought the person was fishing on the pier, but you'd come to place Joe's body in the water."

"Right, we can stop this right here. Mona, do me a favour, just for the craic, lift Ryan there. He's about the same weight as Joe, and see if you can lift him, let alone carry him to the water," Teresa said smugly.

Mona looked as if she were up for attempting the task.

"There'll be no need, Mrs Sweeney," Starrett said, "but a very good point, Miss Sweeney, I grant you. In normal circumstances, it would have been impossible for a woman to carry a mature man any distance."

"Maybe she dragged him?" Bernadette suggested helpfully.

"There were no scrape marks along the gravel, Bernadette, so that rules that out. But I have another solution to that problem. Garda Browne, come over here will you to this mobile Football Special contraption," Starrett said, pointing to the rusted spherical gridwork.

Browne, the one Starrett had prepared earlier, reluctantly did as Starrett requested. Starrett instructed him to lie comatose on the ground by the iron grid, moulded in the shape of a sphere.

Starrett rolled the iron ball until the opening was close to the ground by Browne. He manoeuvred Browne's head, shoulders and right arm into the inside of the ball, then, by slowly tilting the iron grid in an arc towards the remainder of Browne's body, he easily managed to get the body on the inside of the sphere. Starrett rolled the sphere along the ground, slow enough so Browne could find his balance and not end up as bruised as the final orange in the barrel. The inspector also took care to roll the sphere in such a way that Browne never came near the opening.

Browne started to grow visibly nervous as Starrett continued rolling his cage through the gates and out of the courtyard across the pier and in the direction of the water.

"And what's your next trick, Mr Houdini?" Teresa jested. "Can I just stop you here for a moment, Starrett? Say I'd . . . sorry, say *we'd* given Joe the roofies and as a result he was totally unconscious. OK, and say we'd wanted to drown him, then why bother going to all this trouble with your large iron football here? Why would we not just drop him off the side and into the water?"

Her mother seemed to take heart from Teresa's words.

Ryan just looked at the blue sky above; Maeve was holding him tightly and comforting him. If this had been a jury, Starrett figured he already had those two in the bag. Breda and Tom were still on Teresa's side, and, Starrett figured, the remainder of his jury were still undecided.

"I'll give you that," Starrett conceded as Teresa grinned largely for the jury, "except of course that would have meant you wouldn't have had an alibi for the time Joe died."

Silence reigned as everyone considered Starrett's statement.

"I don't understand." Bernadette said what most of them were probably thinking. Starrett hadn't noticed it, but she'd wandered off to be close to her mother and father by this point.

Starrett lifted his crooked finger to the heavens Ryan was still so intent on. Ryan looked troubled and distracted to Starrett, as if he'd already worked it all out and was starting to hurt.

"I'll try to explain, Bernadette," Starrett said, and then, addressing Teresa, "So, you come down here after eleven o'clock, and under the cloak of darkness you wheel Joe's body in this sphere." The detective then started to turn the wheel again, now moving it further along the pier and away from the direction of the town.

Eventually they came alongside the set of stone steps that led down to the water and disappeared underneath. To Browne's immense relief, Starrett ordered him out of the sphere and, as soon as the novice was safely out, Starrett wheeled the sphere down the steps and into the water.

"The high tide was not due until 02.30 the following morning," Starrett said quietly, "so at 23.00, Joe's body would still be above water and he'd have been alive. The trawlermen, as keen as you to make the high tide, passed you on the end of the pier. Unfortunately they were facing the wrong direction to see what you were up to. They actually thought you were fishing. The trawler sailed up the Swilly, leaving you to do your evil work.

"Work done, you scooted back to your bungalow to get your midnight party up and, noisily, raring along; your rave was still going strong at 02.30 and (intentionally) disturbing your neighbours. At this point, the water would have risen to its maximum height of ten feet, at which point Joe, in his comatose state, would have been totally underwater and drowning."

Colette Sweeney wailed. Liam and Ryan rushed to her side.

"No, Mammy, no, it's not true," Teresa cried out.

"Jesus, Teresa! How could you?" Ryan cried.

"It's her fault," Liam said, looking at Sheila, "her and all of her friends and their drugs."

"It's not true, listen to me. It's just not true," Teresa pleaded.

Starrett had two more points he felt he needed to make. The jury, sadly he felt, were on his side, but he still wanted, no, he still *needed,* a confession.

"At 02.43, at the time your brother would have been struggling to catch a breath to try and prolong his life for another split second, you rang his mobile number. You clearly wanted to leave a message so that later you could say, 'How could I have possibly been involved in his death if I was trying to get him on the phone at that precise time?' Yes, as you said, you certainly had rung your brother lots and lots of times on his mobile, but your phone records show you'd never ever rung him after midnight before that fateful night.

"Around 07.00 on Tuesday morning, you came down here again. The tide had dropped, and you wheeled the sphere containing Joe's dead body out of the water and back into the courtyard. You'd learnt from the previous evening how wet you'd get, so you'd brought a towel down with you to dry yourself off, just in case you came into contact with anyone. When you'd removed Joe's body from the sphere and it was lying there lifeless . . ." Starrett paused. He didn't know what came over him, but he could actually see the scenario he was describing clearly in his mind's eye ". . . you were overcome with genuine remorse, and the only thing you could think of doing to gain some redemption was to attend to and dry off Joe's hair using your aqua towel.

"Unfortunately for you, Teresa, some of the fabric from your towel remained tangled up in your brother's hair. These fabrics matched up perfectly with the towel we confiscated from your bathroom yesterday."

"Ach, Teresa," Colette wailed again; "our Joe, our wee Joe, how could you do that? What sort of monster did we bring into this world, Liam?"

At that moment Starrett felt Colette's feelings of immense loss for her youngest were so much stronger than any instincts she might be harbouring about protecting her only daughter.

Liam must have picked up the same vibe, because he said solemnly, "I knew it was our Teresa when I overheard that wee lad, Dr Aljoe's assistant, on his mobile telling his mate that Rohypnol had been found in Joe's body. I knew it was our Teresa, because she was always using Rohypnol to come down from her drugs. You even used it under our roof. I do blame myself, Teresa, I should have been there for you, but there was always something that needed attending to, and before I knew it, the next time I looked around you were too far gone, and I'd lost you and I couldn't . . ."

"Aye, Daddy, I know," Teresa said resignedly; "there was always *something* more important to attend to than your only daughter."

Breda Roche was studying Teresa now with a mixture of disgust and disappointment in her eyes. She turned on her heels and quietly walked out of the courtyard and away from the proceedings. No one tried to stop her.

Mona and Tom huddled closely with their daughter Bernadette. They tried to move her out of the courtyard, but she was stuck to the ground, magnetised to the scene, just like it was a train wreck and no matter how much she wanted to look away, she just didn't have the strength to do so.

Ryan openly wept on his girlfriend's shoulder.

His mother trailed her husband over to Ryan, and soon the four of them were comforting each other. The members of the two family groups were all comforting each other, their family senses rising to help each other out in their time of trouble.

Teresa had no one to turn to, no one to comfort her, no one to help her through this time of trouble. Starrett felt genuinely sorry for her. There were few things as devastating as a family turning on one of their own. It might be for justifiable reasons, and it might not, but the overall result was the same: completely overwhelming for the one being alienated.

"Why, Teresa, why?" Ryan asked.

Starrett thought, *Jurors always need the other jurors to agree with their verdict.* Ryan, having positively made up his mind on his sister, now sought cast-iron proof for his fellow family members.

"My friend at school told me her dad said Teresa owed big bucks to a drug dealer in Dublin," Bernadette offered, showing that school playground gossip is often ahead of the gardaí.

Teresa looked slowly from one of her family members to the next. She shivered, not from the chill of the last Sunday of August air, but from the fact that there was no one holding or comforting her. Her bloodshot eyes eventually settled on Sheila Kelly.

"You," she spat. "You said he'd never work it out."

Chapter Fifty-Five

By the time the first of September's ever darkening evenings had arrived, just over a day later, Teresa had made a full confession. She refused to incriminate Sheila Kelly in any way. Starrett still wasn't sure if the girlfriend was the puppet master or an innocent bystander. He would leave it to the courts to decide the degree of her involvement and her punishment. Either way, Inspector Frank O'Rourke of the Drug Squad was waiting in the wings with his arrest warrant.

A week later, the Sweeney farmhouse seemed very empty to Liam and Colette, but, if anything, it was busier. Joe Sweeney, at the time of his death, had been the only one still living at home, but since the day down in the courtyard, Tom, Mona and their girls, and Ryan and Maeve Boyce were regular visitors. Tom and Ryan were trying to ensure that there would always be at least one of them staying overnight with their parents. Even Finula and Bernadette were being a lot more considerate of their grandmother. Their own mother, well, that was another matter altogether. Breda Roche also promised to keep in touch. On one of her first visits, when the farmhouse was crowded with all the family, she presented Liam with the birthday present Joe (supposedly with input from Teresa) had bought for their father on behalf of the family.

Liam Sweeney studied the present for a few minutes. It was expertly wrapped in beautiful blue paper. The accompanying card was written in Joe's scratchy handwriting: "Happy Birthday, Dad, from the Sweeney Gang and assorted partners, wives and girlfriends."

No one could tell if Liam was going to burst into tears, open the present or put it at the top of his wardrobe to gather dust for a few years until the memory wasn't quite so painful. He surprised the family by declaring, "I love presents. Let's see what you all bought me," as he tore into the paper. When he opened what appeared to be a shoebox, the immediate look on his face was one of disappointment as he spotted several pairs of sober socks, two ties and three pairs of very loud underpants. Then he spotted another small box at the bottom amongst the socks.

"Joe knew how much you hated getting socks and underpants for presents," Colette laughed through her tears.

"What's this though?" Liam asked as he struggled to open the smaller box. Inside he found a beautiful gold pocket watch with matching chain. The farmer flicked open the lid and discovered an inscription on the inside:

"For the real boss of the farm, to ensure we all still run on time. From the Sweeney Family."

Chapter Fifty-Six

"I think it was a master stroke having young Bernadette at the proceedings," Major Newton Cunningham said to Starrett. They met by chance on the steps the following Friday night as they were leaving Tower House for the weekend.

"I'll admit I was a little worried about that," Starrett confessed, as they both walked down the rickety steps in front of the station.

"The fact that her father and, in particular, her grandfather would have been determined that she not only knows right from wrong, but that she could actually witness the process, set the tone for the entire proceedings. When it gets down to it, a family will always instinctively protect their own."

"But then, what about Teresa?" Starrett interrupted.

"What I was about to say was that a family will always instinctively protect their own, *particularly* the youngest."

"I see," Starrett said, and thought he did, as his mind wandered to Moya and Katie Keane.

"What are we going to do with young Romany?" the major asked as he futtered away in his pockets, appearing to count the change contained therein.

"He's keen, he's got a good brain, he's arrogant," Starrett offered and slowed to ponder further, "he's in too big a hurry, he likes the girls a wee bit too much for his own good, he's . . ."

The major dropped the change he was midway through mentally counting and held up his hand in interruption.

"So, he's probably a wee bit like we were at that age then?" he said.

Starrett smiled.

"Well, when you put it like that, I guess you just might be right."

"So, at the very least he's got a chance then?" the major said.

"I'd like to hope so, Major, I'd like to think so," Starrett replied as he found himself distracted and thinking of Joe Keane.

Cunningham showed he still possessed some of his old powers of deduction, not to mention insight, by asking, "How are you and Maggie Keane getting along these days?"

"Very well, Major. Very well indeed." Starrett hesitated, momentarily wondering if he should go further or not. He decided there was no time like the present. "Did I tell you her eldest boy Joe is my son?"

"No, you didn't, Starrett; no, you didn't," the major declared as he headed across Gamble Square in the direction of his parked Vauxhall VX490, "but then again, twenty years ago, anyone who'd at least nine fingers could have figured that one out for you."

The major gingerly strode across the square away from Starrett, muttering quietly to himself.

Starrett had had the key to Maggie Keane's house in his trouser pocket for nearly a week now, and he'd never had to use it once. Every time he called, no matter how late, she'd always be there waiting for him.

"You seem very happy with yourself," Starrett declared, as they disengaged from their first kiss of the evening.

"I am, Starrett, I am," she declared.

"Spill the beans then?"

"Well, Nuala's been telling me, and more importantly, Bernadette Sweeney has been telling our Katie how absolutely brilliant you were last week down at the warehouse solving the murder of Joe Sweeney single-handedly."

"Flattering but not true; the team does the work, and I get the glory. But there's more. There's more in your eyes than that."

"Yes, indeed there is," Maggie Keane, who just didn't do happy, declared in spite of herself. She broke free of Starrett and led him out of the kitchen and into the dining room. There were five places set at the dining table. "Starrett, for the first time, I'm going to have my family, our family, all together for dinner. Joe's up from Queen's for the weekend."

"Bejeepers, Maggie," was all Starrett could say as he went into a panic attack.

He needn't have worried. The evening was perfect. Katie even asked him, in front of the others, when he was moving in.

"As soon as we can get it organised," her mother replied, fondly taking Starrett's hand as she spoke.

A couple of hours later, Starrett found himself and Joe sitting alone together in the kitchen, which was the family room they all tended to gravitate to. On this particular occasion though, Maggie and the girls seemed to have conveniently disappeared upstairs together for something or other.

Starrett and his son were enjoying a natural conversation about life in Belfast in general and Queen's University in particular when Joe said, "You'll have to come down and see me, see my place, see where I hang out."

"Yes," Starrett replied, "I'd enjoy that." And he meant it.

"OK, when do you want to come down?"

"Ehm . . ." Starrett was taken aback at his son's no-nonsense approach.

"Look . . . ah . . . D . . . Starrett," Joe Keane eventually made a choice on how to address his father, "what I was looking to say to you was that it's going to take time for us to get to know one another, but I'd really like to start as soon as possible."

"Bejeepers," Starrett replied proudly, "there's no time like the present. When do you go back to Queen's?"

"I usually get a bus from Letterkenny after lunch on Sunday."

"Right so, why don't I run you down this Sunday and we can have the evening together. You can show me around, and we can start to catch up on lost time?"

"Sounds perfect to me."

"OK, now let me ask you this," Starrett said: "Dylan. Do you prefer the music he made before his motorcycle accident or the music he made after it?"

"Well, if you're talking about immediately after the accident, there'd be no competition; it was much too bland and indulgent for a time, but then it started to get better again, and now the last three albums of new material are amongst the best he's ever done, and certainly my favourites. What's *your* favourite Dylan album?"

"I'd have to say, *Bringing It All Back Home*," Starrett declared, recalling the CD he'd recently borrowed from Nuala Gibson as part of his Bob Dylan crash course. " 'She Belongs to Me,' 'Love Minus Zero,' 'Mr Tambourine Man' and 'It's All Over Now Baby Blue' are amongst the best songs ever written, and to have them all on one album. Bejeepers, it's just unbelievable."

Starrett wasn't absolutely sure, but he thought he might have heard some sniggering from the top of the stairwell.

He wasn't wrong on either that point or on his summary of the master's music.

ALSO PUBLISHED BY BRANDON

PAUL CHARLES

Sweetwater

"Almost like an Inspector Morse without the irascibility and lovelorn aspirations...The puzzle slowly fits together, exposing a rich pageant of human relationships. An exemplary case for the quiet sleuth of British crime fiction."
Maxim Jakubowski, *Guardian*

ISBN 9780863223679

The Dust of Death

"From its killer first line to its last, *The Dust of Death* is compelling and elegant, like a well-woven garrotte." Mark Billingham

"A mystery that's as smooth as a good single malt and none the less satisfying." John Harvey

ISBN 9780863223853

The Beautiful Sound of Silence

"Kennedy is not the clichéd cop of so much crime fiction. He is a well-rounded laconic hero who takes a philosophical approach to crime solving and life in general. Likewise the novels are cliché-free as well and tend to be cleverly plotted stories with the emphasis on character and atmosphere rather than gimmicky twists and turns." *Books Ireland*
ISBN 9780863223983

KEN BRUEN

American Skin

"Ken Bruen's artfully violent and distinctly human voice is in full effect with *American Skin*. There are few crime novelists today who write with such passion and bravado."
George Pelecanos

ISBN 9780863223792

ALSO PUBLISHED BY BRANDON

SAM MILLAR

The Dark Place

"A powerful new crime series from Irish author Millar." *Publishers Weekly*

From the nail-biting beginning to the explosive ending, Karl Kane's nightmarish journey forces upon him a decision that changes his life forever, and forces him to look into the abyss.

ISBN 9780863224034

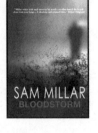

Bloodstorm

"The crossover novel that will propel [Sam Millar] into the mainstream – and not a minute too soon." *Crime Always Pays*

"Gripping…arrestingly violent, *Bloodstorm* is a well-written thriller with its share of disturbing insights into the dark side of the human psyche." *Irish Mail on Sunday*

ISBN 9780863223754

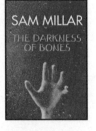

The Darkness of Bones

"Millar writes with such intensity his words can often knock the breath clean from your lungs…A shocking and original voice in a genre crowded by clichés." *Belfast Telegraph*

ISBN 9780863223501

The Redemption Factory

"While most writers sit in their study and make it up, Sam Millar has lived it and every sentence… evokes a searing truth about men, their dark past, and the code by which they live. Great title, great read. Disturbingly brutal. I enjoyed it immensely." Cyrus Nowrasteh

ISBN 9780863223396